"The only thing [...]
InCryptid book. [...]
all the McGuire [...]
    —Charlaine [...]

"Seanan McGui[...]
triple threat—smart and sexy and funny. The Aeslin mice alone
are worth the price of the book, so consider a cast of truly
original characters, a plot where weird never overwhelms logic,
and some serious kickass world-building as a bonus."
    —Tanya Huff, bestselling author of *The Wild Ways*

"McGuire kicks off a new series with a smart-mouthed, engaging heroine and a city full of fantastical creatures. This may
seem like familiar ground to McGuire fans, but she makes New
York her own, twisting the city and its residents into curious
shapes that will leave you wanting more. Verity's voice is strong
and sure as McGuire hints at a deeper history, one that future
volumes will hopefully explore."   —*RT Book Reviews*

"Verity is a winning protagonist, and her snarky but loving observations on her world of bogeyman strip club owners, Japanese demon badger bartenders, and dragon princess waitresses
make for a delightful read."   —*Publishers Weekly*

"*Discount Armageddon* is an exceptionally well-written tale
with a unique premise, fantastic character work, and a plot that
just pulls you along until you finish. This is one for the urban
fantasy enthusiasts out there—as well as for anyone who wants
something different from most anything else on shelves today.
Easily one of my favorite books of 2012."   —Ranting Dragon

"Smart, whimsical and bitingly funny, Verity Price is a kick-ass
heroine that readers will love. Just when I thought she couldn't
surprise me again, she would pull some new trick out of her
hat—or, in the case of her throwing knives, out of her corset. I
would send Verity and my Jane Jameson on a girl's night out,
but I'm afraid of the damage bill they would rack up!"
    —Molly Harper, [...]

"*Discount Armageddon* [...]
what makes a monster [...]
fantasy protagonists walk [...]
lets up, and when the en[...]
wait for the next book!"

DAW Books presents the finest in urban fantasy from Seanan McGuire:

InCryptid Novels

October Daye Novels

*Coming soon from DAW Books

HALF-OFF RAGNAROK

AN INCRYPTID NOVEL

SEANAN McGUIRE

DAW BOOKS, INC.
DONALD A. WOLLHEIM, FOUNDER
375 Hudson Street, New York, NY 10014

ELIZABETH R. WOLLHEIM
SHEILA E. GILBERT
PUBLISHERS
www.dawbooks.com

For Mandy.
Love and ice worms.

Price Family Tree

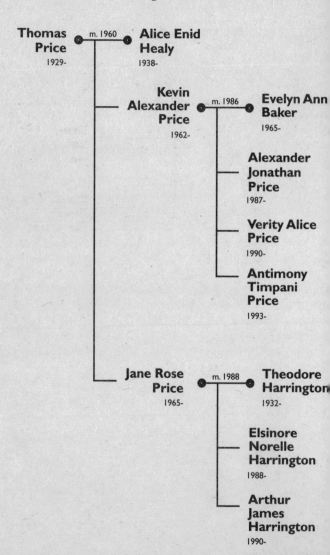

Thomas Price 1929–

m. 1960

Alice Enid Healy 1938–

Kevin Alexander Price 1962–

m. 1986

Evelyn Ann Baker 1965–

Alexander Jonathan Price 1987–

Verity Alice Price 1990–

Antimony Timpani Price 1993–

Jane Rose Price 1965–

m. 1988

Theodore Harrington 1932–

Elsinore Norelle Harrington 1988–

Arthur James Harrington 1990–

Baker Family Tree

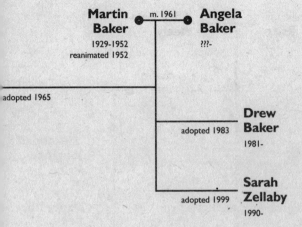

Martin Baker
1929-1952
reanimated 1952

m. 1961

Angela Baker
???-

adopted 1965

adopted 1983

Drew Baker
1981-

adopted 1999

Sarah Zellaby
1990-

Herpetology, noun:

The scientific study of reptiles.

Cryptoherpetology, noun:

1. The scientific study of reptiles and reptile-like cryptids.

2. A specialized branch of cryptozoology.

3. Not a good way to live a long and healthy life.

Prologue

"I'm not saying that it's a horrible monster
here to mercilessly devour you whole. I'm
sure it would chew you first."

—Thomas Price

*A small survivalist compound about an hour's drive east of
Portland, Oregon*

Fifteen years ago

A LEX KNELT IN FRONT of his new terrarium, peering
through the glass as he searched for a sign of his
latest pet.

The problem was the piece of hollow log he'd placed
in the middle of the tank. It had seemed like a great idea
when he was putting the terrarium together, and it
looked pretty boss surrounded by native ferns and nestled down in the spongy moss he'd used as a ground-
cover. It was a totally natural environment, or as close as
he was going to get on his limited budget. He would
never have been able to afford a fifty-gallon tank if it
hadn't shown up at the swap meet.

The tank would still have been outside his price range
if the glass hadn't been cracked on one corner. That
would have been a problem if he'd been planning to
keep fish in it, but that had never been an option. Who
wanted stupid old fish, anyway? All they did was swim

around and flip their fins at you. Reptiles and amphibians were where the *real* fun was. They didn't care about cracked glass, as long as the tank was big enough. And that took him back to the hollow log, which was completely obscuring his new coatl. The little winged snake had slithered into the artificial shelter as soon he released it into the tank, and it hadn't come out since.

If he squinted *really* hard, he could almost make out the edge of one wing. The coatl had it half-spread, preventing most of the light from filtering into the log. Defeated, Alex sank down onto his heels and glared at the carpet. "Stupid snake," he muttered.

"Trouble in paradise?" asked a voice behind him.

"Mom!" Alex scrambled to his feet and spun to face his mother, cheeks burning. "I didn't mean to leave the door open."

"I can tell," said Evelyn Price, surveying the chaos of her ten-year-old son's bedroom. He was a surprisingly organized and scholarly boy. Some people probably assumed that made him easy to clean up after. Those people had never dealt with a smart boy who liked nature enough to bring it home with him. "What's wrong?"

"I put my new coatl in his tank, but he won't come out." Alex sat down on the floor again as he glared at the glass. "I barely even got to *see* him before he hid."

"Oh, is that all?" Evelyn walked over to kneel beside her son. "What do you know about coatls?"

"They're winged snakes native to the Americas, and were named in honor of the Aztec god Quetzalcoatl," recited Alex, without hesitation. "Most known species are nonvenomous and primarily found in forested areas."

"Uh-huh. And they're cold-blooded, right?"

Alex nodded.

"Did you turn on the heat lamp?"

Alex's eyes widened for a moment before he dove under the table that held his terrarium and started fumbling for the cord. Once he found it, he shoved the plug into the wall outlet. Then he crawled back out from under the table and got to his feet, reaching over to flip the switch on the side of the heat lamp. Red light bathed half the tank.

Evelyn stayed on her knees, gesturing for her son to join her. He settled against her side, and she put her arm around his waist. Together, they watched as the bright green little snake with the feathery, olive-colored lumps on its back slithered hesitantly from beneath the log, tongue flicking out to taste the air. It slithered onto the rock directly beneath the light, where it curled in a loose half-circle. Then, almost as an afterthought, it opened its wings, revealing the brilliant gold-and-blue flight feathers it had been concealing while it was in motion.

"It's beautiful," breathed Alex.

"Yes," agreed Evelyn. "It is."

One

"If you find something you truly love, stick with it. There's nothing else in this world that will make you half as happy. There's nothing else that will make you half as miserable, either, but you can't have one without the other."

— Alexander Healy

An unnamed stretch of marshland near Columbus, Ohio

Now

THE THICK BLACK MUD sucked at my boots as I walked, constantly threatening to send me face-first to the murky ground. If I fell, my choices would be "land in brackish water harboring God-only-knows what" or "land in mud harboring God-only-knows what, with the bonus of mud being harder to wash out of your hair." If I was *really* lucky, I might get a third option and find some quicksand to land in. At least that would be a new disgusting swamp experience, instead of a disgusting swamp experience I'd already had several times that day.

Mosquitoes hummed around my head, only somewhat deterred by the rosemary oil covering my clothes and skin. I smelled like one of Mom's casseroles. Commercial mosquito repellent might have been more effective—and it definitely wouldn't have made me as hungry—but it could have frightened away my actual quarry. Once again, I was sacrificing comfort for science. Science is my passion, but sometimes . . .

Sometimes science sucks.

I was dwelling on that pleasantly irritated thought when my left foot snagged on a tree root and I pitched forward into the swamp. I managed to catch myself on one knee, but both hands landed in a deep puddle, sending a wave of brackish water up to soak my shirt. My pack shifted on my back, the collection jars inside rattling. I bit back several expletives, each worse than the last.

There are times when I envy my sisters. Verity specializes in urban cryptids, who tend to wear shoes and have running water. Antimony doesn't specialize in anything yet, unless you count pit traps, explosives, and getting on my last nerve as professional callings. Neither of them finds themselves in swamps on a regular basis.

A loud flapping noise, followed by a thump, announced the arrival of a creature the size of a large corgi. It croaked, somehow managing to make it sound like laughter.

"Thanks, Crow. You're always such a ray of sunshine." I turned. My Church Griffin, Crow, was sitting on one of the few nearby patches of solid ground, looking self-satisfied. His long, extravagantly fluffy tail was wrapped around his feet, keeping it well away from the mud. He croaked again when he saw me looking, now sounding *incredibly* self-satisfied. "Yes, yes, hello to you, too. Did you find the frickens?"

Crow flicked his tail up, displaying the feathered frog clutched in one of his taloned forefeet. One of his claws was pressed through the tiny amphibian's skull. He had probably pierced the poor thing's brain, killing it instantly.

I pushed myself upright. "Give," I commanded, holding out a muddy hand.

Crow churred sulkily.

"I don't care if you're the one who caught it. I know

you ate at least two before you deigned to bring one to me. Now *give*."

Still looking sulky, Crow shook the fricken off his claw. It landed in the mud with a splat. Then he launched himself into the air, splashing swamp water in my face in the process. I swear he was laughing as he flew off into the swamp.

"Real mature," I muttered.

Crow was only acting according to his nature, but that didn't make him any less annoying. As the Church Griffin is a breed of miniature griffin that basically combines the raven with the Maine Coon cat, "acting according to his nature" included playing in the water, mercilessly hunting and killing anything smaller than he was, and generally being a brat. There are people who say that Church Griffins like Crow combine the best parts of the creatures they resemble. And then there are the people who've actually *lived* with a Church Griffin.

(Crow got his name from my youngest sister, Antimony. I originally called him "Poe," as in "Edgar Allen." Antimony took one look at him and demanded to know how I could be so uncreative as to name a black-feathered griffin "Crow." It annoyed me enough that I defended my name choice without pausing to consider the fact that it wasn't *my* name choice, and it stuck. In hindsight, I'm pretty sure that was her intention all along. My baby sister is devious enough to make your average bogeyman seem like an open book.)

The fricken hadn't been dead for long; its eyes were barely clouded over, and rigor hadn't started setting in yet. I scooped it gently into my hand, studying its plumage. It was a common swamp fricken, one of the three varieties normally found in the marshes and wetlands of Ohio. Shrugging off my pack, I dug out a collection jar. Once I got the fricken back to my lab, I could test its skin and feathers for signs of fungal infection.

Exciting? Not necessarily. Essential? Absolutely. Again, science is a cruel mistress.

Something in the unexplored swath of swamp in front of me shrieked. It was a high, shrill sound, like razor blades running across steel. My head snapped up as my hands automatically finished the process of sealing the collection jar and stuffing it into my pack. The shriek was not repeated. I clambered to my feet, watching the trees for signs of movement. When several seconds passed without anything charging out and trying to eat me, I tightened the straps on my pack and started to walk toward the scraggly tree line.

I was about halfway there when someone screamed. I swore under my breath and sped up. That would teach me to complain about a lack of excitement.

My name is Alexander Price—Alex to my friends, family, and people who want to distinguish me from my great-grandfather, Alexander Healy, who was one of the premiere cryptozoologists of his time. (That's not as impressive as it sounds. There weren't many cryptozoologists in his time. He was still a pretty cool guy.) I voluntarily chose a profession where running *toward* screaming is considered a good idea. It is entirely possible that there is something wrong with me. Then again, it's equally possible that the same thing is wrong with my entire family. We breed for it.

Crow flew up from behind and sailed past me, vanishing into the trees. His black feathers and banded brown-on-brown tabby fur granted him perfect camouflage in this sort of environment. That was good; it reduced the odds of his being eaten by whatever was in the wood.

Being the son of human parents, I don't have any such natural defenses, so I have to make do with artificial ones. I drew the tranquilizer gun from my belt and slowed down slightly, choosing caution over certain death as I ran down a mental list of things that were likely to be wandering around the swamps of Ohio and shrieking.

Then I rounded the edge of the stand of trees, and saw the eighteen-foot-long reptilian creature looming over my assistant, who was scrambling backward as fast as traction and the mucky ground allowed. The creature's head was flat and spade-shaped. It looked like an oversized, armor-plated skink with attenuated limbs sprouting from a body that had somehow been stretched beyond all reason. Spikes stood up in a vicious-looking line along its back, their razor edges gleaming in the light that filtered through the trees.

"Well, shit," I said. "Lindworm." Lindworms are predatory, and they'll eat anything they can catch. That didn't mean anything good for my assistant. Or for me, if we didn't handle this correctly.

I put two fingers in my mouth—regretting it pretty much immediately, when I got a taste of the muck all over me—and whistled. The lindworm whipped its head around, mouth opening as it shrieked again. Dee took advantage of its distraction to keep scrambling backward, working to get herself out of strike range. She's not a herpetologist, and she's not certified to handle any of the venomous snakes at the Columbus Zoo, but if there's one thing Dee knows, it's reptile strike zones.

"Took you long enough!" she shouted. She didn't look surprised to see me. Then again, she knew me well enough to know that the sound of screams would attract me like the sound of a can opener attracts Crow.

I pulled my fingers out of my mouth, calling, "Crow! Harass!" before answering her: "I was busy!" And I was going to need something bigger than my tranquilizer gun. This was a mature lindworm, and it wasn't going down for anything less than enough diazepam to kill an elephant. Maybe not even then.

Crow flashed out of the trees like a feathered arrow, aiming for the lindworm's head. His talons glanced off the scales of its cheek. The lindworm turned its attention on Crow, shrieking again, and snapped at him. Crow evaded easily, going into the distinctive series of twists, feints, and sneak attacks that made up his harrying pattern. Usually, it's crows and ravens harrying raptors. A

Church Griffin harrying a lindworm was only slightly stranger.

"I didn't think lindworms were native to this part of Ohio," I said, picking my way through the mud toward Dee. "I'm not sure I've got anything on me that can put it under."

"You know how I always say you need to be more about preserving *us*, and less about preserving the local wildlife?" demanded Dee, scowling at me through the lenses of her specially polarized glasses. The glass was almost clear, with just the faintest touch of yellow hinting that there might be something strange about it.

"Yes . . ."

"This is one of those times!"

Crow squawked as the lindworm managed to catch one of his tail feathers. He pulled himself free and resumed harrying, but Dee was right; this wasn't going to work forever. I shrugged off my backpack and put it down on the mud, crouching to begin rummaging through its contents.

"All right, this is what we're going to do," I said. "Dee, when I give the word, you're going to take off your protective gear."

"Alex—"

"Trust me, get in front of me, and do as I say."

She gave me a flat look. "You're going to get yourself killed."

"Not if you know how to listen." I straightened up, the vial of ketamine in my hand. "Get in front of me."

Dee sighed and moved into position, crouching in front of me like we were about to play a game of touch football with the giant reptile. In a way, we were.

Crow was still harrying the lindworm, but he was slowing down; Church Griffins are more like cats than ravens in many ways, including stamina. He was doing his best. He couldn't have kept that up much longer.

It was a good thing he didn't have to. I whistled again before shouting, "Crow! Home!"

Crow doesn't know many commands, and he doesn't reliably listen to any of them (except for maybe "dinner"), but this was one he both recognized and was glad to obey. He whipped around and flew back toward me, landing heavily on my shoulder. I clamped my free hand down over his eyes, an action that he only protested weakly. There wasn't time to be gentler. The lindworm was already turning, mouth open, shrieking furiously.

"Now, Dee!"

Cool as a cucumber, my assistant reached up, removing her wig with one hand and her glasses with the other. The snakes growing from her scalp in place of hair rose, hissing, as her eyes locked onto the lindworm's. It stopped mid-charge, looking dazed. Then, with an unceremonious "thud," it toppled over to the side.

"Glasses, please, Dee," I said. The snakes at the back of her head were looking at me, their tongues scenting the air. I offered them a pleasant smile. The snakes that top the heads of Pliny's gorgons are venomous, and it never hurts to stay on their good side.

If the snakes cared that they were being smiled at, they didn't show it. "You know, I could have stunned it without you here," Dee said, putting her glasses back on. She turned to frown at me, her wig still held loosely in one hand. "You're the one who asked me not to go and paralyze anything we found in the swamp."

I relaxed as soon as Dee's eyes were safely covered. Only the human-seeming eyes of a Pliny's gorgon carry a paralytic. The snakes atop their heads can't petrify so much as a mouse, although the gorgon's gaze seems to work better when their snakes are exposed. It's just one more quirk in the incomprehensible biology of the gorgon.

"No, I asked you not to paralyze anything I hadn't asked you to paralyze. There's a difference." I took my hand off Crow's head. He launched himself from my shoulder and flew to the nearest tree. Perching on a low branch, he began to preen his feathers, churring sulkily the whole time. I ignored him as I walked over and knelt beside the unconscious lindworm. "Reptiles are delicate. I'd rather not kill anything today that we don't have to."

"So why was it okay for me to paralyze the—what did you call this thing?"

"It's a lindworm, and it was okay for you to paralyze it because very little kills a lindworm. Seriously. The only reliable method of killing them that we have on record is decapitation. Even then, there are some pretty plausible reports of lindworm heads surviving without their bodies for up to a week before they expired, presumably of thirst." I pried the lindworm's mouth open. Filling a syringe with ketamine, I injected the sedative into the lining of its mouth. "If a Pliny's gorgon could kill a lindworm, I'd know."

"Oh." Dee walked over to join me, squinting at the lindworm. "It's big."

"It's male. The female would be over twenty feet, and have slightly more developed hind limbs. She uses them to dig the den she and her mate will hibernate in over the winter. Get my bag, will you? I want to take some measurements on this fellow before he wakes up."

Dee lifted one artfully drawn-on eyebrow. "You mean we're not leaving right now?"

"Of course not." I beamed up at her. "This is the *fun* part of science."

Between Dee's paralytic stare and my tranquilizer, the lindworm stayed sedated long enough for me to get length, estimated weight, some scales, and a blood sample. I slipped a radio tag onto one of its hind legs. If it started eating people, we'd be able to find it and make it stop. If it stayed in the swamps, doing what nature intended it to do, we weren't going to interfere. Lindworms may be unpleasant creatures to share a swamp with, but their presence keeps some even nastier things away. It's a fair trade.

Dee seemed to have decided that the presence of a giant snakelike cryptid made her hair less outré, because she didn't put her wig back on while she wrote down the lindworm's measurements. Crow stayed in the trees, wings drooping as he watched suspiciously. He clearly expected the lindworm to get back up at any moment, and I couldn't blame him. Heck, *I* half expected the lindworm to get back up, and I was the one who'd sedated it.

"So if these things aren't native to Ohio, where did this guy come from?" asked Dee.

"That's the thing. They *might* be native to Ohio. I'm not sure this is a species of lindworm that we've seen before. The first recorded species were in Europe—Sweden and the United Kingdom, mostly—but we've found them all over." I capped my pen and tucked it, and my notebook, back into my bag. "Maybe we just made cryptozoological history."

"Be still my heart," said Dee dryly. Her hair hissed agreement.

"Lindworms are a sign of a healthy ecosystem," I said, straightening. "Now let's get out of here before the healthy ecosystem eats us. I think I have enough specimens for today."

Dee rolled her eyes. "Sure thing, boss."

Side by side, with Crow flying behind us, we squelched our way through the swamp toward the distant road, leaving the lindworm to peacefully sleep off the rest of the ketamine.

Just another day at the office.

Two

"Yes, that's a brilliant idea. Choose the career path most likely to lead to an early, painful death, and you're sure to find job satisfaction."

—Jonathan Healy

The reptile house of Ohio's West Columbus Zoo, visiting researcher's office

EVEN AFTER STOPPING AT home to drop off Crow and change my clothes, I still made it back to the zoo in time for the afternoon shift change. Technically, as a visiting researcher, I didn't have to come in unless I was giving a talk or shepherding a school group through the wonderful world of venomous snakes. In reality, I did the bulk of my research in my small, borrowed office. It wasn't completely secure, but the door locked, and all the really sensitive work was done at home. I'd learned to sleep soundly despite the smell of formaldehyde.

Between Dee, Crow, and myself, we had managed to collect specimens representing three of the fricken subspecies known to be native to Ohio: the common swamp fricken, the greater swamp fricken, and the Midwestern spotted fricken. I'd spend all evening after dinner dissecting their bodies. Hopefully, that would give me enough data to let us stop killing the harmless little creatures.

I was typing up a completely fabricated report of our trip to the swamp—which had supposedly been focused on looking for copperheads, trying to assess the local population density—when Dee stuck her head in from the main office. Her wig was now firmly back in place, and she looked the very picture of the modern administrative assistant.

"Hey, boss, did you see the time?" she asked. "I ask because you told me to, and not because I'm nagging. Please remember the distinction at my annual review."

"You're technically employed by the zoo," I said. "I don't think I get to do your annual review."

"You have a real gift for focusing on the inconsequential part of a sentence, don't you?" She crossed her arms, leaning against the doorframe. "Time. Look at the."

I blinked before glancing to the clock on my computer, which showed ten minutes to four. "So?"

"So you promised you'd attend the tiger show today? The one that a certain Miss Shelby Tanner is in charge of?" Dee uncrossed her arms in order to inscribe an hourglass shape in the air. "Unless you no longer care about keeping your hot Australian girlfriend happy . . ."

"She's not my girlfriend," I said automatically. I was already standing up. Dee, sensing victory, pushed herself away from the doorframe and plucked my jacket off the coatrack, handing it to me. I shrugged it on and smiled, a little wryly. "What would I do without you, Dee?"

"Date less," she replied.

I snorted.

Dee—short for Deanna Lynn Taylor de Rodriguez, a mouthful she thankfully doesn't insist on in casual conversation, or ever—is a Pliny's gorgon, which puts her in the middle range of "potentially deadly cryptids with snakes in place of hair." Lesser gorgons are more common, greater gorgons are more dangerous, and Pliny's gorgons are, as Dee says, just right. She lives with her extended family somewhere outside of Dublin, Ohio. I don't ask her where, and she doesn't offer to tell me. Being a Price might make me a cryptid ally, but at the end of the day, I was still a human. Humans have a long history of chopping the heads off of gorgons who are just trying to get by.

Pliny's gorgons usually have one or two members of their community working in the local human settlements, where they can keep an eye out for any possible mobs with torches, or anything else that might be bad for the family. Always females: most male Pliny's gorgons are more than seven feet tall, which can be difficult to explain, while the females are more human-normal in height. Dee was right around five-seven, making her about four inches shorter than me. She'd been my assistant since the day I arrived at the Columbus Zoo, and I couldn't have done it without her.

"Is there anything else you need, boss, or can you take things from here?"

"I think I can manage." The report to zoo management was essentially finished; all I needed to do was check my grammar and hit "send." I'd write up the encounter with the lindworm and email it to my parents later this evening. Maybe Dad could find something in the family records about lindworms in Ohio—or maybe I was right, and this really was a new species. Either way, I had plenty to get done tonight.

"Good boy," said Dee, and left the office, her hair hissing softly beneath her auburn wig.

I chuckled, shrugged my jacket on, and followed her out.

The reptile house was mostly empty when I emerged from my office. The late afternoon was always our slowest time. The more interesting shows—which we were supposed to call "interactive exhibits," according to the latest flyer from the head office—always took place after lunch, and most people were happier watching koalas or

performing tigers while they tried to digest their pro-
cessed cheese food sandwiches than they were wandering through the dark, snake-infested building where I
worked.

Individual heating lamps lit the various enclosures,
and hooded lights on the ceiling lit the rest of the room,
although not very brightly. Many of the species we had
living there were more active at night, and so we tricked
them into thinking this *was* nighttime. They slithered and
skittered around their artificial environments, exploring
the boundaries they had explored a thousand times before. Crunchy, the aptly-named alligator snapping turtle,
hung in the water of his tank like a floating, bad-tempered
boulder, his mouth hanging open in silent invitation. It
was an invitation I had no intention of accepting any time
soon.

An old fellow like Crunchy can weigh in excess of
three hundred pounds, and can take off a human leg in
one bite. Two boys I judged to be about eleven years old
were standing near his tank, watching him with rapt fas-
cination. I paused, raising an eyebrow.

"You boys need something?" I asked.

"He moved last week," said one of the boys. "He
might do it again."

I smiled to myself. There was a time when I would
have been the one standing patiently outside the big turtle's tank, waiting for that split second when he would
close his jaws and the world would be awesome. "Here's
hoping," I said, and walked on, heading for the front
door. If I hurried, I could make it in time for the show.

As much as I loved the reptile house, it was always a
sweet relief to step out of it and into the zoo proper. Inside, the air smelled of snake, a hot, musty, dry smell that
never quite went away. The air outside smelled like
freshly cut grass and a hundred types of blooming flowers, many of which had been imported solely to make the
zoo seem wilder and more exotic. Tigers looked more
realistic, somehow, when they were framed by flowers

that didn't come from the grocery store florist's department.

Tourists and school groups milled listlessly on the paths, slowed down by their recent meals, while the diurnal animals did basically the same thing inside the open-air habitats. The African wild dogs were barking again, their strange, yodeling cries splitting the air. I sped up, until I was walking at a pace that was just shy of a run.

The big cats had their own private corner of the zoo, with multiple outdoor enclosures spreading out around the main building like the petals on a flower. A small amphitheater of sorts had been constructed between the lion and tiger enclosures, providing a space for the zookeepers to show off their animals. Cheers and applause were coming from that direction. I abandoned the pretense of walking, and ran the rest of the way.

Shelby's tiger show was packed, leaving only a few seats at the rear of the amphitheater. I murmured apologies to the people already sitting on the benches as I sidled past them to get as close to the center as possible. People cast glares and irritated looks in my direction, but no one paid attention to me for long. There were better things for them to focus on.

The stadium-style benches of the amphitheater extended down to ground level, where they gave way to an eight-foot median, followed by a four-foot wall topped with a chain link fence. On the other side of the fence was a grassy lawn spotted with super-sized cat toys—and with super-sized cats to boot, in the form of five orange-and-black–striped tigers. They prowled and lounged just like their smaller cousins, and I couldn't help thinking that Crow would be fascinated.

Three zookeepers in khaki and white moved around the edges of the enclosure, keeping the tigers under close watch, while the woman I'd come to see strutted at the center of the enclosure. Shelby Tanner.

I wasn't the only one in the audience who was watching her rather than the tigers. The tigers were beautiful, but Shelby . . . Shelby was gorgeous. She was pleasantly tall, with long legs that only looked longer in her khaki shorts, and the kind of figure that comes from manual labor and good genetics. Her wavy blonde hair was pulled back into a ponytail, keeping it from becoming tangled in the hands-free microphone that was clipped over her left ear.

"Now this big beauty is Mitya, one of our Siberian tigers," she said, her Australian accent slathered so broadly across the words that it was almost difficult to understand her. "Isn't he a looker? Come on, Mitya, give us a kiss." She tapped her thigh with one hand. The largest of the tigers in the enclosure responded by rearing up onto his hind legs, putting his forepaws on her shoulders, and licking her cheek like a dog. The audience applauded and cheered. I shook my head, wondering how many of them could tell how nervous the rest of the zookeepers were. This was grandstanding, pure and simple. But grandstanding gets butts into seats, and we needed that. As long as Shelby didn't actually get eaten during one of her shows, management would let her decide what happened.

Hell, even if she *did* get eaten, management would probably let the show go on according to her notes. Anything to keep ticket sales up.

Shelby Tanner and I had arrived at the zoo at the same time, me as a visitor from California, no, really, we swear, and her as a visitor from Sydney, Australia. It was only natural for the rest of the staff to shove the two outsiders together. She hadn't known what to make of me at first, and the confusion was mutual. Shelby was boisterous, enthusiastic to a fault once she had decided on a course of action, and prone to leaping before she looked. I was a man of science, and science was always going to be my first love, no matter how attractive the alternatives might be. And Shelby was a *very* attractive alternative. She didn't carry a hunting rifle on a regular basis, but aside from that, she was everything I'd ever wanted in a woman, and I'd been very careful not to pursue her. I don't make promises that I can't keep.

Our first date had happened three months before, and it had almost certainly been a dare. She'd marched up to me after a staff meeting, looked me up and down, and informed me I was taking her out for a drink that coming Friday night. I said no. She laughed and said this might be fun after all, and somewhere in the discussion that followed, my no turned into a yes, and one date turned into two, then three, and then four.

All we really had in common was our work with animals, although I was more on the pure research side, while Shelby was a trainer—as she was showing off even now in the green space beneath me, putting a Bengal tiger through his paces by throwing a medicine ball for him to chase. She was a big cat specialist, and had come to Ohio for the opportunity to study them in North America, where there were more specimens available than in her own cat-free homeland. (Big cats turn out to be surprisingly popular in Australian zoos, maybe for the same reason that kangaroos and koalas are so popular in North America: they're so weird they're unbelievable, if you didn't grow up with them.)

The Siberian tiger reared up behind Shelby, putting its paws on her shoulders. The audience gasped. Shelby reached back and calmly scratched the tiger under the jaw, saying, "These big fellas aren't domesticated, but as you can see, they've got a lot in common with the cats you may have at home, or the ones you love to watch on the Internet." Nervous laughter answered her. "They deserve our respect, and they deserve to be protected, because our world would be a lot poorer without them. Now, if you'll excuse me, it's time we got back to work. These beauties will be back in their enclosures and ready for their adoring public in about fifteen minutes! Thank you all!"

Thunderous applause greeted her announcement. I stood and hopped over the bench I'd been sitting on, heading for the nearest exit before I could get swept up in the crowd. They'd be thronging to the tiger enclosures, trying to get a good spot to gawk at the performers up close. I was doing something similar. I just had a different performer in mind.

The amphitheater was a stand-alone structure, but the green space where the tigers were displayed backed up on the main cat house, allowing the staff to discreetly move the animals back into their individual runs, and then on to their proper places. While the crowds formed around the outdoor enclosures, I slipped into the main building and made my way to the door marked "Staff Only."

The hall on the other side combined industrial tile floors with glossy white walls. It shared certain traits with hospital halls, like the fact that it had obviously been designed to be cleaned with a power hose. There were even drains in the floor. A few interns passed me as I walked toward Shelby's office. They waved. I nodded. We all went about our business.

The door to Shelby's office was standing slightly ajar. I stopped outside, rapping my knuckles against the wood under her nameplate. "Can I come in?"

"That depends," replied Shelby, yanking the door open and glaring at me. Her hair was out of its ponytail, falling to frame her face in disheveled waves. "Are you going to demand I talk like Crocodile Dundee to amuse the tourists?" Now that she was no longer on stage, her accent had faded, becoming more common and less cliché.

"I wasn't planning to," I said. "I just wanted to let you know I actually made it to the show today."

"Really?" Shelby stepped back, making room for me to come into her office. It was the same size as mine, but contained what seemed like ten times as much stuff. I was constantly afraid of an avalanche when I came to visit. "Do you want a medal?"

"Not particularly." I moved into the office. "I was doing the copperhead survey this morning in the swamp."

"Mud and venomous snakes. Sounds like the ideal date." There was a sharp edge to her words, and she still wasn't smiling. I managed not to wince. Shelby was one of those people who looked miserable, almost funereal, when she wasn't smiling. When she did, it seemed like she could outshine the sun.

She hadn't been smiling much at me recently.

"I'm sorry I didn't invite you," I said. "I knew you had a show this afternoon."

"I suppose that's fair," she said, after a pause that left me squirming. Finally, the corners of her mouth tipped upward, and she asked, "How'd you like it?"

I grinned. "I thought it was fantastic."

"Good, because I thought we had some pacing issues during the conservation section," she said, and began chattering rapidly about the structure of the tiger show, leaving me free to listen and enjoy being back in her good graces.

Shelby was possibly the most dangerous opponent I'd ever faced: brilliant, beautiful, and a biologist who knew how to wrestle a mountain lion without hurting either herself or the animal. She hit all my buttons at once. And she didn't even know my real name, or anything else about my real life. That was part of why she was annoyed at me—I kept pulling away every time she got too close, and I was pretty sure she was getting tired of my crap.

Her talk about the tiger show was winding down. I watched her carefully, trying to decide what the appropriate next move would be. Shelby answered the question for me by crossing the room, leaning forward, and kissing me. I reacted without thinking, sliding my arms around her waist and kissing her back, pulling her against me until I could smell the faint wild traces of tiger on her skin.

When she pulled away, her smile had become something sweeter and darker, like cherry cola syrup. "Come on, Alex, what do you say? Take a girl to dinner after work?"

"I'd love to," I said, allowing my honest regret to come through in my voice, "but I can't. I have two school groups coming tomorrow, and I have a lot of work to do on the samples that I collected today. I'm really sorry."

Shelby's smile faded, replaced by a look of profound sorrow. The first few times I disappointed her, I thought I'd broken her heart. It took weeks before I realized that she was just one of those people who looked like the world was ending every time she was a little unhappy. "You and science have the best relationship. I'm not sure there's really room in it for me."

"Shelby—"

"You've canceled six dates on me, Alex, and that's in the last month. I know we're not official or anything, but a girl likes to know that the man she's seeing actually wants to *see* her once in a while."

"He does! I mean, I do! I've just been busy lately, that's all." My words sounded hollow even to my own ears. Maybe Shelby had a point. Maybe it wasn't fair to either one of us for me to keep stringing her along like this. If I was just willing to admit that it was never going to work, I could save us both a lot of pain in the long run. (In the short run, however, I would be dealing with an angry Australian woman who had access to a large number of predatory cats for the rest of my tenure in Ohio.)

And I couldn't do it. I *liked* Shelby. I liked feeling like there was someone in the world who didn't give a damn about my family or our mission, and who just liked me for me. It would all fall apart eventually, but for now . . .

For now, I just wanted to enjoy it.

Shelby frowned. "You're really sure you can't come out with me tonight? There might be ice cream in it for you . . ."

"You have no idea how much I wish I could," I said, shaking my head. "Can I maybe get a rain check?"

There was a brittle edge to her laughter as she said, "At this rate, we'd need a monsoon for you to pay back all the rain checks that you owe. Come on, Alex. Give me a date. I'm begging you here. Have mercy, and tell me when I'll need my rain gear."

I grimaced. It would take most of the night to dissect the frickens. The next night, I was supposed to be watching my cousin so that my grandparents could have *their* date night. But the night after that . . . "How's the day after tomorrow?" I asked. "If you say it's good, I promise you nothing will interfere. I'll be all yours for the whole evening."

"You know, I'm fairly sure I've heard that one before," she said. "What can you offer to sweeten the deal?" Shelby stepped close enough to poke me in the chest. "Well?"

"Um . . . no biology homework?"

"Aw, and see, I was hoping for a bit of biology homework. The practical sort." Shelby leaned up and kissed me, long and slow and with the kind of promise that made me truly regret the fact that I couldn't go home with her immediately. She smiled again as she pulled away, a languid expression that she could almost have borrowed from the cats she cared for. "I'll see you then. Don't you dare be late. And now, you'll be going. I need to change."

She pushed me out of the office and into the hall, where I stood, gaping like an idiot, as she closed and locked the door behind me.

The rest of the afternoon passed in a flurry of school groups and the usual questions about the denizens of the reptile house, many of which were some variation on "can't you make it be less boring?" Reptiles are fascinating things, but you have to be willing to spend a lot of time waiting for them to move.

The kids who passed through the reptile house would probably have been a lot more interested in my private research projects—frogs with feathers and winged lizards that could turn a man to stone. Hopefully, with a little luck and a little more time, we'd be able to bring things like the frickens and the basilisks into the protected valley of mainstream science before they went totally extinct in the hinterlands of cryptozoology.

I was in a rotten mood by the time we closed. I didn't like abandoning Shelby and her interesting notions of biology homework just to spend another night alone with my microscope. I know I've already said that I sometimes envy my sisters, but nights like these are the ones where it gets hard to deal with. Verity chose a field of specialization that regularly brings her into contact with sapient cryptid species who could explain what they were and where they came from. I chose something that looks a lot like traditional biology. Just a little more likely to turn you to stone or melt you or mutate you if you're not careful about what you're doing.

Basically, I chose the specialization that means spending an awful lot of time alone. I drove along the tree-lined streets of Columbus and cursed myself for poor career choices, poor wardrobe choices, poor choices of pet ... basically, if I could curse myself for it, I did. It made me feel a little bit better, paradoxically; after all, if I was doing absolutely everything wrong, I was at least consistent. That was something, right?

My grandparents live in one of Columbus' older housing developments, a place the locals call "Bexley," which was designed back when they still allowed multiple types of homes in every neighborhood. You have to pay close attention to realize that the same six frames repeat over and over again as you drive through the area. If you don't, you could easily mistake their neighborhood for something that occurred organically, rather than being planned by some canny developers out to make a buck. Even if you weren't paying close attention, though, you'd probably realize that there's something a little bit ... off ... about my grandparents' place. It's the only three-story house on the block, for one, and the only house with a widow's walk. But most of all, it's the only house surrounded by an eight-foot fence with spikes on top.

My grandparents have been practicing "blending in with the neighbors" for a long time. Maybe someday, they'll actually be good at it.

The gate was already open, in anticipation of my arrival. Grandma's car was in its customary place by the door, and Grandpa's car was parked behind it. I pulled up behind him.

"Home sweet home," I said, turning off the engine. The porch light was already on as I walked up the pathway to the door. I smiled at that small gesture of hospitality, pulling my house keys out of my pocket.

I didn't start my stay in Columbus by moving in with my grandparents. I originally had an apartment downtown, right in the heart of the city, where I'd be able to experience the nightlife and see the sights. Only after six months, I figured out that all the nightlife did was make it hard for me to sleep, and the only sights I was seeing were either through a microscope or out in the swamp, which was nowhere near where I was living. And then my cousin Sarah got seriously hurt saving Verity's life, and it suddenly seemed like a really good idea for me to take my grandparents up on their offer of a place to stay. We're family. We stick together.

"Grandma, Grandpa, I'm home!" I called, dropping my briefcase next to the coatrack and peeling off my light jacket. Not that I needed one for Ohio in the spring, but I grew up in Oregon; I feel naked without a coat. Crow appeared at the head of the stairs, croaking once in greeting before disappearing again, off on some obscure griffin business that didn't involve coming down for scritches.

"Alex!" My grandfather emerged from the kitchen. He was grinning widely, and had a frilly apron that read "Kiss the Cook" struggling to remain tied around his waist. "You made it in time for dinner!"

I smiled. "That was the goal. I have a lot of work to do tonight, so I figured I should spend some quality time with my family."

"Good," said Grandpa. "I look forward to hearing about your day. Now come give your grandmother a kiss." He motioned for me to follow him. Being an obedient grandson, I did as I was bid, and stepped into the warm, homey-smelling air of the kitchen. Sometimes it's good to go where everybody knows your name . . . and your species.

My grandparents have what could charitably be referred to as "a mixed marriage." Not in the sense that they're of different religions or races, but in the sense that they're actually different *species*, and neither of them is a member of the species commonly known as *Homo sapiens*. (Their daughter, my mother, is human. She was adopted.)

Grandma Angela is a cuckoo, a form of hyperevolved parasitic wasp with annoyingly strong telepathic abilities. They look like pale, black-haired humans, for reasons that only nature can explain. Nature's not talking, possibly because even nature realizes that giving perfect camouflage to apex predators is sort of a dick move. Grandpa Martin is a little closer to human—or at least, he started out that way. He's what we call a Revenant, a construct of formerly dead body parts that has been successfully reanimated through one highly unpleasant mechanism or another. In his case, it was your standard mad scientist bent on denying the laws of God and man in favor of obeying his own twisted muse. The result of that long-dead scientist's tinkering was my grandfather, a six-and-a-half-foot–tall man who looks, charitably speaking, like he's wrestled one too many bears in his day. He's one of the nicest men I've ever met, maybe because he doesn't feel like anything is worth getting too worked up over.

Grandma married him because he was the first man she'd ever met who wasn't affected by her telepathy. This is the sort of thing that Internet dating sites never have a field for. Anyway, they'd settled in Ohio and adopted three children: my mother Evelyn, my uncle Drew, whose room I was currently occupying, and my cousin Sarah, who was my age. (Technically, this makes Sarah my aunt, but "cousin" is a better match for our respective ages and actual relationship.)

Speaking of Grandma, she was taking dinner out of the oven when Grandpa and I walked into the kitchen. She raised her head and smiled. "Alex! You're home early."

I glanced at the clock. "It's almost six. I need to work on my definition of 'early.'"

"But you can't argue with me, now, can you?" She handed the covered casserole dish to my grandfather, who didn't need oven mitts to transport it safely to the table. "Give me a hug and wash your hands before you put your nametag on. We're having shepherd's pie for dinner."

"I love your shepherd's pie." I obligingly hugged her before moving to the sink. I couldn't stop myself from glancing toward the dining room door as I turned the water on. "How is she?"

Grandma sighed. "It's not her *best* day," she admitted. "She's still having trouble remembering who I am. But she's up and moving around under her own power, and she picked her own clothes out this morning. So that's a good sign."

"Grandma . . ."

"I know, I know. But it's not like there's a manual for this, all right, Alex? There's no one I can ask. Sarah will get better at her own pace."

"Or she won't." I tried to keep my words gentle. I didn't quite succeed.

My cousin Sarah is a cuckoo, like Grandma, even though they're probably not biologically related. Like all cuckoos, she manipulates the memories of the people around her as a sort of natural defense, making them feel like she belongs. Well, a few months ago, the Covenant of St. George managed to corner my sister, Verity. If they'd been able to take her back to Europe with them, they could have learned everything there is to know about our family, starting with the part where we still exist, despite being officially wiped out after the Covenant branded us as traitors to humanity. (The Covenant of St. George: assholes with a cause. They want to wipe out all the "monsters" in the world, and the definition they use encompasses most of my family. Oh, and that thing about us being traitors to humanity? That's because we used to be members of the Covenant. Hell hath no fury like a centuries-old organization of zealots scorned.)

Verity couldn't let that happen. *Sarah* couldn't let that happen, and so she stepped in and used what's supposed to be a passive defense in an active fashion, revising the Covenant's memories of what they'd seen in New York. The result was a bunch of brain-blasted operatives ... and one brain-burnt cousin.

Grandma went to New York to bring Sarah home. I moved in with them three days later.

My grandmother looked at me silently for a moment, processing my contradiction. Then she nodded, very slightly, and commanded, "Dry your hands, put on your nametag, and bring the biscuits."

"Yes, ma'am." I've always found it best to do as I was told when dealing with my grandmother. Both my grandmothers, really. Dad's mom isn't any less terrifying when crossed.

The nametag was preprinted, large block letters on a white background. ALEX. Without her telepathy,

Sarah—whose species didn't evolve with the need to recognize faces, thanks to their habit of reading minds—couldn't tell one person from another. That included her family. She could normally have told us apart by voice, but as bad as she'd been lately, that was by no means a guarantee. Nametags made things a little easier on her, and hence a lot easier on the rest of us.

Grandpa had already dished out the shepherd's pie when we got to the dining room. I put down the biscuits at the center of the table and took my seat across from Sarah, pulling my plate closer to me. Her plate was conspicuously empty. That meant this wasn't one of the days when she could be trusted with a fork. This was going to be a fun dinner.

"Hi, Sarah," I said.

She kept her eyes fixed on the table as she mumbled something I couldn't understand. A brief pressure at my temples informed me that she was trying to make contact. I was once again grateful for the anti-telepathy charm Grandma insisted I keep on me until Sarah's recovery was finished. Sarah no longer remembered enough about her own strength to watch her volume, and I didn't need another migraine from her screaming inside my head.

"Here you go, sweetheart," said Grandma, placing a biscuit on Sarah's plate. It was liberally smeared with ketchup. Sarah didn't react. Sighing, Grandma kissed the top of her head. "Just eat when you feel like it, Sarah. That's all we need from you right now." She took her own seat, shoulders slightly slumped.

I know Sarah did what she did of her own free will. I know Verity didn't ask to be captured by the Covenant. But sometimes, when I saw my grandmother looking so defeated, I just wanted to scream at both of them for having been so careless.

Instead, I stuck my fork in my shepherd's pie, and asked, "Have either of you heard anything about lindworms in Ohio?"

"Not in a long time," said Grandpa. "Why?"

I smiled, trying to make the expression seem sincere. Maybe I couldn't make Sarah better or figure out how to balance my duties and my social life, but I could do this. I could be there for my family, and I could help them remember that they weren't alone, no matter how bad things got. "Dee and I went out into the swamp to gather fricken samples today . . ." I began.

This was dinner with my family. Everything else could wait a little while.

Three

"Our relationship with the mice is . . . complicated. Just remember that being a god doesn't actually give you any authority and you'll be fine."

—Kevin Price

A nice, if borrowed, bedroom in an only moderately creepy suburban home in Columbus, Ohio

A MADDENED CHORUS OF exultations greeted me when I opened the bedroom door. It increased in volume when the congregation caught sight of the tray I was balancing on my left arm. "HAIL! HAIL! HAIL THE ARRIVAL OF THE DINNER!" Crow, who was curled up in the cat bed on top of the wardrobe, croaked his amusement at the scene. At least, I hoped it was amusement. The last thing I wanted was a war between my resident griffin and my splinter colony of Aeslin mice.

Yes, mice: talking, intelligent mice that worship the Price men as gods—which is a very long story that no one seems to fully understand, not even those of us in the pantheon. There's a reason Crow is the closest thing to a cat that anyone in my family has ever had.

The rodent rejoicing continued as I stepped into the room and closed the door behind myself, and they reached a fever pitch when I raised my right hand to signal that I was about to speak. There were only thirty mice in my splinter of the family colony, but thirty mice can make a hell of a lot of noise when they feel so inclined, and Aeslin mice anticipating their dinner are *always* so inclined.

"Quiet, please," I requested.

The mice quieted down, ever obedient to the dictates of their gods. They sat back on their haunches and wrapped their tails around their hind legs, fixing their glittering black eyes firmly on me as they waited for me to proclaim some pearls of godly wisdom. That, or feed them. To the Aeslin mice, those concepts were basically one and the same.

"I will need three assistants to help me sort feathers tonight, and three more to help articulate fricken skeletons this coming weekend," I said. "The colony will be paid for the labor in cheese and cake. Is this acceptable?"

Judging by the wild cheering that overtook the Aeslin, it was acceptable. I waited for them to calm down before I said, "This is for science. Science rules will be in effect during the work."

"Science rules" was dealing-with-the-Aeslin shorthand for "no rejoicing, no dropping what you're working on to race off and join a spontaneous parade in honor of the Violent Priestess, no asking complex theological questions when you're supposed to be focusing on your job." It was sort of amazing sometimes, how many rules we needed to keep ourselves sane.

The announcement of science rules was greeted in a rather more subdued fashion. The mice exchanged looks before turning as one to the colony's High Priestess. She was distinguished from the others by her slightly more elaborate attire—a cloak of glossy black feathers harvested from Crow during molting season—and her posture, which was straight and proud, even when facing one of her personal gods. She cocked her small gray head to the side, thoughtfully. Then she nodded.

"It Shall Be So," she intoned, stressing each word so that it sounded like it had been individually capitalized.

That was the cue the mice needed to resume their rejoicing, shouting, "HAIL!" and "ALL GLORY TO THE SCIENCE RULES OF SCIENCE!" I smiled gratefully at the High Priestess as I set the tray on the floor. I barely had time to grab Crow's dish of meat scraps and liver before the colony swarmed over the food, their exultations reaching a fever pitch. Only the High Priestess remained aloof, sitting calmly on the floor near the bed as she watched her people accost the food. They didn't eat it. Instead they picked up the plates, working in teams of five, and began toting them toward the closet. The dishes would reappear in the morning, neatly stacked and ready for me to take back down to the kitchen.

I walked over and put Crow's dish on top of the wardrobe, next to his bed. He stood, stretching languidly, and I gave him a quick scratch behind the ears before he began gulping down his food. At that point, interfering with him might have caused me to lose a finger.

The mice had managed to disappear by the time I finished feeding Crow—all save the High Priestess, who was still sitting patiently, waiting for my attention. I pulled out the desk chair and sat, putting myself closer to her level without doing her the disrespect of kneeling. Aeslin hate to see their gods humble themselves. "Hail," I said, leaning forward with my elbows on my knees. "What's going on?"

"Hail to the God of Scales and Silence," squeaked the High Priestess. "We have done as you bid us do, and have kept Eyes Upon the younger Heartless One."

"Thank you very much for watching Sarah for me." Aeslin mice have their own unique approach to the language. I was the God of Scales and Silence—largely, I think, because I liked snakes and didn't talk as much as my sisters—and Grandma and Sarah were the Heartless Ones. It was a biologically accurate label, if somewhat insensitive-sounding: cuckoos don't have hearts. They have decentralized circulatory systems, and thick, clear fluid that's basically biological antifreeze where most bipeds would have blood. The mice weren't trying to be cruel. Aeslin mice very rarely are.

"It is our pleasure to serve," said the High Priestess. She wiped her paw across her whiskers in a gesture that I had come to learn meant she was upset. "Holiness, I must speak to you frankly. I apologize if my words offend."

"It's okay. Say whatever you need to say."

"The younger Heartless One . . ." The High Priestess hesitated before saying, in a profoundly troubled tone, "She is Not Well, Holiness. I do not know that she will ever become Well. I fear for your safety, and for the safety of the colony, in her presence. The Heartless Ones . . . when they are Unwell, they can destroy so very much, so very quickly. We should not be here. *You* should not be here. We have Faith, Holiness, but there is Faith, and then there is Common Sense. Sometimes the one must take precedence over the other."

I blinked. The Aeslin mice are smart. Sometimes it can be easy to forget that, with the way they carry on, but they'd never have survived long enough to hook up with the family if they weren't capable of taking care of themselves. Finally, I said, "I understand your concerns. I can't leave my family. I wouldn't . . . if I were the kind of man who abandoned his family when they needed him, I wouldn't be worthy of calling myself a God of the colony."

"We understand, but we are still afraid," said the High Priestess.

"I understand the feeling," I said. "Is everyone wearing the charms we made for them?" Getting antitelepathy charms for an entire colony of Aeslin mice hadn't been cheap, and I hadn't regretted it for a moment. The last thing we needed was for Sarah to accidentally mind-control the colony in her sleep.

The High Priestess nodded. "We have done as you have Commanded."

"Good. Sarah is unwell. She became unwell helping Verity—the Arboreal Priestess—to protect the family. I can't refuse to do as much as she did to keep us all safe. Now. What did you see?"

The High Priestess preened her whiskers before saying, "The younger Heartless One engaged in an argument with nothing. We thought at first that she was speaking with her mind, and echoing with her voice, but the elder Heartless One entered and bid her quiet and calm. The elder set the younger a task, to chase the numbers they call 'prime' as far as she could."

"And?"

"And she began to cry and said there were no numbers." The look the High Priestess gave me was frankly terrified. Disney had never animated such fear in the eyes of a mouse. "We have never heard tell of a Heartless One losing the numbers. It Bodes Ill."

I winced. I couldn't help myself. Cuckoos have a racial obsession with math. No one knows why, but every cuckoo we've ever encountered has been easily distracted by numbers. Sarah had been in New York with Verity in part because she wanted an excuse to audit some math classes at the colleges there. Sarah lived for her math classes. If she couldn't do something as simple as reciting primes . . .

She was still family. And family doesn't leave family behind. "I promise you, if it looks like we're in any danger because of Sarah, I'll get us out of here. You have my word. But for right now, we have to stay. I thank you for your report. There will be extra cake tomorrow night to show my gratitude."

The High Priestess sighed. "You are your father's son," she said quietly. "I am glad to know that, even as I fear for your safety, and ours as well. I shall send your assistants to you anon, Holiness."

"Thank you," I said again, and offered her a small half-bow. The High Priestess bowed back, with all the formality of a clergywoman addressing her deity, before scurrying away, vanishing into the closet with the others. I looked at the closet door for a moment. Then I turned to the desk and opened my laptop. There was work to be done before morning, and my report wasn't going to write itself.

The official version of my trip to the swamp had already been written and submitted to zoo management. Now it was time to write the version that would go into the family record. Crow settled back into his cat bed, his head hanging over the edge of the wardrobe so that he could watch my every move. I ignored him. Years of living with Antimony looking over my shoulder has left me essentially immune to suspicious glares. He'd long since forgiven me for leaving him at home alone after our excursion to the swamp—all I had to do was give him his dinner and everything was wonderful again—but now he was angry because I wouldn't let him have the frickens I was planning to dissect.

The dissection itself took about two hours, and is better left to the imagination. If you've ever seen a frog dissected in a high school science class, you know the basics: the details are mostly squishy and unpleasant, even to the scientifically-minded. I had to write up my notes after that, which took longer than expected, largely because I was tired enough to be continually distracted by my research materials. First I had to list the species of fricken we had found still living in Ohio (assuming we hadn't collected and killed the last individuals; it would be bad form for me to render a cryptid extinct in the process of studying it). That meant digging through the field guide to verify my identifications. Mom used to say, not quite joking, that if I touched a field guide, you'd need to send a search party to get me out again. She wasn't wrong.

After the fricken count was done, I had to write up

the encounter with the lindworm, and that meant another trip through the field guide, with a supplementary jaunt into the local bestiary to be sure there really was no confirmed record of a native lindworm species. The one we'd seen in the swamp didn't quite match the description of any known lindworm, although it was close enough to be a relative. There was a good chance that we'd just discovered an entirely new species.

"I love science," I said, and saved the file.

It only took a few minutes to write up a cover letter describing the situation, attach the report, and mail everything off to my parents. I sent a second copy to the printer. I'd give it to the Aeslin, for safety's sake. There is no better backup system in this world than a colony of Aeslin mice. They may demand to be paid in cheese and cake, but once they know something, they know it forever.

With all that done, I checked on Crow—now soundly asleep—and sprinkled some baby bloodworms into the terrarium with my poison dart frickens, which goggled their brightly colored eyes and flared their brightly colored crests in a threat display that was as adorable as it was serious. The neon-tinted little amphibians were incredibly deadly.

"Yes, you're terrifying," I said to the frickens, who ignored me, already engaged in pursuing their dinner. I walked to the closet, where I stopped, cleared my throat, and said, "The Time of Science is upon us."

Live with Aeslin long enough, you learn how to pronounce capitals. It makes things easier. There was a rustling from inside the closet, and then three sleek-furred young temple novices appeared around the edges of the door, whiskers forward and ears up.

"We Are Ready!" they squeaked in joyous unison.

"Great," I said. "Let's sort some feathers."

Aeslin mice excel at small, repetitive jobs that contain an element of ritual. Sorting fricken feathers by species, type, age of specimen, and whether or not they showed signs of fungal infection was fiddly enough and required enough very precise steps that the Aeslin couldn't have been happier. I barely had anything to do once the three of them got involved. That was exactly what I'd been hoping for. I picked up the field guide, sat back in my chair, and started reading.

According to the historical records, there were fifteen subspecies of fricken that could potentially appear in this region of Ohio. Five were considered common, six more were uncommon, and four were rare bordering on "may not be native, but we caught one once, and that means we need to make a record of it." My family has never been what you'd call "restrained" when it comes to maintaining the regional field guides. With good reason. A lot of the smaller, apparently harmless cryptids, like the frickens, can be used as a general barometer of an area's well-being. If they're dying by the dozens, you probably have a problem. It's best to find that out from the little things, rather than learning it from, say, a unicorn attack.

(Unicorns like virgins. That part is true. But being liked by a unicorn is actually not very good for your health, and being disliked by a unicorn is even worse. Unicorns are deadly to things and people that they decide not to like. We'd have a shoot-on-sight order if they weren't so vital to maintaining a healthy water table. Nature enjoys a good practical joke every now and then.)

That was the historical record. Based on the recorded sightings from my fieldwork, my dissection results, and the slowly growing piles of feathers, there were currently *nineteen* subspecies of fricken living in the swamps of Columbus, Ohio.

"Well, hell," I said, staring at the heaps of feathers.

Things exist for a reason. Nature doesn't mess around with things that don't have a purpose. Sometimes those things come into competition. Sometimes they edge each other out. Invasive species have been transforming the world in their own image for as long as animals have been capable of moving from one place to another. Humanity has hastened the process, since we're the first animals to build airplanes and container ships, but we didn't start it, and it won't stop when we're gone.

If the number of frickens in Ohio was going up, they had to be filling a niche that was previously occupied by something else. My money was on the frogs. That was the whole purpose of this study: to prove that the native frogs were being replaced by either an increase in the native frickens, or by an influx of frickens from elsewhere. Not the most exciting stuff in the world, I know, but it was ecologically important, especially if we wanted to continue keeping the frickens from being revealed to the world.

I yawned and reached for my laptop. I needed to make some more notes.

I woke up with my cheek on the keyboard, having already filled several hundred pages with random characters. I sat up, wiping the drool from my cheek. My back ached. I stood, straightening as I turned toward my bed. Then, before I could stop myself, I let out a short, sharp scream, which ended only when I clapped my hand over my mouth. Hopefully, that hadn't been enough to wake my grandparents.

Sarah was sitting cross-legged on my bed.

She was wearing a white nightgown, and had a red ribbon tied in her hair, making her look like a Tim Burton horror movie reimagining of Snow White. She cocked her head when she saw me looking at her, but there was no trace of actual comprehension in her wide blue eyes. She just kept staring at me.

"Sarah?" I lowered my hand, wishing I could stop my heart from pounding against my ribs. "What are you doing here? This isn't your room."

"The moon doesn't approve of the screaming in the

cornfield," she said. She sounded entirely reasonable, as long as I ignored the fact that she was talking like a book of Mad Libs. "Have you seen the Queen of Hearts today? Does she have the treacle tarts?"

"Sarah, you're scaring me. Do I need to go get Grandma?"

"No. No no no no . . ." She started shaking her head viciously from side to side, knocking her ribbon askew. I took a step forward. She grabbed handfuls of her hair, pulling as she continued to chant denial.

"Sarah!" I grabbed her wrists before I could think better of it. Telepathy is easier for cuckoos when there's skin-to-skin contact. Even with my anti-telepathy charm, there was a chance she'd be able to read me while I was touching her. That still seemed better than letting her hurt herself.

Sarah stopped shaking her head. She blinked at me, eyes luminescing with a brief flash of white, and asked, "Alex?"

It was the first time she'd really sounded like herself since she came back from New York. I smiled hesitantly, not letting go of her wrists. "Hi, Sarah."

"Your head is full of scientific classifications and the natural order of things." Well, that answered the question of whether or not she could read me. I was still a little surprised when a relieved smile spread across her face, and she said, "I like it. It's been . . . not so orderly in here for a little while."

I didn't know whether she was aware of how long it had actually been, and I didn't want to think about it too hard. Thinking about it would have been the same as asking her, and that wouldn't have been fair. "We've been worried about you," I said instead, and moved to let go of her wrists.

"No!" Sarah grabbed my hands, flipping the grip around so that she was holding onto me. She bit her lip, and said, "Please, no. I don't want everything to come apart again."

"Sarah . . ."

"I won't push, I promise I won't push, but Angela's filled with worrying about me, and I can't read Martin at all. Please, let me stay and be organized? Just for a little while? Please?"

She looked so anxious—and so exhausted—that I relented. It wasn't like I could keep her out, and at least this way, she might follow instructions. "All right, but I need to sleep. Can I do that?"

"Even your dreams are orderly," said Sarah. She let go of my wrists. "Hurry please. Hurry." She still sounded more coherent than she had before she grabbed me, but there was an edge of harried desperation to it, like she was clinging to her renewed lucidity by her fingernails.

"I'll hurry," I assured her, and grabbed my pajamas from the floor next to the bed before fleeing the room, heading for the bathroom down the hall.

I reviewed my options as I brushed my teeth. I could wake Grandma and ask her to take Sarah back to her own room, possibly with a few strong suggestions about locks. That would prevent things like this from happening again, and also allow me to dismiss the dull but growing concern over how many times Sarah had crept down the stairs to watch me sleep. And yet . . .

And yet Sarah, for all that she wasn't human, was family. Family comes first. The cryptid community comes second. She represented both those things, and she'd been wounded saving my little sister's life. If all she wanted was for me to sleep holding her hand, was that really so much for her to ask? I had my anti-telepathy charm, and I had the mice. If she'd done anything to threaten me, I had faith that they would have woken me up.

Sarah was still sitting on the bed when I returned with my teeth brushed, my pajamas on, and my anti-telepathy charm firmly in place. "Hello, hello," she said, looking down at her crossed ankles. "How's your father?"

"In Oregon," I said, reaching out to take her wrist. "Sarah."

"Yes?" She raised her head, eyes focusing a bit better already.

"A few ground rules for tonight."

"Yes, yes, it's good to be grounded; how are you grounding me tonight?"

"You are sleeping on top of the covers; if you try to come under the covers, I'm sending you back to your room." It wasn't as harsh as it sounded. Cuckoos get some benefits from the clear hemolymph in place of blood; for one, they don't feel heat or cold the way most mammals do. Like I said, Nature likes a good practical joke every now and then. As for why I didn't want her under the blankets . . .

Skin contact made her stronger. If I wanted to keep her from burning my brain out when she had a nightmare, I needed to minimize how much we were touching one another.

Sarah nodded. "That's fair," she agreed.

"If you start feeling like you're going to project at me, rather than just reading, you need to let go and get out." I folded back the covers with my free hand.

"Okay."

"Okay," I said, and got into the bed. It felt strange to trust her like this. It felt even stranger to doubt her. Sarah waited until I was settled before she curled up next to me, resting her head on my shoulder. I dropped our joined hands to my stomach, staring up at the darkened ceiling as I listened to her breathing slowly level out into sleep.

Sometime after that, I joined her in unconsciousness.

My dreams were full of algebraic equations and the sewers of New York, where alligator men danced with ladies made entirely of numbers, and carnival music played on an unseen hurdy-gurdy. Even asleep, I knew that Sarah's dreams were leaking into mine, but it didn't really seem to matter. Together, the two of us slept on.

Four

"The trouble with the word 'monster' is that
it's very much in the eye of the beholder.
Show me a monster, and I'll show you a
man who just didn't know how to explain
himself to you."

—Martin Baker

*Ohio's West Columbus Zoo, home of many exotic species
and way too many geese*

I PULLED INTO THE ZOO parking lot at ten past eight, trying to yawn around the bagel I had clamped in my
teeth. It wasn't working very well, given my desire not to
aspirate chunks of breakfast food. Crow wasn't helping.
He was curled in the passenger seat making throaty
churring noises that sounded suspiciously like laughter.

As soon as I had a hand free, I removed the bagel
from my mouth and waved it at the uncaring Church
Griffin. "You are a terrible pet," I informed him. "My
mother was right. I should have gotten a dog." Any dog
that my parents would have approved of me getting
would probably have breathed fire or transformed into
a dragon on the full moon or something, but at least it
wouldn't have *laughed* at me.

Crow croaked.

"Uh-huh. Out, before I change my mind about bringing you to work today." I opened my door. "Office, Crow."

Crow launched himself from the seat in a flurry of madly beating wings and flew out the open door, smacking me in the face with his tail as he passed. I spat out a small hairball and got out of the car, tucking my keys into my pocket. Time for one more day in the real world, explaining that the existence of House Slytherin in the Harry Potter books doesn't make snakes evil and keeping small boys from climbing into the snapping turtle enclosure.

The Canada geese that infested the pond outside the zoo thronged the sidewalk as they saw me approach, snaky necks bent into S-curves and orange beaks working overtime as they honked frantically. I threw the rest of my bagel into the water. The geese followed it, fat gray-and-white bodies hustling as each one tried to beat the others to the prize. I walked on undisturbed, smothering another yawn behind my hand.

Sarah hadn't been in the bed when my alarm rang. Since she didn't put off as much body heat as a human, I couldn't tell how long she'd been gone by feeling the blankets, but my fingers were stiff, like something had been gripping them for hours. I hoped the night had been more restful for her than it was for me. My dreams had been strange enough to keep me from sleeping well, probably because they weren't *my* dreams. I wasn't mad at her or anything. I was still going to talk to Grandma after work, to find out whether that sort of thing was actually helpful to Sarah's recovery.

(That assumed that she would know. Cuckoo mental health is something of an unexplored territory, since most of them are too dangerous to attempt to psychoanalyze. If anything, Sarah's actions had proven that she wasn't your ordinary cuckoo. After all, an ordinary cuckoo would probably have slit my throat while I was unconscious. All Sarah had done was try to steal a pillow.)

It was almost an hour to the zoo's official opening, and the arrival plaza was empty, the ticket booths stand-

ing deserted. By nine o'clock they'd be thronged by ex-
cited children, harried parents, and even more harried
teachers with their school groups. For now, I could walk
through the area without worrying that I was going to
step on any runaway toddlers. I paused to stroke the
nose of the brass lion statue, murmuring a good morning,
and turned toward the gate.

"Morning, Dr. Preston," said the guard on duty. "ID
please?"

"Does it ever occur to you that 'good morning, person
I know by name, please provide proof of who you are' is
a little silly, Lloyd?" I asked, digging my zoo ID card out
of my pocket and handing it to him.

"Every day of my life, but you know what happens
when you don't do your job." Lloyd was an older man,
tan and thin as a sun-dried lizard, with a battered slouch
hat pulled firmly down over his presumably bald pate. I'd
never seen him without the hat, or without the thick-
lensed glasses that gave his gaze a fishbowl quality that
I knew all too well from my time in my high school science club. I put his age as somewhere between sixty and
eighty, in that timeless country occupied by men lucky
enough to live that long.

"I suppose that's fair," I said.

Lloyd snorted. "Fair doesn't enter into it. Never has,
never will." He gave my ID a cursory glance, handed it
back to me, and unlocked the gate. "I don't check your
ID, you tell the administration, and I wind up another
sad old man trying to take your over-fancy coffee order
at Starbucks. No, thank you, Dr. Preston. You can come
on in now."

"Thank you, Lloyd," I said, stepping through the open
gate.

"You're welcome, Dr. Preston." Lloyd offered me a
friendly nod before turning back to face the plaza, standing at the sort of military attention that had absolutely
no place in a zoo.

At least he took his job seriously. I shrugged, put my ID away, and started down the path that would eventually take me to the reptile house.

About half the zookeepers were out and checking their respective enclosures; a few were in the enclosures, waking or talking to their charges. I waved and kept on walking. We all had work to do before the zoo would be ready to open, and they wouldn't appreciate the disruption.

A little girl in a vibrant orange sari was sitting on the bench outside the reptile house, kicking her sneaker-clad feet sullenly against the cobblestones. I hesitated before walking over to her. "Good morning, Chandi. How did you get into the zoo this time?"

"I'm not telling," she said, in a tone as sullen as her posture. "When can I come in the reptile house?"

"Well, that depends."

She glanced up, eyes narrowed warily. She was a pretty child, and she was going to be a devastatingly attractive woman someday, if we could convince her to stop sneaking into the zoo through whatever cracks and crevices she could find. She'd snuck in via the alligator enclosure a week before, and only the fact that she didn't smell like a mammal had prevented her from getting eaten. And she always did it while wearing her nicest dresses. I was starting to wonder if she actually repelled mud.

"On what?" she asked.

"If you promise me that you won't sneak in for another week, I'll let you in right now, and—" I raised a finger, cutting off the protest I could see forming on her lips, "—I'll let you get Shami out of his enclosure and take him into my office."

"For how long?" she asked.

"I can give you three hours."

There was a pause while Chandi considered my offer. Then, regally, she nodded and slid off the bench. "Okay," she said, and offered me her hand, as guileless as any eight year old has ever been. I took it. It was better for both of us if she didn't seem to be running around the zoo unescorted.

Dee met us at the reptile house door. "Alex—" She stopped herself when she saw that I wasn't alone. "Oh, good morning, Chandi, I didn't realize today was one of your scheduled visits with Shami."

"That's because it's not," I said. "We made a deal." My assistant looked flustered, which wasn't an easy thing to accomplish, and her wig for the day—a lovely red bee-hive style studded with polka-dot bows—was pulsing, signaling that whatever had her upset was bad enough to have also upset her hair. "What's wrong?"

"Wrong? Nothing's wrong. Why should something be wrong?" Dee laughed, a jagged, unrealistic sound. I blinked at her. So did Chandi.

"I thought gorgons were familiar with normal human emotional response," said Chandi, looking up at me for a clue as to what was supposed to happen next.

"They are," said Dee. "I mean, we are. I mean, are you sure you want to let Chandi in early? We have a *lot* of work to do."

"I promised her three hours with Shami," I said. "Unless there's some sort of 'let's panic for no good reason over something that can wait until lunch' problem, I'm fine with bringing her in early. It'll make it easier for me to get Shami out of his enclosure without needing to explain to a human why I'm handing a spectacled cobra to a little girl."

"I could explain," said Chandi demurely.

"I want to get Shami out of his enclosure before I have to explain to *anyone* why I allowed a little girl to bite and kill a member of my staff," I amended.

Chandi pouted.

"That's the problem!" said Dee. "Andrew was supposed to be here an hour ago to feed the turtles. When I got here, the door was unlocked, but Andrew was no-where to be seen."

I blinked. "Oh. That's a problem."

"Yeah, it is."

"I'm bored," said Chandi. "May I see my fiancé now?"

"Yes, Chandi, you can, but I want to renegotiate our deal first."

Chandi's eyes narrowed. "You said I could see him," she said, her voice taking on a faint lisp as her fangs descended. I kept hold of her hand, despite the fact that every mammalian instinct I had was telling me to let go and move away. Being bitten by a venomous snake is never good for you, and the young, who have little to no control over how much venom they expel in a bite, are the most dangerous of all.

(It wasn't until my sister discovered that dragons never became extinct, and that the cryptids we'd been classifying as "dragon princesses" were actually the female of the species, that we stopped to take a long hard look at the wadjet. We'd always assumed they pair-bonded with their human servants, somehow extending their lives through an interaction with their venom. Instead, they turned out to be another form of dragon, one where the males resembled immense cobras, while the females looked like humans. And this is just one more entry on a long, long list of reasons that I never dated much: half the girls I met in the course of my daily life were never human in the first place.)

"Without Andrew, Dee and I are going to need to feed all the reptiles before the zoo opens in," I glanced at the clock above the door, "thirty minutes. If you'll take the venomous snakes while I handle the turtles and lizards and Dee does the nonvenomous snakes, I'll let you have six hours with Shami. Three today, as promised, and three tomorrow, with no argument or attempt to backpedal."

"All I have to do is feed a few snakes?"

I nodded. "You have my word."

"Very well." Chandi turned to Dee and smiled brightly, showing her fangs. "Please take me to the rats."

I let go of her hand. "Dee, we'll talk about this as soon as we're open, all right?"

"All right," she allowed. "I'll go get the feeding schedule."

Getting the reptile house ready to open proved to be a remarkably fast process when we had someone who actually spoke snake helping us out. The fact that Chandi wasn't worried about the prospect of being bitten didn't hurt. (Wadjet are immune to all known forms of venom, and probably a few that we haven't gotten around to officially discovering yet, since venom has a nasty tendency to kill the people who first find out that it exists.) I stowed my coat, briefcase, and lunch in my office, and we got to work with surprising efficiency. Soon, all that was left was for me to hang a "this exhibit is temporarily closed" sign on the enclosure that housed Chandi's fiancé, and we were set to receive visitors.

Just in time, too. The reptile house was one of the most popular early morning destinations for school groups, and no sooner had we opened the door than we were flooded with human children Chandi's age. I spared a thought for how most of those kids would react if they saw Chandi, now happily curled up with Shami on the beanbag chair in Dee's office. I just as quickly let it go, and turned to help a little girl win an argument about whether or not boa constrictors swallowed their prey whole. (I, and science, said yes. Her mother, who was tired of dinnertime attempts to swallow broccoli without chewing, said no.)

It was just another day at the office. The loud, snake-scented office full of wide-eyed children, some of whom were seeing their first really dangerous members of the reptile kingdom up close. Having both Dee and Chandi in the building had the snakes all worked up, and they were putting on quite the show as they slithered around their enclosures and even reared up to flick their tongues at the glass. A large bluegill swam too close to Crunchy's open jaws, and the big snapping turtle did what he did best, slamming his beak closed hard enough that the sound was audible through the side of the tank. The children swarmed in that direction, pressing their faces up against the glass and waiting to see if he was going to do it again. Oblivious to their admiration, Crunchy resumed his normal posture of patient serenity.

Dee caught my eye, nodding toward my office door. "Go," she said. "The first official tour isn't for an hour. Get started on what you need to finish today."

I brightened. "You sure?" I liked watching the kids, but I'd like knowing that my paperwork for the week was finished even more.

"I'm sure." Dee flashed me a quick smile. "If they get out of control, I'll just take off my wig and remind them that sometimes, a trip to the zoo means you get the opportunity to feed the animals."

"Right." I laughed. "You have fun with that, and if you need me, I'll be in my office."

"Sure thing, boss-man." She saluted mockingly. "I will do my best not to burn the building down while you're sequestered in your chamber of scholarship."

Past experience told me "saying good-bye" could last upward of fifteen minutes if we kept going, and by that point, my escape would doubtless be blocked by some group of teenagers who wanted to know whether we ever used Crunchy to dispose of human bodies. (Answer: yes, but it was an emergency, and the guy really, really deserved it.) I answered her salute with one of my own before turning and fleeing the room, heading for the questionable safety of my office.

I had no sooner ducked inside—easing the door carefully shut behind me, since slamming was both immature and likely to draw attention—when I heard a sound that seemed to have been dredged up from the deepest pits of hell. It was a combination of diamond fingernails scraping across a blackboard and the yowling of an angry cat, and it says something about my life choices that I recognized it instantly.

"*Shit*," I said, turning toward the window. "Crow."

My Church Griffin was clinging to the outside of the windowsill, wings flapping wildly as he struggled to maintain his balance, and forelimbs pressed against the glass. When he saw me, he redoubled his yowling, and his flapping, until I was genuinely afraid that he was going to hurt himself.

"Crow! Calm down!" I scrambled across the office, knocking over a stack of paperwork that should have been filed a week ago, and opened the window. Crow slammed through the opening, scolding loudly as he flew a lap around the office. Then he dove into the cat bed atop the desk hutch, becoming a lump of sullen-looking black feathers and banded brown fur.

I sighed and closed the window. "I'm sorry, Crow. It's been a hectic morning."

No response from the sulking griffin.

"If you'd let me leave you home once in a while, we wouldn't have to worry about you getting locked out."

Still no response from the sulking griffin.

This was the sort of thing that could go on all day, and I didn't have time for that if I wanted to get anything done before the tour groups began to arrive. I picked up the jar of dried liver cubes I kept as treats for Crow, shook four of them out, and set them carefully next to the cat bed.

"When you're speaking to me again, let me know," I said. "Right now, I have work to do. I'm sorry I left you outside."

Maybe talking to a pet like it was a person was a sign of loneliness, or stress, or my inevitable impending status as the male equivalent of a cat lady. Whatever it was, I felt better after leaving Crow the treats. I sat down at the desk, reaching for my keyboard.

I was typing the last of my emails to the administrative office—this one listing my supply needs for the next month—when someone knocked on my office door. The sound was followed by the door swinging open just wide enough for Dee to stick her head inside. "One of the teachers reported, quote, 'a horrible racket outside the snake house, I think somebody's being murdered in there,' end quote," she said. "I told security that one of the kids threw a tantrum when we wouldn't let him hug Crunchy."

"Quick thinking."

"You didn't give me much choice." She looked to where Crow was still curled tightly in his cat bed. "Is he asleep or giving you the cold shoulder?"

"What do you think?"

"I think you should have gotten an iguana."

I laughed, glancing at the clock. Then I grimaced. "Is that really the time?"

"Clocks don't lie," said Dee, stepping fully into the office. "Your first tour group will be here in a few minutes. Time sure does fly when you're having fun, huh?"

"Oh, is that what I've been doing?" I pushed my keyboard away. "I thought it was paperwork."

Dee laughed. "It comes for everyone. Chandi is still in my office with her fiancé. They looked so peaceful that it seemed best not to disturb them."

As long as no one from zoo management showed up wanting to show off the spectacled cobra, that should be fine. I nodded. "Good plan. Have we heard from Andrew yet?"

"No. I tried his cell phone, but there's no answer."

I sighed. "Great."

"Okay. I have made small talk, I have asked after your griffin, and I have told you what's going on with our resident wadjet." Dee planted her hands on her hips, painted eyebrows arched high. "Well?"

I looked at her blankly. "Well what?"

"This is where you explain to me what you've learned from the frickens we collected yesterday."

"What? Oh!" I grimaced. "Sorry, Dee. I was distracted."

"I know. You don't usually wander around rocking the absentminded professor look for fun." She leaned against the doorframe, effectively blocking me inside the room. "So come on. What's up, Doc?"

"I drafted the Aeslin mice into helping me last night. Full examination of the subspecies of fricken encountered during our most recent swamp expedition showed that they were healthy, with no outward signs of illness. They all seem to be eating a varied diet, which is actually odd for two of the subspecies—they'd normally be hunted out of certain food sources by larger frogs." If not eaten by the frogs. Nature doesn't play favorites. "Two were females of breeding age and size, only one was carrying eggs, which means the other must have spawned recently."

"Fungal infection?"

"Yes and no."

Dee paused. "Okay, science boy. Try that again, using words of more than one syllable."

I smiled a little. "See, if more girls had made that request in high school, I might not have been forced to take my sister to prom. Just four frickens showed signs of fungal infection . . . on their feathers, and *only* on their feathers. What's more, three of the four had molted recently, and showed very little fungal growth."

Slowly, Dee nodded. "Okay. And one more time, in English?"

"We know that frogs and other amphibians are dying off. There are a lot of reasons, but fungal infection is a big one. The frickens are protected from the worst of the fungus because they're amphibians with feathers. They're enjoying a hitherto unknown supply of food, spawning pools, and unoccupied habitat. They're spreading to fill the spaces the frogs are leaving in the food chain."

"But isn't that a good thing?" asked Dee, frowning. "I mean, there are a lot of things out there that rely on frogs as a food source. If they're willing to eat frickens instead of frogs, problem solved."

"Except that the frickens will breed. They'll fill the open ecological niches."

Dee looked at me blankly.

I swallowed a sigh. "What happens when some enterprising young biologist comes running in with the revolutionary news that frogs with feathers have been spotted in the swamps of Ohio?" Or any other state or province in North America. South America was a whole different ball of wax. I'd need serious funds to know whether the same thing was happening with the frickens down there.

Finally Dee's eyes widened as she got my point. "Oh, hell . . . the frickens are going to get acknowledged by conventional biology."

"Which takes them neatly out of the cryptozoological wheelhouse, yes." That wasn't the problem: more like convenient shorthand for the problem, which was, quite simply, that the formal discovery of the fricken would lead to a whole new school of scientific study. Technically, moving things from "cryptid" to "acknowledged part of the natural world" was something I wanted very much. The Covenant of St. George couldn't exactly lead a campaign against cute little feathered froggies. But when people realized that amphibians could have feathers . . .

It would completely change the way the world looked at amphibians, which would, in turn, change the way we looked at reptiles. It was unavoidable, and becoming more so with every year that passed. That was what made my work so important. If this was going to happen, we were going to try to control it.

"If you knew this was happening, what are you planning to do about it?"

"We didn't know. We suspected." I raked a hand through my hair, pulling it away from my face. "Now I've got proof, which I sent home last night. My father will copy and verify my research and send it off to the rest of the family."

"And after that?"

"Since I can't stop the frogs from dying, after that, we brace for impact." I glanced at the clock. "The school group should be arriving. Let's go teach some kids about snakes."

Dee wisely didn't argue. Crow was still curled in his cat bed when we left the office. I closed the door behind us.

I'll say this about school groups: they can take your mind off practically anything. My concerns about the growing fricken population were forgotten the minute I had to haul two ten year olds away from the rattlesnake exhibit and lecture them for taunting the snakes. Dee hastened to cover the glass before the two snakes that had been goaded into strike position could work themselves up to actually striking. I didn't want to deal with an injured rattler if there was any possible way to avoid it.

One of the chaperones came and whisked the boys away as soon as I was done with my lecture, probably to deliver another, far more "I'll call your parents"-oriented lecture of her own. That was fine with me, and I had other problems, since one of the smaller, cleverer girls— who had equally small, clever fingers—was in the process of removing the lid from a tank of blue-tailed skinks. I raced to stop her. Dee was on the other side of the reptile house, explaining Crunchy's diet to a rapt audience. As vigorous alligator arm gestures were involved, I wasn't worried about her losing their attention any time soon.

I made my way to the door to Dee's office, knocking once before cracking it open and sticking my head inside. Chandi was still seated on the beanbag chair with Shami wrapped around her waist, his head resting on her shoulder and his forked tongue contentedly scenting the air. She didn't react to my presence.

"Ten minutes," I said.

Now she reacted. Her head came up, dark eyes widening in surprise, and then narrowing in irritation. "You promised me three—"

"I promised you three hours. It's been more than three hours. My lunch is in ten minutes, which will give us a chance to get Shami back into his enclosure without anyone seeing. If you're willing to help with that, I won't even deduct today's extra time from tomorrow's visit." That was a bluff: I wouldn't have done that, even if she'd refused to help me. There was trying to keep an enterprising young wadjet from breaking her venomous fiancé out of his tank, and then there was being mean to a little girl. All sapient species go through the period analogous to human childhood. It's one of the things that unify us all.

"Oh." Chandi's lower lip wobbled a little before she pulled herself proudly upright and said, "We will be ready to part in ten minutes. I will see you tomorrow, for my *full* three hours."

"Agreed," I said, and closed the door.

Dee was finishing her alligator pantomime, and the school group teacher and chaperones were gathering their charges, herding them efficiently toward the exit. I sidled over to where Dee was standing.

"Where are they having lunch?" I muttered, sotto voce.

"Main courtyard."

"Oh, thank God." I was supposed to be meeting Shelby in the semi-private picnic garden near the tiger cages. It was small, mostly concealed from the casual eye, and didn't have any vending machines, which you'd think would discourage school groups, but sometimes those were the very attributes that attracted harried teachers looking for a moment's peace and quiet. And I absolutely did *not* want to cancel on her, or have yet another attempt at getting together interrupted.

"Did you talk to Chandi?"

"She'll be ready in ten minutes."

Dee eyed me suspiciously. "With no argument?"

"Miracles happen."

Dee looked like she was going to quiz me further, but was interrupted by the arrival of the midday shift—Kim, an overly-earnest, extremely sweet girl with hair the color of butterscotch and a fondness for terrapins of all kinds (but especially Crunchy), and Nelson, who was nice enough, but terrified of anything that weighed more than fifteen pounds or so (again, especially Crunchy). Dee turned to bring them up to speed on the day so far, including Andrew's ongoing absence. I took advantage of her distraction, waving genially to the pair and ducking into my office before I could be grabbed for any new, exciting emergencies.

Crow was finally out of the cat bed. That was a good thing, except for the part where he was standing on the counter, looking as guilty as it was possible for a cat/bird cross to look, with a dead rat from the refrigerator dangling from his beak. I sighed.

"Did you stop to consider that that might be someone else's lunch?" I asked.

Crow swallowed the rat before turning his back resolutely on me and beginning to preen his left wing. I sighed again, harder this time.

"That almost certainly means no. You're a flying vacuum cleaner, you know that?" No response from my misbehaving pet. I smiled fondly. I'd been wondering for a while if he could open the fridge. Now I knew that it was time to invest in a padlock.

I grabbed my coat off the back of the chair and moved to get my bag lunch out of the fridge, where it had been sandwiched between a sack of dead rats (for the pythons) and cubed raw chicken (for Dee's hair). There was a hole in the sack of rats. "Be good, all right?" I said to Crow. "If you're going to eat anything else, just try not to puke it back up on the rug."

Crow continued to groom himself. Chuckling, I opened the office door and stepped back into the reptile house. It had been a long morning, and I was going to need to do something relaxing after I separated Chandi from her boyfriend. What could be more relaxing than having lunch with my own beautiful, blessedly mammalian not-a-girlfriend?

Things Shelby Tanner didn't specialize in: relaxing. She was sitting atop the picnic table we had claimed as our own, waving a turkey drumstick like a conductor's baton as she punctuated her own points.

"—so I said, Nicole, it's lovely that you're taking an interest, but do you think you could take a step away from the snow leopard enclosure? Possibly before you get your throat ripped out and make a bunch of paperwork for me to handle? There's a good girl."

"Nicole's the new girl, right?" I asked, between bites of my ham-and-cheese sandwich. I was focusing less on her words and more on the way the sunlight glinted off the tiny golden hairs on the back of her knee, where I knew she was sensitive in all the best ways.

"Yeah, the really *keen* one." Shelby said keen like it was a bad thing. From her perspective, it probably was. Being keen in the Australian sense—overeager, enthusiastic, and extremely hungry for praise—wasn't what I'd call a survival trait when you're working with large predators. "She's been nothing but one problem after the other since the start of her assignment."

"So did she get eaten? Because it sounds like that would solve the problem."

Shelby laughed. "Not quite, but not for lack of trying. Mimi, our big female, was almost on her when I finally got her to move away from the bars. Poor kitty looked awfully betrayed, seeing her midmorning snack step out of range like that."

I grinned. "I'm sure she'll find the strength to carry on."

"Don't much care if she doesn't; we've only got Nicole for another two weeks. Then she's off to harass the keepers responsible for the elephants, and good riddance, too." Shelby's smile was fast, and showed far too many teeth to be comforting. "If she disappears after *that*, nobody's going to be looking for incriminating evidence inside my kitty cats."

"That's fast. The transfer, I mean, not the murder plot. If we had someone that careless in the reptile house, I'd probably have fed them to the snapping turtle by now." That was an exaggeration . . . but not by as much as many people would think.

Shelby shrugged. "What can I say? We've got a double crop of interns this year." The big cats saw a much higher turnover rate than the reptile house, since working with the flashy carnivores was a plum position for trainees and interns. We could hold onto people for as much as a year before someone else wanted their slots. Shelby was lucky if she got to keep someone long enough for them to learn not to feed themselves to the lions. It wasn't just the big cats, either. Pretty much anything mammalian was more attractive to your average aspiring zookeeper than a bunch of snakes and snapping turtles, even though I'd never personally seen the appeal.

"Earth to Alex, come in, Alex." I turned to see Shelby leaning forward, elbows on her knees. She looked faintly annoyed. "I've been doing all the talking again, and you've been letting me. I thought we'd talked about this. I want you here when you're here, or we shouldn't even bother."

"Well, you talked about it, mostly," I said, trying to elicit a laugh.

It didn't work. Her annoyance deepened. "If we want this to work out, Alex, we've both got to do our share of the heavy lifting. That means sometimes you've got to tell me about your day, even if you'd rather not."

"Ah. Sorry—distracted." It was hard to talk about my

day when I had to constantly revise it to remove the feathered frogs, the supposedly mythological creatures, and the little girls who liked to cuddle cobras. Shelby was a smart girl. That was part of the problem. She could see the holes. "It was hectic at the reptile house this morning. Three back-to-back school groups, and one of the juniors didn't show up, which meant poor Dee had to do half the feedings for me."

Shelby blinked. "Your assistant? But she's not even a zookeeper. Is that safe?"

"She's been working here for a lot longer than the interns, and you hand them raw meat and put them in front of predators."

"Yes, but they're doing it for college credits. We *pay* her."

I snorted laughter. Shelby shrugged.

"Just being pragmatic, although I'm sorry you've had a lousy morning. Who's on shift now?"

"Kim and Nelson came on just as I was getting ready to start lunch. Dee's finally doing her own job, which has got to be a relief for her. I'll be able to work on my research during the afternoon."

"Oh? Does that mean you might be done in time to grab a spot of dinner with me?" Shelby tried to make the question sound innocent, but I could see the pointed interest in her eyes. I did a quick mental count of the nights since our last official date, and winced.

"I'm sorry," I said. "I really can't. But we're still on for tomorrow, right?"

"Tomorrow," she said. "You can't blame a girl for trying, can you?" She didn't sound happy about it. I could hear the inevitable future beginning to unspool in her tone. One more canceled date and she'd start having better things to do with her time when I asked if she wanted to catch a movie or go out for something to eat. Not long after that, I'd get the "This isn't working" talk, possibly with a side order of "We should be friends, it's better if we can stay friends."

That was probably what was best for both of us. She had her work, her research, and eventually, her life back in Australia, where we wouldn't have been able to meet for dinner if we'd wanted to. It wasn't like we'd ever officially become a couple. That didn't make the thought any easier.

"I guess I can't." I dropped my sandwich back onto the paper bag it had come off of and stood, trying to make it look like a natural stretching gesture. It didn't work. I was too stiff, and too obviously unhappy. Shelby sighed.

"I'm not breaking things off with you, Alex, all right?" she said. "I'm not thrilled that we've had so little time lately, but you've got to stop thinking that every road bump is the beginning of the end. You don't throw out the car just because you've run over an echidna."

I stopped. "Please tell me that isn't something you actually say in Australia."

"What, you don't like my folksy Australian sayings?" Shelby put her turkey leg down next to my sandwich, shaking her head. "It's incredible just how many people around here are totally willing to believe that we really walk around talking like that."

"To be fair, Australia does sound sort of fictional if you've never been there."

"I get told that a lot. Doesn't feel like a very fictional place to me." She picked up a napkin, beginning to wipe the grease from her fingers. "I mean it, though. You need to relax. You're too tense, and you're taking everything far too seriously. Are you having trouble with your research?"

"Not trouble, it's just . . . taking some turns I didn't anticipate, that's all." I began to pace, trying to look like I was raptly drinking in the scenery that I'd seen a hundred times before. Anything to keep Shelby from pressing, and me from being forced to lie to her.

The tiger garden was definitely one of the zoo's better-kept secrets, a picturesque little quirk of the landscaping that no one had yet thought of tearing out in order to install a new enclosure or walkway. It was only a matter of time before somebody looked at an aerial map of the zoo and went, "Hey, that spot is so isolated that it's only going to get used by zookeepers and horny teenagers looking for a place to make out. Let's level it." (Sadly, whatever unnamed bureaucrat was eventually responsible for that decision probably wouldn't take into account the existence of horny zookeepers who didn't like making out right next to where they fed the lions. Such are the trials of the working world.)

Thick greenery ringed the circular garden on all sides, surrounding the brick patio flooring and lone picnic table with a concealing veil. Hardy, just-exotic-enough flowers bloomed riotously among the general wash of green, planted by gardeners who enjoyed their privacy as much as Shelby and I did. Even the noises of the zoo were dampened here, muffled by the vegetation, until we could pretend that we were someplace much less artificially designed. A real jungle, maybe, albeit one with an inexplicable amount of landscaping.

"You want to talk about it?" asked Shelby.

"I honestly don't know where to begin. Do you know much about colony collapse disorder?"

"Isn't that the thing with the bees?"

"Yeah, it's ... the thing ..." I tapered off mid-sentence, losing the thread of what I'd been trying to say as I stared at the object protruding from one of the decorative hedges.

"Alex?" I heard Shelby sliding off the table. She sounded alarmed. I couldn't say for sure that it was the wrong emotional response.

The object in question was a shoe. Just a simple white sneaker, the laces still tied. That wasn't unusual, in and of itself: lots of people manage to lose shoes at the zoo, for reasons that I have never quite understood. No, the problem was what was protruding from the shoe.

The problem was the human ankle.

I stepped closer to the hedge, leaning forward to gently part the branches and look down into the greenery. Shelby stepped up behind me, resting her hands on my shoulders as she craned her neck to get a better view. I didn't ask her to move back, even though all my years of training were telling me that I should be doing exactly that.

"Well," I said, after a long moment of silence had passed between us, "I guess I know why Andrew didn't show up for work this morning." I released the hedge. It mercifully sprang back into its original formation, blocking the horrified, distorted face of the junior zookeeper from view. I turned, and Shelby put her arms around me, folding me into a strong embrace. I closed my eyes. It didn't help. Even with my eyes closed, I could still see his expression.

Worse, I could still see his eyes, which had been gray from side to side. Something had turned them to stone. Something that had killed him at the same time. Something not human.

We had a serious problem on our hands.

Five

"A little knowledge is a dangerous thing. It's much easier to be brave when you don't believe that the monster under your bed is real."

—Alexander Healy

Ohio's West Columbus Zoo, telling polite lies to the local police to avoid panic, institutionalization, or institutional panic

I ADJUSTED MY GLASSES with one hand, resisting the urge to glance toward the unfortunate Andrew's half-calcified body. My fingers itched. I wanted—no, I *needed*—to get my dissection tools and dig into his remains. Whatever had petrified him would have left traces, subtle cues in the striations of the stone that had replaced an undetermined amount of his original substance. The local medical examiner would never be able to decode those markers. Even if I stole a copy of his autopsy report (and let's be honest here: I was *going* to steal a copy of his autopsy report), I wouldn't have all the data. We'd still be essentially flying blind.

"Now, you say that you were simply enjoying lunch with your—what did you say your relationship to Miss Tanner was, again?" the officer asked.

"She's my girlfriend." The words were out before I realized they were a relationship upgrade. I winced, but pressed on, saying, "We've been seeing each other socially for about three months."

"I see. And is your relationship public knowledge?"

I raised an eyebrow. "Are you asking if I arranged for the bizarre death of one of my junior zookeepers because Shelby was some kind of dirty little secret? Zoo management is completely aware of our arrangement. It was the zoo's HR director who introduced us. We don't work in the same part of the zoo, we don't answer to the same managers, and a little fraternization is encouraged if it means we're more likely to volunteer for overtime and double-shifts." Like when your significant other had already been drafted by her own manager, thus canceling yet another in a long string of canceled dates.

Shelby was on the other side of the tiger garden with another policeman, sitting atop the picnic table and giving her version of the story. From the occasional words that drifted my way, I was willing to venture that her version matched mine in the broad strokes, but was both more carnal and more profane in its details.

"Now, I don't know whether I would have said that about your coworker's heritage," I said mildly, after Shelby made a particularly salty comment.

My policeman narrowed his eyes. "Please pay attention to your own situation, and not your girlfriend's, Mr. Preston. Can you account for your whereabouts this morning between eight and eleven?"

"Yes, I can," I said. "I was at the reptile house for most of the morning, along with my assistant, Deanna Taylor-Rodriguez. She's still there now. I arrived at work about a quarter after eight. Lloyd was the guard on duty at the front gate." For the first time, I found myself grateful for Lloyd's slavish dedication to following the letter of the law. He'd have a triple-checked timestamp verifying exactly when I arrived.

That meant he probably had one for Andrew, too. I made a mental note to check with Lloyd once I was done explaining my innocence to the local police.

"Did this Lloyd gentleman walk you to the, ah, snake house?"

"No, he didn't," I admitted. "But if you check with Dee, you'll find that it took me a maximum of ten minutes to cross the grounds to the *reptile* house." I subtly stressed the word "reptile." I wasn't trying to mock him or piss him off. I just wanted him to remember that I knew my own business. "I honestly have no idea what happened to Andrew. Whatever it was, it probably took more than ten minutes."

The first part wasn't entirely a lie: there were a number of things that could have turned my unfortunate junior zookeeper into stone, and most of them were viable suspects, since he was still meat-based enough that he could have been zapped by anything from the bottom to the top of the power scale. The second part was one hundred percent fiction. Depending on the strength of the creature doing the petrifaction, it takes a few seconds, sometimes less. When something that's capable of doing that to living flesh makes eye contact with a mammal . . . game over. I could easily have turned Andrew into stone and still made it to the reptile house on time. Except for the part where I'm human.

The policeman frowned at his notes. I seized the opportunity to add, a little more sheepishly, "Also, if I did . . . whatever it is . . . do you honestly think I would have brought my girlfriend here? I mean, I was hoping to have sex again in this lifetime, and most girls get sort of upset when you take them to see a dead body."

Most girls. Not, apparently, Shelby, who was now laughing with her policeman, both of them appearing to have a grand old time as they reviewed her statement. I didn't know how she did it, but I loved her for it in that moment, just as I'd loved her for every similar thing I'd ever seen her do.

My policeman followed my gaze to Shelby. Then, to my surprise, he smiled. "Yeah, okay," he said. "You're free to go back to work. Please don't leave town, Mr.

Preston, we may need to speak to you further about this incident. I have your contact information, and I assume that your paperwork with the zoo office is up to date?"

"Yes, sir, it is," I said. It was all fake, of course—Alexander Preston had only existed on paper before I brought him to the Columbus Zoo, and he'd cease to exist as soon as I moved on to my next assignment—but everything about him was designed to pass even the deepest of examinations. He had a good college GPA, glowing letters of recommendation from his professors, and even contact numbers for his next of kin. He was a pretty well-liked guy, and I was going to miss him when it came time for me to move on to being someone else.

I didn't have a choice, sadly. Verity could maintain a single identity for her ballroom dancing, because the Covenant wasn't looking for us in that community. Anything related to professional zoology was more likely to catch their attention. No identity was secure enough to risk using twice.

"All right, then," said the policeman, and turned his back on me, moving toward the cluster of EMTs and police personnel who were examining Andrew's body. Shelby waved, mouthing the word "later," and went back to talking to her policeman.

I waved back, a little hesitantly, and left the tiger garden, heading back to the reptile house as fast as I could. I kept my eyes away from the ground as I walked, just in case a cockatrice had been responsible for what had happened to Andrew. Cockatrice like to stay low, and for all that I knew, it was still at the zoo. Under the circumstances, avoiding an accidental staring contest was the safest thing I could have done.

Let's talk about things that can turn you to stone.

There are a surprisingly large number of them extant in the world, and there used to be even more, before the

Covenant of St. George compared notes with some Greek gentlemen and figured out all those spiffy little tricks with smoked glass and reflective surfaces. That cut down on the things-that-turn-you-to-stone population both dramatically and quickly, but "cut down" is not the same thing as "eradicated." Good thing, too, as many of the things that can turn flesh to stone serve very important roles in the world's ecology. This probably doesn't make it any nicer to lock eyes or swap venom with them.

My original purpose in coming to Ohio actually involved things that turn people to stone. When I wasn't counting frickens, I was supposedly administrating a basilisk breeding program. Technically I still was. It was just that my breeding pair of basilisks were currently hibernating—or had been as of ten o'clock the previous night; I'd been so busy dealing with the reptile house when I got to work that I hadn't checked on them yet—and basilisks can hibernate for ten years at a stretch. It's part of what made them so hard for the Covenant to eradicate. It's hard to kill something that can go off and be a small boulder when it wants to take a long nap.

(Of course, they're so sensitive to changes in their environment that moving them can cause them to hibernate even longer, which is why the breeding program had to take place in Ohio, where my pair had acclimated enough that they were unlikely to sleep for more than a year at a time—plus, with my middle sister on the East Coast and my parents and youngest sister on the West Coast, it was good for me to be in the Midwest. I could react quickly if there was an emergency, and it helped increase the number of air strikes required to wipe us all out.)

But back to the larger subject. All known petrifactors (IE, "things that can convince the minerals in your body that they really want to change formation and become different types of mineral") are members of the Ophion family, a group of synapsids which includes everything from gorgons to cockatrice. This is more a matter of convenience than any strong scientific evidence proving their evolutionary relationship. They range in size from the greater gorgons, who are substantially larger than humans, to basilisks, which are the size of irritated chickens. Really, they only have one absolute unifying feature. All of them are capable of turning flesh to stone, to one degree or another.

Lesser gorgons stun with their gaze and petrify with their bite, although you'd have to work to find traces of petrifaction in most of their victims. They prefer their meat to be, well, meaty, not filled with delicious veins of silicate and carbon. Pliny's gorgons like Dee could stun *and* petrify with their eyes, although they were better at the stunning part, and needed to have their hair uncovered if they wanted to petrify, or even stun something particularly large. They needed the extra eyes. Greater gorgons . . .

If we had a greater gorgon, I was going to be tempted to grab Shelby, my family, and anyone else that I was fond of and declare that it was time for a month-long vacation somewhere very, very far away. Like Hawaii. Or the moon.

Petrifaction can be stopped if you catch it early, but once it's gone far enough, there's no known treatment. If it happens, it's happened, and there's no force in this dimension or any other that will undo it. It's supposed to be a very painful way to die. Personally, I never want to find out.

But Andrew found out. On that somber note, I reached the reptile house, pushed the door open, and stepped inside.

Kim and Nelson were working with the latest school group, a bunch of bored-looking sixth graders who clearly thought of themselves as far too cool for anything as jejune as a bunch of stupid snakes. I waved to the other zookeepers and kept walking, noting in passing that Shami was back in his tank.

Dee's office door wasn't locked. Good; that meant she hadn't let her hair out of its confinement. I opened the door and stepped inside, closing it behind me. "We have a problem," I announced.

"You just came into my office without knocking," said Dee, lowering the sandwich she'd been about to bite into. It was dripping red. I was willing to bet it wasn't because she'd used too much ketchup. "I'll say we've got a problem. We've discussed privacy and appropriate boundaries before, Alex, and this is—"

"Andrew's dead."

Dee froze. Seconds ticked by while she stared at me, apparently too stunned to move. I waited as long as I could before snapping my fingers. She jumped in her seat, an audible hissing sound coming from beneath her wig.

"Earth to Dee, come in, Dee," I said, only realizing after the words were out of my mouth that I was unintentionally parroting Shelby's words to me in the tiger garden. "I need you alert and tracking, so if you could stop being stunned and useless, that would be *awesome*."

"Little heavy on the sarcasm there, boss," she mumbled, still sounding half-present. She shook her head, eliciting more enraged hissing from her hair, and looked at me pleadingly. "Is this some sort of really shitty joke? Because if you say it is, I'll laugh. I promise to laugh."

"I wish. The police are in the tiger garden now. They'll be showing up here soon, to verify that I arrived when I said I did." Belatedly it occurred to me that my beeline for Dee's office could be seen as an attempt to solidify my shaky alibi. I sighed, forcing myself not to dwell. If they were going to try and pin Andrew's murder on me, there wasn't much I could do about it, aside from being innocent. Since I hadn't killed him, I figured I had that part in the bag. "Look, Andrew's death isn't the problem. It's the way he died."

Dee's eyes widened behind the tinted lenses of her glasses. "Oh, God, he was murdered, wasn't he?"

"I don't know. It'll depend on what killed him. If it was a sapient being, then yes, he was murdered. If it was a nonsapient, then no. He was just killed."

"Wait . . ." Dee paused, cocking her head to the side as she frowned at me. "Are you saying that a cryptid of some sort did this?"

"Worse, at least from your perspective. I'm saying that a petrifactor did this."

This time, the agitated hissing that rose from beneath Dee's wig needed no translation. I turned and flipped the lock on the door, guaranteeing our privacy at least until the police arrived. "Do you need to let them out?"

"Yes, I think that would be best. I'm sorry." Dee reached up and pulled her wig from her head, allowing her serpentine hair to uncurl and hiss fiercely in my direction. A few of the smaller snakes dropped to frame her face, hanging so that they mimicked human curls. It was pretty, in a reptilian sort of way. "Are . . . are you sure?"

"His eyes were stone, Dee. Most of him was still flesh, so I can't be sure what killed him, but his eyes were stone. Only a petrifactor could have done that."

"If it started with his eyes, he probably met a gaze-based petrifactor," said Dee slowly, clearly selecting her words with care.

I nodded. "I thought of that immediately. I'm not here because I think you did it."

"Oh, thank Athena." Dee groaned, slumping back in her chair and sliding her hands up under her tinted glasses so that she could rub her eyes. "You scared the crap out of me, Alex. I was half-waiting for you to whip out one of those giant knives of yours and kill me on the spot."

"Do you really think that little of me?" I asked quietly.

"No. But I think that little of the Covenant, and sometimes it's hard to remember that your family isn't associated with them anymore." Dee removed her hands from her face, checking to be sure her glasses were still in place before she opened her eyes and offered me a wan smile. It faded quickly. "What are we going to do?"

"I'm going to go home and tell my grandfather that he needs to get me a copy of Andrew's autopsy file. Maybe he can get samples at the same time, and we can figure out what did this before it strikes again."

Dee nodded. "That poor man. It's a horrible way to die."

"So I've been told. Look, Dee, I hate to ask you this, but . . ."

She put up a hand to cut me off. "*No*, Alex. I can't take you home with me. Please don't ask."

Pliny's gorgons tend to live in isolated communities, close enough to human neighborhoods for them to commute, but far enough away to allow them to relax and let their hair down, so to speak. I knew that Dee lived somewhere outside of the city limits with her husband and daughter, as did the rest of their extended clan, although I didn't have any idea how large the population of their community might be.

"If this happens again, you know I'll need to ask," I said, as gently as I could. "And I won't be able to take no for an answer."

"I know," said Dee miserably. "Just please don't ask me yet if you don't have to."

"All right," I said. "We'll table it for now. I'm going to go check on the basilisks before the police get here."

"I'll get ready," said Dee, reaching for her wig.

I tried to smile reassuringly. It felt more like a grimace, but I was hoping that the intention would get through even if nothing else did. "We'll be okay, Dee."

"Tell that to Andrew."

There was nothing I could say to that. I unlocked the door at the rear of her office, the one that connected to the back halls of the reptile house, and let myself out.

When I was a kid, I always wondered why buildings at the zoo seemed so much bigger on the outside than they were on the inside. Once I started working in zoos, I realized it was because the part the visitors see—the animal exhibits and the attractively designed public areas—are just the tip of the iceberg. You need feeding pens and bathing areas, storage closets and research labs, places for the animals that aren't currently on display, the gravid females, eggs or cocoons, and babies too young to handle being stared at all day. The reptile house was unusual because our offices, of which there were three, were connected to both the public and private areas. That was a design choice based on necessity: after all, our offices were where we stored the antivenin.

I moved down the hall to the research labs, pulling the key to lab number two out of my pocket. The door I wanted was locked twice, once with a deadbolt and once with a combination lock. I shielded it with my body as I turned the dial to the appropriate numbers. Not even Dee knew how to get into this lab without me, and that was exactly as I wanted things to be. Gorgons and basilisks don't get along, and they're not immune to each other's abilities.

The inside of the lab was lit only by the red glow of the heat lamps. I shut the door, locking it from the inside, and took down the protective eyewear from the hook by the light switch. The smoked glass lenses would block the effects of the basilisks' eyes if they were awake. *Please let them both be here, and don't let them be awake,* I thought. *Please don't let this be my fault.*

Moving the heavy plywood sheet away from the basilisk enclosure was difficult, but I'd done it before, and after a few moments of tugging, I was able to lift it down and lean it up against the wall. I peered through the glass.

It was a good-sized enclosure, about eight feet on all sides, with a twelve-foot vertical clearance. Basilisks liked to roost in trees when they were courting, which just added to their resemblance to weird, scaly chickens. Ferns and other leafy plants surrounded their artificial stream. The trees were empty. As for the basilisks themselves, they were still asleep, curled up in hard little balls of what looked like granite.

This was the dangerous part. I picked up one of the feeding sticks and slid open the hatch at the side of the basilisk enclosure. Neither basilisk moved, not then, and not when I threaded the stick through the opening and used it to nudge them gently. They were both as hard as, well, rocks, and entirely unresponsive. I removed the stick and shut the hatch before allowing myself a very small sigh of relief.

The basilisks hadn't killed Andrew. Judging solely by their surface hardness, they'd been asleep for months.

My relief passed as quickly as it had come. Dee didn't kill Andrew. The basilisks didn't kill Andrew. And since that accounted for all the known petrifactors on the zoo grounds, that raised one very large, very unpleasant question:

If they hadn't killed him, then who had?

Six

"Everything is dangerous when looked at from the right angle. Mice fear cats, cats fear dogs, dogs fear bears, and bears fear men with guns. It's often just a matter of perspective."

—Thomas Price

Ohio's West Columbus Zoo, attempting to surreptitiously search the zoo grounds for a creature capable of converting living flesh into stone

I WALKED SLOWLY DOWN the path connecting the tiger garden to the main courtyard, trying to keep my eyes on the ground without being too blatant about it. My glasses weren't helping. I'd swapped my normal pair for a pair with tinted lenses, and the prescription was slightly off, making it harder to be sure of the details in the bushes around me. I made a mental note to visit the optometrist as soon as possible. I hadn't been hunting petrifactors in the wild since arriving in Ohio, and I'd allowed my tools to get outdated. That was a good way to get myself killed.

My current search was running off one major assumption: that Andrew had been killed by something low to the ground, like a cockatrice, rather than something arboreal, like a basilisk, or something human-shaped, like a gorgon. I was basing that assumption on the area where he'd been found, which had had plenty of bushes, but no trees and very little foot traffic.

We'd be able to narrow down what had killed him after I got a look at the autopsy report. If I was wrong, all I would have lost was a few hours. It was a risk. It was also a necessary short-term decision. If Andrew had been killed by a gorgon, they were probably long gone by now, or else had an agenda I didn't understand yet. Either way, if our petrifactor was a gorgon, no one else was likely to be in immediate danger.

But if I was right—if the local gorgons were too smart for this kind of stunt, and there was a wild basilisk or cockatrice loose in the zoo—I couldn't afford to wait for the results. I needed to find the thing that had killed Andrew before anyone else got converted into garden statuary.

At least Lloyd had confirmed my guess about when Andrew arrived at the zoo, and hence when he was likely to have been petrified. The old security guard had looked at me oddly for asking. Hopefully, he wouldn't tell the police that I'd come to him to tighten up my alibi. And if he did . . .

Well, I'd figure something out. That was part of my job, after all.

Something rustled in the bushes to my left. I tensed, my hand tightening around the mirror in my coat pocket, and prepared to spring . . . only to see one of the zoo's endless supply of Canada geese waddle into the open. It looked at me disinterestedly before waddling on, feet slapping against the brick pavement, and vanishing into the bushes on the other side of the path. I let out a breath, feeling some of the tension slip out of my shoulders.

"Little on edge, aren't you, sweetheart?" asked Shelby, directly behind me.

I jumped as I whirled to face her, and only years of training prevented me from pulling one of the knives I had hidden inside my coat. Heart pounding, I forced my hands to unclench as I offered her my best sheepish "oh, it's nothing" smile. "I was just thinking," I said. "Are you finished with the police?"

"A bit ago, yeah," she said. My obvious distress must have leavened my smile into something she could believe this soon after the death of one of my coworkers, because she put her hand on my elbow, a sympathetic look on her face. "I came looking for you, but Dee said you'd already gone. She was pretty shaken up, the poor dear."

"I think we all are at the reptile house." I didn't know if that was true—I hadn't spoken to Kim or Nelson before racing out of there and starting my search of the grounds. I pulled my hand out of my pocket, wishing there was a way I could keep hold of the mirror without being obvious about it. "How are you holding up?"

"Not thrilled about the situation, obviously, but I didn't know him as well as you did." She left her hand on my elbow. I stifled the situationally inappropriate urge to put my arms around her. "I'm assuming you left for your walk before the police got there to chat with Dee?"

I nodded. "I didn't think they'd appreciate my presence, given the whole 'maybe we suspect you' vibe that they were giving off during my interview."

"Aw, pish, that's just their job," said Shelby, waving my concern away. "Look, though, that means you didn't hear that we're closed."

"What?" I blinked at her.

"The zoo. We're closed. Everyone's going home, since there's just been a death in the family, as it were." Now it was Shelby's turn to smile, a trifle wryly. "Don't tell me you were thinking so hard that you didn't notice there was no one else about."

"Um . . ." I rubbed the back of my neck with one hand. I didn't have to work to look sheepish. "Like I said, I was thinking. You know how I get."

"Yeah, it's a good thing you're not Australian. You'd have been eaten by a bunyip by now."

"Probably not, since I don't usually hang out near the

edges of billabongs smelling like fish," I said automatically, and winced when I saw the look on Shelby's face. "Er, a bunyip is a kind of crocodile, right?"

"Not quite, but nice try." She looped her arm through mine and started walking, pulling me along in an odd two-person *Wizard of Oz* formation. "So our working day has just ended several hours early, with the tragic loss of a peer. There are two ways we can deal with this."

"Those being?" I asked cautiously.

"Option one, we go out to a local pub and get righteously smashed before stumbling to our beds. We wake up tomorrow with hangovers the size of Queensland, and a feeling of satisfaction over a death well-mourned."

"Uh-huh," I said. "And option two?"

"We go back to my place, order in a pizza, and have a more private wake for poor Andrew."

Given what I knew about ghosts, there was a more than reasonable chance that "poor Andrew" would show up and haunt her apartment looking for a show if we did that. "I can't," I said. "I wish I could, but . . ."

"Whatever plans you have tonight, I'm sure whoever they involve would understand you needing to spend a little time with your *girlfriend* in the wake of a coworker's death, Alex," said Shelby. The way she stressed the word "girlfriend" made it clear she'd heard me talking to the police. "Unless you're ashamed of me for some reason?"

"God, Shelby, no. I am . . . believe me, I am anything *but* ashamed of my hot, brilliant, capable, uh, girlfriend." I was going to pay for that label later. I could see it in her eyes. "But I'm supposed to look after Sarah tonight. I promised my grandparents I'd stay home with her." I realized guiltily that I wasn't lying. This was supposed to be their date night, and I was about to ruin it by coming home and telling them that we had a petrifactor loose at the zoo. "They've had these theater tickets for weeks. I can't back out on them, and Sarah won't tolerate a sitter she doesn't know."

Shelby sighed. "Your dedication to your family is one of the things I love about you. Maybe if I keep reminding myself of that, my needing to go home and spend the night sitting alone in my apartment, right after I've seen a dead man . . . well, maybe it won't sting as much."

It was a statement calculated to make me feel bad. It was sincere enough that I didn't mind. She had every right to fling that particular arrow at me: if I was supposed to be her boyfriend, I was doing a shitty job of it. "I'm really sorry," I said. "Look—I'll call, okay? I'll get Sarah settled with a video or something, and I'll call."

"If you don't, I shall hunt you down tomorrow in the parking lot and remove your kidneys with a spoon," she said blithely.

"Deal." I kissed her cheek. Anything else would have required us to stop walking, and I wanted to get to my . . . I stopped in my tracks, hauling Shelby to a stop along with me. "Oh, hell. Shelby, I'm sorry, I forgot something back at the reptile house. I gotta go." Whatever had rustled in the bushes would be long gone by now, if it had ever been there in the first place. My imagination was playing tricks, and I wasn't properly equipped to do this on my own.

She blinked at me. "That's all right, I'll walk with you."

"No!"

She blinked again, eyes widening. Then they narrowed into a stubbornly murderous expression that I knew all too well, since I'd been seeing it from most of the women in my life since I was born. "No? What did you forget, Alex, your pet monster?"

Considering that what I had forgotten was Crow, the guess was closer than I was comfortable with. "No, but you're not certified for venomous snake handling, and I forgot to milk our tiger snake in all the excitement. We're supposed to make a delivery to the local hospital tomorrow. We can't do that if I don't milk the tiger snake."

"I'm Australian, and you're seriously telling me I'm not safe around snakes."

"I'm sorry, zoo rules, I'll call you tonight." I kissed her cheek again. Then I turned and ran, putting her behind me as quickly as I could. I didn't want to see the betrayed expression I knew was on her face.

Running through the closed zoo right after a man had been found dead might have looked suspicious. I was willing to risk it, since it could also just look like normal human discomfort over hanging out where a corpse had recently been. "Reacting normally around dead things" had been one of the hardest lessons for my parents to teach to my sisters and me, since frequently, after we'd reacted normally, we were expected to take the dead things home for further study. My being a scientist alleviates that somewhat; I'm expected to react oddly, and a little morbidly, when I encounter bodies. I've never been sure how Verity manages. As a ballroom dancer, she's pretty much expected to flip her shit if she sees so much as a rat.

I burst back into the reptile house. Kim and Nelson were gone. Dee was still there, turning off lights and peering anxiously into enclosures. She turned at the sound of my footsteps. "Anything?"

"No," I said. "The zoo is—"

"Closed, I know. I'm just double-checking the cages."

"I came back for Crow." I started for my office door. "Do you want me to walk you to your car?" I felt guilty as soon as the offer was made. I'd left Shelby alone, with a monster or a killer potentially loose in the zoo, and here I was offering to escort my assistant.

"I'm good," said Dee. She tapped her glasses. "This isn't my first rodeo. I'll call you when I get home tonight, just so you know I got there safe."

Pushing away the images of a petrifactor rodeo— which would probably be very slow—I said, "Can you also ask around and see if anyone knows anything?"

Dee nodded. "I can, but people are going to assume you're accusing them. You're braced for that, right?"

"I'd rather they make a few assumptions than we

wind up with a bunch of dead bodies on our hands. I mean . . . any death is horrible, but what if it hadn't been a staff member? What if whatever petrified Andrew had found a bunch of school kids on a field trip?"

"I'll never understand the human idea that children are invariably more valuable than adults," said Dee. "If you have twenty adults and twenty children, and half of them are going to die, you can't save just the kids. They'd all starve to death."

Pragmatism is a gorgon trait. That sort of thing is important when you've spent centuries being hunted down and slaughtered for being something that humans think of as monsters. "I don't disagree with you," I said carefully, all too aware of my own human prejudices, "but remember that we're in a human-dominant culture. If it had been a dead kid, or worse, dead *kids*, we'd have news crews crawling all over this place looking for answers, in addition to the police. That would make it a lot harder for us to find the killer and make it stop."

"Do you really think it's still here, whatever it was?"

"I think it would be stupid to assume it wasn't."

Dee sighed heavily. "This isn't what I signed up for when I took this job, you know. I thought the worst thing I'd have to deal with was my hair biting someone."

"Welcome to my world." I unlocked my office door, stepping inside, and crossed to the window. It was still light outside: that made this trick a little more dangerous, but I couldn't leave Crow in the office overnight. He'd freak out when he realized I wasn't coming back, and the amount of damage he could do was limited only by his imagination.

Crow was curled in my desk chair. He lifted his head, watching my progress across the room. The rat bag was on the office floor. It was empty.

"At least that means I don't need to worry about feeding you," I said, and opened the window. "Crow, car."

Crow made an inquisitive croaking noise. He could see as well as I could that it was still daylight outside.

"Crow, *car*."

He stood, performing a languid cat stretch before flattening and stretching out his wings like a raven. I stepped hurriedly to the side, and even then, he barely missed me as he took off and launched himself at the open window. I shut it behind him and left the office, moving fast now that I needed to race my griffin to the car. He'd beat me there, of course—he had wings, I had feet and gates I couldn't just fly over—but I wanted to minimize the amount of time he was likely to spend sitting out in the open, casually preening himself.

Wild miniature griffins move in flocks, and the ones that have survived into the modern day have learned to hide from humans, since natural selection—and men with guns—took all the ones who didn't hide out of the gene pool years ago. Crow had none of those instinctive reactions. He was more like a house cat, raised from birth to believe that all humans existed solely to be a source of food and entertainment for him. If he tried to make friends with one of the other zookeepers . . .

That was a bad thought. I set it aside and kept walking.

I didn't see Shelby again as I made my way to the parking lot. I was still feeling guilty about having lied to her, and I could recognize the start of a vicious cycle. My guilt would grow and grow until I saw her next, and then, just as I was getting it under control, I'd need to lie to her again. The conflict between what I could say and what I wanted to say was becoming a serious problem—and worse, it was messing with my focus. I couldn't prioritize her life over anyone else's. That didn't stop me from wanting to.

It wasn't fair. My father found a woman who'd been raised by cryptids and saw nothing in the least bit unusual about them. My Aunt Jane married an incubus, which neatly sidestepped the issue of "how do you explain that not everything that looks human actually is." And my sister went and hooked up with a member of the

Covenant of St. George. Shelby was the first girl I'd met in a long time—who was I kidding; the first girl I'd met, period—who seemed right for me. She was perfect, except for the part where if she met my family, she'd scream and run away.

Crow was nowhere to be seen when I reached my car, but judging by the angry squawks of the geese, he was definitely nearby. I unlocked and opened the door before calling, "Crow! Home!"

He shot out of the midst of the gray-feathered waterfowl like a charcoal-colored missile, arrowing past me and through the open car door to land on the passenger seat. He had several goose feathers clasped firmly in his beak. Dropping them, he turned to me, beak open in what I would have sworn was silent laughter.

"Yes, you're a mighty hunter," I said, and got into the car. "Come on, mighty hunter. Let's go home."

Driving through Columbus during the middle of the workday was strange. Doing it with Crow wide awake and spun up from playing with the geese was nerve-racking. I kept waiting for the moment where he would pop up in the window like a demented jack-in-the-box and scare the holy hell out of the drivers around me. To my surprise, he did no such thing. Instead, he compacted himself into the classic cat loaf position, tail wrapped tight around his entire body, tucked his head under his wing, and went to sleep. I smiled a little. The world could end, and anything morphologically feline would find a way to take a nap.

Grandma's car was gone, but Grandpa's car was parked in its place. I scooped the still-snoozing Crow out of the passenger seat and made my way up to the house, unlocking the door and letting myself inside. It was even stranger to come home and not smell dinner in progress, or hear my family moving around.

Speaking of family ... I paused and looked uneasily around the hall. Sarah sometimes liked to lurk in corners, perfectly still, waiting for something to attract her attention. It wasn't normal cuckoo behavior, but what about Sarah was normal these days?

She wasn't there. I walked into the living room, put Crow down on the couch, and went looking for my grandfather. Date night was always on the evening of his day off.

I found him upstairs in the office he shared with my grandmother. He was seated at his computer, glasses perched on his nose and sleeves rolled far enough up that I could see the faint discoloration where one body's skin ended and the next began. He was usually careful to conceal his seams, unless he was certain that he wasn't going to be seen by anyone who might find them strange.

I rapped my knuckles against the doorframe. He turned toward the sound and blinked, frowning slowly. "Alex? What are you doing home?"

"They closed the zoo early."

There was a pause as he ran through the reasons this might have happened. Finally, he said, "Either a kid got into one of the big predator enclosures again, or there's been a murder."

"We don't know yet whether it was actually a murder, versus an accidental death, but yes." I walked across the office and sat down in Grandma's chair, explaining the situation with Andrew as quickly and succinctly as I could. Grandpa only interrupted a few times, asking terse questions about where the body had been found and exactly what the vegetation around it had looked like.

When I finished, he sighed. "You realize what this means, don't you?"

"That a man is dead?"

"That's a problem for him, but for the rest of us, it means there's an increased chance we'll catch the Covenant's attention. That's not good."

I nodded. "I know. I'm going to need you to get me a copy of the autopsy report. If it doesn't say anything particularly shocking, maybe they won't catch wind of this death." Grandpa was a coroner for the City of Columbus. Dead bodies didn't bother him, since he'd been one (or two, or three) himself at one point, and while he didn't need replacement parts—all the ones he had were good for at least another forty years, barring accident or assault—others weren't always so lucky. By working where he did, he was able to keep the Revenants, ghouls, and other humanivores of the city from bothering the living population. It was really a public service, and one that was helped along by the number of people who got into truly stomach-churning automobile accidents.

"I assumed you'd be asking for that," he said. "Although we may have a problem."

"What's that?"

"They may decide to send his body someplace like the CDC for autopsy, since this is the sort of thing that qualifies as 'unusual circumstances,' and petrifaction could be mistaken as some sort of strange new disease. If that's the case, we're going to need to work much harder to get those results."

"And there's a much higher chance the Covenant will get involved," I said slowly. "Is there any way you can find out who's going to do the examination?"

"I can make a few calls." Grandpa made a small "shoo" gesture with his hand. "Go get some food in you and call your father."

"What?"

"We both know that as soon as you're done with me, you're going to call home and update everyone on what's going on. I endorse this, since it will allow me to check in with the morgue without you hovering over my shoulder. Now go on, scat." He smiled, making the scar on his cheek pull upward. "I can take care of this part by myself."

"You're the best, Grandpa," I said.

"I know."

Feeling better than I had since we found Andrew's body in the bushes, I turned and left the office. Grandpa was right. It was time for me to work on my part of the plan.

Dad picked up the phone on the third ring. "This is an unlisted number," he snapped.

"You know, Dad, I don't mean to push, but there's this thing called 'caller ID' that you can get these days. It might mean being a little less rude to your children when they call home." I reclined on the bed, watching the Aeslin mice systematically dismantle the plate of cheese and apple slices I'd prepared for them.

"Ah, but what if someone steals your phone?" Dad countered. "What then? Maybe I answer with 'hello, beloved only son, how are you today,' and that confirms your identity as my eldest child to the horrible monsters that have kidnapped you for their own nefarious purposes."

I laughed. It was impossible not to. "Nefarious purposes, Dad? Really?" My parents raised us to answer the phone like we hated the entire universe and wanted it to go away. It was supposedly part of the smokescreen that protected us from the Covenant of St. George. Given how memorable it was, I suspected that Dad actually just enjoyed having an excuse to snarl at people for a change.

"It could happen," he said serenely. "Verity got taken by the Covenant last year."

"Yeah, and she called us after she'd kicked their asses." One of the mice led a conga line across the floor, all of them singing the praises of cheddar. "Is Mom there? I've got some information, and it'll be easier if I don't need to repeat myself."

"She's at the flea market with your sister."

"Mom and Antimony at the flea market? Really? Is there a betting pool on what the body count is going to be?" It's not that I thought my baby sister was a danger to life and limb, exactly. It's that I *knew* my baby sister was a danger to life and limb, and I was happier when my mother wasn't the only member of the family inside her potential blast radius. Mom wasn't very good at defusing an angry Antimony.

"We needed more cleaning supplies."

"Got it." Given the family business, it was no surprise that we went through enough bleach, lye, hydrogen peroxide, and other questionable chemicals to pass ourselves off as a crime scene recovery service. Most of those things are traceable when bought in large quantities . . . unless you happen to, say, buy them off the back of a truck at the local flea market. It's amazing what you can obtain without leaving a paper trail if you're willing to put the hours in. The dealers we bought from most frequently probably thought we were a family of serial murderers, but hell. That's not the worst thing that's been said about us.

"So what's going on that's important enough for you to need to call? I'm afraid I didn't have time to read your report. Did you find conclusive evidence that the fricken population is increasing?"

In all the chaos, I'd almost forgotten about the frickens. "I can't prove an increase, but I can prove some new species in the area—previously native to surrounding states, never sighted in Ohio before—and that they're not suffering the same sort of fungal infections that the frogs are. If the frog population continues to decline the way it has been, I'd say we're looking at reclassification of the fricken from 'cryptid' to 'normal' within the next five years. Maybe less if this is a worldwide phenomenon."

"Which it almost certainly is," said my father grimly. "That's bad news."

"I know. It's still not the reason I called."

There was a pause. Then, tone sharper, he asked, "Did Sarah get out?"

Sarah escaping from the house was currently the family's greatest nightmare: an uncontrolled, unstable cuckoo who we had nurtured to adulthood getting loose amongst the local population. There was literally no telling how much damage she could do. We'd never dealt with a case like hers before. But since the only way to be sure she wasn't going to hurt anyone was to kill her, we were living with the fear. Sarah was family.

"No, Sarah's fine, or as fine as she gets right now," I said. "One of the other keepers from the reptile house was killed sometime between closing time last night and lunch today."

"Murder?"

"Unclear. Whatever killed him was a petrifactor."

There was another pause, longer this time, before he said, "Alex, the basilisks . . ."

"Are still hibernating. I checked them myself, and their skins are too calcified for them to have woken up—or been woken—left the enclosure, turned a man partially to stone, and gone back to sleep. Not that they would have gone back to the enclosure anyway. They didn't do this. And before you ask, yes, I also talked to Dee. I don't think she had anything to do with it."

"That's a relief."

"It is, except for the part where I started out with three petrifactors who could have been responsible for this and promptly eliminated all three of them as possible candidates."

"So what are you thinking?"

"If it was a gorgon, it was murder. The victim's eyes were definitely stone. Lesser gorgons can't *truly* turn you to stone, and Pliny's gorgons can't always stone you with a glance; they'd need to have either uncovered their hair and locked eyes with him for long enough, or milked their hair beforehand for venom and sprayed him with it. I can't rule out a Pliny's gorgon, but it's more likely that we're looking for a purely glance-based petrifactor."

"The greater gorgon is glance-based."

"Yes, I'm aware. You'll forgive me if I try to find any other possible answer before I go to the place where I get eaten alive, won't you?"

"Your mother would never forgive me if I encouraged you to take any other course of action. There's always the simpler answer, you realize."

"I thought of that. A cockatrice would fit the situation as I currently understand it. It's glance-based, it likes to hide in low bushes . . . it's perfect." And it wouldn't be murder. Your average cockatrice makes an iguana seem like a super-genius. When animals kill people, it's tragic, but it's not malicious. "There's just one problem with that theory."

"Lots of things aren't native to Ohio, Alex. You've just said that some of the frickens you've caught aren't native to Ohio."

"Yes, but there's a big difference between something moving into an open ecological niche and something like a cockatrice showing up for no good reason."

"So maybe there's a good reason."

That wasn't the sort of statement that inspired confidence. I sighed, removing my glasses and putting them on the bedside table before pinching the bridge of my nose. "Maybe. Grandpa's going to see about getting me access to the autopsy records. We should know more after that happens."

"Keep us posted. You know we'll be right there if you need us."

"I do." I also knew a family invasion of Ohio would mean things had gotten very bad. I wasn't too proud to ask for help, but mobilizing the troops was the sort of thing that should only be used as a last resort. "Tell Mom I said hi and send my love when she gets home."

"Any messages for your sister?"

"Tell her to stay out of my room."

Dad laughed. We exchanged farewells and I hung up, slumping over backward onto the bed. Crow hopped down from the dresser to curl up, catlike, against my side. I stroked his wings absently, and he purred in response.

"It's a mess, Crow," I said.

He made a contented churring noise. I sighed and closed my eyes, continuing to stroke his wings. I had a lot of work to do, but other than preparing my notes on the situation, there wasn't much that I could do *now*. I lay on my bed and listened to the joyful songs of the mice, trying to let my worries slip away, just for the moment, just for now. I needed to get some food in me like Grandpa had instructed. I didn't want to move.

If this situation turned out to be as bad as I was afraid it was going to be, I wasn't going to have any more moments like this one for a while. So I stayed where I was, and tried to enjoy the moment while it lasted.

I tried.

Seven

"Perhaps you misunderstand me. I am not afraid to die. Neither am I afraid to kill you. Now how about we put down the guns and discuss things like breathing men, rather than continuing this conversation in the afterlife?"

—Jonathan Healy

An only moderately creepy suburban home in Columbus, Ohio, waking up after an impromptu nap

CROW WAS CURLED UP on my stomach when I woke up. I blinked at the ceiling, only gradually coming to realize that I'd been woken up by the sound of someone knocking on my bedroom door. I sat up, sending Crow tumbling, and rubbed my face with one hand while he squawked in irritation.

The knocking continued, now accompanied by my grandmother's voice calling, "Alex? Are you awake?"

"I'm up, Grandma," I called back, giving my face one more good rub before I swung my feet around to the floor and stood. I grabbed my usual glasses off the table as an afterthought. It wasn't like I needed to worry about being turned to stone in my own home. "Crap. I didn't mean to go to sleep. What time is it?"

"Seven."

"Crap." I pulled my phone out of my pocket as I walked across the room, and found a text from Dee telling me that she had made it home. That was a relief, at least. I opened the door to find my grandmother standing in the hall, still wearing her work clothes, a concerned look on her face. I forced a wan smile. "Did Grandpa tell you what's going on?"

"He did," she said, with a nod. "Are you all right?"

"I am. Andrew's not."

"Now, you don't know that. He could be getting his afterlife orientation right now."

My Aunt Mary used to babysit my grandmother, and she died decades before I was born. That doesn't stop her from showing up at every family reunion and Christmas party she can get to. I shook my head. "Breathing people like to keep breathing. When you stop, you're not all right anymore, even if you get to have a new existence as a semi-corporeal houseguest. Has Grandpa heard back from the morgue?"

"He has," she said. "The autopsy is being performed locally, which is good news—"

My stomach sank. "But it's not being performed until the morning, is it?"

Grandma shook her head. "They've already ruled out contagion—there's nothing to indicate that turning into stone is something you can *catch*. So while it's being treated as a chemical attack for the moment, it's not urgent."

"Then we have to break into the morgue. I need to see the remains." I shook my head, wishing I was the telepathic one, so that I could make her understand why this mattered so much. "Petrifaction isn't a thing that just happens in the human body. We need to know how it happened so that we can determine what did it, so we can stop—"

"Alex, *you* need to stop." Grandma folded her arms, looking at me gravely. "I love you, but you have the same problem your father does. You assume we haven't been fighting this battle without you for centuries. You're not the only answer to every problem."

Her words stung, but she was right. I frowned before allowing my shoulders to sag. "I'm sorry, Grandma. I just want to help. This could be my fault."

"Because of your basilisks, or because it happened at the zoo where you happen to be working? Sometimes a coincidence is just a coincidence, you know."

"And sometimes it's the start of something very large, and very unpleasant. I can't bank on one and ignore the other."

"I know." She smiled slightly. "You're my grandson, after all. Come on down to the kitchen. We have a proposition for you."

Grandpa was waiting in the kitchen. Grandma led me to the table and pushed me into a chair, and Grandpa set a tuna fish sandwich in front of me. "Eat," he commanded.

"Yes, sir," I said, and picked the sandwich up.

They waited until my mouth was full and I couldn't protest before Grandma said, "You're staying home with Sarah tonight while we go on our date. You'll get your autopsy results in the morning."

"And no, we're not breaking into the city morgue," added Grandpa.

I swallowed my half-chewed mouthful of sandwich, managing not to choke, and said, "But I need to see—"

"You need to learn patience," said Grandpa. "There's no good reason for us to see this as anything other than an isolated incident right now, and there are quite a few good reasons for you to stay home."

"For instance, we only have two tickets to the theater, and I'm not going to buy another one from a scalper just because you don't feel like waiting here," said Grandma. "And there's Sarah to be considered. Someone has to stay with her. That's why we arranged this date night in the first place. I know you want to serve the cryptid community, sweetheart. Well, tonight, you serve the cryptid community by babysitting."

"I don't believe this," I said.

"The autopsy isn't going to happen any faster if we cancel our date," said Grandpa. "He's scheduled for the morning. Learn patience."

"Can you at least promise I'll get the file as soon as the autopsy is complete?" I asked. My head was spinning. Of all the possible solutions I'd considered, "you stay home and babysit because patience is a virtue" wasn't on the list.

"Yes," said Grandpa firmly. "As soon as he's released to the city morgue, I'll call you, and we'll examine him a second time together. But tonight, we need you to stay home. Please, Alex, can you do that for us?"

"I *really* don't believe this," I said, pinching the bridge of my nose. Finally, against my better judgment, I nodded. "Yes, I'll stay at home with Sarah so you can have your date night. But you have to *promise* I'm getting those autopsy reports."

"I swear," said Grandma.

I sighed and dropped my hand. "I guess I'm staying at home, then."

"Yes, I suppose you are," said Grandpa, and smiled.

An hour later, they were heading out the door, having delivered the usual list of instructions for the care and feeding of my cousin, most of which involved the word "don't." Don't let her go outside, don't let her answer the phone, don't let her answer the door, don't let her get into philosophical debates with the pizza delivery man, don't let her eat chocolate chips. (To be fair, that last one was for medical reasons: chocolate is mildly poisonous to cuckoos, and she'd make herself sick before she remembered she wasn't supposed to have it.) Sarah stood halfway down the stairs, clutching the banister and swaying slightly as she watched them go.

"Be good!" called Grandma, and closed the door behind her, leaving us alone. I turned to Sarah.

"What do you want to do?"

"Ignite the heart of a dormant sun and resolve the impossible fractions," she replied.

"Well, since that's not going to happen tonight, how about some television?" With her telepathy mostly blocked, TV was actually more soothing for her than live interaction. She knew she couldn't read the minds of the people on the screen, and most of the time, the characters were easily distinguishable by hair color and wardrobe—two of the things she *could* pick up on.

"Television is good," she agreed, descending two more steps. "What's the menu?"

"I have season one of *Numb3rs*, or some downloads of *Square One* that Artie sent for you. Whichever you like."

"PBS is better," she said serenely, and finally walked to the bottom of the stairs, proceeding into the living room. I shrugged and followed her.

"*Square One* it is," I said.

It didn't take long to get her settled on the living room floor with a bowl of ketchup-covered popcorn in her lap and math-based edutainment programming playing on the television. Sarah stared raptly, swaying to the beat as two would-be rappers began singing about prime numbers.

"I'll be in the kitchen if you need me," I said.

She flapped a hand, dismissing me from her presence. I smiled.

"Yes, Your Majesty," I said, and left, pulling my phone out of my pocket as I walked. I'd promised Shelby I would call her. Sure, it was originally going to be a little later, since I was hoping we might be breaking into the morgue, but I hadn't specified an exact time.

Shelby picked up so fast that I wasn't sure the phone had actually completed its first ring. "Alex? Is that you?"

"Caller ID probably says it is," I said. Then I paused, and laughed.

"What?" she asked, tone turning suspicious. "What's so funny?"

"I just talked to my father a little while ago, and I was making caller ID jokes with him, that's all. What's going on? I'm calling like I said I would."

"What do you want, a cookie?" Shelby paused and sighed. "I'm sorry, that was nasty of me. I just don't want to be alone right now. I keep waiting for something to jump out of the shadows at me, and it's making me incredibly uncomfortable."

I grew up waiting for something to jump out of the shadows at me. I sighed as I sat down at the kitchen table. "I'm sorry."

"So I was wondering . . ."

"What?" I should have heard the danger in her tone, which had sweetened and taken on a faint wheedling quality. But I was worried about her, and anxious about the possibility of a cockatrice rampaging through Columbus, and I suppose I just wasn't listening clearly.

"Could I come over? Tonight, I mean? I know I've never been to your place, but you can't leave your poor sick cousin, and I won't be any bother, I swear. I just . . . I really don't want to be alone right now. Please?"

"Shelby . . ."

Her voice dropped to a whisper. "I keep thinking about Andrew."

I pinched the bridge of my nose, fighting the urge to groan. "Give me a second."

"Of course."

It wasn't technically against the rules for me to have company—Grandma would have encouraged it if it hadn't been for Sarah, since she really wanted me to have more of a social life. As long as I put away anything incriminating before Shelby arrived, and could convince Crow and the mice to stay upstairs for the duration of her visit, I wouldn't have to worry about anything except for my cousin.

About that . . . Sarah was happy in front of the television, and lots of people eat strange things on their popcorn. One of my college roommates used to put baker's yeast on his. Ketchup was nothing. I could give Shelby a telepathy blocker, say it was a piece of jewelry that made me think of her. The charms were pretty things, copper disks suspended in little glass balls filled with water. She'd probably believe me.

Shelby sounded honestly distressed, and I wanted to be a good boyfriend, no matter how bad at it I was. Certain that I was making a mistake—and less certain of exactly what it was—I said, "Come on over. I'll text you the address. Just . . . give me twenty minutes to clean up?"

"What, disposing of the bodies, are you?" she asked, a bit of her normal playfulness seeping back into her tone.

"Something like that." If she thought body disposal would take me twenty minutes, she'd clearly never watched me clean a snake cage. I could get rid of an average human body in ten minutes, tops.

. . . and maybe that would be a bad thing to brag about to the nice girl that I was dating. Clearly, "normal" was still a bit beyond my capabilities. I shook my head and quickly added, "Only a bit less gruesome. Mostly it's just dishes and making sure Sarah understands we'll be having company."

There was a pause. "She's really quite ill, then?" said Shelby, sounding unsure.

"Nothing contagious, I swear." It occurred to me that Shelby might have taken my constant excuses about needing to care for a sick cousin as exactly that: excuses. I glanced at the kitchen door. "She's watching television right now. I'll talk to her before you get here."

"All right," said Shelby. The uncertainty was gone, re-

placed by her normal good cheer. "See you soon, then."
She hung up.

I smiled to myself as I texted the address to her number, put my phone away, and began the process of removing any obvious "nonhumans live here" markers
from easy view. The kitchen was easy: tuck a few of
Grandma's cookbooks into a drawer, hide Grandpa's
bottles of formalin behind the wilted lettuce in the vegetable crisper and presto, a normal kitchen for a normal
human family. The front hall was harder—I had to take
down several pictures—but it was still nothing compared
to what it would have taken to do the same thing at
home.

I stuck my head into the living room, where Sarah was
still staring raptly at the television. Nothing in there really screamed "hide me," except for maybe Sarah herself,
and that wasn't an option. "Sarah?" I asked, stepping
fully inside.

She didn't react. It was possible she couldn't tell me
from the voices on the TV. I walked toward her, careful
to stay at a nonthreatening distance. Trying to approach
her when she was focusing on something else was a lot
like dealing with the venomous snakes at the zoo, and
about as dangerous. "Sarah, it's Alex. Can you look at me
for a second?"

"Math is happening," she scolded, not turning her
head.

"Math has a pause button. Please, can we talk for a
second? I'll make you an ice cream sundae."

That got her attention. She turned her head toward
me, and asked, "Vanilla? With ketchup and curry powder?"

I managed to repress my shudder. She probably
wouldn't have recognized it anyway. "Yes, vanilla ice
cream with ketchup and curry powder."

"All right." Sarah twisted to fully face me instead of
the television. "Talk."

"I have a . . . friend. Her name is Shelby. She works

with me at the zoo. We had a bad day today, and she doesn't want to be alone. So I told her that she could come over here. Is that all right with you?"

A line formed between Sarah's eyebrows as she frowned. "Oh," she said. "No. No, I don't think that's okay at all. Won't I be here? Won't she see me?"

"Yes. She'll see a pretty girl who's having some medical trouble, and that's all." I touched the chain around my neck that held my anti-telepathy charm. "I'm going to give her a charm so that you can't accidentally hurt her, because I know you'd be sad if you did. And it'll be good for you to see someone who isn't a relative."

Sarah shook her head. "I don't want to."

"Sarah . . ."

"What if it doesn't work? The charm? The math doesn't always add up, you know. What if I get confused and I hurt her? You'll hate me, and Angela will finally say 'that's it, oh well, we tried, but cuckoo is cuckoo is cuckoo,' and then the knives in the night, and nothing ever after."

"Sarah . . ." I moved closer before crouching down. "That's not going to happen, I promise. Now, I can call Shelby and tell her not to come if you need me to, but I want you to be sure you need that. Please, Sarah."

She bit her lip. Then, finally, she said, "I want two ice cream sundaes, and I want to sleep in your room tonight."

If my little sister had tried bargaining like that, I would have been annoyed. From Sarah, it was a sign of recovery, and so welcome that I almost hugged her. I restrained myself and smiled instead, straightening back up as I said, "It's a deal. Shelby will be here soon; I'm going to go and tell the mice they need to keep quiet."

Sarah snorted, and for just a moment, she looked like her old self again: focused, smarter than me, and laughing at my pain. "Good luck with that, Alex."

"Thanks." I walked out of the room as she turned

back to the TV. I didn't want to see the moment when the presence slipped out of her face, as I knew it inevitably would.

She was getting better. She had to be.

Bribing the mice required an entire package of Oreos and half a pound of cheddar cheese, with the promise of more to come after they'd kept their word and stayed in the bedroom until Shelby was gone. Bribing Crow was easier: a package of raw chicken livers and he was happy to stay right in the middle of my bed, getting bloodstains on the duvet. It wouldn't be the first time.

I was walking down the stairs and buttoning a clean shirt when the doorbell rang. "Coming!" I shouted, almost tripping over my own feet in my hurry to answer. "Coming," I repeated, and opened the door.

Shelby blinked. Then she grinned. "You're lopsided," she said.

"What?"

"Lopsided." She gestured toward my shirt. I looked down and reddened. I had managed to miss a button in the middle, leaving me off-kilter.

"Oh," I said.

"Don't worry about it." Her hand brushed my chin, pushing it gently upward until we were eye-to-eye. She was still grinning. "I think it's cute. Are you going to invite me inside?"

"Oh," I said again, and stepped to the side, indicating the front hall with a wave of my hand. "Please, come in."

"Don't mind if I do," said Shelby, and stepped over the threshold.

She was wearing a knee-length blue dress with an almost 1950s-style skirt, the kind that would flare out if she spun around. The six inches around the neckline and bottom foot or so of the fabric was white, meeting the blue in a series of scalloped curves that looked almost

like clouds. It was the sort of dress most women would
have paired with heels, but she was wearing blue ballet
flats. I silently approved. Shoes like that wouldn't get her
killed in a firefight. Her only jewelry was a pair of opal
stud earrings and some sort of pendant on a silver chain,
currently hidden by the neckline of her dress.

Shelby was looking at me, smirking slightly. "You
done staring, there, or shall I stand here a bit longer before you show me around?"

"Sorry." I grimaced and closed the door, turning the
deadbolt. "Um, kitchen's to your left, bathroom's down
the hall, living room's to your right. The upstairs isn't
currently fit for human habitation. Sarah is in the living
room watching PBS. Did you want some coffee, tea, cocoa, something stronger . . . ? Like maybe a boyfriend
who doesn't babble incessantly?"

"I like the babbling all right, and cocoa'd be nice,"
Shelby said. "Thank you. For everything, really. I truly
didn't want to be at home alone tonight."

"It's my pleasure. Come this way." I started for the
kitchen, casting one last nervous glance over my shoulder at the closed living room door. Sarah had promised
to be good. I needed to take her at her word.

Shelby followed me, and sat down at the kitchen table
while I busied myself with preparing two cups of hot
chocolate and a plate of Grandpa's snickerdoodles.
Touching the cookies would normally have triggered an
avalanche of mice, but like Sarah, they had promised to
be good. I had to take them at their word, too.

I handed Shelby a mug, and was rewarded with another smile. "Thank you," she said. "You really do have
a lovely home. What I've seen of it, anyway."

"My grandparents believe that a healthy mind begins
with a healthy environment."

Shelby paused with her mug half-lifted to her mouth,
expression turning skeptical. "This isn't hot carob with a
soy-based 'whipped cream' on top, is it? Because I'm
afraid I'll have to pour it on you if you say it is."

"Not that kind of healthy, I promise." Grandma had no arteries to clog, and Grandpa regularly flushed his circulatory system with acids. "Health food" wasn't a risk in their kitchen. "I meant more that they really think a home should be a home, and not a house where you're temporarily living."

"They sound like clever folks," said Shelby, and finally sipped her cocoa before asking, "Is that why you agreed to move back home? I remember you used to have an apartment, even though I never saw it."

"That was part of it, yeah," I agreed. Back in Portland, the house was always full of people—my parents, my sisters, my paternal grandmother, and whoever among our allies and extended family had followed us home that week. In Columbus I'd lived alone, in a one-bedroom apartment that didn't allow pets. Its layout made it essentially indefensible. I hadn't slept well once while I was living there. "And then there was Sarah. My grandparents couldn't take care of her on their own, so they asked if I'd come and help them out."

"Family first," said Shelby.

"Yes, exactly," I agreed. "Family first."

Shelby took another sip of her cocoa. For a moment, it felt like she was watching me over the top of the cup. The hairs on the back of my neck rose. Then she raised her head and smiled, and I knew that I was just being silly. "I'm glad you're all right."

"Me, too." I reached across the table and took her free hand. "I was really worried when the cops shooed me off and kept on talking to you."

"They mostly just wanted to know if I thought you might be a serial murderer."

I raised an eyebrow. "I hope you told them that I was your beloved boyfriend who would never murder anyone." Without good cause.

"I told them you were a bastard who canceled dates and refused to let me see his home and probably had a wife hidden in the attic, but that you weren't the type to commit murder in cold blood," said Shelby sweetly, before taking another sip of cocoa.

"Hey," I protested. "I haven't canceled *that* many dates."

"Any woman in the world will tell you that one date canceled is one too many," Shelby said, and took a cookie. "I told them you almost certainly were not a serial killer, and that they were being horribly sexist by assuming that of the two of us, only you were capable of committing murder. That may have been a tactical error—it got me rather a lot more questioning that I hadn't exactly been planning on."

"Well, yes. It's usually unwise to tell the police you could be a serial killer if you really, really wanted to." I took a cookie of my own, dunking it in my cocoa. "But everything is okay otherwise?"

"You mean beyond the dead man in the bushes and our ruined lunch? Yes. Everything is fine. How was your staff?"

"They're not technically my staff. I don't run the reptile house."

Shelby snorted. "Come off that, Alex. You run Dee, and Dee is the force that holds that place together. Before they hired her on to keep records, it was like a bunch of children playing at being a serious research institute."

I raised an eyebrow. "And you would know this how? We arrived at the zoo at the same time."

"Yes, and you brought Dee with you, and while your staff may have been too grateful to go telling tales, the rest of the zoo wasn't so restrained. If you stuck your head outside the snake box every once in a while, you might have heard a thing or two."

My cheeks reddened. "I was busy getting settled into my new position." Rearranging the labs so that no one would notice my basilisk enclosure had taken months, shifting things one piece at a time while Dee adjusted the paperwork and kept the rest of the staff distracted with her streamlined schedules and improved feeding

processes. She wasn't a zookeeper, but she knew her reptiles.

"I know; the gossip had died down before you stuck
your head aboveground, and by that point, it seemed a
little silly to tell you everyone basically assumed you
were in charge. Where's the harm? Means no one's mon-
itoring your lunch hours, unlike me." She grimaced. "I'm
thirty seconds late and it's another lecture from the head
keeper on punctuality and pride and lots of other words
that start with the letter 'P.'"

"Still. I didn't know." And I didn't like it. I was supposed to be keeping a low profile, not setting myself up
as the new god-king of the Columbus Zoo reptile house.

"I know. That's part of what made you so interesting."
Shelby grinned.

After a pause, I grinned back. She started to lean
across the table toward me. I did the same—and froze,
pulling away just before our lips could meet. Shelby
blinked at me, smile fading into a puzzled frown.

"What is it?" she asked. "Is something wrong?"

"I'm sorry—I was going to give you something. Hang
on just a second." I bolted from the table before she
could argue with me, running back into the front hall.
The kitchen door swung shut behind me. "Stupid, stupid,
stupid," I chanted, wrenching open the drawer on the
hallway table and digging through the mass of protection
charms, rope, and old batteries that had built up over the
years. (Why the old batteries, I don't know. Maybe there's
some sort of natural law that says every drawer without
an exact defined purpose has to contain a certain number of batteries.)

I *knew* Shelby needed an anti-telepathy charm if she
was going to be in the house. I'd *planned* for it. So how
was it that the second I saw her standing there in her
pretty blue dress, I forgot about everything important?

The TV in the living room was still on, and Sarah was
unlikely to have moved as long as her show was playing.
That was something, anyway.

The anti-telepathy charm was wedged into the bottom of the drawer, next to an anti-hex charm and a basilisk's claw. I grabbed the thin cotton cord of the charm I'd been looking for and slammed the drawer, running back to the kitchen. I slapped a smile across my face and pushed the door open.

"Sorry about that, Shelby; I just didn't want to risk forgetting—" I stopped mid-sentence.

Shelby was no longer at the kitchen table. She was standing near the sliding glass door to the backyard, frowning out into the darkness. "I think I saw something moving out there," she said, stepping closer, so that her face was practically pressed up against the glass. "It didn't look like a raccoon . . ."

I didn't think: I just moved, racing across the room and shoving her out of the way just before the creature she'd seen lunged toward the door. I caught a glimpse of madly flapping wings and a tail like a whip before a searing pain lanced through my eyes.

The world went gray.

Eight

"The natural world has a place for everything. It's just that some of those things make me think that Nature isn't very fond of people."

—Martin Baker

In the kitchen of an only moderately creepy suburban home in Columbus, Ohio, trying not to collapse from the sudden intense pain

"ALEX!"

Shelby's shout snapped me out of my shock. I clapped my hands over my face—too little too late—and kicked the door, sending reverberations through the glass.

"Shoo!" I shouted. "Go on, get out of here! You're not welcome!" I kicked the door again. The pain in my eyes was immense, burning and freezing at the same time. I kicked the door a third time before staggering backward, bellowing, "*Sarah!*"

I had asked her to be good. She had promised. Being good meant staying out of sight, and Sarah kept her promises. She didn't answer me.

"It's gone, Alex, whatever it was, it's gone." Shelby grabbed for my elbow, trying to find purchase on my moving arm. "What's wrong? Let me see."

"No." I closed my eyes tightly, gritting my teeth

against the urge to shout for Sarah again. "Can you please get me to the kitchen table?"

"Alex, this really isn't the time—"

"Please!"

She went momentarily silent before she said, "All right, Alex. There's no need to shout." Her hand caught my elbow. "It's this way."

"Thank you." The pain was like nothing I had ever felt before. It was definitely something I never wanted to feel again.

"What's going on? What was that thing? What's the matter with your eyes?"

"I don't know what it was, but you're going to need to trust me for a minute, okay?" If only the backyard had been better lit. I hadn't been able to see the thing that got me well enough to tell whether or not its wings had feathers. Feathers would mean basilisk; lack of feathers meant cockatrice. "My cousin is in the other room. She can't hear me with the TV on. Go get her."

"Alex . . ."

"Please." The pain in my eyes wasn't getting better, and in this situation, that was a good thing. Stone doesn't hurt.

There had been a thick pane of glass between me and the creature, even if it wasn't properly polarized, and petrifaction is known to be less effective at a distance. Those factors combined might be enough to save my vision.

"I don't understand *any* of this." Shelby sounded more irritated than frightened. Good. Irritation was easier to work with.

"Just go get Sarah, please. She'll be able to get the first aid kit."

"All right—but you're going to explain *everything*," snarled Shelby. I heard footsteps as she moved away, followed by the sound of the kitchen door swinging open. I slumped in my chair, resisting the urge to rub my eyes. That would just cause me more pain, and might result in structural damage.

Everything was dark. I tried to focus on the last thing I'd seen, the creature on the back lawn with the wildly flapping wings and the serpent's tail. Feathers or no feathers? The more I thought about it, the more convinced I became that its wings had been more like a bat's than a bird's, but that could have been wishful thinking, me refusing to acknowledge that this could be my fault. If its wings weren't feathered, it wasn't one of my basilisks.

How would one of the basilisks get this far from the zoo? The thought was compelling. Basilisks aren't fast movers, and they're extremely territorial, especially when the females get broody. If the zoo basilisks had managed to escape, they should have gone to ground on the spot, refusing to be budged.

The door banged again as Shelby returned. "Alex? Are you all right?"

"I'm fine. Did you find Sarah?"

"This is a positively appalling way to make an introduction, but yeah, I found her," said Shelby. "She's getting that first aid kit you wanted. Now are you going to tell me what's going on?"

"Can we take this one step at a time for right now? Can you go to the fridge, please? There should be a bunch of bottles of water with different colored caps on the second shelf. Get one of the green-capped bottles. Please."

"I know they say 'please' is a magic word, but it doesn't actually control the universe, you know."

"Shelby! I'm trying to not freak out right now, so *please*, can you go along with my seemingly irrational demands until we reach the point where I am capable of explaining myself in a calm and rational manner? *Please?*"

There was a pause. Finally, Shelby said, "The green lid, you say?"

"That's the one."

The kitchen door swung open again, followed by the

soft sound of bare feet against the floor. "I found the first aid kit. It was not in the land of talking bluebirds, although they're very loud right now. Alex, what did you *do*?"

"I locked eyes with a petrifactor," I said. "Sarah, can you read right now?"

There was a momentary pause before she said, "Not reliably. Numbers are easier."

"Okay. We can work with this. Shelby, give the bottle of water to Sarah and take the first aid kit. I need you to look for a vial labeled 'belladonna.'"

"What in the world would belladonna be doing in your first aid kit?"

The pain in my eyes was starting to fade. I couldn't tell if that meant my nerves were becoming overloaded, or if it was a sign that the damage was getting worse. Either option was bad. "Hopefully, saving my vision. Once you've found the belladonna—it should be a clear liquid—look for a jar of bilberry jam."

"You keep *jam* in your first aid kit. Alongside the *belladonna*." Now Shelby sounded outright skeptical. That wasn't good. I wanted her to help me, not call the authorities to report my nervous breakdown.

"It's a very specialized first aid kit," I said, as patiently as I could. "Once you have the belladonna and bilberry, you need to mix them into the water Sarah's got. Then—"

"What, there's more? Should I be getting a cauldron?"

"A cauldron would be lovely," said Sarah.

"We're getting off track here," I said sharply. "There is a small refrigerator in the pantry. Open it. On the second shelf you will find a rack of antivenin. Get the vial labeled 'P. cockatrice' and bring it here."

"Alex, this is madness. If you're really hurt, we need to get you to a hospital, not sit about playing chemistry lab with your cousin."

"A hospital wouldn't help me," I said. "Now *please*."

Something about my voice must have gotten through; maybe it was the desperation. There was a pause before

Shelby sighed and said, "Oh, what the hell. It's not like I had anything better to do this evening."

I groaned, and stayed where I was, hands clapped over my face, as I listened to my girlfriend and my cousin mixing the substance that might—if fate was kind and I'd been correct in my split-second taxonomical classification—save my eyesight. It was the longest five minutes of my life. Sarah occasionally offered murmured corrections, equally divided between "useful" and "complete non sequitur." It would have been entertaining if I hadn't been in so damn much pain.

"How much jam?" asked Shelby.

"Three large tablespoons full."

"And how much belladonna?"

"The same."

Shelby muttered something that sounded suspiciously like "moron" and kept rattling around the kitchen, the clatter of her shoes followed by the softer padding of Sarah's bare feet. I heard the pantry door open. "Second rack?"

"That's the one. Be careful with the vial. It's all we have, and there's none back at the reptile house."

"I can't see why you think you need antivenin, you only *looked* at the thing—"

"*Please.*"

Shelby sighed. "I'm a fool for not loading you straight into my car and rushing you to the emergency room," she said. There was a soft thud on the table in front of me. "The gunk you asked us to mash up is near your right elbow. Mind you don't spill it, although what else you're going to do with it is a mystery to me."

"I'm going to apply it to the affected areas," I said. I lowered my hands. The unyielding darkness that had replaced the room did not change.

Shelby's gasp was followed by Sarah saying serenely, "Don't worry, Alex, I caught the antivenin before it could hit the ground."

"Well, that's my nightmares sorted for the next week,"

I said sourly as I began feeling around the table for the jar of jam, belladonna, and purified unicorn water.

"Alex, your *eyes*," said Shelby.

"I know." My right hand found the jar. I picked it up, sticking the first two fingers of my left hand into the thick goop that it contained. Scooping out a generous dollop of the stuff, I began smearing it on and around my eyes. It didn't sting, but the pain was still there, burning and freezing deep inside. I kept scooping and smearing until I had practically covered the top half of my face. Gingerly, I set the near-empty jar aside.

"The antivenin, please," I said, holding out my left hand.

"Oh, Alex . . ." whispered Shelby. The familiar shape of an antivenin vial was pressed into my hand. I unscrewed the cap with my right hand—the one without sticky fingers—and said, as cheerfully as I could, "Let's hope this works, okay?"

Then I drank the contents of the vial in a single long gulp that burned all the way down.

The trouble with many cryptids—the trouble, and the reason we cryptozoologists sometimes resist allowing them to be reclassified as part of the so-called "natural world"—is that their capabilities defy many of the things we currently pretend to understand about science. How can anything turn flesh to stone? No one knows, but the petrifactors still manage to do it. Why do bilberries counteract petrifaction? Again, no one knows, although there were some fascinating rumors about bilberries improving eyesight during World War II. (They weren't entirely false. Eastern Europe has a terrible basilisk problem, and anyone who wanted to avoid being taken prisoner behind enemy lines needed to be prepared for a few unpleasant encounters. Bilberries could save your life, if you swallowed them while you still had a throat made of flesh.)

Unicorn water isn't actually the cure-all that legend claims it is, but it's the purest thing known to man, cleansed down to the molecular level. That makes it the perfect sterile solution for something like this, since there was no chance of contamination before the seal on the bottle had been broken. I had applied the topical ointment. I had used the right ingredients. Now I just had to hope that I was as good at this as I thought I was.

If I die this way, Antimony is going to decorate my statue for the holidays for the rest of time. I could practically see myself turned to solid gray stone, standing on the front porch of the family home, with tinsel and Christmas lights wrapped around my neck. The thought was horrible and hysterical at the same time. I laughed.

It hurt.

That was a good sign. I kept laughing, and it kept hurting, until I figured out where in the pain I had left my hands and used them to push myself upright. Peeling my cheek away from the kitchen table took some doing; I had been slumped over long enough for my jam-based facial mask to start turning sticky and trying to gum me down.

"Can I get a wet washcloth please?" I rasped. Speech hurt even more than laughter. I swallowed hard before adding, "And a glass of milk? I need to counteract some of this acid."

"Alex!" Shelby sounded like she couldn't make up her mind whether she wanted to be stunned, delighted, or furious. "Are you all right?"

"We'll know in a second. I don't want to open my eyes until I've wiped this stuff off."

"I'll get it," said Sarah. There was a scrape as she pushed back her chair, and she went padding away across the kitchen. The water in the sink started a few seconds later.

"I thought you'd just committed suicide," said Shelby in a hushed tone. "Alex, your eyes . . ."

"It's an allergic reaction to the thing that was out back. I'm just glad you didn't see it."

"A *visual* allergy? Alex. Don't treat me like I'm an idiot. There's no such things as visual allergies."

"Sure there are. Haven't you ever seen a pattern that made you feel dizzy, or an optical illusion that gave you a headache? Visual allergies exist. This is just a little more severe than most." Something warm and wet was draped across my hand. "Thanks, Sarah."

"Okay," she said serenely.

"That's Sarah for 'you're welcome,'" I said, and began using the towel to wipe away the jam that covered my face. I kept my eyes closed while I was working, trying to pretend that the sinking feeling in my stomach was anything but terror. If we'd been too slow getting the treatment prepared, if the proportions were off, if any one of a dozen things had gone wrong . . .

The pain had stopped. I clung to that. Even if my eyesight was gone, I wasn't going to turn to stone. That was better than the alternative.

Wiping the last of the jam away, I cautiously cracked my eyes open. I immediately slammed them shut again as the light assaulted my retinas. "Okay, *ow*," I said.

"Alex?" demanded Shelby.

"The petrifaction didn't have time to penetrate his retinas, but there's still strain," said Sarah, sounding distracted, like she was explaining something that really didn't matter. "It's going to take time for his eyes to adjust to the kitchen's light levels. There's no dimmer switch. There was a clapper for a while, but Angela likes to watch opera on DVD. The applause would make the lights go wild. Martin took it out."

"Is that so?" said Shelby. She sounded faintly baffled. Not an uncommon reaction when Sarah decided to go off on a tangent.

"I'm okay," I said, and raised one hand to shade my

eyes as I carefully opened them again. The kitchen came into view, blurry and over-bright, but *visible*, beautifully, blessedly visible. I could have laughed, except that I was afraid that if I started, I wouldn't be able to stop again until I had all the panic out of my system. I did cry, both from relief, and from the pain of the light lancing into my eyeballs. It was a good pain, though, a clean pain, far removed from the grinding agony of petrifaction.

"Alex?" said Shelby.

"That *sucked*." I lowered my hand and reached for my glasses, blinking as I tried to clear away the blurriness. The table, cluttered with items from the first aid kit, was the first thing to come into focus. Then came Sarah, who was sitting across from me with a quizzical expression on her face, like this was the most interesting thing she'd seen all week. I managed a faint smile for her. "Hi, Sarah. Thanks for your help."

"There's a period of adjustment that comes with the sudden loss of a primary sense," she said. "You would have had difficulty making the ice cream sundaes you promised me."

"That's true," I said. I realized that she could just as easily be describing herself: without easy access to the telepathy she'd depended on since birth, she was essentially "blind."

"Are you really all right?" asked Shelby.

I turned to her, and blinked, suddenly struck by just how beautiful she was. The faint blurriness of my vision made the white hem of her dress look like actual clouds, and the kitchen light was reflecting in a corona around her head. All that, and she'd just saved me from an unidentified cryptid. If I hadn't been afraid I'd topple over if I tried to get out of my chair, I would have been tempted to propose on the spot.

"I'm going to be fine," I assured her. "We got the antivenin into my system fast enough, and the stuff you mixed up with the jam was enough to fix the superficial damage."

"So you're fit? Intact and stable?"

"I think so."

"Oh, good." Shelby was abruptly on her feet, sending her chair toppling over backward. It was still falling when my eyes focused on the important part of this scene: the pistol she was holding in her hands, with the barrel aimed squarely at Sarah's chest. "Now that we've got that taken care of, let's move on to the important things. Like extermination."

Well, crap.

Nine

"Expectations are dangerous things. They've probably killed more people than any creature or cryptid that you care to name."
—Kevin Price

In the kitchen of an only moderately creepy suburban home in Columbus, Ohio, dealing with a suddenly homicidal girlfriend

IF SARAH WAS UPSET about having a gun aimed in her direction, she didn't show it. I wasn't even sure she realized the thing in Shelby's hands was a gun, as opposed to a stapler or something similar.

"You can leave the kitchen if you like, Alex," said Shelby. "I know this must be very confusing for you, but I promise, it's all going to start making sense soon."

"What are you—"

"You never gave it to her, but I couldn't hear her," said Sarah, blinking her enormous blue eyes with Disney princess guilelessness. "I didn't even know she was in the house until she started talking to you. She should have been here until you gave it to her, and she wasn't."

"Gave *what* to her? Sarah—" I glanced at Shelby, who was holding her perfect shooter's stance with a casual ease that implied she could do this all night if she needed to. I was in favor of that. As long as she was standing still, she wasn't shooting my cousin. "Maybe this isn't the best time to talk about what you could and couldn't hear, okay?"

"But you never *gave* it to her." Sarah's eyes stayed fixed on Shelby, but her tone turned petulant. She seemed more perturbed by me than she was by the woman with the gun. Oh, priorities. "You promised."

"Gave *what* to . . . oh." I froze, feeling the blood drain out of my face.

I had never given Shelby the anti-telepathy charm. I left the kitchen to get it for her, but I'd been distracted by the cockatrice in the backyard, and I'd never given it to her. I risked a glance over my shoulder, confirming that the little glass-and-copper pendant was still lying on the floor. I'd dropped it and then forgotten about it in the scramble to keep me from turning to stone. Shelby couldn't be wearing it—but if she *wasn't* wearing it, Sarah should have been able to "hear" her presence. Having a stranger in the house should have been driving my cousin's telepathy into a frenzy.

And instead we were all gathered calmly in the kitchen, except for the part where Shelby had a gun. I looked back to Shelby, trying to assess the distance between us. What had I invited into my home?

More importantly, what could I do to fix things?

"Shelby . . ." I began.

"It's all right, sweetheart," said Shelby, in the sort of wheedling tone she normally reserved for her charges at the zoo. She never took her eyes off of Sarah. "We're going to get you all sorted out, and then I'll explain everything about what's happening here. Assuming you remember there's anything *to* explain. You may not."

There was a gun strapped to my calf. I bent casually forward and reached for the holster, trying to make it look like I was just scratching an itch. *Please don't make me shoot you, Shelby,* I thought. That would be a bad breakup, even by my admittedly low standards. "I don't understand what you're talking about."

"No, you wouldn't, would you?" The sympathy in

Shelby's expression died, replaced by a sneer as she focused her attention back on Sarah. "Where's the rest of your flock, you filthy brood parasite? There's no point in protecting them. I'll find them with or without your help."

Sarah looked bemused. "I don't have a flock," she said. "They abandoned me on a doorstep, and they never came back. Fly little bird, fly and be free. But I'm not a bird, you know. Biologically, I have nothing in common with birds. Well. Lungs, I suppose." She looked to me, sudden curiosity lighting up her eyes. "Do birds have lungs?"

"Yes, Sarah, birds have lungs," I said, as soothingly as I could manage when I was trying to unclasp my holster without Shelby realizing I was going for a gun.

"Stop prattling and answer the question," snapped Shelby.

The gun came free in my hand. I sat up straight, pulling it out from under the table and aiming at Shelby's shoulder. I flipped the safety off with my thumb. I'd be shooting to wound, not kill, as long as she didn't move. *Please, Shelby, don't move.* "Put down the gun."

Shelby—who had stiffened at the small, clean snap of the safety being released—didn't move. "How far has she managed to get her claws into you, Alex?" she asked. She sounded almost regretful. "I'm so very sorry. I didn't realize what was happening to you at first, and by the time I did, it was too late."

"Put down the *gun*," I repeated. "I don't know what you're talking about. I do know that we're not having a rational conversation about it until you stop holding a gun on my cousin."

"She's not your cousin, Alex. She's not even human."

Oh, crap. I stiffened in my seat, considering half a dozen solutions and rejecting each one before I said, "I don't know what you're talking about. I think today may have upset you more than I realized."

"She's messed with your mind, Alex. That's what her

kind does." Shelby kept her gun trained on Sarah, who was still sitting calmly in her chair. Thank God for small favors. "They scramble your perceptions until you don't know right from wrong, up from down, or your family from the things that would destroy it."

"Shelby . . ." Sometimes you have to take risks—and I was willing to bet that I was a faster shot than Shelby. Taking a deep breath, I said, "Sarah's not human, but she's still family. Her being what she is just means we have to clean ketchup out of the toaster every now and then."

"*What?*" Shelby finally turned to stare at me, although her aim didn't waver, and she didn't take her finger off the trigger. "You *know* she's a Johrlac?"

My family calls Sarah's species "cuckoos," but their real name is "Johrlac." I nodded slowly, my own gun staying raised. "She always has been, and she's not messing with my mind. She's *family*." Shelby, on the other hand . . . she'd been a better girlfriend than I deserved, maybe, but I didn't really know her. I stood, adjusting my position as necessary to make certain that my aim never wavered. "Who are you?"

"What?" Shelby blinked, eyes going wide as she did her best to look innocent. "I'm your girlfriend. Don't tell me she's forced you to forget me."

"Sarah isn't capable of forcing me to do anything. I'm wearing an anti-telepathy charm that keeps her from getting into my head without my permission." I steadied my gun hand against the opposing wrist. "I know who you've been to me for the last few months. I know who I think you are. But who are you really?"

"I could ask you the same question," Shelby shot back. "All those nights you said you weren't available for dinner, all those dates you canceled, and for what? I was getting ready to break it off with you, write you off as a bad deal, when I realized what was happening. Your Johrlac 'cousin' isn't here because she loves you. She's here because she's a brood parasite, and you're her latest nest. So what are you to *her*? Are you her next meal, or are you some sort of collaborator, luring her prey into range?"

"They call us 'cuckoos' here, but you got the rest right," said Sarah. She leaned back in her seat, looking at the ceiling. "We infect nests that should belong to other birds. Just a crack in the eggshell . . ." She started humming to herself.

Shelby glanced at Sarah, frowning. "Is this some kind of trick?" she asked. "She's not acting like a normal Johrlac."

"That's because she's *not* a normal Johrlac. She's my cousin, and she's not well. She was injured saving my sister's life. She's here in Columbus to recover." I shook my head. "She's not a danger. Unlike you."

"Me?" Shelby actually looked shocked. "What did I do?"

"You came into my house and drew a gun on my cousin. I find that pretty damn dangerous."

"You're the one who had a gun hidden in your trouser leg!"

"Shoulder holsters mess up the line of the shirts I'm supposed to wear to work."

Shelby blinked. Blinked again. And then, apparently against her will, she snorted in amusement. "Right," she said. "Fashion. That's what ought to be the concern here. Whether or not something looks good under a tweed professor's coat."

"Tweed is a valid lifestyle choice," I shot back. "Now please answer my question: who *are* you?"

"My name is Shelby Tanner," she said, without inflection. I'd never heard her voice so dead. "I am a visiting naturalist from Australia."

I stared at her in horror. There's only one group of people I know who are that bent on destroying cryptids, even to the point of following them home. "Oh, God," I said. "Covenant."

I've mentioned the Covenant of St. George, but I haven't explained them very well, and a little understanding is important if you want to know why having a Covenant operative in my home was such a terrifying concept.

Several hundred years ago, relations between humans and what we'd later come to call "cryptids" were . . . well, strained. The fact that all nonhuman intelligences were referred to as "monsters" may give you some idea of how bad things were. This was exacerbated by the fact that many cryptids didn't regard eating humans as *wrong*. If we could eat cattle, why couldn't the occasional meat-eating cow eat us? It was an egalitarian approach to the problem, and naturally, some people didn't like it. The Covenant of St. George was founded to rid the world of dragons, werewolves, basilisks, and anything else that might threaten mankind's dominion.

I can't exactly call their original mission statement "wrong." It's a lot easier to be live-and-let-live about ghouls and harpies when they aren't sneaking into your home and stealing your children in the middle of the night. The problem arose when the mission statement expanded, coming to serve as an order of execution for anything that wasn't explicitly listed as accompanying Noah on the Ark. (Where they got a full shipping manifest for the contents of a boat which may or may not have actually existed is anybody's guess.)

The Covenant of St. George never tried to understand the things it killed, and the modern Covenant still doesn't make the effort. They slaughter whatever they judge unnatural, and leave history littered with the bodies of those who crossed them. If it seems like there's a little resentment there, it's because I'm descended from two good Covenant families—the Healys, who were among the best assassins in a society filled with killers, and the Prices, whose scholarship and devotion to the cause helped move the Healys into position. Killing is in our blood. My great-great-grandparents turned their back on the cause, but they couldn't change who they were, or who their children would grow up to be.

My sister, Verity, met a Covenant operative in New York City, and true to family form, she promptly seduced him, convinced him to abandon his holy calling, and brought him home to meet the parents. Talking to Dominic had just confirmed what we'd believed for years: the Covenant of St. George thought that the Price-Healy bloodline had died out in Buckley, Michigan, but they were more than willing to be proved wrong if the opportunity arose.

And the orders regarding our family weren't friendly ones.

If Shelby was Covenant, I wasn't going to have any choice about what I did next. I was going to hate it, possibly forever, but I was going to do it anyway. Family comes first. That's the one good lesson that we took away from our time with the Covenant. Family *always* comes first.

*

Shelby blinked, expression turning quizzical. Then, to my surprise, she burst out laughing. "You—I—you really—oh, *Alex*." She raised a hand to wipe her eye, and somehow turned that gesture into a full-body turn, bringing her gun around to aim at my chest. I guess saying the word "Covenant" had rendered Sarah the lesser threat. Bully for me. Face gone suddenly cold again, she demanded, "What do *you* know about the Covenant? Are you working for them, is that it? A double agent? Because don't think I won't shoot you where you stand."

"Wait—what? One second you're threatening my cousin for being a cryptid, and the next you're threatening me because you think I'm with the Covenant? Don't you think you should make up your mind before you shoot me? And if I were with the Covenant, why the hell

would I be asking if *you* were with the Covenant?" I
frowned. "You're not with the Covenant, are you?"

"Are you mad? I'm from *Australia*!"

That seemed to answer everything for her. It just
raised more questions for me. "What the hell does Australia have to do with anything?"

"The Covenant tried to have the entire *continent* declared anathema and cleansed, you moron!" Shelby was
yelling now. "They'd have wiped out our ecosystem and
replaced it with things they considered 'acceptable'! Idiots. Destructive, shortsighted idiots. I can't believe you
work for them!"

"Oh, no, we don't work for the Covenant." Sarah's
tone was light, almost dreamy, like she was working on
getting in touch with her inner kindergarten teacher.
Shelby and I both whipped around to look at her. Judging by the look on Shelby's face, she'd almost forgotten
Sarah was there. I couldn't blame her; so had I. Sarah
looked down from her study of the ceiling, a beatific
smile on her face. "The Covenant broke me like a hammer breaks an egg. That's why the eggshell is cracked,
and we're putting Humpty together again. They wouldn't
have us if we wanted to go back."

"Back?" echoed Shelby. She swung back around to
me. I realized belatedly that I'd just missed my best
chance at disarming her. "What does the Johrlac girl
mean, 'back'?"

"Her *name* is Sarah," I said. "As far as the rest
goes . . ." I paused, studying Shelby.

Either she was an enemy or she was an ally. If she was
an enemy, I had nothing to lose by telling her the truth:
she might still shoot me and Sarah, but there was no way
she'd be getting away with it for long if she did. The mice
would tell my grandparents what she'd done, and
Grandma would track her down, and Grandpa would
make her understand why it wasn't okay to hurt his family. That assumed she was prepared to shoot me at all.
She hadn't done it when she had the element of surprise,

and now? She was on my home turf. I knew where all the weapons were, and I was ready to disarm her if she got distracted again.

Of course, all that assumed that she was an enemy. If she was an ally, she'd only stop lying to me if I stopped lying to her. One of us had to go first.

"The only thing I lied to you about was my last name. It's not Preston: it's Price," I said. "I'm not part of the Covenant of St. George. My family quit several generations ago. If you're against them, then it looks like we may be on the same side."

Shelby blinked. "You're a *Price*?" she said, disbelieving.

"Yeah."

"As in Thomas Price, the author of *The Price Field Guide to the Cryptids of Australia and New Zealand*."

I vaguely remembered seeing that book in the library at home. "Yes," I said, with more certainty than I felt.

"You're lying. He didn't have children."

"I think that's something you should take up with my grandmother, since she's pretty adamant about us being his, and he married her before my father was born, which means we're all legitimate in the eyes of the law."

Shelby blinked again. Then, much to my relief, she lowered her gun. Her shoulders started to shake. I worried for a moment that she was crying, until I realized that the shaking was from the effort of keeping her laughter contained. "All these weeks . . . all those nights of being afraid you'd catch me out, or you'd start asking questions . . . all the times I worried you'd stumble over something on one of your field trips and get yourself eaten . . . I've been worrying about a *Price*. That's worse than worrying over nothing. That's like worrying about the well-being of the crocodile in your billabong!"

"Um," I said. "Sorry about that?" I lowered my own gun. Playing fair is important, especially when there are firearms involved.

"I thought you were completely clueless and just

didn't know how to deal with women!" Shelby shook her head. "I truly believed you were a dead man walking!"

"Getting less flattering by the second, but thanks," I said. "Now do you want to explain what the hell you're doing pulling a gun on my cousin? Since we've established that we both had a little bit of a smokescreen going on?"

"A *little bit* of a smokescreen? What would you term a *large* one? Convincing me you were a Martian?"

"Alex would make a terrible Martian," said Sarah. "He doesn't have a giant laser and he's not planning an Earth-shattering kaboom." She slid out of her seat and wandered toward the fridge. Apparently, once we'd lowered our weapons, she no longer felt the need to remain seated. That was sort of reassuring, in a way: it meant she recognized the guns for what they were.

Shelby tracked Sarah's movement, but she didn't raise her gun. That was also reassuring.

"I'm not a Martian, and the only thing I ever lied about was my last name and my state of origin—we don't live in California." I didn't tell her where we *did* live. There's feeling out an ally in the hopes that no one has to get killed, and then there's being stupid. "I do sort of feel like the information exchange is a little one-sided right now, though, so if you could please explain how you know what a Johrlac is, or why you've read my grandfather's work, that would be awesome."

"I belong to the Thirty-Six Society," she said, with an almost prim air. "We've got our reasons to be interested in your movement, although it's been decades since any member of your family set foot in Australia."

I blinked at her. "You're a Thirty-Sixer?"

"Just said that, didn't I?"

"You . . ." The urge to laugh at the sheer improbability of it all was high. "Don't you think it's a little, well, bizarre for the first Australian I meet to be a Thirty-Sixer?"

A smile tugged at the edges of Shelby's mouth. "I

don't know. How bizarre is it for the first American biologist I really get to know to be a Price?"

"It's zebras all the way down," said Sarah agreeably, as she walked back to the table. She was holding a can of V8. At least that would keep her occupied for a little while. We both turned to look at her. Then, as one, we turned back to each other and burst out laughing. Shelby sat back down, placing her gun on the table. I did the same.

"All right," she said. "Story time. We can decide whether anyone's getting shot later."

"Deal," I said. "I came to Ohio to oversee a basilisk breeding project ..."

Telling Shelby my life story—edited to remove details that could be used to track down my family or otherwise do us harm—took a while. Sarah occupied herself with the V8, and Shelby listened attentively, fingers never twitching toward her firearm. I chose to view that as a good sign, rather than as proof that she considered herself fast enough that she didn't need to twitch.

"...and then you asked if you could come over, and here we are," I finished. "My grandparents should be home any time now."

"I want to go over the autopsy reports with you when they come in," said Shelby. It sounded just like every request she'd ever made for dinner or a movie, except for the suddenly morbid content. I blinked at her. She shrugged. "I was there when you found him. You can't expect me to sit idly by and let you have all the fun."

"Since you didn't tell me until tonight that you had any idea about any of this stuff, I can absolutely expect that." I wiped a bit of gravel out of the corner of my eye.

"Ah, but by the same token, I expected *you* to keep your nose out of things that you couldn't possibly understand. So we're really in the same position as regards each other."

I sighed. Growing up with two sisters has given me a highly-advanced ability to know when I've been beaten. "I'll talk to my grandfather."

"The equation hasn't balanced," said Sarah suddenly.

"What do you mean?" I glanced over at her. "Do you need more juice?"

"Yes," she said. "But no. I mean, yes, I need more juice, the good kind, please and thank you, but I also mean the equation isn't balanced. You've given one half of the numbers. She needs to provide the other, or we'll never know what it equals."

"What?" Shelby looked from Sarah back to me. "Are all Johrlac like this?"

"You knew what she was well enough to come hunting for her," I said, picking up my gun and flipping the safety back on before I stood and stuck it into my belt. I started for the fridge. "Haven't you ever talked to one before?"

"No. I don't like getting this close, even with blockers to keep them out of my head." She fingered her necklace, finally cluing me in as to the location of her anti-telepathy charm. "They're tricky."

"That's true, I suppose. No, most Johrlac aren't like Sarah. She's from the rare 'not a sociopath' segment of the population, and she really is ill. I wasn't making that up." I pulled the orange juice and A-1 sauce out of the fridge as I spoke, combining them in one of the large juice tumblers. Sarah was aware enough of her current limitations that she didn't mix her own drinks, but I knew what she meant by "the good kind."

"Then you should let nature take its course."

I slammed the orange juice down on the counter, making both Sarah and Shelby jump. "She's ill because she telepathically injured herself saving my sister's *life*," I said, barely restraining the urge to yell. "If she'd been willing to let 'nature take its course,' I'd be short a sibling right now. So you'll excuse me for feeling like I owe her."

"Okay, I'm sorry," said Shelby, eyes very wide. "I didn't know."

"No, you didn't. So back off." I shook my head, picking up Sarah's drink. "Besides, I think you'd like Sarah under normal circumstances. When she's feeling herself, she's a lot more linear and a lot less like trying to have an argument with a prerecorded phone tree. Right now, she's getting better. It's just a slow process."

Shelby looked dubious. "I'm sorry. I just can't imagine caring for one of them this much."

"Stop that *right* now," I snapped. I stalked to Sarah, put her juice down in front of her, and rounded on Shelby. "You are in *my* home, which means you are in *her* home. Yes, you were invited, but I don't recall saying 'bring your own bullets' when I called you. Stop acting like she's not a person. She's done nothing to hurt you. If anything, she's helped you. Now leave her alone."

Shelby blinked at me. "You really mean all that. She's not toying with your mind, is she?"

"Didn't I just spend the last twenty minutes telling you my life story so you'd believe me on this?"

"That was my concern, yes: that you were telling me what you thought I wanted to hear in order to keep me from harming her. Again, Johrlac can be tricky."

"Right now, Sarah's about as subtle as a bull moose in the middle of a shopping mall." I reclaimed my seat. "Now it's your turn. Explain what you're doing here, and why you're so bent on shooting my cousin."

"Why should I?"

"Because if you don't, we're going to have to shoot each other, and that would be a lousy end to an already lousy day." I shook my head. "Also that would officially be my worst breakup ever, and that's not a bar I was looking to exceed. So please. What are you doing here?"

Shelby sighed, leaning forward a little to rest her elbows on the kitchen table. "How much do you know about the Thirty-Six Society?"

"Um . . . Australian organization, *very* territorial, successfully drove the Covenant of St. George out of the country during my grandparents' time, although according to the family records, the Covenant has been trying to get back in since the door was slammed in their faces."

"Hence you thinking I might be a member; you thought the Covenant had succeeded and taken us over while your family wasn't looking."

"Something like that," I agreed. "I mean . . . no offense, but you guys are awfully far away, and we've always had other things to deal with here at home. I guess you just fell off our radar."

"That's always what happens to Australian ecological concerns, if you're not Australian, isn't it?" There was a faint bitterness in Shelby's voice, but it wasn't aimed at me: more at the whole world. "There have always been cryptozoologists in Australia. They predate the word 'cryptid' by quite a lot, but for a long time, we weren't organized. The Covenant never found us easy targets, but they could still make headway against us. The Thirty-Six Society was founded after the death of the last officially known thylacine—the Tasmanian wolf—in 1936. They were hunted to extinction over a relatively short period of time, and a lot of the incentives that were used to goad people into killing them were provided by the Covenant of St. George. Your Covenant always hated my country. Everything in the ecosystem looked like a monster to them."

"They're not my Covenant," I protested. "We quit generations ago."

"Some things take a long time to stop mattering, if they ever do." Shelby shook her head. "We'll never forget the thylacine. My parents were both members of the Thirty-Six from as far back as I can remember, and so were my grandparents. I grew up understanding that if I didn't help protect Australia's more . . . esoteric . . . flora and fauna from humanity, no one would."

"It's a big world," I said, feeling obscurely bad. I shouldn't have: North America is large enough that my family can't patrol it all on our own, even as we enlist allies from the human and cryptid communities. Covering Australia as well would have been impossible, and would have stretched our already overtaxed resources to the breaking point. That didn't stop me feeling like I should have helped.

"It is," Shelby agreed. "Trouble is, we're an island ecosystem. Sometimes things get in and turn out to be a great deal more destructive than they ever were in their original habitats. Game animals, mostly, imported by idiots thinking that Australia needs a native population of manticores or tailypo. But sometimes that extends to beings that can get their own passports and trick their way through immigration." Her gaze slipped back to Sarah, who was peacefully drinking her sewage-colored orange juice and A-1 combination, seeming to ignore everything that was going on around her.

"Johrlac," I said.

Shelby nodded. "Yes. A hive came over on a cruise ship about ten years ago. I don't know why, or how they tolerated one another long enough to make it across the ocean without multiple murders, but they made it. We'd never *seen* a Johrlac in Australia before that. No one realized what they were until it was too late."

Any story that started with "until it was too late" wasn't going to end well. But if I wanted it to end without Sarah getting shot in the head, I needed Shelby to keep going. "What happened?"

"What always happens when Johrlac introduce themselves into an unprepared population: nothing remotely good. They spread out, and then one of them found a member of the Society." Shelby stole another glance at Sarah. "She looked just like your cousin."

"Cuckoos have minimal visual variance within the

species," I said. "It's probably because they evolved from insects, not true mammals." Every female cuckoo we had a record of looked enough like Sarah and Grandma to be their sister. Every male cuckoo we had a record of looked like their brother. Just one more clue that they didn't handle mammalian biology the same way the rest of us did.

"Doesn't make her look any less like the woman who killed my brother," said Shelby calmly. She looked back to me. "She took out six Society members before someone found the anomaly in our records and we realized what was happening. Six! And she wasn't the only one. There were eight Johrlac in Australia. It took us five years to catch them all."

"I'm sorry."

"Sorry doesn't bring back the dead." Shelby shook her head. "All of us juniors wound up in field positions years before we expected, and for what? Because some horrible brood parasites wanted a vacation? It wasn't fair. It was never going to be fair."

"No, it wasn't, and I'm sorry. But killing my cousin won't bring back your dead." I frowned. "If all your juniors got promoted to seniors, why are you here? Why aren't you back in Australia, making sure that nothing starts eating people?"

"Manticores," she said, with a shrug.

"Manticores?" I echoed.

"Some damn fool imported three breeding clusters around the turn of the century, to use as game animals. They ate him and got loose—"

I groaned. "Of course they did."

"—and now we have manticore issues in Queensland and the Northern Territory. I was hoping that by coming here, I could learn more about how manticores behave in the wild, and maybe find a few solutions."

"There are manticores in Ohio?"

"Oh, yeah." Shelby frowned. "Hadn't you noticed?"

"No, I hadn't. I've been studying the local fricken

population, and trying to convince my basilisks to breed. Which they are absolutely refusing to do, the lazy stoners."

"Why would you want to breed basilisks?" asked Shelby.

"They're big ratters, for one thing, and they tend to avoid humans whenever possible. They're also the only known predator of stone spiders. So they have their uses, as long as we can keep them out of the cities."

"You had me at 'spiders,'" said Shelby. She took a deep breath, letting it out through her nose. "So. Here we are."

"Yes," I agreed. "Here we are."

The sound of a crossbow bolt being notched into place drew our attention toward the kitchen doorway. Grandma was standing there, a pistol crossbow in her hands, the point aimed solidly at Shelby. Grandpa was a dark shape in the hall behind her. If I squinted, I could just make out the cudgel in his hands.

"Great," said Grandma. "Now that we've established where we are, let's move on to the part where no one ever finds your body."

I put my hand over my face and groaned.

Ten

"Yes, dear, it does seem unwise to stand here and calmly wait to be devoured by the ever-expanding maw of the netherworld. If you have a suggestion as to how better to handle the situation, I'm quite eager to hear it."

—Thomas Price

Still in the kitchen of an only moderately creepy suburban home in Columbus, Ohio, now dealing with a heavily-armed grandmother

"HI, GRANDMA," I said, without taking my hand away from my face. "Have you met my colleague, Shelby Tanner? I'm pretty sure I've mentioned her. I'm sort of dating her. She's with the Thirty-Six Society. I know I didn't tell you that part before. I just learned it myself."

"She has a gun and she's in my kitchen," said Grandma. She sounded very calm. That wasn't a good sign.

"Well, I have a gun and I'm in your kitchen," I said, trying to be reasonable. "And technically, right now, the table has her gun."

"You're *allowed* to have a gun in my kitchen," said Grandma. "Young women to whom I have not been properly introduced most emphatically are *not*."

"Your grandmother is Johrlac?" squeaked Shelby, sounding more unsettled than I'd ever heard her.

Confused, Grandma asked, "You know what I am?"

"She knew what I was, and threatened to shoot me several times to avenge her brother's death," said Sarah blithely.

There was a moment of silence. I uncovered my face to find Grandma looking at Sarah, although her crossbow was still pointed at Shelby. Using the voice she reserved for my cousin, Grandma asked, "Sarah, sweetheart, did you kill this woman's brother?"

"I didn't kill anyone that I'm aware of," said Sarah, and took another sip of juice. "But she helped mix the goo to make Alex's eyes stop being stone. I like her."

There was a long, dangerous pause before Grandma said, "*What*?"

"The cockatrice!" I'd been so preoccupied with more immediate issues—keeping my eyes from turning into balls of granite, keeping Shelby from shooting Sarah—that I'd forgotten about more potentially long-term threats. I shoved myself away from the kitchen table so fast that my chair went clattering to the floor. Running to the sliding glass door, I hit the switch that would flood the backyard with light. I didn't look to see whether I had disturbed anything; I just grabbed the hanging curtain and pulled it closed, blocking the yard from view.

I turned to find everyone, even Sarah, staring at me like I had just grown a second head. "Er," I said, and released my fistful of curtain. "I can explain."

"I think that might be a good idea," said Grandpa, finally stepping into the kitchen. Shelby gasped, a small, strangled sound that she clearly tried to swallow. It didn't do her any good. Grandpa looked down at her, frowning. "This is my home, young lady. Be polite."

I forced myself to stop looking at Grandpa Martin as my beloved grandfather and to see him as Shelby would: a hulking giant of a man with subtly uneven facial features and heavy cords of scar tissue running along the joins where flesh from his various donors met. He'd removed his sweater before he and Grandma realized there was a problem, and the different skin tones of his hands and forearms were very apparent. Honestly, looked at like that, I couldn't blame Shelby for gasping. Especially when he was carrying a cudgel too large for most men to safely lift, much less wield.

She recovered fast. "I'm sorry, sir," she said, remaining seated. Good call: she was less threatening if she wasn't moving. "I didn't realize ... I mean, we've never been properly introduced, and I thought ... I mean ..."

"She thought you and I were being held captive by Sarah, who she'd somehow managed to get a look at ..." I glanced at Shelby, curiously.

Looking abashed, she shrugged. "I stole your phone the day the skinks got loose in the reptile house, and went through your pictures. I wasn't jealous!" she added, seeing the look on my face. "I didn't think it was another woman or anything, but you kept canceling dates to look after a 'sick cousin,' and it was the sort of excuse I'd heard before. I wanted to figure out whether I could break it off with you and still keep the moral high ground."

"I don't have any pictures of Sarah in my phone," I said, confused.

"No, dear, but you have pictures of me," said Grandma. "Cuckoos have so little facial variation."

Again, I paused to look at my grandparents, trying to see them as a stranger would. Grandma looked older than Sarah, but not enough older to reflect her true age. I would have placed her in her mid to late thirties if forced to take a guess. When looking for a single cuckoo ...

"I guess that's true," I allowed.

"If I'd known there were two Johrlac present, I would never have brought a gun into your home," said Shelby fervently.

Grandma turned to Shelby, eyeing her sternly. "Oh, no? What would you have done instead?"

"I would have chained the doors shut while you were sleeping and burned the place to the ground." Shelby stole an apologetic glance at me. "It would have been the only way to be sure."

I blinked. Grandma blinked. And then, to my surprise, my grandfather burst out laughing.

"She's got you there, Angie," he said, putting his cudgel down on the counter. "Now come on. Put down the crossbow and let's hear about this cockatrice that's made such a mess in our kitchen."

"I'd like more juice, please," said Sarah.

I knew my cue when I heard it. "Shelby called and said she was uncomfortable being alone after what happened to Andrew . . ." I began, as I stood and walked to the fridge. I continued as I prepared Sarah's mixture of orange juice and A-1, summarizing the events of the evening. I tried to hit the high points without dwelling too much on things like "letting Shelby into the house." As I put Sarah's juice down in front of her, I said, "I didn't get a good enough look at the cockatrice to tell you subspecies, age, or gender, but as soon as I locked eyes with it, I felt a stabbing pain all the way to the back of my retinas, and . . ." I shrugged helplessly.

"His eyes began turning to stone," said Shelby.

"I didn't see it happen, but I sure as hell felt it," I said. "I walked Sarah and Shelby through preparing the bilberry poultice and combined it with the appropriate antivenin. It worked, because the petrifaction was reversed. If Shelby hadn't been here, I think I would have lost my eyes." And possibly my life. The petrifaction hadn't been able to progress to its natural limits, and it was hard to say how large a dose I might have received.

"She saved his life, Angie," said Grandpa gently. "Put the crossbow down."

"I like her," said Sarah. "Blonde ladies with guns remind me of Verity. I miss Verity. Will she be back from dance camp soon?"

This time the silence that fell over the kitchen was sad, the brief, shared quiet of a family that had, for just a few seconds, managed to forget that it was broken.

Grandpa was the one to break it, saying, "Alex, why don't you take Sarah up to her room? We'll stay here with your little girlfriend, and make sure she doesn't run off before we can finish having this talk."

"Grandpa . . ."

"I promise we won't kill her and dump her body in the nearest ravine," said Grandma, sounding annoyed. "Just go, all right?"

"Okay." I cast Shelby a half-worried, half-apologetic look as I stood and walked back to Sarah's chair. "Come on, Sarah. Let's go upstairs."

"Why?"

"Because that's where we left your math notebooks, and you have homework for tomorrow."

"But I never got my sundae."

"After the homework is finished. I promise."

Sarah lit up. It was the only way to describe the smile that suffused her face, making her look heartbreakingly like her old self. "Okay!" she said, and stood, clutching her juice glass in one hand. I took the other, and led her out of the kitchen, leaving my grandparents and my girlfriend behind. Hopefully they would all be alive when I got back.

Getting Sarah situated in her room was relatively easy, made easier by bringing Crow across the hall and dropping him onto her bed, where he curled up, stuck his head back under his wing, and went to sleep. Sarah sat down next to the "kitty" with her math workbook open in her lap, happily starting to fill in fractions with a number two pencil. I stayed long enough to see that her answers were almost entirely wrong, and then left the room, shutting the door behind myself.

She was getting better all the time. She was still a long, long way from being *well*.

I returned to my room, shutting the door behind myself, and fished my cell phone out of my pocket. Grandma's specific non-threat — "we won't kill her and dump her body in the nearest ravine" — had been a coded instruction to do something I really didn't want to do right now. She wanted me to call my sister.

Verity had left New York after defeating the Covenant field team that had been sent to begin the Manhattan purge. She felt staying in the city would be tempting fate, and she was ready to go home. Of course, flying is hard when you carry an arsenal on your person at all times, and it's harder when you have your own private colony of talking mice. So she'd packed her belongings, her mice, and her (ex-Covenant) boyfriend into a U-Haul and set off for Oregon the long way. She called it a road trip. I called it an exercise in self-indulgence.

Then again, Verity had survived being shot in the stomach and helped save untold cryptid lives when she and Sarah convinced the Covenant that the denizens of New York were not the droids they were looking for. I guess she'd earned a little self-indulgence.

The phone rang twice before Verity's voice came on, informing me with sugary sweetness, "This is an unlisted number. Now hang up before I call the police."

"Hello to you, too, Very," I responded. "Where are you?"

"Alex?" She sounded puzzled, trending into pleased. "Is that you?"

"In the thankfully unpetrified flesh. Do you have a minute?"

"Sure! We're just rolling into New Orleans to check out a party that Rose told us about, but I can always make time for you."

I paused. "Rose as in Rose Marshall, the hitchhiking ghost?"

"Uh-huh."

"Very . . ."

"It's a dead man's party. Don't worry about it. Everybody's welcome."

I swallowed the urge to groan. My sister was a grownup. She could take care of herself. "Okay, well, try to keep your soul inside your body, I don't feel like going wandering around the afterlife trying to put you back together. Is Dominic there?"

"What?" Verity's tone turned suspicious. "What do you want Dominic for?"

"I need to ask him a question, okay? Now can you put Dominic on the phone?"

"What—"

"The girl I've been sort of dating is in the kitchen right now, and she says she's with the Thirty-Six Society. Since I don't have any contacts in the Society right now, I just need to confirm that she's not Covenant. So please, can you put Dominic on the phone?"

"Oh, um, sure. One sec." I heard Verity put her hand over the phone, followed by the muffled sound of her voice as she relayed the situation. There was a louder scuffing noise before Dominic's voice came on the line, briskly saying, "Hello?"

"Dominic, hey. It's Alex."

"Yes, Verity told me," he said, his faint Italian accent growing stronger as he started to get impatient. "What did you need to discuss with me?"

"Do you know of any Australian Covenant agents currently on assignment in North America?"

There was a pause before Dominic said, sounding bemused, "No, because there *are* no Australian Covenant agents. Not unless they've managed to recruit an expatriate—and that would be unusual enough that I would have heard about it if it had happened before I quit the Covenant. Since I didn't hear about it, any Australian recruits would have to have joined quite recently, and would not have completed training, much less been given field assignments. Why?"

"My girlfriend, Shelby Tanner. She says she's with the Thirty-Six Society. I don't have a way of confirming that for sure."

"Well, I can assure you she's not one of o—one of theirs." He stumbled a little as he finished the sentence. I felt bad for him. Dominic's resignation from the Covenant was still recent. Maybe sometimes, he even managed to forget that he'd turned his back on the only life he'd ever known. "Miss Tanner may not be who she claims, but she is not Covenant."

"Couldn't they be trying some sort of double agent scenario? Train a British operative to act Australian and send her here to . . ." I stalled out. I was reaching, and I could tell.

So could Dominic. He chuckled. "If the Covenant knew you were there, you would have more than a lone pseudo-Australian agent to contend with, and if they were going to try something so complicated, they would have sent her to Australia, not to the middle of nowhere."

"Gee, thanks."

"It is only the truth. She cannot be one of the Covenant's agents. It makes no sense."

"Good to know. Thank you."

"You're very welcome. Now, if you will excuse me, a dead woman is trying to convince me to drink something that comes in layers." Dominic sniffed. "I expect to be carrying your sister back to the motel."

"Thanks for not adding the 'again' on that sentence," I said dryly. "Love to Verity, ongoing tolerance to you." I hung up. Phone manners have never been a big thing in my family.

So Shelby wasn't likely to be working for the Covenant. That was a little bit of a comfort. Now I just had to hope that she was still among the living.

I trotted down the stairs, half eager to get back to the gathering in the kitchen and half afraid of what I was going to find when I got there. I didn't *think* they could fit an entire human body in the garbage disposal. Maybe more importantly, I didn't want them to kill Shelby for the crime of wanting to protect me from a deadly predator. It wasn't her fault she'd decided to protect me from the one Johrlac in the world who truly wouldn't hurt a fly if she had any choice in the matter.

"Is everything all right in here?" I asked, pushing open the kitchen door.

"Of course, Alex," said Grandma, who was seated at the table across from Shelby. Grandpa was at the stove, stirring a pot of what appeared to be milk. No one was bleeding or even visibly injured, and the mess from our first aid adventure had been cleared away. All good signs. Grandma smiled encouragingly, motioning for me to take the chair next to Shelby. "We didn't shoot her or threaten her or anything."

"Your grandfather's making us more cocoa," said Shelby, sounding faintly stunned. "He's heating the milk for it now."

"Grandpa makes really good cocoa," I said, trying to be reassuring. I turned back to Grandma. "I talked to our Covenant expert, and he confirmed that they don't have any Australian recruits. We may not be able to reach the Thirty-Six Society directly, but the odds are good that she's not Covenant."

"That's nice, dear," said Grandma. "Sit down and have some cocoa."

I eyed her as I slipped into my chair. "Does the fact that she's not Covenant and we're all having a second round of cocoa mean you've decided not to threaten Shelby anymore? Because seriously, that is not the way to help me have a healthy relationship."

"We've come to an agreement," said Grandma. "She doesn't attempt to kill anyone who lives in this house, I don't arrange for her sudden disappearance. Largely because you'd be a suspect, and I'd rather not get you taken in for police questioning."

"*Angela.*" We turned to my grandfather. He was standing with his hands on his hips, scowling at his wife. "The

young lady explained her reasons for being here, and
even you have to agree that they were good ones. Your
species does a lot of damage. No one knows that better
than you do. Now stop tormenting the poor kids. Alex has
already been punished enough for having company over
without permission, what with the whole, ah," he gestured vaguely at his face, "eyes getting turned to stone
business."

Grandma sighed. "I'm sorry, Martin. I just don't appreciate having my house rules violated like this." And
there was the glare I'd been expecting.

I put up my hands. "I would never have invited her
over if there hadn't been a petrifactor at the zoo—which
brings us back to the cockatrice, if you don't mind talking
about something other than how much trouble I'm in or
how much you'd like to be allowed to kill my girlfriend."

"How sure are you that it was a cockatrice?" asked
my grandfather.

"I took a direct hit," I said, letting my hands drop to
the table. I leaned back in my chair, feeling suddenly
tired. "The lighting and the circumstances meant that I
didn't get the best look at it, but when we prepared the
treatment, I used the cockatrice antivenin."

Now it was Grandma's turn to blink. "You didn't use
the general gorgon? But, Alex—"

"I was sure it was a cockatrice! Well, almost sure.
Eighty percent sure. If we'd used gorgon antivenin, my
eyes would have remained partially petrified. I couldn't
risk it." There's no place in the field for a cryptozoologist
who can't see. Oh, I'd have opportunities for work—if
nothing else, I'd be better equipped than anyone in the
world to continue my basilisk studies—but I'd be removed from active duty for the remainder of my life. That
wasn't something I'd been willing to let happen. "So I told
them to use the cockatrice antivenin, and it worked."

Shelby looked at me, horrified. "You mean you were
guessing?" she demanded.

"You got almost as good a look at the thing as I did,

Shelby, and you didn't contradict me." I shrugged. "That seemed like a good sign."

"Of course I didn't argue, you idiot! *There are no cockatrices in Australia!*" Shelby grabbed the front of my shirt as she shouted at me. "You could have been killed! You could have been turned to stone, and it would have been my fault, you — you — you *Price!*"

"I can see why you like her," said Grandpa, putting a cup in front of each of us. "She's enthusiastic about her work."

"And definitely understands that you've been bred to take idiotic risks in the name of science. That'll serve her well," said Grandma, accepting her own cup. The liquid inside was a toxic-looking orange rather than brown.

"The key word here is 'science,'" I said, scowling at both of them. "I made a determination based on what I had observed, and I was correct. My eyes are fine."

"Better yet, we know what probably killed your co-worker," said Grandpa. He walked back to the counter, picking up his own cup of cocoa. "I doubt we have two petrifactors running loose in this town."

I froze in the act of reaching for my cocoa. "Say that again."

"I said that I doubt we have two petrifactors running loose in this town. Not counting the local gorgons, of course. They've been good neighbors for decades. They've got no reason to stop now."

"But we're miles from the zoo." I stood. "The average cockatrice has a range of less than a square mile. They're not migratory, and they don't like to move too far from their dens."

"Alex . . . ?" said Grandma.

It was Shelby who realized what I was saying first. She reached for her gun, saying, "Either this isn't the same cockatrice, or — "

"Or someone brought it here," I finished grimly. "Somebody brought it here and set it loose in our backyard. This wasn't a random encounter. This was an attack."

There was a long moment of silence before my grandmother said, uneasily, "You can't be sure of that."

Cuckoos aren't fighters. They weren't built that way, unlike us monkeys, who were basically born to defend our territory. To my surprise, it was once again Shelby who spoke first. "Are they clever things, these cockatrices?" she asked.

"Not particularly," I said. "Why?"

"Back at the zoo, Andrew's body was pushed into the bushes. There's no way he was that well-covered from just falling," said Shelby. "Whatever turned him to stone could have been a dumb animal, but he was moved by someone who was smart enough to know what they were doing."

I paused. "Are you sure?" I'd been so focused on the unusual circumstances of his death that I hadn't been looking for signs that anything else was involved.

"Lions and tigers usually bring down prey and then drag it a ways before they eat it, right? There's always a trail when that happens, and there was a trail today. Andrew was dragged into those bushes. Trust me, I know what a dragged kill looks like."

"Cockatrice aren't big enough to drag a dead human, and they don't work together well." I glanced to my grandparents. "There's a cockatrice loose in the neighborhood, and it may have a handler. We need to get out there and stop it before anyone else gets hurt."

"I was wrong about you, Alex," said Shelby, with a small smile. "You really do know how to show a girl a good time."

Eleven

"Shoot first, but aim for the foot, hand, or other non-life-threatening extremity. That way you'll still be able to ask questions later."

— Alexander Healy

In the basement of an only moderately creepy suburban home in Columbus, Ohio, getting ready to go on a cockatrice hunt

I MIGHT BE WILLING to go out at night hunting for a creature capable of turning me into solid stone. I wasn't willing to do it without proper preparation. On a normal day, I have the gun on my calf, three or four knives, and a garrote. This called for something a little less, well . . . basic.

Shelby looked around the basement with the saucer-wide eyes of someone who has just been allowed to glimpse the hills of Heaven, and has found them to be very pleasant indeed. "This is an *armory*," she said.

"Not compared to the weapons room at home, but it does well enough," I said, picking up a brace of throwing knives and making them disappear, one by one, into my coat. "Check the drawer underneath the pole arms. There should be some polarized glasses in there. You'll need a pair if you don't want to become a really confusing new lawn ornament."

"This is all horrible," said Shelby, even as she obediently opened the drawer and started rooting through the assorted forms of protective eyewear. "I don't understand how you can be so calm about people being turned to *stone*."

"Grandpa?" I picked up a second pistol and started loading it.

My grandfather, recognizing a request for information when he heard one, sighed and said, "Petrifaction is the process of flesh or plant matter being converted into stone." Shelby looked at him blankly. "Basilisks, cockatrice, and stone spiders are all petrifactors. They can, one way or another, turn flesh to stone." Shelby continued looking at him blankly. "Don't you have any of these things in Australia?"

"I think the crocodiles ate them," she said flatly. "Can we go back to the core question here? How can a person be turned into *stone* when nothing's been injected or dumped on them?"

"You saw my eyes," I said, tucking my new pistol into the waistband of my pants. I rubbed the corner of my right eye with a finger, dislodging another bit of gravel. I was going to be putting in eye drops for the next few weeks, while I waited for the moisture levels to get back to normal.

"You explained that, though," she said. "Visual allergies."

"Calling petrifaction a 'visual allergy' is pretty accurate, but it doesn't describe the whole process," said Grandpa.

"You'd be better off calling it poison that you see," said Grandma, stepping into the room with a jar of bilberry jam in her hand. "In the case of visual petrifactors, like the cockatrice, it enters via the eye—making it most dangerous to actually lock eyes with one of them—and travels down the optic nerve to the rest of the body. From there, it will begin petrifying whatever it encounters."

"Cockatrice petrify from the inside out, starting with the eyes and internal organs, while basilisks petrify from the outside in, starting with the eyes and skin," added Grandpa. "A basilisk will actually leave most of its prey unchanged, counting on suffocation to provide the killing blow."

"Why?" asked Shelby.

"Crunchy outside, chewy inside," I said, taking the jar of jam from my grandmother and shoving it into my pocket. "They peck their way through the hard stone shell and have a nice meal all pre-packed and waiting for them. The two species do have one thing in common, though."

"They're horrible?" ventured Shelby.

I laughed. "No. They both start with the eyes."

"So do some gorgons," said Grandpa pointedly.

"I know." I shook my head. "I think the presence of a cockatrice in our backyard is a pretty strong indicator that a gorgon didn't kill Andrew. Yes, a Pliny's gorgon could have turned him partially to stone. It can't have been a greater gorgon. There would have been no flesh left." I didn't want to think of a Pliny's gorgon being responsible for this. Dee had been as shocked as the rest of us.

Dee had spent her entire adult life pretending to be human, and doing it well enough to fool almost everyone she'd ever met. Dee disguised her history, her culture, and her species on a daily basis. If she was a good enough liar to manage all that, why wouldn't she be good enough to fool me by looking surprised when a dead man was found on zoo property?

"You know you have to consider it," said Grandma.

"I know," I said miserably.

"Hang on a second," said Shelby. "There's different kinds of gorgon?"

I turned to eye her. "What do they teach you in the Thirty-Six Society?"

"Not *that*," she replied. "You may have a Eurocentric view of the cryptid world—which doesn't make much sense to me, mind you, since you lot are living in North America—but it's not the only view there is, and we're an island ecology. Mostly, we try to keep the native species from eating each other, and we only worry about the non-native ones when they turn invasive."

Given the climate and geographical isolation of Australia, I'd be stunned if there weren't at least a few families of gorgons living there. That doesn't necessarily say anything about the skill of the members of the Thirty-Six Society. The chupacabra predates European colonization of the Americas, and we didn't know they existed until about fifty years ago (as far as I know, the Covenant still thinks they're just werewolves with a skin condition). When something has good reason to stay hidden, it finds a way.

"Since we're about to go looking for a cockatrice that we know was responsible for partially petrifying at least me, is it okay if we save that particular natural history lesson for later?" I asked.

Shelby nodded. "Yes, although I suppose I ought to ask: is there a way to *find* a Pliny's gorgon? Are there any in this region?"

My thoughts went to Dee again. "There are a few," I admitted.

"That makes them strong suspects," said Shelby. Then she paused and eyed the three of us, expression turning suspicious. "You're being awfully forthcoming with all this information, you know. With as long as you've been living under the radar, I'd expect more restraint."

"It's simple." Grandma smiled sweetly, showing more of her teeth than she really had to. Something about that expression triggered a reminder at the back of my mind, telling me that I was basically a very advanced monkey, and that even very advanced monkeys need to worry about bigger predators. "We can always kill you later if it turns out you can't be trusted."

"*Grandma*," I said sternly. "Please stop threatening my girlfriend."

"I'll threaten anyone I want to," said Grandma.

Shelby laughed. We all turned to look at her. She shook her head. "I'm sorry. I know I should be taking this all terribly seriously, but this is so much like listening to my own family argue that it's actually very relaxing. Do let me know if we reach a point where I should be running for my life, all right?"

"Good lord, there's more than one of them," said Grandpa.

"Okay, well, that's a disturbing concept for all of us, but I think we should get moving if we want to track this thing before it disappears again," I said, sliding a pair of polarized goggles on over my glasses and motioning to Shelby to put hers on. "Shelby, you're with me. Grandma, I want you to stay here and keep an eye on Sarah. Grandpa—"

"I'll go out front and look for suspicious cars," he said.

"Great." I grinned. I couldn't help myself. "Let's go commit some senseless acts of science."

⬩

Even with the kitchen lights on, the backyard was dark enough that Shelby and I had to pause for several minutes in order to let our eyes adjust. She stuck close beside me, her gun in her hand. I would have told her to put it away, but she seemed to be treating it more as a security blanket than a weapon. I couldn't blame her for that. Even coming from a cryptozoology background, this had to be a pretty major shock to the system.

It had definitely been a shock for me. I adjusted my polarized goggles and began walking slowly forward, stepping as lightly as I could. "Cockatrice have internal ears, like snakes," I said, pitching my voice low. "They'll hear you coming mostly through vibrations in the ground."

"So it's safe to talk, yeah?"

"Yes. Just don't stomp." My grandparents had chosen

their home partially for its spacious yard, which had seemed perfect when they were planning to start a family. Now, it seemed too large, and the old swing set by the back fence was surrounded by strange shadows, where anything could be lurking.

"I'm not much of a stomper," said Shelby.

She matched my pace step for step. I took my eyes off the ground long enough to steal a sidelong glance at her. In the moonlight, her hair seemed to almost glow, and the expression of intense concentration on her face was one of the sexiest things I'd ever seen. I frowned, forcing myself to look away. She was a distraction. I didn't need that. Not here, not now—and maybe not ever.

"So were you really planning to break up with me when you realized I had a Johrlac nearby?" I tried to keep the question light. My bitterness still seeped through.

"You meant it when you said we could talk, huh?" Shelby shook her head, a quick blur in my peripheral vision. "This doesn't seem like the best time ..."

"Really? You don't think this is the best time?" We had reached the bushes that grew up against the fence. I stooped, pulling the LED flashlight out of my pocket. It had a red lens, to protect our night vision and hopefully keep from startling the cockatrice if we found it.

"No, not really."

"Well, I think that the aftermath of you threatening to shoot a member of my family is the *perfect* time for a relationship discussion. Since most people who threaten my family don't have much time for conversation afterward." There was nothing under the bush, not even tracks. I straightened, turning the flashlight off again.

"You know, threats make it a little hard to have a conversation."

"Then you *should* break up with me. This is how we communicate." The cockatrice had been standing in the middle of the yard when it locked eyes with me. I backtracked to the place where I estimated it had been, crouching down to study the grass. Here, at least, there were signs of its passage: bent grass, churned-up bits of earth. "I wish the damn thing didn't have wings. It's always harder when they can fly ..."

"Dammit, Alex, you're not making this any easier for me."

"I'm sorry, Shelby. I didn't know that 'making it easier' was part of my job." I turned my flashlight back on, sweeping it across the grass. The faint indentation that marked the cockatrice's passage swerved off to the left. "It went this way."

She sighed and followed as I straightened and started toward the fence. "All right, yes. I was planning to break it off with you. Happy now?"

"Not so much, no, but thank you for being honest." I kept my eyes on the ground. No matter how much I wanted to be looking at Shelby, I wasn't going to let myself be distracted again.

"I started seeing you socially because it seemed like a laugh, and I was bored. You weren't the same kind of boring."

"Not making me feel any better, Shelby." The tracks stopped about a foot before the bushes on this side of the fence. I walked a little faster, running my light along the top of the bush. There were broken twigs there. The cockatrice had left the lawn, landed on the bush, and then taken off again.

"Still being honest, like you asked. You're not ..." Shelby made a frustrated noise. "You cancel dates. You keep secrets. You talk about lizards at the dinner table. You're a geek, Alex, and that's fun for a while—I like smart men—but you weren't willing to let me see anything deeper. You wouldn't even watch bad science fiction shows with me, and most geeks love that sort of thing."

"I should introduce you to my sister." I squinted at the fence. It was about eight feet high, and the neighbor on that side didn't have a dog. "Come here."

"Why?" asked Shelby suspiciously.

"I'm going to boost you up so you can see into the next yard. It looks like our cockatrice went over the fence."

To her credit, Shelby came right over, putting her hands on my shoulders as I stooped to form a basket for her foot. "I didn't stay with you only because your cousin was a Johrlac, if that's what you're thinking."

"Then why?"

She stepped into my joined hands, smiling impishly before she said, "The sex has been amazing." She pushed off the ground before I could formulate a reply. I straightened automatically, boosting her until her head cleared the top of the fence. Shelby put her hands on the wood, steadying herself.

Silence fell. She wasn't getting heavier, so she wasn't in the process of turning to stone—good. Finally, when I could restrain myself no longer, I asked, "Well?"

"We need to go next door," she said, voice sounding strangely hollow, like she was trying to divorce herself from the scene. "There's a dead man on the back porch."

This time, the pause was mine. "All right," I finally said. "Let's get you down." It was time for a little recreational breaking and entering. If it's not one thing, it's another.

My family has always had what can most charitably be called a complicated relationship with the law. We understand the need for laws that cover an entire population. We just get cranky when those laws are applied to *us*. It's hypocritical as hell, but when you're trying to balance the needs of several dozen nonhuman species against the needs of the human population, sometimes hypocrisy is the only answer. In the four generations we've been active in North America, we've racked up charges ranging from breaking and entering and vandalism to assault with a deadly weapon and murder. So far, we've been able to make all those charges go away. Our luck isn't going to hold forever, and every time we stretch the law, there's a chance that this will be the time that things fall apart.

All this ran through my mind as my grandfather boosted me over the fence and into the yard of Bill O'Malley, aka, "the dead man on the porch." He'd been living there alone since his wife had died some eight years previously, which was a good thing for us; it lowered the odds of someone coming in and finding us creeping around the property. I'd already been questioned by the police once today. I really wasn't in the mood for a second conversation.

I hit the grass in a crouch, straightening and turning to help Shelby lower herself down. Then I grabbed her hand and pulled her farther into the yard, moving away from the fence as fast as I could without actually running. Shelby frowned at me.

"What's the hurry?" she asked.

"Grandpa's coming."

She opened her mouth to ask another question, before Grandpa answered it the easy way, vaulting one-handed over the eight-foot fence and landing on the grass so hard that it seemed to vibrate the ground. I winced. The thump made by his impact meant that we weren't going to be finding a cockatrice in this yard—the vibrations would have driven it as far away as its wings could take it.

"That's amazing," said Shelby.

"That's engineering," said Grandpa. He started toward the porch. I moved alongside him, watching the ground for signs that the cockatrice wasn't as far off as I thought. Nothing moved within my field of vision, and so I turned my attention to the body.

Bill O'Malley had been in his seventies, still the kind of man who could manage his own house, although he'd been using a yard service for the past few years, accord-

ing to my grandparents. He was lying facedown on the
brick of his back porch, one arm straight out in front of
him like he was pleading with something. I moved closer,
crouching for a better look.

The tips of his fingers were gray.

The door was still open. Looking through into the
kitchen, I saw nothing that seemed out of the ordinary
or even out of place. He'd probably heard a noise and
gone to investigate. There had been no one there to mix
a poultice for him. He'd never had a chance.

"Poor bastard," I murmured, straightening. "Grandpa,
do you think you can jump the fence while carrying Mr.
O'Malley? I want to examine his body under better
light."

"How invasive?" he asked.

"We won't be able to put him back." I felt a pang of
guilt at that, and knew I had some sleepless nights ahead.
Any family he still had would never know what had happened to him. But I needed to confirm, once and for all,
that this was a cockatrice, and that meant a physical examination. This was how we'd save lives. I tried, with
only limited success, to put the thought of his grieving
family out of my mind.

Sometimes it can be hard to reconcile being a Price
and a scientist with being a decent human being.

"What are you going to do with the remains?" asked
Grandpa.

"Crunchy." Alligator turtles are immune to petrifaction, as are all true reptiles. He'd enjoy the meaty bits,
and any rocks that wound up in his dinner would just be
spat out like so much unwanted roughage.

Grandpa nodded. "All right." He cast a regretful look
at the house. "He was always a good neighbor. Never
asked too many questions. I like that in a man."

"I'm sorry."

"So am I, Alex. So am I." With that, Grandpa knelt
and scooped Bill O'Malley into his arms. The old man's
face was uncovered in the process, revealing eyes the

solid, unwavering gray of granite. Grandpa carried him like he was light as a feather, walking back toward the fence. Shelby and I followed. With no reason to suspect foul play, our footprints would be gone long before the police came to check on Mr. O'Malley. Even Grandpa hadn't been able to dent the sunbaked Ohio ground.

One by one, we climbed and boosted each other over the fence into our own yard, leaving the dead man's empty house behind us, lights burning in the windows like signposts, trying to beckon their departed owner home. But he was never coming home again.

Twelve

"I knew Evelyn was the one for me the very first time I met her. She slapped me so hard that my jaw hurt for three days, and all because I'd said that sometimes, werewolves could be dangerous. Love is a painful thing."

—Kevin Price

In the kitchen of an only moderately creepy suburban home in Columbus, Ohio, preparing to perform an autopsy on the kitchen table

"No," said Grandma. "Absolutely not. Martin, what were you *thinking?*"

"That we sold the Ping-Pong table at the rummage sale last summer, so if we're going to cut a man up, this is the best place to do it." Grandpa sounded slightly sheepish. "I told you we shouldn't have sold it. Things like that always come in handy when you least expect it."

"Sorry, Grandma," I said, without looking up from the complicated business of cutting Bill O'Malley's clothes off with the scissors from the junk drawer. His joints had stiffened enough to make it hard to bend his arms and legs, and I wound up removing his pants in small pieces, dropping them into the trash can I had ready for just that purpose.

"Angela. I know this is inconvenient, but we don't have a better place to perform the autopsy." Grandpa's voice was level but firm. He walked over to her, putting one massive hand on her shoulder. "Mr. O'Malley is already gone, God rest his soul, and it's not like we could use him for spare parts when he's been half-petrified."

"Excuse me?" said Shelby.

Grandpa continued like he hadn't heard her. "Now at least this way, he can teach us something before we dispose of his mortal remains."

"But does he have to teach us on my kitchen table?" Grandma asked petulantly. Then she sighed. "I suppose you'll want the autopsy kit."

"That would be nice," I said.

"I'll go get it," said Grandma. "You three, stay here, and try not to get any gore on my kitchen."

"I'm coming with you," said Grandpa. "I think this one is going to require the big tarp." The two of them turned and left the kitchen, leaving me alone with Shelby and the dead man.

The dead man was honestly the least of my problems. Shelby crossed her arms, glaring at me, and demanded, "Spare parts?"

"Grandpa's a Revenant," I said, as I resumed cutting off the last of Mr. O'Malley's clothing. "He was originally several different dead guys. Now he's one living guy. You should ask him about it sometime. He tells the best dumb mad scientist jokes."

Shelby looked at me blankly for several seconds before she said, "You're a hell of a lot cockier than I'm used to you being, you know that?"

"That's because you're finally seeing me in my element. Work cocktail parties, not so much my thing. Dead bodies? I'm your boy." I pulled the last of Mr. O'Malley's clothing off of his body, covering his genital region with one of Grandma's good hand towels. She'd probably yell at me for that later, but the man deserved at least a little dignity.

"Disturbing yet endearing," said Shelby. "What do we do now?"

"Hmm?" I dug my phone out of my pocket. "Now we examine the body. Have you done this before?"

"I've never done a proper autopsy, but I've done plenty of necropsies, and a few cryptid dissections. None where the victim was partially turned to stone, but I know how to hold a scalpel."

"Good." I handed her my phone. "I'm going to want you to take pictures for right now. Once we get into the more invasive procedures, I may need your hands."

"Got it," said Shelby, with a mock salute. "Why are we doing this again? I thought your grandfather was a coroner."

I saluted back, motioning for her to follow me as I began to circle the body. "He is, but this isn't really an autopsy so much as it's a game of hide-and-seek with the petrifaction. He understands the human body. I understand turning it to stone."

"So it doesn't matter if you butcher the poor man as long as you find what you need, yeah?"

"Yeah. On that note, there's some petrifaction of the fingertips and discoloration of the skin to the first knuckle, but the rest of the hand looks normal." I picked up Mr. O'Malley's hand, turning it gently. "Normal pliability for this stage of rigor. No signs of internal petrifaction."

Shelby dutifully took a picture of Mr. O'Malley's stone fingertips.

My next stop was Mr. O'Malley's head. As expected, his eyes had been fully petrified, becoming hard round balls of stone. His tongue was also petrified, and his lips were discolored, showing the progress of the petrifaction through his system. His cheeks remained fleshy and skin-toned, the tips of his ears and bottoms of his earlobes had been petrified. Shelby dutifully took pictures of all the grayish spots.

"So is all of this telling you anything?" she asked.

"It was definitely a visual petrifaction—poison moves with the bloodstream, but this was targeting the extremities as much as it was the eyes and internal organs. That's a sign of the whole 'visual allergy' thing."

"Cockatrice, yeah?"

"Probably. At this point, I'm hoping so." I looked up long enough to flash her a strained smile. "I'm not really in the mood for another scientific mystery right now."

Shelby nodded. "All right then," she said. "Let's get back to the dead man at hand."

We had almost finished our initial, noninvasive examination of the body by the time my grandparents came back. Grandma was carrying the plain brown briefcase that contained our home autopsy kit, as well as a pair of rib spreaders, a bone saw, and a chisel. I raised an eyebrow at the chisel. "You don't know how far the petrifaction has spread internally," she said.

"Fair point," I replied.

Grandpa, on the other hand, was carrying an armload of protective gear. He dropped smocks, gloves, and non-polarized goggles on the counter before walking to the kitchen table, putting a hand beneath it, and lifting the whole thing casually off the floor. "What have you learned so far?" he asked, as he began spreading a tarp across what would become our autopsy zone.

"Visual petrifaction confirmed; some damage to the extremities, but the main damage seems to have been to the eyes and throat. His trachea is completely blocked by what looks like concrete. He probably suffocated."

"What's this?" I turned to see Shelby looking at the dead man. She pointed. "Look at the underside of his knee. See? Right there."

"I noticed those during the initial examination," I said, moving to stand beside her. From here, we had a perfect angle on the wound: two messy punctures, each a little less than five millimeters in diameter, surrounded by a thin ring of petrified flesh followed by a thick ring of bruised and damaged tissue. The marks were spaced about as far apart as a human's canine teeth, although whatever made them was clearly longer and thinner than a human tooth. I looked at them for a long moment, frowning. Finally, without moving, I said, "Put the table down now, Grandpa. We need to get started."

"What did she find, Alex?" asked my grandmother.

"Those puncture wounds are petrifying."

The table hit the floor with a "thump," and Grandpa frowned at me across the body. "Cockatrice don't inject venom into their prey."

"No," I said. "They don't." But lesser gorgons did. So did Pliny's gorgons. *Oh, hell, Dee,* I thought. *What did your people* do?

Grandma opened the autopsy kit as the rest of us moved to put our smocks and gloves on. And then, with no further discussion, we got to work.

As dates go, "come join me and my family in dismantling the man who used to live next door" ranked high in memorability, and low in normalcy. Shelby proved to be as well-trained as she'd claimed to be, and didn't even wince when my grandfather used the rib spreaders to crack Mr. O'Malley's chest, revealing the half-petrified surface of his heart. The arteries connecting it to the rest of his body were an equal mix of flesh and stone, striated almost like the bands of fat in bacon. Cutting it loose would have been a difficult, time-consuming process, and so we didn't bother. Instead, we simply took samples from the heart tissue and the equally damaged lung tissue, placing them in sealed vials for later study.

Since we already had cause of death—petrifaction— we were able to skip several of the standard autopsy steps, such as weighing the individual organs and examining the contents of Mr. O'Malley's stomach. Grandpa did make some disparaging comments about wasting good organs, and Shelby somehow managed to keep herself from asking for details about how he would have used them. It was almost peaceful by the time we were ready to devote more attention to the puncture marks behind Mr. O'Malley's knee.

The ring of stone around the wounds had expanded during our examination. I frowned as I uncapped a venom extraction syringe and fitted it over the first puncture wound. Shelby frowned too, catching my expression.

"What's wrong now?" she asked.

"The wounds imply a venom-based petrifactor, but the progression in the eyes, throat, and internal organs implies a glance-based petrifactor," I said, pulling back the plunger. The suction this created would pull any remaining venom from the wound, allowing me to analyze it at my leisure. "It doesn't make any sense."

"Not unless you've got one of each, like a sine and a cosine," said a dreamy voice from the doorway. We all turned to see Sarah standing there, one hand grasping the doorframe, the other pushing her hair out of her eyes. "I woke up and I didn't know who I was, so I came down here so I could find me."

"Angie . . ." said Grandpa.

"I'm on it." Grandma set down the pan she'd been holding and shucked off her gloves, dropping them onto the counter before she rushed to put an arm around Sarah's shoulders. "Come on, sweetheart. You need to get back to bed."

"Will you tell me a bedtime equation?"

"Sure, honey. Sure." Then they were gone, allowing the kitchen door to swing closed behind them. I sighed. Shelby turned to look at me.

"I'm sorry," she said quietly.

"So are the rest of us," I said, and moved the venom extraction syringe to the other puncture. "I'll compare these wounds to the field guide after we dispose of the remains."

"Right—body disposal." Shelby looked briefly unsure. "How were we going to manage that, exactly?"

Despite my distress over Sarah, and the whole situation, I smiled.

Breaking into the zoo after hours was surprisingly easy: I had a key card, and there were no guards on duty this late at night. The security camera next to the south employee gate had been broken for months, and so there wouldn't even be a tape to destroy. Grandpa carried the plastic garbage bag of what had been Mr. O'Malley, before his body met a bone saw and a deadline. Shelby followed him, and Grandma brought up the rear, having finally talked Sarah into going back to bed. We'd need her if anyone found us before we were finished.

Sometimes it's a little depressing to realize how simple it is to make a person disappear. I tried not to dwell on that as we walked across the deserted zoo to the reptile house. I watched the bushes the whole way, searching for a sign that the cockatrice had been transported back to its original stomping grounds.

I didn't see anything.

Inside the reptile house, the nocturnal animals were wide awake, slithering and skittering around their enclosures . . . and then there was Crunchy, who hung as still and patient as a stone in his tank, waiting to be rewarded for his persistence. I pulled out the stepladder and positioned it in front of the glass, climbing up to the top step. Once I was stable, I unlocked the panel that kept foolish kids from going for a swim, pushing it off to the side. Then I held out my hand.

"Give me a leg," I said.

If Crunchy was surprised by this sudden manna from heaven, he didn't show it. His neck lashed out as the leg drifted by, and with dismaying speed, what had been a piece of a human body was nothing but a thin red cloud in the water. In a few seconds, even that was gone. I held out my hand again. Grandpa passed me the next piece of Mr. O'Malley. Bit by bit, we fed the old man into the tank, until there was nothing left but a bloody plastic bag, which my grandfather solemnly folded and tucked into his coat.

"Let's go home," said my grandmother, sounding subdued.

"Alex—" began Shelby.

"Tomorrow, all right?" I locked the panel over Crunchy's tank before climbing down from the stepstool and turning to look at her. She was beautiful in the reddish light of the heat lamps on the reptile enclosures. She was dangerous.

I needed to get her the hell away from my family.

"Promise?" she asked.

"I promise," I said wearily. "Now come on. We'll drive you back to your car."

Together—hopefully for the last time—the four of us walked out of the reptile house and started across the empty zoo. It had been a long day. It had been a long night. And the next few days didn't look like they were going to be any shorter.

Thirteen

"I have always enjoyed the company of dangerous women. Fortunately for me, many of them seem to enjoy the company of dangerous men."

—Thomas Price

The reptile house of Ohio's West Columbus Zoo, about an hour and a half before the zoo is supposed to open, waiting for a gorgon to come to work

BETWEEN THE BODY DISPOSAL, cleaning the kitchen, and analyzing the samples we'd taken during our makeshift autopsy, I was too spun up to sleep. Oh, I tried. And when four o'clock in the morning arrived without my catching so much as a wink, I gave up. I'd spent the hours between then and leaving for work doing research, drinking coffee, and emailing home to ask for more details about the Thirty-Six Society—which I didn't have, naturally, since everyone else in my family was smart enough to go to bed.

My car was one of the first into the parking lot. I got out and started down the path to the front gate, noting as I passed the pond that even the geese were still asleep. It was like I had the place to myself. Then again, that could have been a side effect of sleep deprivation.

I walked around the curve in the path and smiled, the feeling of isolation dissipating as I saw Lloyd already manning his position at the gate. "Good morning," I called.

He jumped, coffee slopping over the lip of his mug as he turned to stare at me. "Dr. Preston?" he asked.

"I know, I'm early." I shrugged. "I couldn't sleep. How about you, Lloyd? They always make you come to work this early?"

"My shift starts as soon as there's staff on the grounds," he said, recovering some of his composure. He put his coffee down and reached for his clipboard. "ID?"

I shook my head as I pulled out my ID card and handed it to him. "Every day."

"There were police here yesterday," he said, in an overly patient tone. "Management wants to be extra sure they know who's coming and going." He found my name on his clipboard, checked it off, and handed my ID back to me. "Welcome to the zoo, Dr. Preston."

"Thanks, Lloyd," I said, and waved as I walked through the gate. He didn't wave back. When I glanced over my shoulder he looked away, and I frowned. I must have been really early if my presence was this confounding to security.

The zoo was as deserted as the parking lot. I walked quickly, scanning the ground. I was wearing my glasses with the polarized lenses and carrying a hand mirror, just in case. Crow was still at home. If things went as badly as I feared that they might, he didn't need to be here.

Unlocking the reptile house was like coming home after an annoyingly short absence. Many of the reptiles were still active after their long and exciting night. Some of them froze when they saw me walking by, their instincts kicking in and causing them to pretend to be bits of fallen wood or pieces of the wall. Others ignored me completely, so accustomed to humans that I was no more important to them than an empty room. If I came back with food, maybe then they'd give a crap about me.

Shami rose in the classic cobra "stand" position when I passed his enclosure, flaring his hood slightly as he looked at me. I stared into his unblinking eyes, trying to guess what he was thinking. It was easier with wadjet females. At least they looked mostly human, and could be counted on to show their emotions in the same way.

"Alex?" Dee sounded confused, like I was the last person she'd been expecting to find in the reptile house at this hour. The sound of the front door swinging shut followed her question. I turned to face her.

She was wearing a smart-looking blouse and pencil skirt combination, one that was just a little old-fashioned, and hence went perfectly with her impeccable beehive wig. Only the uneven curves of her painted-on eyebrows told me that she was as exhausted as I was. That was a good sign. I didn't want it to be Dee. Whatever was going on, whoever was involved with it, I didn't want it to be Dee. I somehow mustered a smile.

"Hi, Dee," I said. "How are you this morning?"

"What are you doing here? It's not even seven o'clock." she asked, walking toward me, and then continuing on past me as she made her way to her office. "You never beat me into the office. Is everything okay at home?"

"We had sort of an exciting night last night." My eyes were still dry, and I'd found sand on my pillow when I'd finally given up and gotten out of bed. "Do you have a minute to talk?"

"Sure. Come on in."

Dee's office was impeccable, unlike mine: every surface was cleaned to within an inch of its life, and only the most essential items were allowed to claim territory. There were a few carefully curated "personal touches," including a forced-perspective picture of Dee, her daughter Megan, and her husband, whose name I realized I didn't know. The camera angle had been chosen to make it harder to tell that he was in the neighborhood of seven feet tall, and it worked, mostly, if you didn't know what you were looking for.

"Did you sleep last night?" she asked, putting her

purse on her desk and leaning over to switch on the computer.

"Not really," I said, following her into the office and closing the door. "I had a lot to do. Sleep wasn't on the agenda."

"Oh?"

There were a lot of places I could begin. I didn't want to tell her about Shelby—not yet. That wasn't my secret to share, and as long as Shelby wasn't endangering the local cryptids, I didn't have to force the issue. Instead, I went for the biggest shock value: "There was a cockatrice in my yard last night. I looked into its eyes."

Dee's gasp woke her hair. It hissed softly beneath her wig. "Alex! Oh sweet Athena! Are you all right? You're all right, aren't you?" She paused, almost visibly moving on to the next thought. "How are you all right? If you met its eyes, you should have . . . you should . . ."

"Luckily, my cousin was on hand, and I got a good enough look at it before my eyes started turning to stone that I was able to tell her which antivenin to use on me. It was a closer thing than I enjoy, but I'm fine now. A little dehydrated. Nothing a few bottles of Gatorade can't fix."

"So a cockatrice turned Andrew to stone?" Her voice was heavy was bald relief . . . and with eagerness. The only question was whether she was eager to have the mystery of Andrew's death resolved, or eager to have me convinced of what had killed him.

"Yes," I said, and watched her brighten. "Also, no." She dimmed just as quickly, expression turning puzzled.

"I . . . I don't understand. How was it a cockatrice if it wasn't a cockatrice?"

"It wasn't alone." I pulled out my phone, opening my gallery. The most recent image—the puncture wound on Mr. O'Malley's leg—filled the screen. I held it toward Dee, like Perseus holding his mirrored shield between himself and the fabled Medusa. "Look familiar? Because I checked these against the field guide, and they have the same diameter and spacing as the bite of a Pliny's gorgon."

The hissing was louder now, her wig beginning to pulse as her snakes worked themselves up into a fury. "I...I don't..."

"We found this wound on my next-door neighbor's leg after he died of petrifaction. I took venom samples from the surrounding tissue. They tested as gorgon. I didn't get enough to tell the subtype, but we both know this bite wasn't made by a greater gorgon, and the bite radius is pretty compelling." I lowered my phone. "So you tell me, Dee. Please. How was this man killed by a cockatrice if he was bitten by a gorgon? Why was there a cockatrice in my yard? I can't imagine the two things are unconnected. Then again, I'm the least imaginative member of my family. Maybe I'll believe you, if you can explain."

"I..." Dee's shoulders slumped as she reached up to steady her pulsing wig. "I swear to you, Alex, I don't know. I can't say for sure that I'd tell you if I knew it was a member of my community who'd done this, because I've never been in that position, but I *can* tell you it's not any member of my community who I know. They would never have done this."

"You have to know how this looks."

"Yeah, well, maybe so does somebody else, did you consider that?" She glared at me, the familiar fierceness back in her eyes. "Anybody who knows I work for you could have mocked up those bite marks as a way to make you accuse me."

"To what end?"

"To keep you from looking for the real killer."

I paused. "That's not a bad theory," I said, after a moment of thought. "There's just one problem."

"What's that?"

"We're right back at it being something other than just a cockatrice. So if it wasn't a Pliny's gorgon, what was it?"

Dee stared at me for a moment, eyes wide behind her tinted lenses. She started to open her mouth, presumably to offer an answer.

The sound of someone knocking on the office door stopped her cold.

With me and Dee both inside her office, the reptile house wasn't officially open; what's more, unless I'd been more careless than I thought, the outer door shouldn't have been unlocked. We exchanged a glance. I nodded, and she reached up to put one hand on the arm of her glasses, clearly ready to pull them off. I couldn't draw a firearm on zoo property without doing a lot of explaining, and so I just turned to the door, prepared to leap out of the way, and opened it.

Chandi didn't flinch. She had eschewed her fancy clothes today, instead wearing blue jeans and a T-shirt advertising a brightly colored, presumably age appropriate puppet show called *Lazy Town*. There were alligator-shaped barrettes in her hair. "Am I going to be allowed to see my fiancé as we agreed?" she demanded, frowning.

"Chandi." I returned her frown. "The reptile house isn't open yet. How did you get in?"

Her eyes darted to the side. "The front door was unlocked."

"No, it wasn't," said Dee, stepping up behind me. "Chandi, do you have a key? I thought we discussed this . . ."

"I have a key for emergencies," said the little girl sullenly. "Humans being murdered inside the safe haven we arranged for Shami constitutes an emergency. I am allowed to use my key under these circumstances."

"Okay, hold on a second," I said. "Chandi, did you knock before you let yourself in?"

"No," she admitted.

"So that's where we draw the line, all right? You need

to knock before you assume you're allowed to let your-self in, whether or not you think we're having an emer-gency." I paused. "Wait—the *zoo* isn't open yet. How did you even get to the reptile house?"

"I just told you that," said Chandi. "Humans are being murdered."

The thought struck me and Dee at the same time. We exchanged a horrified look. "Lloyd," she said.

"Chandi, I need you to listen to me *very carefully*." I turned back to her. "Was the man at the front gate alive or dead when you came inside?"

"He was dead. Now may I see Shami?"

"Dee?"

"I've got it." Dee stepped past me, putting her hands on Chandi's shoulders and steering the little girl firmly away from the office door. "You can see him for a mo-ment, sweetie, but if there's been another murder, they're going to close the zoo, and you don't want to be here when that happens, do you? It would come with so many inconvenient *questions*, and I don't think you want to explain them to your parents . . ." Her voice faded into so much reassuring muttering, punctuated by Chandi's objections.

I didn't stay to listen. I was already running for the front door.

The zoo was still deserted. *What did I just do?* I thought, racing down the main trail toward the gate. Lloyd had been alive when I arrived at work. Dee came in after me. If she was the killer, then I had decided to leave her alone with a little girl.

A little girl with venomous fangs of her own. We weren't even sure wadjet could be harmed by gorgon venom, given their immunity to everything else. Chandi had a finely-honed sense of self-preservation, and an even more finely-honed sense of entitlement. If Dee at-tempted to attack her rather than giving her access to her fiancé, I was betting on the wadjet.

The sound of voices told me I was on the right track.

I jogged to a stop where I would be concealed by a large patch of shrubbery and peered through the branches at the crowd that had gathered around Lloyd's body. I hadn't realized that many people came to the work this early. His clipboard was on the ground, its utility finally at an end. Although I supposed that if the police went looking for a murderer, it would give them a convenient list of suspects.

There were too many people there for me to risk approaching. They'd ask questions, and later they'd remember that I not only came in to work early, but appeared to conveniently "discover" the body with the rest of them. I turned away, pulling my phone from my pocket, as I walked slowly back toward the reptile house. I didn't want to get her involved. I wasn't even sure I wanted to *speak* to her right now. And that didn't matter, because I needed the backup.

"Shelby? Hi, it's Alex. We've got a problem at the zoo . . ."

Chandi and Dee were both alive when I stepped through the reptile house doors. That was a comfort. They were shouting at each other. That wasn't.

"—can't keep me out! I'll tell my father! I'll tell everyone! I'm allowed—"

"—believe your parents will be mad at me for looking out for your best interests? You need to think about your safety—"

"—am I supposed to develop a proper immunity if you don't let me—"

"—will be time for that—"

I put two fingers in my mouth and whistled shrilly, bringing both sides of the argument to a crashing halt. The two turned to stare at me, eyes wide. For a moment, the only sound was the hissing of Dee's hair.

"Both of you, listen up," I said. "Lloyd is dead.

Chandi, did you notice anything about the body when you came in?"

"Just that his eyes had turned to stone," she said, as dismissively as a human child might report an adult with a visible booger.

"What?" said Dee. "But that's—"

I cut her off. "That's what I was afraid of. Dee, is there any way we can smuggle Chandi out of the zoo before the police get here?" I raised a hand to cut off her protests before they could begin. "You didn't check in at the gate, Chandi, because if you'd tried, Lloyd would have made you wait until we opened. That means the police will be *really* interested in how you got inside, and why you didn't call 911 as soon as you saw the dead man. Do you want to go through all that?"

"No," she admitted sullenly.

"I can probably get her out one of the delivery gates if I take her now," said Dee. "But, Alex, really, we need to talk about this."

"We'll talk about it when you get back here. Right now, getting Chandi to safety is more important."

"I thought you might say that." Dee frowned. "What are you going to do?"

"Isn't that obvious?" I shrugged. "I'm going to get us ready to open."

Dee looked briefly like she wanted to protest, but thought better of it. Instead, she took Chandi by the shoulder and walked her to the door. For once, the young wadjet didn't object or try to bargain for five more minutes. She just went with Dee, leaving me alone with the reptiles.

I looked at the enclosures around me, sighed, and said, "All right, fellows. Let's get ready for an opening that's never going to happen."

Shelby showed up five minutes before the reptile house doors were supposed to officially open. She was wearing her uniform and looked as fresh as a daisy, even though I knew she'd been awake almost as long as I had the night before. "The zoo's closed," she announced without preamble. Then she paused, looking around the open space. "Is Dee in her office?"

"No," I said. "Dee had to deliver a package to one of the gates. She should be back any minute."

Shelby's eyes widened. "You let her go out there alone? Alex—"

"Why shouldn't he have let me go out alone?" asked Dee, stepping through the door behind my girlfriend. "I'm his assistant, not his prisoner."

"Oy!" Shelby whirled, taking a large step backward in the process, so that the three of us wound up standing in a loose circle. A loose, extremely *tense* circle. Shelby eyed Dee suspiciously. "Don't sneak up on me like that!"

"Don't stand in front of the door and maybe I won't," snapped Dee. She took a deep breath, calming herself, and said, "I'm sorry. That was rude. Did you hear about Lloyd?"

"What do you know about Lloyd, then?" asked Shelby.

I pinched the bridge of my nose. "That's about as subtle as a hammer, Shelby."

"Sometimes subtle isn't the best plan," Shelby shot back. "Sometimes subtle gets you killed. But you didn't let me go on. The dead man—it's not Lloyd."

"What?" I lowered my hand. "What do you mean?"

"I mean it's not Lloyd. It's one of the other guards. They must have traded off before whatever happened."

"Oh, thank God." I realized how bad that sounded as soon as it was said. I didn't waste time trying to take it back. Someone I knew and liked was alive; someone I didn't know as well was dead. Being relieved was only human. "Dee, did you get Chandi out of the zoo without her being seen?"

Dee nodded, looking incredibly relieved for some reason. "She was really unhappy about it."

"We'll make it up to her somehow."

Shelby blinked, looking more confused than suspicious as she asked, "Chandi? Isn't that the little girl who's always lurking about in here?"

"Every chance she gets," I confirmed. I looked back to Dee. "Do you trust me?"

"You're the boss," said Dee.

"Okay. If that's the case . . . the zoo's closed. The police should be coming to talk to us all soon, since we were some of the last people to come into the zoo before the murder. Do you have my address?"

Dee nodded.

"Good. When we're done here, we meet up at my place. All of us." I could explain the situation to Grandma during my drive home, and Sarah would be fine as long as we distracted her somehow. This was getting bad. This was no longer the sort of thing I could take care of on my own, if it ever really had been—something I now sincerely doubted. Shelby was the closest thing I had to backup. I was going to be stuck with her for the long haul.

Dee's eyes widened, and she darted an uneasy glance at Shelby. "All three of us? You know, if I'm not going to be working today, I have some things at home that could really use—"

"The man at the gate wasn't Lloyd, but he was still turned partially to stone," I said. "So was Andrew. So was Mr. O'Malley. I don't think you can stay out of this one, Dee. Will you come to my house, or do I need to find yours?" The unspoken threat hung in the air between us, only Shelby's politely puzzled expression keeping it from turning truly menacing. If Dee wasn't on our side, if she wasn't an ally, there was every chance she was an enemy. I couldn't afford to take that chance.

"I . . ." Dee hesitated. Then her shoulders slumped, and she nodded. "I'll be there."

"All right. Shelby? You want to head back to the big cats? Maybe it's best if the police don't find us together again."

"Aye-aye," she said, snapped a sloppy, mocking salute, and jogged back out the door to the zoo. In a matter of seconds, it was me, Dee, and the reptiles, alone again.

"I hope you know what you're doing," she said, with a mistrustful glance. Then she walked away, heading for the closet where we kept the lizard food.

I grimaced and followed. Even if the zoo was being shut down for the day, even if we had a petrifactor to stop, the animals still needed to be fed.

The police arrived while I was tossing trout into Crunchy's tank. The big alligator snapping turtle was still full from the night before, and took his time making the fish disappear. The officer responsible for taking my statement didn't look happy about that. It could have been worse; he could have been talking to Dee, who was feeding our rattlesnakes.

The time line I'd guessed at from Chandi's arrival was confirmed by the interviewing officer: Dee and I were among the last people to enter the zoo before the man at the gate had died. Not, I was relieved to realize, the *very* last—we were getting the same treatment Shelby and I had received the day before, and I doubted that would have been the case if either of us had been a prime suspect.

"Where can we find you if we need to ask additional questions?"

"I'll be at home," I said. If I wasn't, well. There would be one or more cuckoos at home, and that would keep any policemen who showed up from walking away thinking I'd been uncommunicative.

"Your girlfriend, Shelby Tanner, works here at the zoo, does she not?"

"Yes, in the lion house. She's a visiting researcher from Australia."

The officer nodded. "You're a visiting researcher yourself, aren't you? California?"

"Yes. I'm on loan from the San Francisco Zoo." My credentials would check out. The reptile house there was operated by one of the rare dragons who had chosen to go into something other than professional money-making. The rest of her Nest tolerated her bizarre interest in research because it gave them easy access to heated sand for incubating their eggs. "I'm doing a survey of the native amphibians of Ohio."

"Fascinating stuff," said the officer, flipping his notebook closed. "We'll call you if we need anything."

"Thank you," I said, and tossed another trout into the tank.

The officer who had interviewed me walked toward the door, beckoning the officer interviewing Dee to follow him. My assistant stayed where she was, freezing with one hand still halfway in the timber rattler enclosure as she waited for the door to close behind the two blue-clad men. I was privately glad she hadn't frozen like that until their backs were turned. There was something impossibly static about her stillness, a reptilian quality that screamed her inhuman origins more loudly than anything else about her disguised appearance.

Only when we were alone did she relax and start breathing again. She replaced the lid on the rattlesnake enclosure, stepping down from the stool she'd used to reach the opening, and said, "Alex, I don't know how much of this I can take."

"You'll take as much as you have to." I threw the last of the trout in with Crunchy and closed the hatch above his tank. Hopping down from my own stool, I grabbed it and carried it back toward the closet. "We'll get through this, Dee. I promise."

"You don't honestly think I had anything to do with this, do you?"

I hesitated before shaking my head. "No. I admit, I had a few moments of doubt when we saw the puncture marks I showed you, but there's no way you'd kill all these people. They've all been harmless so far. There's nothing they could have done to you."

"They could have found out where my community was located and threatened to expose us," said Dee. She opened her lips wide enough to let me see the fangs that had unhinged from the roof of her mouth. They folded again before she said, "Because anyone who threatened my family would find themselves between a rock and a bad place."

"I understand the sentiment," I said.

"Do you really expect me to come back to your house and talk about this in front of your *girlfriend?*"

I allowed myself the thinnest stripe of a smile. "I think you'll be surprised."

Ambulances and emergency response personnel clogged the front plaza of the zoo as Dee and I walked out and past them. No one looked our way. They all had their own problems to worry about and their own jobs to do; we were just so much moving background noise. I walked smoothly but with the appropriate amount of hesitation as I passed the place where I knew the body had been found, trying to mirror the normal responses of a human male in my situation. The last thing I wanted was for someone to remember me in this moment, or to remark upon my behavior as having been in any way odd.

The upbringing I shared with my sisters didn't make us monsters, any more than someone like Dee or Chandi was inherently a monster. It just instilled us with a different set of priorities and responses. The man I was pretending to be, Dr. Alexander Preston, had probably never seen a dead body. He worked with his snakes all day and went home to a normal life, a normal world, one that didn't have anything nasty lurking in the shadows. I was normally pretty good at pulling Dr. Preston across me like a mask, but here and now, I itched to examine the body for clues that might have helped me determine my next move.

Dee was parked across the lot from me. I paused before separating from her, asking, "You're sure you remember the address?"

"I've got it," she said. "You're sure you want me to come over?"

"Trust me," I said. "This is what's best for all of us."

She didn't look like she trusted me. She looked like she wanted to cut and run for the hills. But she wouldn't have been my assistant if she hadn't been too smart to pull a stunt like that. Looking uneasy, she nodded. "All right," she said. "I'll be there."

"Thank you." I turned and walked toward my car, trying to show I believed her by not looking back. It was difficult, and not just because I was half-afraid she wouldn't come. Another man was dead, this one killed in broad daylight, and I was allowing Dee and Shelby to run around without backup. It had nothing to do with gender, and everything to do with the fact that I didn't know how good their training had been. Dee was a gorgon. They're not immune to basilisks, so what about a cockatrice? Would she even know how to handle one? And Shelby — she'd said there were no petrifactors in Australia. What would happen if she was attacked while she was alone?

Those thoughts were bad thoughts, and they would only take me to bad places. I forced them out of my mind, got into the car, and drove.

I waited to call Grandma's cell until I was halfway home. She picked up almost immediately, greeting me with a cheerful, "Alex! How are things at work?"

"Dee's clean, or probably clean, and we have a problem," I said. "One of the guards was found dead this morning. Killed by a petrifactor, *after* both Dee and I had checked in for work. The zoo's closed for the day, and Dee and Shelby are planning to meet me at the house so we can discuss our next steps."

There was a brief pause before Grandma sighed.

"You know, I want to ask you why you and your little friends need to have your meeting here, but since three humans are dead, I suppose discussing the situation in public would be a bad idea."

"Unless we feel like being accused of murder and maybe terrorism, since they've got that whole 'unknown chemical agent' angle, yeah." Most of the time, events and issues relating to the cryptid world can be talked about virtually anywhere, since no one will believe you're talking about anything real. Unicorns? Bogeymen? The thing in the closet? Whatever. Anyone who happens to listen in will assume that you're a fantasy nut or talking about something from a television program.

That changes when people get dead. It's not that the fantastic becomes any more believable. It's just that everyone starts listening differently, and that sort of thing can get you in trouble.

"All right. I'll get Sarah settled in front of the television. Have you kids had lunch?"

"We were sort of distracted by the whole 'dead man, closing the zoo, police interrogation' thing."

"Swing by the Tim Horton's on your way, then," she said. "If Dee or Shelby beat you here, I'll make them wait in the kitchen."

I laughed. "Are you asking me to do this because you need donuts to make up for the invasion of your home?"

"I am," she said. "Get double blueberry." The connection died as she hung up on me. I laughed again, and kept on driving.

Dee's car was in front of the house when I pulled up; Shelby's was nowhere to be seen, which concerned me slightly. I parked in my usual spot behind Grandma, balancing the bag from Tim Horton's as I got out and walked to the front door. It was unlocked. The sound of laughter greeted me as I pushed it open.

The voices were coming from the kitchen. I stuck my head inside. Grandma and Dee were sitting at the table, each with a mug of what looked like herbal tea (and technically was, if you took a broad enough view of the word "herbal") in their hands. They looked over as I stepped inside. Dee was grinning, and her fangs had dropped, pushing little indentations into her lower lip.

"You really tried to hug a manticore? Alex, I never thought you had it in you."

"I was six," I said, trying to recover my dignity as I put the Tim Horton's bag down on the table. "It looked like a puppy crossed with a scorpion. Of course I wanted to hug it."

Something about my frosty tone struck them both as funny, because they started laughing again, even harder than before. Grandma reached out and freed the box of Timbits from the rest of my lunch order, popping it open to reveal the donut holes inside.

"You're my favorite grandson," she cooed, popping one into her mouth.

"I'm your only grandson," I said sourly. Then I paused, looking around the kitchen in alarm. "Grandma, did you remember to bribe—"

"HAIL! HAIL THE RETURN OF THE GOD OF SCALES AND SILENCE!" exulted the mice, emerging from behind most of the appliances on the kitchen counter.

"—the mice." I groaned, putting a hand over my face. "You asked me to bring home baked goods. You didn't bribe the mice to stay upstairs. Are you setting me up for a musical number, or do you just hate me?"

"If this Shelby girl is going to be involved with the family business, she's going to need to handle whatever that involvement might entail." Grandma took another donut hole out of the box and smiled at me. "Hence the mice."

For her part, Dee blinked, looking baffled. "Excuse me, but what's going on?" she asked, in her usual calm, reasonably even tone. She'd been to the house before, and she'd met the mice, but that had been the mice in company mode: three of them had come politely to the kitchen, thanked her for her visit, and asked if she'd like to attend that night's catechism. This was the mice in full-on celebration. It was a pretty daunting sight even for me, and I grew up with it.

"Grandma doesn't approve of Shelby, so she's arranged for an Aeslin bacchanal to convince her to back off." I pushed my glasses up, glowered at my grandmother. "This is dirty pool, you understand."

"All's fair in love, war, and not inviting representatives of barely vouched-for cryptozoological organizations into my home." Grandma flicked her donut hole into the ocean of mice, where it disappeared, accompanied by the sound of redoubled cheering.

The doorbell rang.

Grandma turned her face to me and smiled serenely. "You'd better get that," she said. "You wouldn't want to leave your little girlfriend waiting."

"We're going to talk about this later," I promised, before turning and heading for the door, fighting the whole way not to glower. Intellectually, I knew my grandmother was being reasonable. She was protecting her home. Shelby was a barely-known quantity, and until she could be trusted, embracing her fully was a terrible idea. Grandma had always been a little mistrusting. Being one of the few nonsociopathic members of an entire species had influenced her views of everyone else in the world, and having Sarah home and essentially defenseless wasn't helping.

At the same time, I needed the help. If Shelby was qualified—which she was—then having her on my side was the best thing I could hope for. I opened the front door. Shelby smiled at me, and held up her Tim Horton's bag.

"I stopped for donuts," she said.

I blinked. "There is a God." I stepped to the side to let

her in, and closed the door behind her. "Okay, look. I need you not to freak out. Can we agree on that? That you're not going to freak out?"

Shelby's smile faded. "Why would I be freaking out? Has someone else been turned to stone?"

"Not quite. Can I have the donuts?"

"Um, sure?" Shelby handed me the bag.

I took her hand. "Just trust me, okay?" On this confidence-building note, I turned and pulled her with me into the kitchen.

As soon as we stepped inside, the mice began cheering again. It was sort of a reflex with them. "HAIL! HAIL THE RETURN OF THE GOD OF SCALES AND SILENCE!"

"I have returned with company, and with donuts," I informed them, after waiting for the cheers to die down. "I request a bargain."

"What bargain?" squeaked one of the mice, its identity obscured by the throng.

"I will give you this bag of donuts," I held up the Tim Horton's bag, "the contents of which are a mystery *even to me*, if you will take it upstairs and stay there until such time as I give you leave or the evening meal arrives, whichever comes first."

There was a long pause while the mice consulted among themselves. I caught the words "holy," "mystery," and "towels." I didn't ask. The Aeslin mice were better at making decisions when no one tried to help them do it. Finally, the muttering stopped, and one of the mice stepped forward. "Your Bargain is Accepted," said the mouse.

"Thank you," I replied, and placed the bag on the counter. The colony surged forward like a single creature, enveloping the promised treats, lifting the whole thing over their heads, and finally marching out of the kitchen with their prize. There was some singing involved. The whole process took less than a minute.

Grandma took another donut hole from the surviving assortment. "Oh, well," she said.

Dee and Shelby exchanged a stunned look, briefly united by the sudden understanding that everyone else in the house was seriously weird. Shelby recovered first, asking, "What in the fuck was all that about?"

"The mice have to be bribed if we want them to leave us alone once they've gotten interested in something," I said sheepishly. I rubbed the back of my neck with one hand. "I don't suppose you've heard of Aeslin mice?"

"Those can't be Aeslin mice," Shelby said. "They're extinct."

"Wait," said Dee. "Why isn't she freaking out?"

"They're not extinct," I said. "They just don't get out much."

"She's supposed to be freaking out," continued Dee.

"That's remarkable," said Shelby. "Do you think I could talk to them later, see if they know of any colonies in Australia?"

"I don't see why not," I said.

"Can we focus on the important thing here, like *why isn't she freaking out*?!" Shelby and I turned. Dee was standing, her palms flat on the table, her eyes wide and a little wild behind her tinted glasses. A faint hiss escaped her wig.

I sighed. "I think we should bring everybody up to speed, don't you?"

Explaining the situation took about half an hour. It would have been faster, but everyone had a different understanding of what was going on, and piecing it all together took more work than I had expected. We ate our way through the donuts I'd picked up from Tim Horton's. Everyone drank too much coffee, mine and Shelby's mixed with milk and sugar, Grandma's mixed with ketchup and pepper, and Dee's spiked with rattlesnake venom. Since we hadn't yet reached the "Dee isn't human" bombshell, her coffee was prepared when Shelby wasn't looking.

But the bombshell was coming. I was trying to be respectful of Dee's rights as a sapient individual and not go around blabbing her inhuman nature to anyone who looked like they might be open to a team up. (Discretion isn't just my watchword: it's a good way to keep myself from being punched by my friends.) At the same time, I needed help if I wanted to deal with this situation, and the only help I had readily at hand was Shelby. Dee would have to trust her eventually.

Shelby herself was quite forthcoming about her history with the Thirty-Six Society and reasons for coming to this country, now that she knew it was okay for her to talk about that sort of thing in front of Dee. She took a mouthful of coffee and beamed at my assistant across the table. "It's nice to know that there are so many cryptozoologists in the area," she said. "Although I have to ask—why Ohio? I'm here because there used to be prides of manticore around here, and I know Alex is here to try and convince basilisks to get it on, but what brings you to the middle of the continent?"

"I grew up in this area," said Dee vaguely.

"And your husband, is he a cryptozoologist, too?" Shelby continued. "I've seen that charming photo in your office. Did you meet through work?"

"Oh, no," Dee said slowly. "Frank's a doctor. We didn't meet until he . . . that is . . . he was the best husband my parents could find, and normally I would have been sent to join him, but he didn't like the overcrowding where he grew up, and we needed a doctor, so he came out here."

"Arranged marriage?" Shelby blinked. "I didn't know that was an American tradition."

"Not . . . quite." Dee worried her lip between her teeth, glancing at me. I nodded encouragingly. She looked back to Shelby. "There's something I should show you. Will you please promise me that you'll stay in your seat, and not make any sudden or hostile moves?"

"Unless you make sudden or hostile moves toward me, sure," said Shelby.

"All right," said Dee, and reached up, and removed her wig. Freed of their confinement, the snakes growing from her scalp uncoiled, stretched, and settled into a loose halo around her head, their tongues scenting the air. The rest of us turned toward Shelby to see what she would do.

Shelby blinked. Then she blinked again, and finally, looking somewhat nonplussed, she asked, "Is *anyone* in Ohio human?"

"I am," I said.

"You're a Price, you don't count," Shelby shot back. She returned her attention to Dee, or rather, to Dee's snakes. "They're beautiful. Do they bite? Have they got minds of their own? Does this make you a gorgon, then, or is there another species that comes with snakes in place of hair? Do you have *any* hair? You draw your eyebrows on, and your eyelashes have always looked fake to me, so I suppose not . . ."

Now it was Dee's turn to blink. "You seem pretty relaxed about all of this."

"I'm from Australia. I see stranger than women with snakes for hair when I look out my bedroom window." Shelby shrugged. "Besides, Alex trusts you, and I trust Alex, at least for the moment. So if I've already decided to trust you, I may as well focus on the natural marvel which you represent." She broke into a broad grin. "Evolution is so *cool*."

"That's something I think we can all agree on," I said, relaxing. "Now that we've got that out of the way, can we please focus on the problem at hand? Three men are dead, and whoever—or whatever—killed them either *is* a Pliny's gorgon, or is trying to implicate the local community in the deaths."

"Whoever *or* whatever?" asked Shelby. "Don't we already know the answer to that one?"

"If a Pliny's gorgon is using a cockatrice to commit

the murders, or is committing the murders on their own and somehow pinning it on a cockatrice, we're looking for a who," I said. "If it's a cockatrice that's somehow being covered up for, it's a what. That's going to change our hunting strategies dramatically."

"Pliny's gorgons don't like cockatrice any more than anyone else does," said Dee. "They're spiteful, smelly things, and being immune to their glance doesn't make us immune to being pecked and scratched." She shook her head. "Every group has its fringe element. Ours thinks we should be self-sufficient, which means farming. They keep trying to cultivate things that can't be petrified. That includes cockatrice. No, thank you."

"Is there one of those fringe groups around here?"

Dee hesitated before nodding. "Yes. They live about a mile from the main community, where they won't interfere with anyone else."

"We need to see them."

"Alex—"

"Three people are *dead*, Dee." She flinched. I continued: "The police only know about two of them. There's a chance it won't make the national news if it stops now. It'll be a blip on a few of the blogs that specialize in weird news, and it'll go away. But if it continues, it's going to get some media play, and the Covenant is going to notice. Do you want to risk that?"

Dee paled. "No, but . . ."

"We need to visit the community, Dee. You know that's how this is going to end."

There was a moment of silence before she nodded, slowly. "I suppose I did know that. I'd just been hoping there was, well . . . some other way." She glanced to Grandma before she said, almost guiltily, "I'm sorry, Angela, but I can't bring a cuckoo where we live. I know you're, well . . . you . . . but I can't."

My grandmother, who could be stubborn sometimes, but who had lived her entire life with the reality of what she was, nodded. "I understand, Dee," she said, with a small, almost regretful smile. "I never expected you to bring me along." Unspoken was the fact that out of all the cuckoos in the world, my ailing cousin included, Grandma was the least dangerous. She was a projective telepath, like the rest of her kind, but she didn't receive. It was why she'd grown up with a normal code of ethics, rather than being overwritten by her mother's sociopathic nature while she was still in the womb.

"We'll take two cars," I said, pushing my coffee away as I stood.

Dee blinked. "What, *now?*"

Andrew, Mr. O'Malley, and the guard—I still needed to learn his name—weren't getting any less dead while we sat around and talked. I nodded firmly. "Yes, now," I said. "Before it's too late for anyone else."

"Oh, lovely," said Shelby. "I've always enjoyed field trips."

Fourteen

"Try to let go of the idea that humanity is the pinnacle of evolution. There are creatures in this world that can kill you with a look, people with wings, and mountains that walk. Humanity is amazing, but have a little perspective."

—Martin Baker

Driving through the woods half an hour outside of Columbus, Ohio, struggling to remain positive about the situation

DEE HAD ALWAYS STRUCK me as a careful driver, someone who obeyed traffic laws and tried not to attract the attention of the police. What I hadn't considered was that she might be different when stressed out and taking us to meet her family. Once we reached the woods, it was every man for himself: Dee hit the gas, and I was forced to violate several local and state ordinances if I wanted to keep up with her. (She'd been unwilling to give directions to the local gorgon enclave, saying we could follow her home if we insisted on coming for a visit. I was starting to wonder if that wasn't because she thought she could lose us before we got anywhere near the rest of the colony.)

"What the fuck is wrong with you?" I muttered, following Dee as she took a sharp turn across two lanes of freeway and down an exit with a name I couldn't have pronounced if you paid me.

"Sorry?" asked Shelby.

"No, I'm sorry," I said, keeping my eyes on the road. If I looked away for so much as a second, I was going to wind up slamming into a tree and killing us both. "I swear I thought she could drive."

"Alex. Have you ever driven down the Great Ocean Highway?"

"Uh . . . which would be where, exactly?"

"It's in Australia."

Dee took another sharp turn, onto a narrow road I hadn't seen through the trees until she was already heading down it. She hadn't even used her blinker. I hauled hard on the wheel. The tires squealed as we changed direction and went rocketing after my runaway assistant.

When I was breathing normally again, I said, "Then, no, I haven't. I've never been to Australia."

"Oh, we'll need to fix *that*," said Shelby, with a degree of joy that would have been disturbing if I hadn't been focusing so intently on keeping Dee in sight. Maybe that was a life lesson in disguise: when there's any chance your girlfriend is going to exhibit an unnatural amount of glee over something that seems perfectly mundane, take her on a high-speed car chase. It'll take the edge off. Then she sobered. "Didn't expect you to call me today."

"Shelby, is this really—"

"You made me have a relationship talk while we were hunting monsters, I think this is fair. Thought we were probably finished after last night."

"I needed your help."

"Is that all we are now? People who help each other?"

"I don't know," I said honestly. "I'd like to be more, maybe. But I can't afford to be distracted right now. And then there's the whole thing where your introduction to my grandparents involved waving a gun at their adopted daughter, so . . . yeah. I recommend not pulling out any more firearms unless there's a really excellent reason."

"I suppose 'being a Johrlac' isn't an excellent reason, right?" Shelby's tone was unsteadily wry, like she was trying to make a joke but wasn't quite sure how appropriate it was or how it was going to be received.

I sighed, still focusing on the road, where Dee was doing her best to set speed records. "No, it's not. They're my *family*, Shelby. If we want this to work out, knowing what we both know now, you're going to need to learn to be okay with that. They're not the Johrlac who came to your country and hurt the people that you cared about. They've been here this whole time, not hurting anybody."

"Are we, then?" asked Shelby.

"Are we what?"

"Are we going to try and get this to work out?" Shelby twisted in her seat to face me.

I was silent for a moment. "Do you want to?" I finally asked. I knew it was unfair of me, but I needed to know.

"It's different, now that we don't have to hide anything. But . . . I don't know if I would have gotten involved with you if I'd known you were a cryptozoologist."

"Ah, but if you had, I wouldn't have needed to make nearly as many excuses." I shook my head. "I've said it before and I'll say it again: we need a dating service."

"How would you keep the Covenant from signing up?"

"That is why we're never going to *have* a dating service." I laughed. It felt good. So did Shelby. That felt better.

And then Dee turned again, this time into what looked like a wall of solid green. There was no opening there: nothing but undifferentiated trees and the broken, rocky ground between them.

Illusions happen. Whispering a quick prayer to anyone who might be listening, I followed her, tensing myself against a crash that never came. Instead, the turn ended with us driving onto a smooth, gently curving private road. Dee was just ahead, and she'd slowed down enough that I had to slam on the brakes to keep from rear-ending her. Apparently, we no longer needed to drive like maniacs to avoid being followed.

"Holy . . ." breathed Shelby. I glanced to the side. She had her hands pressed flat against the passenger side window, and was close to doing the same thing with her nose. I craned my neck, trying to get an idea of what she was looking at.

The road followed a natural curve in the landscape, winding down into a bowl valley of the type that are common in some forested areas. The trees had been cleared within the valley itself, opening up a wide swath of farmable land. In the middle of the bowl was what looked like a small mobile home park. The individual homes were arranged in a circle that mimicked the bowl itself, and would be a great mechanism for reducing traffic jams if they ever needed to drive out of here. They could start up the lead mobile home and unwind the whole community like a vehicular snake, slithering its way up the road and on to some new safe haven.

I chuckled. Shelby turned away from the window, raising her eyebrows.

"Something funny?" she asked.

"Just that I'm already starting to think in really tortured reptile metaphors," I said. "Don't let me try to talk dirty until we've been away from here for a few hours."

"Don't be silly, Alex. I never let you talk dirty to me if I can help it. You're a great kisser, and you're better in bed, but your idea of romance has *always* been way too centered around reptiles." She pressed her nose back against the window. "I see corn, tomato plants, there's even a small apple orchard. These people must have been living here for *years*."

"At least twenty, I'd say." The road was well-maintained, but it must have been put in before wide Internet surveillance was possible. If it were more recent, people would have noticed the construction, illusions over the entrance or no. "I wonder if this place appears on Google Earth..." I made a mental note to check when I got home.

"I've got cell service in here, if that makes a difference."

"That makes sense, actually. A lot of Pliny's gorgons go into day trading or technical writing or other professions that don't necessarily bring them into contact with people on a regular basis." I smiled a little. "There's at least one romance writer who never goes to conventions, because she's actually an eight-foot-tall grandfather."

"Why do they do that? Dee does fine with humans. I'd never have guessed." Shelby grimaced. "Although to be fair, I wasn't looking. I should probably have suspected something."

"Dee's very good at fitting in. And as for why Pliny's gorgons arrange their lives that way, well, it helps them hide the fact that they—the males at least—are a lot taller than humans. Females top out between five and seven feet, but males can be up to nine feet tall. Not so useful if you want to pass for human, so they get jobs that don't require them to try."

"So what, they've got their own cell tower?"

"I wouldn't be surprised. They probably had DSL before most of the rest of the state." A surprising number of telephone company technicians are cryptids, or know cryptids exist and have simply chosen not to care. Once you've determined that the giant ball of fangs and tentacles isn't going to eat you, there's no good reason not to fix its phone service.

"Huh."

"Pretty much." We had reached the bottom of the hill. The road continued around the base of the bowl, avoiding the farmed areas, to wind its way into the mobile homes. I kept following Dee. It seemed like the only safe thing to do.

People were starting to emerge from the trailers to either side, looking curiously toward my car. A few of them were wearing baseball caps, and most of them were bareheaded. Why shouldn't they be? This was their home, and Shelby and I were the invasive species. One little girl had red bows tied around the necks of her snakes. Their scales were so pale that they looked almost white. I wondered whether they would darken as she aged. Immediately after, I wondered how rude of me it would be to ask.

Dee parked in front of a trailer. There was another space next to her, and so I slid into it, killing the engine. Shelby reached for her door. I put a hand on her arm, stopping her.

"Hang on," I said, and produced a pair of polarized goggles from my pocket. She looked at me quizzically. "The gaze of a Pliny's gorgon can stun if they're not wearing specially tinted glasses. These will keep you from getting hurt."

"And you think you weren't planning to get me involved in all this," she said, taking the goggles and sliding them on. "What about you?"

I tapped the arm of my glasses. "I'm already set. These are specially polarized. So is the reflective coating on my car windows. I plan ahead."

"You say the sweetest things."

"I try," I said, reaching for the door. "Come on. Let's go see how much trouble we're in."

The gorgons had started to move as soon as we stopped. By the time Shelby and I were out of the car, we were surrounded. Size didn't seem to be a factor: even the little girl with beribboned snakes was standing there, clearly confident that she could take us if she had to. Given her natural advantages, she probably could.

"They're with me," Dee announced, stepping between me and the rest of the gorgons. That left Shelby alone between the two cars. I wasn't sure I was comfortable with that. We should probably have planned this better.

A thin man with bronze skin and black-scaled snakes pushed his way through the crowd. He was wearing blue hospital scrubs that left the bottom foot or so of his legs exposed. He must have been seven feet tall. My animal hindbrain began a vigorous argument with the rest of my mind over the virtues of running vs. asking if I could perform a physical examination.

"And who, exactly, are 'they,' Deanna?" he demanded.

"They're my guests, Frank," said Dee, sounding unruffled. She reached up and removed her wig, causing her own brown-and-red snakes to uncoil and stretch to their full length. Several of Frank's snakes stopped writhing in order to watch hers intently. "If that's not enough for you—"

"It's not," said Frank dangerously.

"—allow me to present Alexander Price, and Shelby Tanner. Shelby belongs to the Thirty-Six Society."

"Cheers," said Shelby, solving the "separated from the group" issue by sliding across the hood of my car and landing on her feet beside me. "Nice . . . village? Village works as well as anything, I suppose. Nice village you've got here. How often are you doing crop rotation?"

"Every season," said Frank automatically. Then he scowled. "Hang on. I'm not going to answer any questions about how we're living. You're the ones who should be answering questions."

"Frank." I could practically hear Dee roll her eyes. "They're my guests. Behave."

"They're humans," said one of the children—a little boy in a Pokémon T-shirt. Some things are apparently universal. He looked curious. The reason was revealed as he continued, "I've never seen humans before. Can we keep them?"

"No," said Frank. "They won't be staying. Or at least, they won't be staying alive."

"Do you lot always threaten company?" asked Shelby. "Like, is this a normal social thing, and I should start threatening you back if I want to be civil?"

"Please don't," said Dee.

"Go right ahead," said Frank.

"When in doubt, we uninvited humans like to listen to

the people who have a known track record of not trying to kill us," I said hastily, before things could get any worse. "Look: we're here because I asked Dee to bring us. She's been a good friend, and I'm really glad to have been able to assist your community by supplying anti-venin and other needed medical supplies. I take it you're the community doctor, Mr. . . . ?"

"Franklin Javier Lusczando de Rodriguez," said Frank, drawing himself up to his full height and looking haughtily down his nose. He had a lot of height, which made the gesture more impressive than pretentious, although it was a narrow margin.

"Ah, so you're Dee's husband." I stole a glance at Dee, who wasn't looking at me at all. This was probably not the top of her list of "ways I want my boss to meet my husband." I looked back to Frank. "Anyway. Dee has been a huge help since I came to Ohio, and I want to help her in return. I know it would be devastating for you if a Covenant purge were to get started over all this silly cockatrice business."

As I had expected, saying the word "Covenant" in the middle of a gathering of gorgons was like dropping a lit match into a barrel full of salamanders. Hissing filled the air as people turned to their neighbors, talking in quick, panicked voices. I held my ground, watching Frank. His snakes were still mostly calm, although they were twisting together in a way that could have indicated anything from confusion to guilt.

Finally, he frowned. "Silly cockatrice business?"

I blinked, glancing toward Dee again. She still wasn't looking at me. "Well, this is going to be fun," I muttered, and turned back to Frank. "I can see we have a great deal to discuss. Is there someplace we can go to talk about this, preferably where we won't start a panic?"

Frank kept frowning as he studied me. At long last, he nodded and said, "I have a place. Come with me."

Frank's "place" turned out to be one of the larger mobile homes, set off from the rest by almost fifteen yards—unheard of privacy in a community where everyone shared the same open space as both a common area and a means of getting from one place to another. The reason for the privacy was apparent as soon as he opened the door to reveal the gleaming operating table and state-of-the-art dentist's chair. There was even a maternity area, with several large incubators and a comfortable bed for mothers recuperating from their labor.

"This is your hospital," I said, looking around with a practiced eye. Everything was clean and well-maintained. If more than one person was sick or injured at a time they would need to share the same room, but apart from that . . . "This is fantastic. You could give my parents tips on how to maintain a private emergency room."

As I had expected, Frank preened a bit, walking past me to stand in front of the operating table. It came up to his waist. "It can be hard, getting equipment that's large enough for us to use here," he said. "It doesn't help that we need two sets of everything. My apprentice and both our nurses are under six feet tall."

"Did you go to medical school, then?" asked Shelby.

Frank nodded. "I was young. I still fit in the desks." The snakes atop his head made a noise that sounded suspiciously like a snicker.

"Good for you," said Shelby.

"Apprentice?" I asked.

"Yes. Our physiology isn't exactly like yours, and as you need a license to practice human medicine if you want to get access to most of the stronger painkillers and antibiotics in this country, he and I both went to human schools. Now he's studying with me to become a proper doctor. When his training is done, he'll be able to move to another community, and be a great asset to them."

Given the way Pliny's gorgon communities handled their families, "great asset" probably meant "attract a better wife." I nodded. "It's a good arrangement."

"We think so. Now." Frank's expression turned grave. "What do you mean by 'silly cockatrice business'?"

"Two men have died at the zoo where Dee and I work, and another died near my home," I said. "All have shown outward signs of petrifaction. I was able to gain access to the man who died outside the zoo. There was internal petrifaction as well, although it didn't continue much past the point where it would have been fatal."

"Then it could have been any number of things. Stone spiders—"

"There was a cockatrice in my backyard last night." That stopped him. I shrugged as I continued, "We locked eyes; petrifaction began. If I hadn't had someone with me, I wouldn't have survived long enough for the solution to be assembled. I'm not going to be able to pull off a trick like that again. Keeping me from losing my eyesight—or my life—meant using most of the cockatrice antivenin we had in stock."

Frank blinked. "You *saw* the cockatrice."

"Yes."

"Forgive me if this seems a bit . . . blunt . . . but are you lying to me right now? You're human. You can't have locked eyes with a serpent and lived."

"He didn't," said Shelby. "He locked eyes with a cockatrice. I know. I was there. It would have been me, but he pushed me out of the way before the bugger could get close enough to do any damage." She hesitated before she added, "I could have been killed."

"Serpent is slang for both cockatrice and basilisks," I explained. To Frank I said, "If Shelby hadn't been there and able to follow my instructions, I would have died. Believe me, I have no reason to lie to you about this."

Frank nodded slowly. "You'll excuse my dubiousness."

"Absolutely. I'd think you were full of it if you were the one telling this story. But there's more."

"More?"

"In examining the body we were able to obtain, we found fang marks." I pulled out my phone, opened the gallery, and scrolled to the picture of the back of Mr. O'Malley's leg. I held it out for Frank to see. "In your professional opinion, what bit this man?"

Frank frowned. "May I?" he asked, half-reaching for my phone.

"You may." I let him take the phone, and waited as he studied the picture, his eyes darting from side to side as he took in the small cues to scale and perspective. His snakes even got in on the act, darting forward until their noses nearly brushed the screen, tongues flicking in and out the whole time.

"I want to tell you that you have no business here," he said finally, and handed the phone back to me. "I want to tell you that you are not only wrong and misguided, but you are trespassing and possibly in danger of your lives."

"But you're not going to tell me any of those things," I said.

"No." Frank shook his head. The snakes curled back against his scalp with the motion, hissing and slithering against each other. "I can't. These marks . . . they could have been made by my own fangs." He paused, eyes widening as he realized what he'd said—and who he'd said it to. "I didn't mean—"

"I know," I said. "It can't have been you. It's literally not possible. Not only would your bite radius be substantially bigger, but there's no way a man of your stature could have come into my neighborhood, bitten my next-door neighbor, and gotten away without being seen. Someone would have called the police about 'that really tall guy,' and we'd have more to talk about right now."

"See, honey," said Dee, sounding relieved. "I would never have brought them here if I thought there was a chance you were involved."

I would have been annoyed by that announcement if I hadn't understood it so very well. Family has to come first in this world. Sometimes that means making decisions that you really don't want to make. "So the problem becomes clear," I said. "There's a cockatrice somewhere in Columbus, and we don't know where it's going during the day, or how it got there. I think someone brought it there, and is recapturing it somehow. There's no other reason it would have been at both my place of work and where I live."

"So you think someone is trying to kill you?" asked Frank, frowning.

"That's the problem: I've got no idea." I shook my head. "It's hard to see the cockatrice showing up at my house as anything other than an attack, but who was it an attack *on*? I don't live alone, and Shelby was there. If we're talking about someone who keeps a cockatrice crammed into a cat carrier, they would have had plenty of time to tail her, dump it in the backyard, and get out of sight."

"Gosh, I'm going to sleep *great* tonight," said Shelby.

"Sorry." I shrugged. "So maybe they're trying to kill me, or Shelby, or they're attacking the zoo and having two employees in the same building was too much to resist. Or maybe it was a coincidence. I guess we'll find out when the cockatrice shows up at my house again. Until then, I'm more worried about who's using a poor dumb animal like a weapon."

"You're not here to kill it?" asked Frank, frowning.

"If you're Dee's husband, you know I'm running a basilisk breeding program at the zoo," I said. "I'm not in the business of killing innocent creatures because they were temporarily inconvenient." The three dead men probably wouldn't have liked me calling their deaths "inconvenient," but it was true as far as it went: the cockatrice hadn't meant them any harm. It was whoever put the cockatrice into their paths that I wanted to get my hands on.

"What will happen if you capture it?"

"If it's been partially tamed, enough that it's going to keep wandering into human habitations, I'll see if there's anyone with a breeding program or private facility who we can trust and who's currently looking for a cockatrice," I said. "There are a few carnivals still running traditional sideshows, and most of those have both the enclosures and the equipment needed to safely display a cockatrice. It's not the best solution. The poor thing will never be free again. But it won't have to die, and it won't kill anyone else. If it's still wild, all of this is moot; we'll relocate it to one of the cockatrice ranges in the Appalachians, and forget that it was ever here."

"And what of the one who made those bite marks you showed me?"

This was going to be the tricky one. "Whoever bit my neighbor was a 'who,' not a 'what.' The thing about 'whats,' like the cockatrice, is that they don't do what they do out of malice, or out of anything other than instinct. 'Whos' are different. They're people. And people should know what's right from what's wrong."

Frank narrowed his eyes. "So you get to make that determination all by yourself? That sounds suspiciously like Covenant thinking."

"Not unless there's an immediate threat to the lives of those around me. I'm not Covenant. I don't think like that. But I'm not going to let the sins of my fathers keep me from reaching for a gun when someone is trying to kill me." Belatedly, I realized that the gorgons hadn't taken our weapons away. They were that confident about their ability to overpower us. "At the same time, if I find out that it's someone from this community doing the killing, I will expect you to stop them, through whatever means are necessary. I don't care if you exile them, imprison them, or what, but you can't let this go on. It's *going* to attract the attention of the Covenant. That wasn't an idle threat."

"I never thought it was," said Frank. He turned to face the back of the trailer, where a blue curtain walled off whatever was on the other side. "Have you heard enough?"

"I have," said a mild female voice with a thick Saskatchewan accent. The curtain was pushed aside, and a female gorgon with skin the color of rattlesnake scales in the moonlight stepped into the main trailer. I couldn't tell her subspecies on sight. Her snakes were long, falling all the way down to the middle of her back, and Frank's head only came up to her collarbone, making her at least nine feet tall. She didn't look old, but she felt it. I swallowed the urge to bow.

The older gorgon studied us through narrowed, sand-colored eyes. Finally, she offered me her hand, and smiled, showing teeth that were more like an alligator's than a human's. "Hello," she said. "My name is Hannah. You are Jonathan's boy, are you not?"

I took her hand. Her skin was cool. "Jonathan was my great-grandfather," I said. "It's a pleasure to meet you."

"Great-grandfather? How time flies." She shook my hand gently, only squeezing a little before she let me go. "He was a good man. He helped my parents to wed. I am grateful for that." She turned searching eyes on Dee and Shelby. "You are the newest Healy girl?"

"Sorry?" said Shelby.

"She's my partner, yes," I said. If Hannah had known my great-grandfather, then she must have also known my great-grandmother, Fran. Until that moment, I hadn't considered quite how much Shelby looked like her, and like every other woman in the last three generations of my family, with the possible exception of Antimony, who looked more like my grandfather than anyone else. One more thing to talk about with the therapist I didn't have.

"Hmm." Hannah nodded. "She will do. Now, Deanna. Did you really think that bringing humans to our home was the best choice you could have made?"

"Under the circumstances, yes," said Dee.

"So long as we are not lying to each other." Hannah turned back to me. "Because you are Jonathan's boy, I will trust you enough to listen. You will be my guests for dinner this night. Once we have eaten, then we will discuss what will happen next."

"Thank you, ma'am," I said.

She smiled, displaying the sharp tips of her lower canines. "Thank me after we have eaten," she said. "Anything less would be folly." She turned and walked out of the trailer, leaving us all staring after her.

Frank's wide hand fell heavily on my shoulder. I looked up at him.

"Well, I hope you were planning on sticking around," he said. "You're about to have an interesting evening."

I managed not to gulp.

Fifteen

"Gorgon society is fascinating in its complexity, especially since, until you know what kind of gorgon you're dealing with, there's no way of knowing whether the society is polite or not."

—Jonathan Healy

At a hidden gorgon community in the middle of the Ohio woods, where no one is going to hear the cries for help

"THIS IS BAD," said Dee.

"It's certainly not good," agreed Frank. "Does anyone know you brought them here?"

"My grandparents," I said. "Which means that the rest of my family will know in short order if I don't come home."

"Nobody knows I'm here but Alex and his folks," said Shelby cheerfully. I blinked at her. She shrugged. "No point in lying about it. I figure if I'm going to be eaten, I'll get avenged when your people come riding in with their guns blazing. Although speaking of guns, this feels like a good time to point out that anybody trying to eat me had better be prepared for a face full of bullets. It's not a very friendly thing to do, but neither is eating your company."

"No one's eating *anyone*," said Dee firmly. "We don't

eat humans. Pliny's gorgons are . . . well, we're not vege-
tarians, but we're not people-eaters either."

"But Hannah's not a Pliny's gorgon, is she?" I asked
slowly. Dee and Frank both turned to look at me. I shook
my head. "Not entirely, I mean. She's too tall. Female
Pliny's gorgons don't get that tall. And her snakes . . .
something about the shape of their heads is wrong."

"Her mother was a Pliny's gorgon," said Frank. "Her
father was of Medusa's breed."

I gaped at him. "Pliny's gorgons are cross-fertile with
greater gorgons?" I realized how insensitive the question
was as soon as it was out. I winced. "Sorry. That was rude
of me. I just didn't realize . . . anyway. There's nothing in
the books to indicate that's possible."

"Then you haven't read your great-grandfather Jonathan's notes very carefully. Hannah speaks very highly of
him. He spoke in favor of the marriage of her parents,
when it became clear that they were going through with
their union."

"I may have missed a few things," I said. It was a little
white lie: whatever I'd missed wasn't in the house to be
read. There are big holes in the information we got from
Great-Grandpa Healy's notes, and they can almost certainly be blamed on his daughter—my maternal
grandmother—who burned a lot of his things after he
died. In her defense, she had good reason. That doesn't
justify losing whatever knowledge she'd destroyed.

"Hannah's status as a crossbreed has been debated
many times, and is actually viewed as an asset, now," said
Dee. "She's a bit more . . . potent . . . than the rest of us,
and she does a very good job of guarding the community."

"And as she has no children of her own, she looks
after all the children of the community with the fierceness of a mother defending her own clutch," said Frank.
There was something weary in his tone, which I thought
was better left uninvestigated—at least for now. "She has

been a good leader. You are fortunate to have the opportunity to dine with her."

Most crossbreeds are infertile. That probably explained why Hannah was so happy to take care of the children of the community. I had the presence of mind not to say that out loud. Instead, I nodded and said, "It'll be good to learn more. In the meantime . . . does this mean we have to stay here until dinner is served, or are we allowed to look around?"

"You are not prisoners," said Frank. "It would be a great insult if you were to attempt to leave, but apart from that, you are free to move throughout the community. Within reason. I would not recommend going out alone, and it would be rude to enter a private dwelling without permission."

"Oh, neither of those things is going to be an issue, I assure you." I turned to Dee. "Remember those fringe groups you told me about? The ones who may be trying to work with dangerous animals in the name of self-sufficiency?"

"Yes," said Dee, looking uneasy. She clearly knew where this was going.

There had never been any real question. "This seems like a good time for you to take us there."

Shelby completely failed to suppress her expression of delight.

We left the medical trailer in a group, Dee at the front, me and Shelby in the middle, and Frank at the rear. Attempts to tell him that he didn't need to come had been met with a dangerously blank stare. We were taking his wife into what he clearly viewed as unsavory territory. He was coming along.

Privately, I was glad of the extra muscle. It's hard to make diplomatic inroads after you've shot someone. Having Frank with us might help to avoid that. If the farmers got violent, he at least stood a chance of subduing them in a non-fatal manner.

A crowd had formed outside the trailer while we were talking to Frank and Hannah, and while most of them didn't follow us as we walked away, they weren't subtle about their staring. I counted at least two dozen adults, plus the children. They were the ones who *did* follow us, running behind the trailers and peeking out at us as we passed. Shelby stuck her tongue out at the little girl with the bows on her snakes. The girl squealed with glee. Shelby smirked.

"Kids are kids," she said. "All the rest is just details."

"Remind me to introduce you properly to Chandi after all this is over," I said. "Dee? Do we need to move the car?"

"No. You're parked in front of our house, and that's perfectly fine. We have two parking spaces allotted to us."

"Why?" I asked, before I thought better of it. "I mean—"

"You're pretty good about hiding the fact that you want to study me most of the time, Alex, and I appreciate that, but that doesn't mean I don't *know*," said Dee, sounding wearily amused. She kept walking as she continued, "Megan is away at school right now, but when she's home, she needs a place to keep her car. After she graduates and becomes a full adult, she'll either get a home of her own, or find a husband in another community and move away from us. I admit I'm kind of hoping she'll choose to stay. Even with the Internet and the changes in rapid transit, each community is fairly isolated."

"I can't imagine never seeing my parents," I said. "It seems like it must be really hard."

"It is, but it is the only way," said Frank. His tone was sharp, accompanied by a warning glance at Dee. "If no one can betray anyone else, then there need be no fear of betrayal. We keep communication to a minimum when not bartering or making marriage arrangements."

"Still. It sounds lonely."

"It is." Frank increased his stride, outpacing the rest of us. Now it was Dee following him, and our back was entirely unguarded. That didn't worry me as much as it might have; we were almost to the edge of the spiraling mobile homes, striking out across the green farmland.

"He knows where we're going?" asked Shelby.

Dee nodded. "Everyone knows where the fringe is."

"From the way you talked about them before, I was expecting them to be the only farming around here," I said, and gestured to the left, where a large patch of ground had been dug into furrows and planted with what looked like some sort of melon. "What's all the rest of this?"

"We do as much of our own agriculture as possible. It can be hard to buy enough produce, and we appreciate the self-sufficiency, even if it isn't absolute. The issue is livestock." Dee shook her head. She should have looked incongruous; a woman in business casual clothes with snakes growing from her head, walking into what was basically an amateur farm. She looked like the most natural thing in the world. "There are very few creatures that can share space with a petrifactor without being in danger. None of them are what I'd call 'friendly.'"

"My basilisks are okay," I said, feeling oddly defensive toward the little feathered bowling balls.

"Basilisk eggs are toxic, or they'd be a viable candidate. As it stands, we could eat them, but we'd have to devote a lot more time and money to raising them than we spend just buying bulk raw chicken at Costco."

"That's a problem."

"It is."

We stopped talking for a while after that, and just walked. The patches of farmed ground gave way to fields with people in them, weeding and hoeing as they worked the land. They straightened as we passed, watching us go. Most were bareheaded, but a few were wearing straw hats with the tops cut out, providing them with a small measure of shade while also allowing their "hair" to move freely. I saw one man thrust his head suddenly into the corn, and come out with the back half of a mouse squirming in the jaws of one of his larger snakes.

Shelby followed my gaze. "Bet that's a mouse that's not going to be singing any hosannas any time soon."

"This is why the Aeslin mice stay home," I said.

"Quiet," said Frank, looking back over his shoulder. "This is where we are quiet, and stealthy, and hope that we are not attacked. Yes?"

We were approaching the woods. I frowned. "Your own people would attack us?"

"I'd like to think not, but Frank's right," said Dee. "Strange things have been happening in this stretch of wood. The fringe farmers swear it isn't them, and yet . . ."

"Strange things like what?"

"Men being bitten in two," said Frank. "Is that strange enough for you?"

"Maybe." I looked to Dee. "You couldn't bite a man in two—"

"I appreciate the vote of confidence."

"—but that lindworm we saw earlier could, and we're only about five miles from where we tagged it. That's well within a lindworm's normal territory. Do you have any wild onions growing around here?"

Dee blinked. "Yes. We passed a patch a little ways back."

"Can we get some? I think six bulbs or so would be sufficient."

"And that will keep the lindworm from attacking us?"

"If it's the lindworm, yes. If it's something else, we can at least make it cry as it eats us." I shrugged. "If we have to go through this patch of trees regardless, we may as well try for the solution that doesn't end with us being digested slowly in the stomach of a giant lizard."

"I appreciate non-digestive solutions," said Frank. "Deanna, you wait here. I'm faster." With that, he turned and trotted back toward the promised onions.

I shook my head. "If it's not one thing, it's something else."

Minutes ticked by while Frank gathered onions in the distance. The sun was high enough to make me wish that I'd thought to bring sunscreen. Portland isn't really sunburn country. I slapped at a fly that had landed on my arm, and said, "Hey, Dee? While we're waiting, you want to fill us in on what we're walking into?"

"Sure," said Dee. "It's not like I'm going to convince you to turn around now."

"Pretty sure that ship has sailed," said Shelby, who was eyeing the nearby foliage with trepidation, as if she expected it to attack at any moment. Then again, she came from Australia: she probably *did* expect some sort of vegetable ambush.

(Australia. The only continent designed with a difficulty rating of "ha ha fuck you no.")

Dee took a deep breath, appearing to gather her thoughts, and said, "Most Pliny's gorgons live in communities like this one, close enough to mid-sized human cities to be able to blend in, but far enough away to have some autonomy. We tend to move on when the cities get too large, since the alternative is discovery, and that never ends well for anyone."

"I can see that, what with the," Shelby made a snaky gesture in the air above her head, "and all."

"Yes, that," said Dee, clearly not sure whether or not she should be offended. "This particular community was founded by Hannah and some of her cousins from her mother's side, about fifty years ago. I won't tell you where they came from originally, although you can probably figure it out if you read those notes of your great-grandfather's."

"Er. Yes." Somehow, I didn't think that telling her the

notes had been destroyed was going to help. "Was it a matter of relocating an older community, or . . . ?"

"Hannah had issues fitting in with her original community," said Dee delicately.

"Because she's gigantic?" asked Shelby.

"Something like that. Pliny's gorgons and greater gorgons don't historically have the best relationship, and when it became clear that she needed to move if she wanted to keep the peace in her family, she took some of the younger, more flexible cousins along with her. This," Dee waved a hand, "was intended to be the first of a new breed of community. A permanent one."

"Hence all the illusions and distractions on the way in," I said.

Dee nodded. "We pay every year to have them renewed. The idea is that the cities can grow up around us until we're just one of those strange little patches of forest that seem to exist in every major metropolitan area. Then we'll always have a refuge. Not all our children can stay, of course—the limited footprint of the settlement means that we have population caps—but we know they're safe as long as they're with us."

"So what about the fringe?" I asked. "How did that start?"

"The farming aspect was always a part of the community ideal," said Dee. "Originally, there were some who wanted to see this turned into a multi-cryptid settlement. Plant vegetable lambs and bring in some manticore for protection, start growing bird-fruit and get a few tailypo to come and hang around doing whatever it is that tailypo do . . . but it didn't work out. No one really liked needing to wear eye protection every time they left their trailers, and non-gorgons could never quite relax around us, knowing that all it would take was one slip for them to be at risk. We settled into being a normal gorgon community."

I frowned, eyeing her, and waited. There had to be more to the story.

Sure enough, after a few seconds of silence, Dee sighed and continued, "Some members of the community, though, felt like the leadership had rejected them by even implying that cohabitation was possible. They said we would never be free until we were able to exist entirely independent of human culture and human resources. They moved to the edge of our protected land and started their current farming projects."

"Which eventually expanded to include things like 'happy fun time with cockatrice,'" I said. "Okay, I'm starting to understand the situation. How much do they mingle with the rest of you?"

"More than we'd like, not as much as would probably be good for them," said Dee. "I think — " She cut herself off mid-sentence. I turned to see Frank trotting back toward us, his hands now full of small purple onions.

"This is enough?" he asked.

"That's more than enough," I said, and produced a knife from inside my pocket. "Pass them over." He handed me the onions. "Shelby, give me your hands."

"Righto." She stuck her hands obligingly out toward me, cupping them to make a rough bowl shape.

I started trimming the green tops off the onions before cutting the onions themselves into quarters. The leafy parts I dropped to the ground, while the onions went into Shelby's hands. "Everyone take a few chunks of onion and rub them all over your skin. I know it's not the world's most pleasant perfume, but as much as it bothers you, it'll be ten times worse for the lindworm."

"My eyes are already burning," said Shelby.

"I have more eyes than you do," countered Dee, and took a piece of onion.

"Regardless, if we're covered in onion, we won't smell like food. If we don't smell like food, the lindworm won't eat us. Since I'm opposed to being eaten, I'm okay with being a little onion-y." I finished cutting the last onion, and wiped my knife on my sleeve before tucking it back into my pocket. "Be sure to get the back of your neck, ears, and anything else that isn't covered by your clothes."

"You really do know how to party," said Shelby, dumping half the onions back into my hands before she started scrubbing herself down with the remainder.

"Ain't no party like a Price party," I said. Dee and Frank were covering each other in onion, moving with a careful efficiency that spoke to long years together. I glanced over at Shelby as I rubbed onion on my cheeks and neck. She didn't look like she needed any help. I still wanted to offer it.

This was exactly the wrong place to be wondering about the state of my relationship, which didn't do anything to make me stop doing it. Shelby and I had both been lying to each other, even if only through omission, and while that wasn't the most comfortable thing in the world, it was the level of commitment I'd been both comfortable with and ready for. Now that I knew she wasn't as much of an outsider in my world as I'd assumed, where did that leave us? She'd said that things were "different" between us now, but was that good or bad?

Sometimes I think things would be a lot easier to deal with if I didn't think so damn much.

"Done," announced Shelby, dropping the wrung-out shells of her onions to the ground. "Never seen a lindworm before. What color are they?"

"Greens and browns, mostly. Some of them have blue tails." I dropped my own onions. "Dee? Frank? How are you two doing?"

"Ready," said Dee.

"Great. Let's go hope that whatever's been attacking people in your woods is a lindworm."

"And if it isn't?" asked Frank.

"Well, then we've just seasoned ourselves nicely to be something's dinner."

The trees were silent as we moved from the open farm-land and into their leafy shade. Nice as it was to have a brief respite from the sun, I still tensed. There should have been frickens singing in the trees. Given the num-ber we'd found in a relatively accessible swamp, this stretch of protected, gorgon-occupied forest should have been the epicenter for a fricken population explosion. If they were missing—or worse, if they were silent—then something here was very wrong.

The only warning we had of the attack was a rustle in the bushes to the left. I turned toward it, one hand cheat-ing toward the gun I had tucked into the waistband of my pants, and the lindworm's tail caught me across the knees, whipping out from the right. I yelped and fell, the shouts of the others following me to the dirt.

The lindworm might have caught me off-guard, but that didn't mean I was going to stay that way for long. I turned the fall into a roll and bounced back to my feet, pistol drawn and in my hand as I scanned the foliage for the lindworm's head. "Back-to-back!" I shouted, hoping the others would get the point and move into a defensive position.

Shelby's shoulders hit mine almost immediately, their warm, reassuring weight accompanied by the strong smell of onions. "I thought you said these things didn't like onions!" she shouted.

"Lindworms won't *eat* onions, and they don't usually attack what they're not planning to eat!" I said. "I don't know what's going on with this one!" I'd only been able to catch a glimpse of the tail that hit me, but it had looked more mossy green than electric blue; this was ei-ther a female or an immature male, and either way, it wasn't the lindworm Dee and I had seen earlier. "Any-one have a line of sight on it?"

"No, and we're looking," said Dee tersely.

"Try to stun instead of killing if you can." Neither gor-gon was wearing any sort of eye covering. If they looked into the lindworm's eyes, it was going to be sorry. And yet I couldn't be, because it was going to kill us if we didn't find a way to stop it.

The tail lashed out again, this time cracking in the air like a whip before it withdrew into the bushes. A few seconds passed in silence—and then, with no more warning than that, the lindworm charged.

Its body was long enough that the tail hits had been coming from almost directly behind the head; it had been curved in a vast C-shape, using the brush for cover. When it came at us, its open mouth was pointed almost directly at me. I fired twice, aiming for the back of its throat. At least one of my shots struck home; the lindworm coughed, mouth slamming shut, and began to slither off to the left, either trying to flank or flee. It was impossible for me to tell which it was.

"I've got it!" shouted Dee, just as the lindworm's head flashed past my position, and my blood went cold.

Its eyes were granite-gray from side to side, with no pupil or sclera.

"You're not going to be able to stun it!" I whirled, firing twice more into its side. The lindworm hissed horribly and whipped around again, jaws snapping shut on the place where I would have been standing if Frank hadn't effortlessly yanked me out of the way. I fired at the lindworm again. Thanks could wait until we were no longer in immediate danger.

There was a whoop, and Shelby was abruptly sitting on the lindworm's back, straddling it like a cowgirl riding a bucking bronco at the rodeo. She hooked the fingers of one hand under the broad scales at the back of its skull, drawing a gun from her waistband with the other hand. Her grin died as she glanced my way, meeting my eyes.

Clenching my jaw, I nodded.

Shelby nodded back before pressing the muzzle of her gun against the soft membrane that protected the lindworm's inner ear. The lindworm bellowed, trying to shake her off. Shelby pulled the trigger.

It was a small report, mostly muffled by the lindworm's skull. The two that followed it were only a little louder. The lindworm fell. It didn't do it gracefully, and it didn't do it all at once; that wasn't possible for a creature of its size and bulk. Shelby leaped free before she could be pinned under the falling reptile, and I hurried away from Frank to help her catch her balance and pull her back from the lindworm's death throes.

It thrashed madly in the underbrush for several minutes, each part of its body seeming to get the news about its death at a slightly different rate. When the tail had finished twitching, I finally let go of Shelby. She looked at me, wide-eyed.

"What in the world is going on?" asked Frank.

"Just give me a second, okay?" I moved away from the group and toward the lindworm, my gun still out and at the ready. It didn't move. I prodded the side of its jaw with my foot. It didn't move. Finally, cautiously, I crouched down and touched the stone surface of its left eye.

The petrifaction was advanced enough to have converted the lindworm's entire eyeball. I peeled back the eyelid, feeling the inside edge, and found small, sandy protrusions marking the places where the conversion had begun in the soft interior tissues. It wasn't as advanced there—if it had been, the eyelid would no longer have been capable of moving flexibly—but it was spreading.

"Alex?" said Shelby.

"It's dead. I'm in no danger." The fact that it was dead said a lot about how far the petrifaction had spread. A bullet to the brain shouldn't have been enough to kill a lindworm.

I let go of the eyelid, pulling a knife from the lining of my sleeve, and began trying to pry up the edge of the lindworm's eyeball. Normally, eyes are pretty easy to pop out of their sockets, once you have the proper leverage. They're designed to move freely within their limited space, after all; an eye that can't be budged isn't going to be much use. Petrifaction had reduced the lindworm's ability to move its useless eyeballs to practically zero, but "practically zero" wasn't the same as nothing. I managed to wedge the tip of my knife under the eye in relatively short order, and pressed down, shifting the entire sphere up enough for me to get a good grip. I yanked. It came loose in my hand.

"Oh, my," breathed Dee.

"You took the words right out of my mouth," I said. Maybe with a little less swearing; what I'd been about to say would have been a good deal saltier.

You can't catch petrifaction from skin contact, but I was still careful as I turned the eyeball, studying it. The ocular nerves dangling from the base of the eye were still flesh, red and raw and dripping. The spot where they joined up with the eyeball itself was white and squishy, if inflamed; the tissue looked infected, and when I pressed my knife against it, the vitreous humor that leaked out was gray, cloudy with silt.

"Look at this," I said. "The vitreous humor has partially transformed. I'd need a hammer or a bone saw to tell how solid the interior of the eyeball is."

"You know, it's sort of nice to be surrounded by adults for a change," said Dee, with a nervous giggle. "At work, you'd need to follow that statement up with 'I mean the eye goo.'"

"Yeah, well, if I were dissecting a post-petrifaction lindworm at work, I'd have bigger problems than the vocabulary of today's youth." The inside of the lindworm's eye socket was red and raw and angry, with only small patches of petrifaction.

"That poor sweet baby," said Shelby. "It must have been hurting so bad. No wonder it attacked us."

"Marry me," I said distractedly, turning the eye over in my hand to study the front again.

"What was that?"

"Nothing. This lindworm is a female. Probably the mate of the one Dee and I tagged earlier. You should still be careful in this stretch of wood—the male is likely to come looking for her." I put the eye down next to the lindworm's head and stood. The knife went back into my sleeve. I wiped my hands against my pants, trying to get rid of the faintly sticky, gritty feeling the lindworm's vitreous humor had left behind. "All right. Can a cockatrice petrify something this size?"

"No."

The answer was very soft. It took me a moment to realize that it had come from Frank. I turned to face him.

The snakes atop his head had coiled themselves, tucking their heads under their bodies and going still. From my work with Dee, I knew that this was the gorgon equivalent of looking ashamed. "When you showed that picture I thought you were surely lying. That you had come to make trouble, and that there was no way one of us could be involved in any way. But this . . ." He indicated the lindworm. "A cockatrice is a fearsome predator. It can do a great deal of damage without any assistance from anyone, or anything, else. A human is nothing to a cockatrice. It will lock eyes and move on, never caring about the damage it has done."

"A lindworm is different."

Frank nodded. "Lindworms are larger, more solid . . . and not mammalian. Not even as much as a gorgon can be said to be mammalian. To petrify a lindworm takes something more powerful than the gaze of a cockatrice."

"I'm guessing from the look on your face right now that the venom of a Pliny's gorgon would be enough to do the job."

Expression grim, Frank nodded. "Yes. It would be enough to assist the process, if nothing else."

Shelby cleared her throat. "All right, this is all very fascinating, in that 'we're finally solving the murder mystery, aren't we clever' sort of way, but we're standing in the middle of a forest where a giant lizard just tried to eat us. Worse, we had to kill the poor thing to make it stop. So in the interest of not being eaten, and not killing anything else that doesn't absolutely have to be killed, how about we move on to where we were going in the first place, hmm?"

I stiffened at the reminder of how exposed we really were. The frickens were still silent; they still sensed danger in the trees. They could have been reacting to our presence.

They could have been reacting to something else.

"How much farther?" I asked Frank.

"This way," he said, and waved for us to follow as he turned and led us out of the woods. The body of the lindworm remained behind, a gruesome reminder that not all the deaths in this conflict were going to be human—and not all the victims were going to go down without a fight.

Sixteen

"Rules only matter if everyone understands them, agrees to them, and can be trusted not to break them. Bearing those irrefutable facts in mind, rules never matter at all."

—Thomas Price

At a hidden gorgon community in the middle of the Ohio woods, emerging from the tree line, having not been eaten by a lindworm

WE WERE ONLY A short distance from the other side of the trees. If the dead lindworm's mate was around, he didn't attack us as we walked. The frickens started singing again after we had passed, their tiny, cheerful cries of "creep, creep, creep" signaling that the danger had passed. To them, we must have been as frightening as the lindworm, at least in the aftermath of our fight. Hopefully, they'd get over their fear of us. I didn't want to walk through those woods again without an early warning system.

Then we stepped out of the trees, and I stopped thinking about the frickens. I was too busy staring.

When Frank and Dee called this area of the community "the fringe," I naturally pictured the worst: ramshackle sheds, rusted-out trailers, and a few unkempt farmers with broken shovels in their hands, telling us to get off of their land. It was a terrible stereotype of something that had probably never been invented before—the redneck gorgon—and seeing the reality just made me feel worse about harboring those thoughts.

The main community was mostly mobile homes, designed to move at a moment's notice. Here on the fringe, everything was built to last. A half dozen small brick houses were spaced around the edges of a wide green space, and more were half-hidden by the trees on the other side of the clearing. There was a grain silo, and three separate buildings that were either barns or stables of some sort. People worked in the field, bowed over their hoes and shovels. Like the gorgons back in the main community, they were bare-headed, allowing their snakes the freedom to taste the air. Unlike those gorgons, they were mostly bare-chested as well, exposing the scaled patches on their backs and shoulders. What clothing they did wear was plainly homemade, the sort of thing that could be stitched by hand.

If not for the snakes growing atop the head of every farmer and field hand we saw, this could have been taken for a human farming community, albeit one that should have existed a hundred years ago, or two hundred years ago, not in modern-day Ohio.

"Welcome to the fringe," said Frank, not bothering to smother the disdain in his voice. "Come, this way." He struck out across the field. Lacking any better plan, Shelby and I followed, with Dee bringing up the rear.

Shelby stepped close enough that she could drop her voice and murmur, "This isn't what I was figuring on."

"You're not alone there," I said, matching her tone. "They don't look . . ."

"Friendly? No, they don't, at that." A few of the nearer farmhands had spotted us and stopped their work in favor of glaring. Shelby offered one of them a jaunty wave. He kept glaring. "But you notice, they're pointing most of the unhappy at our guide? It's like we've already been vetted to know that they exist, so they're focusing their nasty on the other gorgons."

"That makes sense." A community this size would have to have human allies, even if they didn't know that they were dealing with gorgons. Local farmers, garden supply stores, even feed stores, if they were serious about keeping livestock. They could pretend to be independent, but they were still connected to the greater world, just like the rest of us. "The fact that we made it this far means they know we're not Covenant. That's probably all that matters."

"Low bar."

"You work with what you have."

"Guess that's true." Shelby's tone changed, turning amused, as she asked, "So what was that about proposing marriage back there in the woods? You *were* talking to me and not the lindworm, right?"

My ears reddened. I pushed my glasses back up and said primly, "I don't know what you're talking about. You probably heard something wrong while we were trying not to be eaten."

"You mean while *you* were trying not to be eaten. I was doing pretty okay. And my ears are fine."

"Yes, about that. How did you know how to fight a lindworm?"

Shelby shrugged. "I didn't. I just assumed that what would work on a crocodile would work on one of these big fellas, too."

I stared at her. "You didn't."

"What are you complaining about? You're alive, aren't you?"

Try as I might, I couldn't come up with a response to that.

As it turned out, I didn't need to. A door opened in the nearest brick house and a man emerged. He was wearing a shirt and vest, but his head was bare, and the snakes growing there were long and healthy. Their scales were a pale silver that accentuated his dark tan. He was carrying a hoe. It seemed like a threat, rather than a farming tool. His size helped with that; he was almost a foot taller than Frank, with the solid build of a man who made his living from the land.

Frank stopped walking, motioning for the rest of us to do the same. "Walter," he said coldly.

"Franklin," Walter replied. He stopped several yards away, eyeing first me and then Shelby with open disdain. He didn't look at Dee at all. His gaze lingered on Shelby's hair, lip curling slightly, the way a human man's might if he were looking at road kill or something else disgusting. "This is my land. Why are you here?"

The question seemed directed at all of us. I cleared my throat. "My name is Alexander—"

"I know who you are, *human*." He spat the word between us. "I knew as soon as you set your filthy feet in this state. You have no business here, and yet here you stand. Why are you here?" His gaze flicked to Frank, then finally to Dee. "Unless you've brought me a breeding pair as a peace offering . . . ?"

"Don't be disgusting," said Dee. She was lisping slightly. I glanced to the side, unsurprised to see that her fangs had dropped. "These people are our allies."

"You're seeking allies among the apes now? You've fallen even farther into disgrace than I feared."

Frank shook his head. "There is no talking to you, is there? There never has been, and there never will be."

"Yet here you stand, like there's some purpose in trying," said Walter. "Which of us is the fool?"

"Sounds to me like you are, but I'm just a monkey, so what do I know?" All of us turned to look at Shelby. She shrugged broadly. "It's a little silly not to listen to someone who's come all the way here to see you, don't you think? Oh, and fought the dragon-worm-thing that was living in your woods, mustn't forget that. It was big, too. You should be quite impressed and happy to talk to us."

Walter blinked, the snakes atop his head stirring and beginning to taste the air. "You saw the lindworms and lived?" he asked. "How is that possible?"

"Onions will usually keep lindworms from attacking,

but in this case, we saw the lindworm—singular, it was the female—and lived mostly because it had already been blinded," I said. "It was half petrified. That made it easy to kill, and that's why we're here. There's a cockatrice running around Columbus, and there's a gorgon helping it turn people into stone. Deanna brought me, and my associate, to talk to you and see if there was anything you might know about this."

"To accuse us, you mean," said Walter flatly.

"Easy to kill?" said Shelby.

"Sir, I'm a Price. Do you really think I would risk everything my family has built solely for the chance to accuse you of something we both know you didn't do?"

Walter blinked again. Then his eyes narrowed. "Come again, son?"

"No, I'm back on 'easy,'" said Shelby. "You think that was *easy* to kill?"

I tried to ignore her, focusing on Walter. "You're too tall to have come into the city without being noticed. Maybe—*maybe*—you could have driven the cockatrice to the city limits and dropped it off, but you'd have had no way of catching it again, and you wouldn't have been able to bite the second man we found. We're here because we need help, and because I heard you've been trying to work with gorgon-safe livestock. I wanted to talk to you about that."

Walter eyed me for a few moments more before he turned to Frank and Dee. "Is he telling the truth?"

"Alexander Price is one of the worst liars I've ever met," said Dee. "Mostly he just tries not to say anything that might get him questioned."

"I've been dating him for months, and I can back up everything she just said," said Shelby, raising her hand. "I thought he was shy at first. Then I thought he was being controlled by a telepathic murder-bitch. It's much better now that I know he's just a terrible liar."

"Yes, that's much better," I mumbled, and turned back to Walter. "Have you ever kept cockatrice here?"

"Yes," he said, without hesitation. "They can meet our eyes without harm. That's more than you can do."

"That's absolutely true," I said. "Can you show me where they were kept?"

His chuckle was slow and deep, like rocks shaking beneath the surface of the earth. "I can do more than that," he said. "I can show you where they are."

Following a Pliny's gorgon I barely knew into a cockatrice coop could probably be moved straight to the top of my list of The Dumbest Things I Have Ever Voluntarily Done. It helped that I was armed, but it only helped a little; gorgons and cockatrice are armed by definition. They wouldn't even need to draw their weapons.

Shelby stuck close to my side as we entered the darkened building. It smelled like a combination of reptile house and pigeon roost, the hot, dry stink of too many reptiles jammed into an enclosed space mingling with feathers, dust, and the unavoidable oceans of bird shit. The ceiling was high enough for both Walter and Frank to stand upright. Light filtered in through cracks between the boards, turned smoky by the dust that hung suspended in the air.

The walls were lined with roosting boxes, and black lumps filled them, occasionally making sleepy clucking noises. I couldn't get an accurate population count in the darkness. I tried, reached "many" as a final number three times, and gave it up as a bad plan. "Many" was terrifying enough.

"You may want to stay back," said Walter, and picked up his pace, using his longer legs to get to the middle of the coop while the rest of us were still hanging back by the door. He grabbed the rope that dangled from the ceiling and gave it a solid yank. A trapdoor swung open, hinges creaking, and revealed the chicken wire dome that we had passed through on our way to the building. I had to give the fringe gorgons this much: they were being careful with their cockatrice (although being really careful would have meant not keeping cockatrice at all). The coop, and a decent amount of the area around it, was completely surrounded by chicken wire, reinforced and double thick. Nothing was getting out of here accidentally.

The lumps in the roosting boxes began to stir as the light hit them. They didn't make the usual broody noises of suddenly-wakened chickens; these sounds were more like the small screeches of angry parrots, combined with an unnerving amount of hissing. Shelby's hand found mine, grabbing hold and squeezing tightly. I squeezed back, trying to be reassuring.

Then the first cockatrice jumped from its brooding box to the floor of the coop, ruffling its feathers as it bobbed its head in a distinctly avian way. It turned to look at us, first with one eye, then with the other, before opening its mouth and hissing. It was a sound more suited to a dinosaur than anything that should have been walking the earth in this day and age.

I stared, caught between horror and awe. "It's *beautiful*."

The cockatrice was about the size of a wild turkey, with a pointed, reptilian head that shared more attributes with a small predatory dinosaur than it did with a modern bird. Its teeth were a jagged sea of points and tearing surfaces, and its only concession to a beak was the hardened "egg tooth"-like scale on the very tip of its snout. It would use that egg tooth-like protrusion to chip away petrifaction inside the bodies of its victims. The feathers started about halfway down its neck, brown and green with hints of yellow, and continued all the way down its birdlike body to the long whip of its serpentine tail. The feathers on its tail-tip were shockingly red. It opened its wings and flapped them in a threat display, revealing more red feathers. Only its leathery wings were completely devoid of plumage. It didn't advance, and none of the other cockatrice came down to join it.

With the trapdoor in the ceiling open, I could finally get an accurate count. There were fifteen cockatrice in the room. That was fifteen cockatrice too many.

"We're not missing any, if that was going to be your next question," said Walter, reaching down and picking up the cockatrice that was currently trying to intimidate us. It hissed and struck at his arm. He responded by wrapping one big hand around its muzzle, effectively removing the threat of its teeth. It locked eyes with him, continuing to stare as it waited for him to turn to stone. Cockatrice aren't very bright.

"This is . . . a lot of cockatrice," I said, trying to mask my discomfort. It wasn't working.

"We'd have more if we could get them to breed," said Walter. "Cockatrice meat can be quite tasty, and their eggs work well in anything that you'd use chicken eggs for."

"Pass," said Shelby instantly.

Walter snorted, sounding more amused than annoyed. "Can't get them to breed, though, no matter how much we try. I'm starting to think it's a matter of space—they want more territory before they're willing to reproduce. As it stands, we have to buy new pullets every time we eat one."

"How much do they taste like chicken?" It was an odd question, on the surface of things. It was also a serious one. People say that everything tastes like chicken, but they're quite wrong. Rattlesnake, for example, is spicy even if prepared with no seasonings at all, and goat tastes more like venison than anything else that people regularly farm.

"I don't know," said Walter. "What does chicken taste like?"

That was the answer I was afraid of. "I'm sorry to have to be the one to tell you this," I said, "but someone's been stealing your cockatrice."

Silence reigned . . . but only for a moment. Shelby put up her hand while the gorgons were still staring at me and asked, in a small voice, "Could we maybe have the earth-shaking revelations somewhere that *isn't* in the coop filled with demon chickens? Because I come from the deadliest place on the planet, and these things are giving me the heebie-jeebies."

Walter blinked at her. Then, ruefully, he laughed.

"All right," he said. "Let's take this inside."

Walter's home was quite nice, and would have fit right into most Amish farmsteads, as long as they were willing to overlook the terrified cage of fancy mice in his pantry, next to the potatoes. He saw me looking and closed the pantry door.

"Every man's allowed his little vices," he said, in a challenging tone. "I trade for them with the community."

"White mice taste better," said Dee. She smiled at me, a slightly frayed air behind her apparent cheerfulness. She didn't like being here, on the fringe, in the home of a man who represented an ideology she didn't believe in. But she was trying, and I respected that.

"I'll take your word for that," I said, and turned back to Walter. "When did you begin keeping cockatrice?"

"Three years ago," he said. "We get them from a family of Bigfoot who live upstate. They trap cockatrice for us, we give them organic produce. They're very fond of 'organic.' I didn't know most people grew inorganic tomatoes."

Lecturing this man on the local and organic food movement seemed like a bad idea. Instead, I nodded, and asked, "When did you start trying to breed them?"

"Right from the beginning. It hasn't worked yet, but we keep trying." He shot a poisonous glare at Frank, the snakes on his head stirring themselves to hiss. "It might go faster if we could get some books on animal husbandry to reference."

"Buy them yourselves," snapped Frank. "Or get on the Internet and order them like normal people."

"You're allowing human culture to corrupt you," Walter snapped back.

"You want human books. How is that any different?"

"We don't *need* them!" Now the snakes atop both men's heads were standing erect, hissing loudly and showing their fangs.

"You may not need human things, but you're both doing an excellent job of embarrassing yourselves in front of the humans," said Dee quietly. The men turned to look at her. "This isn't their fight. Perhaps we should stop providing them with a free demonstration of why it's ours."

"Ah." Walter leaned back in his seat, composing his expression. His snakes kept hissing, but otherwise stood down. "My apologies to our guests."

"But not to your brother-in-law?" asked Frank.

"No, Franklin. Never to you." Walter looked to me. "Why do you think we are so incompetent as to have lost a cockatrice?"

"I don't think you were incompetent," I said, trying not to react to the revelation that Dee was Walter's sister. "I think you were tricked. If you don't know what chicken tastes like . . . the bones are similar. It would be easy to purchase a chicken or small turkey at a grocery store, make soup, and claim that it was cockatrice. With enough wild garlic and onion, the flavor would be even more confused. You'd never know. The count in your aviary would remain accurate, and whoever hatched the plan would be free to do what they liked with the cockatrice."

"None of my people would enter your city, or attack in such a vulgar way."

"No. But they might be willing to trade a cockatrice for something they wanted and couldn't otherwise have."

Walter stood abruptly, his chair legs scraping against the wooden floor. "Come with me," he commanded, and strode toward the door. He didn't look back. Shelby and I exchanged a glance, and then we followed after him.

There was a brass bell outside Walter's door, old and battered and streaked with verdigris. When he rang it, it sounded like it should have been audible all the way into the next county. The echoes were still fading when the fringe gorgons came, walking in from the fields, from the houses, and from the various outbuildings. They were all dressed like the ones we'd already seen, in home-stitched clothes and plain, simple colors. The impression that we'd wandered into the world's strangest Amish farm-stead kept growing, even though I knew it was wrong.

"These people," said Walter, in a booming voice, "have come from the community, with news of the human cities. One of our cockatrice is loose. So I ask: who has given a cockatrice to an outsider? Do not lie to me. I will know." He scanned the crowd, focusing his attention on a group of teenagers who stood slightly apart from the others. One of them was staring at the ground, the snakes atop her head virtually braiding themselves as they twisted together.

Walter stepped away from the porch, walking over to her. "Marian," he said softly. "What is it that you want to tell me?"

"I . . ." She raised her head, biting her lip before she said, "I'm sorry, sir, I'm so very sorry, I didn't know he was going to keep it, and he offered . . ."

"Marian." The gorgon girl stopped talking. Walter crouched down so that his eyes were level with hers. "What did you do?"

She took a deep breath. "A man came through the forest, past the lindworm. He said the community had sent him. Said they needed a cockatrice, but that they were ashamed to ask it of you. He brought payment. A dead bird in a bag for the stew, and sweets for the children, and good yarn for the knitters. All he asked was one of the young males, and we had too many . . ."

"And you gave it to him?"

Marian's voice seemed to desert her. She bit her lip again, and nodded.

"I see." Walter's hand lashed out almost too fast to follow, grabbing a fistful of her snakes and yanking. The rest hissed madly, but didn't try to bite him. I guess even snakes can be smart, under the right circumstances. He turned back to the rest of us. "You should go now. You have done enough damage."

"Walter . . ." began Dee.

"You are as much of an outsider here as these apes that you sully yourself by traveling with," spat Walter. "Our father would be ashamed to see what you've grown into. Go."

I took Shelby's hand, sparing one last glance for the girl, Marian, who was weeping as she hung limply in her captor's hand. If he'd been human, I would have tried to do something—but it's not my place to criticize the culture of the cryptids we work with. Gritting my teeth to keep from saying something I would regret, I turned, and let Frank lead us away from the fringe, back across the fields to the woods.

The lindworm's body was still sprawled where we had left it. It was still too fresh to have attracted any large predators, and its partially-petrified state was probably confusing the bugs. I stopped to pick up the eye I'd pried loose earlier, shoving it into my jacket pocket. Maybe I could learn more about the petrifaction process by studying it. It was worth the effort.

We'd been gone long enough for the frickens to forget what had happened earlier. Their small, piping voices escorted us back through the woods, and no more lindworms came to kill us. After what we'd been through so far today, that was enough for me.

Seventeen

"Try your best. That's always been enough
for the people who love you."
—Alexander Healy

Finishing dinner in a hidden gorgon community in the middle of the Ohio woods

DINNER WAS SERVED AT a long table in the middle of the community's "town square." It consisted of root vegetable stew with unidentified chunks of meat that I suspected were either rabbit or jackalope, home baked bread, and suspicious looks from virtually everyone around us. I couldn't blame them, considering the situation. It had probably been a very long time since Hannah had invited humans to dine with her chosen family. Shelby and I might have impeccable table manners and the best of intentions, but we were still mammals, and hence not to be trusted. Also, we smelled like onions.

Some of the gorgon teenagers cleared our plates when we were finished eating, despite not having dined with us; they had their own table, set a little ways off from the adults, where they wouldn't be scolded or looked at funny for the crime of being teenagers. They cast sidelong looks at Shelby and me as they removed dishes from the table, and more than a few of the girls looked longingly at her hair. Not in a "I wish I were human" sort of way—more in a "what a wonderful fashion accessory" way.

Dee smiled as the last of the girls left. Leaning toward Shelby, she confessed, "When I was thirteen, I dreamt about starting a wig shop just for gorgons. Hair is so much *fun.* You can't style snakes. They pretty much style themselves, and you just get to learn to live with it."

"Bet you save a mint on shampoo, though," said Shelby.

That was the right thing to say. The other gorgons at the table—five in all, bringing our total number to ten— laughed, some of the tension slipping out of the gathering.

One of the men looked at me, and asked, "So you're really Jonathan Healy's boy?"

"I'm his great-grandson," I said. "Forgive me for my ignorance, but ... you look way too young to have known him. He died before my father was born."

"I am the only one here who actually knew dear Johnny, but all of us know of him," said Hannah. "He was a great friend to the gorgon community. To all of the gorgon communities, really, in the places where we were divided as well as the places where we came together."

I blinked. Hannah smiled a little.

"My tales do not match what you know of your own history, do they? Does your family still keep Aeslin mice?"

"Yes, ma'am," I said. It seemed best to be respectful when speaking to a gorgon hybrid whose age and capabilities were unknown to me. Respect is rarely the thing that gets you killed.

"Ask them. They may have moved some of the celebrations and festivals into the background, but they will remember who he was, and what he did for the people who put their faith in him. That is the beauty of the Aeslin." Her smile grew a bit, turning almost wistful. "They never forget anything; they never leave anything behind."

"Speaking of forgetting things," I said, as delicately as I could, "weren't we supposed to be discussing what our next move was going to be?"

"Don't worry: it was not forgotten, merely ... set aside for a short time, to allow us to remember that we are all friends here. We *are* all friends here, are we not?" Hannah's smile suddenly seemed to contain a few too many teeth, and those teeth were very, very sharp.

There are times when no amount of reminding myself that I am a trained professional can override the small, frightened part of the mammalian brain, the one that is always six inches away from being eaten by something larger. I managed to swallow my shudder, but I couldn't stop my skin from breaking out in goose bumps. "I'd certainly like to be, ma'am."

"Good." Hannah turned her attention on Dee, and I suddenly found it much easier to breathe. It's never fun to be reminded that humans aren't necessarily the apex predators on this planet. "What did your brother have to tell you?"

"That he's lost a cockatrice recently, although he didn't realize it until we came to see him; one of his little farmhands sold it to someone who came through the woods claiming to have been sent by us."

"I see. Please do tell Walter that I am displeased with his ability to mind his people. I expected better of him than this. Your father always kept the fringe separate and safe. Your brother should do the same, if he expects to be allowed to keep it."

Dee flinched, and nodded. "I'll tell him."

"So we know where the cockatrice was acquired, and better, we know that it is unlikely whoever is responsible will have access to more than one." Hannah turned back to me as the gorgon teens returned with trays of cheese and fruit. "Are you satisfied that none of us is responsible for this horror?"

Every instinct I had shrieked at me to tell the nice giant snake-lady that yes, of course I was satisfied, now if she would please just refrain from eating me, that would be swell. Sometimes, training wins out over common sense. "Respectfully, ma'am, I am convinced of the exact opposite. I do believe you have not, as a community, declared war on the city of Columbus with nothing more than a single cockatrice. If you chose to break the peace, you would be much more efficient, and we wouldn't be sitting here now. But Walter—who seems to keep his people on a *very* tight leash—was able to lose a cockatrice without realizing it. Dee comes and goes with impunity, and she can't be the only one. I can't say for sure that someone here is responsible for this. I can't say for sure that the opposite is true, either." I decided not to mention the lindworm. No cockatrice could have petrified it, but that would just complicate things in the here and now.

"What Alex means to say is 'no,'" said Shelby. "Forgive him. His mother was a dictionary, and he feels like he's dishonoring her if he uses simple words."

I opened my mouth to protest, and stopped as I saw that Hannah was laughing silently, her mouth open and her fangs on casual display. Sinking back in my seat, I blinked and waited to hear what she would say next.

"Your point is a valid, if long-winded, one," she said finally. "Go, then, Alexander Healy, and I will speak to those who dwell here with me. If there is a traitor or a misguided crusader in our midst, I will find them."

"And will you tell me?" I asked. I didn't bother to correct her on my last name. If she was a fan of my great-grandfather's, I might as well take advantage of whatever goodwill that was going to buy me.

"I will," she said. "I will not surrender them to you, but I assure you, justice will be done, within the standards of our law."

Based on what I knew of gorgon law, that meant the offender would either get a stern lecture, or a swift death. I took a breath. "If there is any danger remaining to the people of Ohio—"

"There won't be," she said, and this time, when she smiled, there was no mistaking her fangs for teeth.

"I think that went well," said Shelby amiably, as Dee and Frank walked us both out to my car. Faces peeked at us through the darkness; the gorgon teens who had served during dinner, trying to get one last look at their interesting guests. "No one got bitten and we didn't need antivenin, so I'm calling it a victory."

"You have an interesting definition of 'victory,'" said Dee. She sounded exhausted.

"I'm with Shelby here, actually," I said. "We've learned a lot, we've established that we mean no harm, and nobody got hurt, unless you count the poor lindworm."

"We put that creature out of its misery," said Frank. "Nothing reverses petrifaction that has gone that far. It would have died anyway, writhing and in pain."

"Cheerful," I said. I turned to Dee. "See you at work tomorrow?"

She blinked, and the snakes atop her head hissed in genuine surprise. "You still want me to come to work?"

"Dee, I knew you were a gorgon when I hired you, and I know neither you nor your husband is responsible for what's happening at the zoo. I don't think I can manage a cockatrice hunt *and* keep the reptile house running if I don't have my assistant. Not to mention the part where I'm pretty much expecting the rest of the staff to stop showing up any day now. Most folks don't like going to work when they're afraid it will get them killed."

Dee smiled a little. "I'll see you tomorrow."

"Good." I extended my hand toward Frank. "It was a pleasure to meet you. If you ever need a source for larger medical supplies, let me know. My mother knows a Bigfoot metalworker who makes his own extra-large tools and equipment. She swears by his products."

Frank looked pleased as he took my hand, his fingers

eclipsing mine completely. "I will keep that in mind, Mr. Price," he said. "This has been a very ... edifying ... evening. I look forward to seeing you again under less troubled circumstances."

"Nice meeting everyone," said Shelby. "You throw a good party. I wish everyone would arrange for giant lizard fights as an icebreaker."

Dee laughed. There didn't seem to be a better farewell than that, and so I got into the car, waiting for Shelby to do the same before I fastened my seat belt, started the engine, and pulled away.

Shelby stayed quiet as we drove out of the small gorgon community and up the winding path that would take us to the main road. Only when we were back on the highway, pointed toward Columbus, did she relax, and I realized just how wary she had actually been.

"Shelby? You all right over there?"

"I hope you won't think less of me for admitting I've been scared out of my mind for the last few hours."

"Only the last few hours?" I merged smoothly with the oncoming traffic. "'Cause see, I've been scared out of my mind since the lindworm tried to eat us."

"That was about the only thing that *didn't* scare me," said Shelby, with a ragged-edged laugh. "Australia's not all crocodiles, no matter what the movies try to tell you, but I went to university as a zoology major. I worked in animal conservation in Queensland. Giant lizards that want to eat me are familiar enough to be almost comforting."

"I'd think less of you if you hadn't been afraid," I said quietly. "Fear is natural. It's a close cousin of respect, and between the two, we don't forget that this isn't our world. We can police the edges, we can keep things from getting more unpleasant than they need to be, but we're never going to belong to places like that. And that's okay. We were born human. There's no shame in that."

Shelby laughed. "I think I like you better now that you're being honest with me."

"That's good. I know I like you better."

"Alex . . ." Shelby took a breath. "Are we going to get any more work done tonight?"

"It's late. We have to work in the morning, and we won't have a copy of the autopsy report for the second guard until tomorrow afternoon."

"No midnight cockatrice hunts?"

"Not for me, thanks. We've confirmed that the cockatrice has a handler, and by now the handler is probably on his guard. This isn't an ordinary wild animal hunt anymore." I chuckled a little. "Because 'ordinary' was totally the word before this."

"I see." Shelby's hand was somehow resting on my thigh, her fingers slipping a little higher than could be explained by a friendly pat. "You know, it'd probably be best if neither of us went about without backup for a little bit. Just for now, you understand, until nothing's trying to kill us."

"I'm a Price," I said. "Something's always trying to kill me."

Shelby's smile was a white slash against the darkness. "Then it's a good thing we're giving our relationship another go, isn't it?"

I broke speed limits all the way home.

My place had my grandparents, either of whom could hold their own in a fight; Crow, whose contribution was mostly in the "making a lot of noise" area, but which could very well be enough to frighten off a cockatrice; and Sarah, who, even wounded and occasionally discombobulated, could at least confuse anyone who intended to do us harm.

It also had the mice.

In the end, there was no question of where we were going to wind up. I parked in one of the visitor spots at Shelby's apartment complex, pausing to text Grandma with my location before I got out of the car. She sent back an immediate one-word reply: "FIGURES." I snorted, shaking my head.

"Something funny?" asked Shelby, looking back over her shoulder as she walked up the short path between the parking area and the building. Her key was already in her hand, but she wasn't watching the bushes for signs of movement. I'd have to talk to her about that.

Later. Much, much later. "Just checking in with home," I said, scanning the landscaping as I moved to stand behind her. "Grandma says 'hi.'"

Shelby laughed as she unlocked the door. "Bet that's not *exactly* what she said."

"No, but she didn't say anything nasty, so I'm calling it a win." I caught the heavy door before it could slam on my foot, shouldering my way past it. It slammed behind me with a bang that sounded like it should have shaken the whole building. "Oof. Has that thing ever killed anyone?"

"Don't know, didn't ask. The rent was low enough to make it tolerable. You know what kind of money I make." The air in the hall was hot, with that strange pseudo-humidity that only seems to materialize in housing complexes and zoo buildings. Following Shelby up the stairs to the second floor was a lot like walking into the big cat house in the morning, even down to the distant smell of boiled meat.

"I save most of my salary by living at home," I admitted. It made a huge difference. When I was trying to maintain my own place, I'd been calling home to ask for ammo at least twice a month. Now I could afford my own supplies, even if I couldn't stretch my funds to pay for much more than that.

"Not an option for me, I'm afraid," said Shelby. She opened the door to the second-floor hall, freeing another gust of hot air to slap us across the faces. "The commute would be *murder*."

"And it's best to avoid murder when possible," I agreed.

The hallway carpet was worn so thin it provided no cushion at all; you could actually hear our footsteps as we walked the thirty or so feet between the stairwell door and her apartment. Shelby undid the locks and stepped inside, one hand going to the gun I now knew she had concealed beneath the waistband of her tan business casual slacks. She scanned the darkened living room before clicking on the light and scanning again, visibly searching for anything that had been moved or taken.

After a few seconds, she relaxed, flashing me a smile. "Come on in, then. We're safe."

"You realize I believed you when you told me your little 'checking the room' routine was born out of the fear of huntsman spiders," I said, closing the door. I flipped the deadbolt with my thumb, and it locked with a satisfying "snick."

"That part was sort of true," she said, shrugging out of her jacket and slinging it over the back of her Goodwill-brand couch. She grinned sharp and quick as she un-belted the holster from around her waist. "If you'd ever seen a huntsman spider, you'd be as paranoid about them as I am. Bastards can hug your entire face with all their horrible, horrible legs."

"I bet they're fascinating," I said.

"Yeah, a spider that can hug a human face, 'fascinating' is absolutely the word for it." Shelby stepped closer to me, close enough that I could smell the remnants of her deodorant under the wild onion that we had rubbed all over ourselves back in the field. I'd almost stopped noticing it.

I smiled, reaching out to smooth back a lock of her hair. "You smell like onion field."

"You're no bed of roses yourself," she said, raising her eyebrows. "You proposing a way to fix the problem?"

"I think I am, yes," I said, and told her.

Fitting two full-sized adults into Shelby's shower was difficult, but not impossible, as long as we were willing to be very, very friendly with one another. After we finished with the all-important business of washing off the onion, we found being very, very friendly to be an easy task indeed.

Shelby pushed me up against the wall once the ... friendliness ... had scaled back a little, resting her elbows on my chest and smiling at me like a cat with a mouthful of canary. I put my hands on either side of her waist, lending just a little bit of extra stability.

"Hello, Mr. Price," she practically purred. "My, that name suits you. Got any more lies you want to stop telling me?"

"Um ... I probably *was* checking out your ass at the work Christmas party, but in my defense, you asked me to."

"Mmm. So just the normal lies, then." She leaned in and kissed me, her breasts a distracting pressure against my skin.

Almost as distracting as the water that was running down my face. I tried to surreptitiously shake some of it away.

Shelby pulled back, and snorted. "Little damp, are you?"

"That's the point of the shower, isn't it?" I reached around her, fumbling until my hand found the faucet. Shutting the water off, I continued, "But sometimes dry can be nice."

"You sweet-talker, you," said Shelby, delivering another kiss before she peeled herself away from me and opened the shower curtain. Her bathroom was small, and with her clothes, my clothes, and my weapons covering every available surface, it looked even more cluttered than the rest of the apartment.

Shelby stepped out of the bathroom long enough to grab two towels from the adjacent closet, dripping all the way. As she came back, she thrust one of the towels out toward me, and said, "You know, this is the first time you've let me see you undress."

"I'm sure you can see why," I said, with a nod toward the tidy array of knives, handguns, and other accoutrements that I had made atop her toilet tank.

"I would have looked at you a bit askance when you pulled the brass knuckles out, it's true," she said, beginning to rub the side of her head. She was still naked, and if the weight of her breasts had been distracting, the way they jiggled as she towel-dried her hair was downright enthralling.

Pulling my eyes away from her breasts, I wrapped my own towel around my waist and reached for my glasses. "I'm always armed. That's been hard to explain sometimes. One of the girls I dated in college was convinced I belonged to a very strange branch of Mormonism, since I was perfectly happy to let her see me naked, and even happier to see her naked, but I never let her see me take my clothes off."

"Discussion of ex-girlfriends, eh? I guess fighting a giant lizard really is the sort of thing that brings a couple closer together."

Shelby's tone was light, but that didn't tell me much—Shelby's tone was almost always light. She was the sort of girl who could sound laid-back and utterly pleasant as she was removing your spleen with a claw hammer. I put my glasses on as I turned to look at her.

She was still holding the towel, but she wasn't making any effort to dry herself off. Instead, she was just looking at me, a complicated mixture of sadness and exhaustion in her face.

"Shelby?"

"I just . . ." She shook her head, slinging her towel around her shoulders. "No. It's silly, and it'll just spoil a pleasant evening."

"Shelby." I took an awkward half-step around the sink, reaching for her hand. "What's wrong?"

"Nothing. Everything. I just . . . oh, come out of the bathroom, will you? This is a terrible place to have any sort of conversation that isn't about soap." She turned, moving a little faster than was strictly necessary, her wet feet leaving a trail of dark spots on the plain brown carpet.

I raked wet hair out of my eyes as I followed her to the apartment's lone bedroom. It was as small and hastily-furnished as everything else, with a queen-sized bed that was really just two mattresses stacked on top of each other and left in the middle of the floor. But she had plenty of pillows, and her linens always smelled like eucalyptus, thanks to the essential oils she added to the laundry every time she had to wash the sheets. (She said it made her feel more like she was home when she was trying to go to sleep. I couldn't fault the sentiment; I didn't add pine oil to everything, but I'd been known to buy scented Christmas candles for the sole purpose of pretending that I was back at home in Portland).

Shelby dropped her towel into the hamper next to her bedroom door as she walked to the bed. She smoothed the duvet with an almost fussy motion before she turned to face me and sat, folding her hands tightly together in her lap. Something about the solemnity of her pose made me feel like I was the one who was exposed, even though I had a towel around my waist, while she was completely nude.

"Alex, what are we doing?" she asked.

I froze. There were half a dozen possible answers to that question, ranging from flippant to overly serious, and I had no living clue which one was appropriate. After standing silent for what felt like way too long, I settled on the most honest answer of them all: "I don't know."

"And here I was hoping at least one of us did." Shelby shook her head. "I thought we were having a bit of fun, you know? You were the American zoologist who didn't know anything about anything—not even that he'd got Johrlac preying on him—and I was going to go home with a clear conscience when everything was done. At least you'd have gotten laid, and that's payment enough, for most men. Only now you're a Price. You're part of the world I come from."

Suddenly, I understood what she had been trying to tell me earlier in the car. "I was your vacation fling, and now I'm not, and you're not sure how to deal with that," I said.

Shelby bit her lip and nodded.

"Look, Shelby . . . if it helps at all, I didn't expect things to go this way either. I'm not suddenly going to propose," even though I sort of had, back when we were standing over the lindworm's carcass, "and I'm not going to hate you forever and badmouth you to all the American cryptozoologists if we break up."

"You promise?" she asked, looking up at me through her eyelashes.

"I promise. This just means I don't have to come up with stupid excuses when I have to work. Maybe you and I can even help each other out sometimes. You can learn more about North American cryptids before you have to go back to Australia." I walked over to the bed and sat down next to her, taking her hands. "Does this change things? Well, yeah, and it's probably good that we're talking about it, even if I might have waited to have the conversation until there wasn't a cockatrice running around the zoo and—anyway, what I'm trying to say is that we can make this work without it turning into anything we don't want it to be."

"I'm glad you think so." Shelby turned her head enough to smile at me, suddenly radiant even in the harsh white light of her bedroom, and my heart gave a lurch.

Oh, hell, I thought, almost distracted, even as she leaned over and pressed her lips against mine. My body, noting the lack of guiding intelligence coming from the brain, decided to get on with things. Even as she pushed me over backward on the bed, I was thinking, and what I was thinking was simple and complicated all at the same time:

I could tell her I wasn't going to make things serious on her, and I could tell her I was done lying, and I could do both those things as much as I wanted.

I was still lying.

I was in love, and I was so screwed.

Eighteen

"Love doesn't care what you want. Love doesn't care if it's convenient. Love pursues its own agenda, and there's no bullet in the world that can take it down. More's the pity."

—Jonathan Healy

A rundown apartment in Columbus, Ohio, sometime after midnight, waking up on a bed that could really use more lumbar support

SHELBY WAS NESTLED AGAINST my side when I woke up. Some subtle change in the atmosphere of the room had disturbed me, although I had no idea what it was. Grainy gray light filtered in through the half-closed blinds, providing enough illumination for me to find my glasses, fumble them open, and slide them onto my face. Shelby made a small protesting noise, her arm still draped across my chest. I moved it carefully out of the way. This time, the protesting noise was louder, and continued as she rolled over, taking the blankets with her. By the time I finished standing, she had formed a cocoon, with only the crown of her head proving that there was a woman inside the mass of bedclothes.

Clothes . . . our clothes were in the bathroom, along with all my weapons. Swearing softly but steadily under my breath, I crept out of the bedroom and started down the hall, listening for clues as to what had so abruptly awakened me. I'm not a heavy sleeper—no one in my family is a heavy sleeper; waking easy comes with the job—but I don't wake up for no reason at all. Something in the apartment was wrong.

Whatever was making the hair on the back of my neck stand up didn't put in an appearance as I made my way to the bathroom. A pair of pants, three knives, and a handgun later, I felt confident enough to slip back into the hall.

I took a glance into the bedroom. Shelby was still sleeping soundly in her blanket cocoon. Holding my gun in front of me, muzzle to the ground, I stepped into the living room. The blinds were open, letting the streetlights shine right into the room. That made it a little easier for me to assess my surroundings, looking for anything that was out of place. I found nothing.

I was starting to think I was being paranoid, and that Shelby had kicked me in her sleep or something, when I heard a sound from the hall. It was soft, and probably would have been inaudible if the carpet had been less than twenty years old: just a foot striking against the floor. Not that unusual—people walk—but most people don't walk with the distinctive gait of someone trying not to be heard. This late at night, whoever was out there should either have been hurrying to their door, or drunkenly weaving without giving a damn who they woke up. This person was creeping.

Shifting my gun to my right hand, I crossed the living room, undid the deadbolt, and opened the door with my left hand—or tried to, anyway. The deadbolt turned easily, but when I tried to twist the knob, it refused to move. The whole mechanism had somehow been jammed from the outside.

"Shit," I muttered, and put my gun on the knickknack table before dropping to the floor and trying to peer under the door. I couldn't quite manage it, but my change in perspective did let me do one thing: it let me smell the gasoline soaking into the thin carpet of the hall.

"*Shit*," I said again, with more fervency. Shoving myself back to my feet, I grabbed my gun and ran for the bedroom. "Shelby! You have to wake up now! Shelby!"

She didn't respond.

Only the fact that she had rolled herself in blankets when I woke up kept me from panicking, deciding she was dead, and making things even worse. Instead, I clicked on the light, shoved my gun into the waistband of my pants, and crossed to shake her shoulder through the blankets. "Shelby. Wake up. We have to move, it's not safe here anymore."

"Fuck off," she mumbled sleepily.

It says something about me that I found that endearing. This wasn't the time or the place, however, and so I shook her again, harder this time. "*Shelby*. I'm not kidding. Your door is jammed, and someone's getting ready to set the building on fire. Wake. *Up*."

"What?" She finally stirred, pulling an arm free of the cocoon in order to push herself into a half sitting position. Her hair was a tangled mess, covering her eyes. "Alex? What are you yelling about?"

"Building. Fire. Get dressed, we're leaving."

She shoved her hair back as her eyes widened. "The building's on *fire?*"

"No, but it's about to be. Now move!" I ran back to the bathroom to grab the rest of my things, trusting her to at least find pants before I got back. This was not a situation that I wanted to go into without as many knives as I could carry, and possibly a few more, just in case.

Panic is a remarkable motivator. By the time I had my shirt on and my weapons tucked in the appropriate places, Shelby was running down the hall, fully clothed, with an old-fashioned travel suitcase in one hand. Before I could say anything, she snapped, "I'm not running around naked for the rest of the week if this place burns down."

There was no point in arguing with her, and if my house were on fire, I'd have a lot more to worry about saving. "Do you have an ax?"

"What?" She stared at me. "The building's about to burn, and you want to know if I have an *ax*? Are you sure you're not just having a really odd nightmare?"

"You got dressed," I pointed at her. "The door is jammed. Someone broke the knob so that we can't escape." I sighed. "I'm going to need to kick the door down."

"Oh, brilliant, that's not dangerous at all," said Shelby.

"Got a better idea?"

She looked away.

The smell of gasoline was stronger when we walked out into the living room; there was no way to pretend that I was just having a very vivid nightmare. I moved toward the door and fell into a position I'd learned during my long-ago karate classes, hoping I wasn't about to splinter my ankle.

"Stop!"

"What?" I turned to see Shelby shaking her head frantically. "What's wrong?"

"Just hold on, all right?" She stepped in front of me, shoving me aside as she leaned forward and pressed her hand against the door. She pulled it quickly away, looking grimly back at me. "It's hot."

"What?"

"I said, it's hot." She dropped to the floor, pressing her cheek to the carpet. "I smell smoke. Not much, not yet, but enough. We can't go out this way. The building's already on fire." She rolled back to her feet, grabbing her discarded suitcase.

"Of course the building's already on fire," I muttered. "Call 911?"

"On it."

While Shelby dialed, I ran to the living room window, looking outside. The lawn was clogged with people, some of them pointing up at the building like everyone else might have come outside for a nice midnight stroll, instead of fleeing from the fire. I tried to open the window, and groaned as it refused to budge. "Shelby?"

"Fire's already been reported, firemen are on their way," she replied, running to my side. She frowned. "You can't open that, Alex, it's been painted shut."

"*Shit*." Smoke was starting to come through the crack under the door, finally overwhelming the smell of the gasoline. "What about the bedroom windows? Do those open?"

"Yes!" Shelby realized what I was really asking before I could voice it. This time, she grabbed my hand, pulling me after her as she whirled and ran back to the bedroom.

There was no crowd of people outside the bedroom window. Instead, it looked out on the roof of the parking area—which was, naturally, on fire.

"Better outside on fire than inside on fire," I muttered. "Wait here."

"What? Alex!"

I ignored her as I grabbed our discarded towels off the floor, running with them back to the bathroom, where a few seconds under the showerhead soaked them—and me—all the way through. I ran back to where Shelby waited, flinging one of the towels at her. She squawked when it hit her, glaring at me.

"What—"

"Follow me!" Before I could lose my nerve, I stepped up onto the windowsill, wrapped the towel around my shoulders, took a deep breath, and jumped.

It was a ten-foot fall to the carport roof. The impact would have been enough to jar every bone in my body if I *hadn't* been leaping into the middle of a blazing inferno. As it was, even my sister, Verity, who never met a building she didn't want to jump off, would have been impressed. I began slapping the roof around me with my towel as soon as I landed, trying to clear something of a safe zone for Shelby. The smell of burning hair wasn't as bad as the smell of smoke, but it was more immediate, since it meant that part of my body was on fire.

My shoes were waterlogged, but the fire was stronger than thirty seconds in the shower. It bit through the thin fabric, and I yelped, the last of my clean air escaping. Breathing in would mean getting a lungful of smoke, and then . . .

Well, there wouldn't be much "and then." I glanced up, still flailing around with the towel, and saw Shelby standing on the ledge, clearly trying to find the nerve to follow me. I beckoned with one arm, hoping that she would see the need to move. I could see the fire now, consuming the building all around her. Whoever had jammed our door had done us a favor: if we'd opened it, the fire would have come into the apartment, and we'd already be dead.

Shelby, please, I thought.

She jumped.

It was not a graceful fall; she pinwheeled her arms madly all the way down, and she landed hard, hitting her knees on the burning roof. But she bounced back quickly, swinging her towel hard as she fought to beat out the flames.

We were never going to defeat this fire on our own, but we didn't need to; all we needed to do was get away. I grabbed her wrist, still struggling not to breathe, and pulled her with me as I jumped again, this time off the carport roof.

After a ten-foot fall into a blazing fire, an eight-foot fall into a puddle of rainwater was almost a blessing. My ankles didn't agree, and they folded beneath me, pitching me to my knees on the pavement. I didn't care. I was too busy scrambling to my hands and knees, turning to check on Shelby. *Please be all right,* I thought frantically. *Please, please be all right . . .*

She was sitting on her butt in the middle of the puddle, her suitcase lying off to one side. The latches had popped, but the lid had fallen back into the closed position after only half a bra had managed to make good its escape. She looked stunned, and the bottom few inches of her hair had been badly singed, probably during the first fall, when she dipped too low to bleed off the force of her impact.

"Shelby? Are you okay?"

"I . . . we just jumped out of a burning building in the middle of the night. That's a thing which occurred in the actual world." She tilted her head back, looking toward her apartment window. Flames were finally visible inside, going industriously about the business of consuming everything she hadn't been able to shove into her emergency bag. "My apartment is on fire."

"Yes," I said. I wasn't sure what else to say. My hands hurt. So did my feet, and my knees. I was going to have some incredible blisters; I was lucky if that was the worst thing I was going to have. I needed to get home and get some medical attention. I needed to help Shelby first.

"The door was jammed." She looked back down, focusing on me as a new emotion overwrote her confusion: anger. Shelby Tanner looked like she was about to start a second fire through nothing but the power of her rage. "Somebody just tried to kill us."

"Yeah, they did." I staggered to my feet, offering her my hand. "Want to go find out who it was, and maybe kick their ass?"

"I thought you'd never ask."

Leaving wasn't quite that easy, of course: if we were seen driving away from the fire, which was most definitely going to be ruled arson, we'd make ourselves suspects. So Shelby and I gathered her things, patted one another's hair until we were sure it wasn't going to spontaneously combust, and went to meet with the emergency responders—after a brief stop at the car to drop off our weapons, of course. I was pleased to see that Shelby had managed to grab two guns and a hand-sized sickle in the process of getting her clothes on. Yes, every second had been important while we were still inside, but sometimes you need to be prepared in order to be safe.

Walking hurt, and was probably going to hurt for the next several days, but it was nothing time and some analgesics wouldn't take care of. Shelby had a nasty burn on one arm that was probably going to scar, and both of us needed haircuts and showers, unless we wanted to walk around smelling like bonfire for the next few weeks.

Shelby's neighbors had mostly gathered on the sidewalk and the grass closest to it, putting a safe distance between themselves and the building. Shelby looked anxiously around the crowd.

"Is that everyone?" I asked.

"I don't know." She turned to look at me, eyes wide and sad. "I've only been here a little while, and I barely know any of my neighbors. There could be a dozen people burning in there, and I'd have no way of knowing."

She'd have no way of saving them, either, but bringing that up wouldn't do either of us any good. I put my arms around her, careful of her burns, and sighed. "We can't save everything, Shelby," I said quietly. "But we each saved one person tonight. You should be proud of that."

"Who'd I save, then?"

"Me. I would have opened that door."

". . . and I wouldn't have woken up until it was too late." We were surrounded by strangers, but the way she looked at me made me feel like we were totally alone. "You saved me."

"And you saved me. So see? You did everything you could have done." I looked at the burning building, and added, "You did everything anyone could have done."

The arrival of the fire trucks cut off any further conversation. Men in uniform shouted for the crowd to fall back, and the crowd did as it was told, clearly relieved to have *someone* taking control of the situation. Shelby sagged against me, exhausted. I held her up, scanning the crowd for anyone who didn't look appropriately upset.

There were a few tall, curvy blonde women who looked more annoyed than traumatized, but I dismissed them as dragon princesses and moved on, looking for a better target. Someone who didn't fit, someone who hadn't just watched what little they had in this world burn away to ashes . . .

Someone moved at the edge of the crowd, ducking their head and quickly stepping backward into the shadows, where I wouldn't be able to see their face. I started to release my grip on Shelby, preparing to go after him, and stopped as a familiar face in a blue police uniform stepped between me and my mystery figure.

"So, Dr. Preston, it seems we're fated to meet again," said the officer who'd taken my statement after we found Andrew's body. His gaze flicked to Shelby and then back to me, assessing. "And Dr. Tanner. The two of you sure do show up at a lot of emergencies these days."

"Dr. Tanner lives here," I said. "Or lived here, I guess. How bad is the damage?"

Shelby lifted her head, wobbling as she looked at him, like even the air weighed too much for her. I would have applauded her performance, if the situation hadn't been quite so dire. "Unit 2-L," she said, voice unsteady. "Officer, what happened? I thought there were fire doors on the stairways to prevent this type of thing."

"We'll have a full report in the next few days. Is either of you hurt?"

"A little," said Shelby, and sniffled, eyes suddenly full of tears. "It's not so bad I need to bother the EMTs. Can Alex take me to the hospital? Please?"

The officer looked torn. I couldn't exactly blame him: first we find a body, and then we show up at a suspicious fire. At the same time, we weren't suspects in anything—at least not yet. Finally, his training won out over his suspicions, and he nodded. "Go ahead," he said. "Just don't leave town for the next few days, all right?"

"We weren't planning to," I said. "Come on, sweetie."

Shelby sniffled again and allowed me to lead her away

from the crowd and the police, back to the dubious safety of my car.

We had no way of knowing whether the arson had been intended to kill me, Shelby, or both. I searched the exterior of the car thoroughly for bombs or signs that someone had tried to break in and, when I found nothing but a little goose shit from the zoo, I unlocked the doors. Shelby got into the passenger seat, and we drove away.

As soon as we had turned the corner and the apartment building was no longer in view, Shelby straightened, all signs of vulnerability gone. "Where are we going?" she asked, wiping away her crocodile tears. The motion smeared the ash on her face, making her look like a chimney sweep from a modern remake of *Mary Poppins*—one where Mary was armed to the teeth and out for blood. "Hospital?"

"Not unless we really need to. I don't know anyone in the local ERs, so we wouldn't be able to dodge the paper trail, and I'd rather we didn't wind up as a human interest story on tonight's news." I kept an eye on the rearview mirror as I turned down another street, watching the road behind us for a tail. "We're heading back to my grandparents' place, as soon as I can be sure that we're not being followed."

"I hope you have a truly monumental first aid kit," she said, wiping uselessly at her face again. Then she winced, as the motion apparently pulled on her burns. "I actually mean that."

"The first aid kit was enough to stop me being turned to stone," I said.

"So it's pretty good is what you're saying."

"We do okay." I drove to the end of the block, pulled off to the side, and turned off the engine.

Shelby blinked at me. "What are you—"

"Just give it a second."

Frowning, she subsided, and we sat in the dark car for several minutes, waiting to see if anyone drove past. When the road remained empty, I turned the engine back on and pulled away from the curb.

"Do you think we're being followed?" Shelby asked.

"Honestly, I think someone dropped a cockatrice in my backyard and tried to burn down your apartment building with us inside, so right now, a little healthy paranoia is the way to go."

"I wish I could argue with that," sighed Shelby.

We didn't talk the rest of the way back to the house.

All the lights were on when I pulled into my customary spot, and both cars were there; if nothing else, we would be well-defended from any additional arson attempts. I got my things and helped Shelby out of her seat. Now that the adrenaline was wearing off, she was having trouble standing. I was doing somewhat better, if only because I was still running in crisis mode. Once we were inside, with people to defend us if things turned sour, then I could fall apart.

"It's a really, *really* good first aid kit, right?" asked Shelby, through gritted teeth.

"The best," I assured her, and together we half-walked, half-limped up the front walkway.

Grandma opened the door before I could reach for my key. Her eyes were glowing a lambent white, all but obscuring her irises and pupils. "Alex!" she gasped. "What happened?"

"Someone burned down Shelby's apartment building," I said, stepping inside. Grandma was right there to help support Shelby's weight, and suddenly walking seemed, if not easier, at least a lot less hard. "We had to jump out the window to get away. How did you know we were coming?"

"I told her," said Sarah. I looked past Grandma to the stairs, where Sarah was standing, pale in her blue night-gown, eyes glowing even more brightly than my grandmother's. "I heard the screaming from all the way down the block."

Sarah shouldn't have been able to hear anything from that far away; we'd both grabbed our anti-telepathy charms along with our weapons. That Sarah had heard me anyway said something, both about how attuned we were as family, and how badly hurt I really was.

"We're here now," I said, trying to project reassurance and calm. "Go back up to your room. Grandma will get us patched up, and then we can have breakfast in the morning, and I'll tell you all about it."

"Listen to your cousin, Sarah," said Grandma, and began pushing us toward the kitchen. "Look at you two. Martin!"

The kitchen door opened, revealing my grandfather. "I'm almost ready for them."

"Good." She half-led, half-shoved us through the kitchen door and to the table, where the first aid kit was already assembled and waiting. There was a straight razor next to the stack of bandages. "Who's hurt worse?"

"Shelby," I said, grabbing a piece of clean gauze and using it to wipe the soot off my glasses. The world suddenly became a lot easier to see. The realization that I'd driven through downtown Columbus while half-blinded followed, and I fought back the urge to be sick. There would be time for that later. "Her arm's worse than any of my injuries."

"Let me see," said Grandma.

Thankfully, Shelby didn't argue. She turned, showing Grandma the red, raw skin of her right bicep.

"We can deal with that," said Grandma, and picked up the straight razor. She flipped it open before neatly slicing open the back of her own hand.

Shelby shrieked, too startled for composure, only to calm and stare as she realized Grandma wasn't really bleeding. A thick, viscous fluid was leaking from the cut, virtually clear, with only a hint of blue. "What in the . . . ?"

"Cuckoos don't have hemoglobin, dear," said Grandma.

"Do they feel *pain*?"

Grandma laughed. "Yes, but sometimes we have to work past that," she admitted, and put down the straight razor before dipping her fingers into the "blood" and beginning to lather it onto Shelby's wound. Shelby squawked again, only to subside, looking puzzled, when there was no pain. Grandma smiled. "As I was saying, we don't have hemoglobin. What we do have is a natural antibiotic, with preservative and painkilling properties."

"They're very popular with the kind of men who like building men like me," said Grandpa. "Alex, let me see your feet."

I stuck them obediently out, managing not to wince when he pulled off my shoes and started examining my blisters. "It's all right, Shelby, honest. Cuckoo blood won't heal you, but it'll make the pain a lot less immediate, and we have drugs to help with the rest."

"It should reduce scarring, though, and that's a good thing, as Martin tells me you're a very pretty girl," said Grandma, finishing her finger-painting and reaching for the gauze. "You should both have showers, but I want you to leave this on for at least an hour before you wash it off, and I'll make up a kit for you to use after you get dry."

"She means she's going to bleed into a jar," said Grandpa. "Don't sugarcoat it for the kids, Angie."

"I got that, thanks," said Shelby, closing her eyes. "Alex? You all right?"

My feet looked mostly intact. "I'm fine," I said. Judging by the tightness in my back and shoulders, I might not *stay* fine, but right here and now, I could give the reassurance. "Grandma . . ."

"Yes, she can stay here." Grandma began to wrap gauze around Shelby's arm. "I don't want either of you sleeping somewhere undefended until this is taken care of. Do you have any idea who may have attacked you?"

"No," I said grimly, "but we're going to find out."

Grandpa's hand landed on my shoulder, heavy

enough to keep me in my seat, even if my feet hadn't already been giving me good reason to keep still. "In the morning," he said. "You need sleep, both of you."

I thought of my room, where the mice were probably preparing a grand celebration to commemorate my getting set on fire. "About that . . ."

"I already bribed them to relocate to the attic for tonight, and leave you alone," said Grandpa. "It was the second thing I did after Sarah woke us."

Curiosity demanded to be satisfied. "What was the first thing you did?"

"Arm the exterior traps. Nothing's getting through any of these windows tonight."

It was the exact right thing to say. I smiled. "Thanks, Grandpa."

"Any time, kiddo," he said, and patted my shoulder one more time before he took his hand away. "Any time."

We didn't shower before we went to bed; we didn't do anything but peel off our smoky, ruined clothing and collapse onto the mattress, with Shelby on the inside, and me closer to the door, so that anything that tried to attack would have a slightly harder time of it. She was already half-gone, thanks to the Vicodin my grandmother had left out for her. I had refused to take anything but a few aspirin. One of us needed to be aware of our surroundings.

That was a foolish fantasy. My eyes were closed before my head hit the pillow, and the last thing I remembered was the warm, familiar weight of Crow settling on my chest. He cawed once, tone inquisitive, and then there was nothing but the dark and my own exhaustion pulling me under.

Nineteen

"Playing fair is for people who don't mind playing to lose."

—Kevin Price

A nice, if borrowed, bedroom in an only moderately creepy suburban home in Columbus, Ohio

I WOKE TO THE sound of shrieking. I was out of the bed and on my feet in less than a second, already reaching for the gun that I kept in the nightstand. The fact that I was stark naked hit me mid-motion, followed immediately by another shriek. This time, I identified the voice as Shelby's. It was coming from the floor on the other side of the bed.

"I'm coming!" I shouted, and ran around the bed, already searching for a target . . .

. . . only to find my girlfriend, who was wearing my bathrobe, lying on her back with Crow sitting proudly in the middle of her chest. His wings were half-mantled, and when he moved them the tips of his primary flight feathers dragged against her arms, tickling her. He moved them as I watched, and another shriek was the result. I lowered my gun, blinking in bemusement, and wished I'd thought to grab my glasses before coming to her rescue.

"Er?" I said.

"You!" Shelby sat up, performing a complicated maneuver with her arms, so that Crow wound up in the classic feline "forepaws on shoulder, hind legs resting on arm" position. He turned to look at me over his own shoulder, and I swear the feathery bastard actually looked smug. "Why didn't you tell me?"

"Shelby, there is a *list* of things that can be used as answers to that question. It's annotated. There's even an index. How's your burn?"

"Hurts like a bitch and a half, but I'll live; hope you like girls with interesting scars. You're moving away from the point."

"I'm naked, I'm sore, and I just woke up. I don't know what the point *is*, ergo, I cannot be moving away from it on purpose."

"This fellow!" Shelby shifted her arms again, presenting Crow to me like he was an adoption drive puppy. He put up with it admirably, telegraphing his mild annoyance at being held that way with nothing more than a swishing of his tail and a ruffling of his feathers.

"When he pecks your eyes out for manhandling him, I'm not going to be as sorry for you as I should be," I said. With that, I turned around and walked back to my side of the bed, where I sat down, stowed my gun in the nightstand, and finally put on my glasses. The room snapped into blessed clarity. I'm not blind without my glasses, just nearsighted, but that doesn't mean I enjoy everything being blurry around the edges.

The mattress jolted as Shelby pulled herself up from the floor and plopped down on the edge of the bed. "Did I wake you?"

"Given the last few days, not only did you wake me, but I thought you were being murdered." I twisted to scowl at her. She was still holding Crow, and her torso was mostly concealed by the mass of black feathers and tawny fur.

"Sorry," she said. Giving Crow's head a scritch, she added, "But you could have told me about this big fellow. I woke up with him sitting on my chest, trying to sort out who I was and what I was doing in bed with his monkey."

"Oh, hell, I didn't warn you about Crow? I'm sorry." Anger transitioned to contrition in an instant. "It was late, and I was crashing so hard, I didn't even think. I hope he didn't freak you out too much."

"If by 'freak me out' you mean 'absolutely delight me,' he did that in spades." She kept scritching Crow's head. He let his beak hang open, eyes closing in bliss. "I had to leave my poor Flora back home in Australia. There was no way I'd have been able to smuggle her through customs, but I've missed her every day since, you've no idea how hard it's been on me." Crow's purring was loud enough to be audible from across the bed.

I blinked. "You have a miniature griffin?"

"No, they're not native to Australia, and while they're certainly handsome creatures, they threaten the ecosystems of several of our indigenous species." The subtext was clear: if miniature griffins were spotted in Australia, and couldn't be relocated or contained in private collections, they would be destroyed. I couldn't find any fault with that. There's a cost to maintaining an island ecology, and sometimes that cost can be unpleasant.

"So Flora is . . . ?"

"She's a garrinna. A very pretty one, too."

"I'd love to see her." Garrinna are sometimes referred to as "marsupial griffins," even though the title is completely inaccurate and doesn't describe anything about them beyond their shape. They're about the size of Welsh corgis, which makes them larger than most species of miniature griffin, and they're very social creatures. As in "a flock of them can and will dismantle a car, given the opportunity." They're virtually extinct, for much the same reason. Well, that, and the part where they look like bright pink parrots crossed with stripy cats. Not much in the way of natural camouflage, there.

"What's this one's name, then?"

"Crow. He's a pest, aren't you, Crow?"

Crow opened his beak and made a self-satisfied churring noise, seemingly content to remain in Shelby's arms all day long, if that was an available option.

Sadly for all of us, it wasn't. I stood, more slowly this time, and winced as my ankles and knees took this opportunity to object to the way I'd treated them the night before. "What time is it?"

"Half-seven. I called the zoo before I settled in with this fellow. They know not to expect us today. I think the fact that the fire was on the news last night made my story just that little bit more believable." Shelby grimaced. "That does take away any chance there might have been that the management doesn't know we're sleeping together, though. Sorry about that."

"It's not a problem. I wasn't really trying to hide it, and what are they going to do, fire us when the rest of the staff is dropping dead?" I stretched, trying to make the muscles in my lower back release. "I need a shower. I smell like forest fire and antiseptic."

"Mind if I join you? I don't mind you running about naked, but I feel like a trash heap."

"Not if you promise to remember that while my grandmother may not be a receptive telepath, my slightly scrambled cousin *is*, and she's likely to come into the bathroom and start asking inappropriate questions if we make any mental noise that interests her."

Shelby wrinkled her nose. "That's a libido killer, but no, I promise, I just want to clean off right now, and I'm not much in the mood for being on my own. Something about my apartment combusting around me has rather put me off solitude."

I paused in the act of reaching for a pair of clean sweatpants to stop and look back at her. "I guess things have gotten a little exciting, huh? I'm sorry about that."

"Don't be. I'm a big girl; you didn't drag me into anything I didn't force you to allow me to be a part of." Shelby put Crow down on the bed, where he wrapped his tail around his feet and croaked in irritation. "I wouldn't be a cryptozoologist if I didn't like a bit of excitement every now and again. I just didn't expect the excitement to be quite so flammable, that's all."

This time, I managed to swallow the marriage proposal before it could escape. "Okay, then. Let's go shower."

Twenty minutes, a lot of soap, and only two accidentally poked bruises later, we were clean and semi-presentable. Shelby scooped Crow off my bed before following me downstairs to the kitchen, where Sarah was attempting to eat a bowl of oatmeal, under the watchful eye of my grandmother. At least, I thought it was oatmeal. Oatmeal isn't usually that red, but the color could be explained by the ketchup bottle that was sitting off to one side.

Grandma looked up as we entered, and smiled. "Good morning, sleepyheads. Shelby, how's the robe?"

"Quite good, thank you, but er . . . where are my clothes?" Shelby shrugged, expression sheepish. "I got up this morning and my suitcase had gone."

"Your clothes are at the dry cleaner's, along with Alex's. You'd never have been able to get the smell of smoke out otherwise." Grandma stood, patting Sarah once on the shoulder, and crossed to the stove. "There's toast and oatmeal, if either of you are hungry."

"I'm starving," I said. "Shelby?"

"I could eat. But er, if the clothes are at the dry cleaner . . . you didn't just hand over the suitcase, did you?"

"Your knives are in the box on Alex's dresser," said Grandma, beginning to dish up two large bowls of oatmeal. "Didn't you have a gun before?"

"It's upstairs with my clothes. I put it on before we left the apartment." Crow squawked. Shelby obligingly put him down, and he began twining around Grandma's ankles, churring to be fed.

"That was probably wise of you." Grandma ignored the begging griffin as she turned, holding out the bowls. "Brown sugar, raisins, and curry powder are on the counter, butter and ketchup are on the table. Can I get you anything else?"

"Er . . . is there coffee?"

"I'll take care of coffee," I said. "I've never heard you say 'er' so many times before."

Shelby glared at me. "Shove off," she suggested. I laughed.

Things were calm for a little while after that. Shelby and I doctored our oatmeal—neither of us added ketchup, although she did add a pinch of curry powder— and sat to devour our breakfasts. Sarah ate about half her oatmeal before pushing the bowl aside and leaning back to stare at the ceiling. I paused with my spoon halfway to my mouth, waiting to see if she was going to do anything else. When several seconds passed without her moving, I shrugged and went back to the food.

I was finishing my coffee when Grandma said, "I think it's about time we started talking about what happened last night, don't you?"

"Do you mean the visit to Dee's neighborhood, or someone deciding to burn down Shelby's apartment while we were still inside?"

"Both, if you would be so kind." Grandma took the seat next to Sarah, folding her hands primly on the table. "I would have asked last night, but it was clear you needed to sleep. So you're going to tell me now. And then you can call your parents."

"This day just gets better and better," I muttered. "We started by following Dee to the local gorgon community . . ."

Twenty minutes seems to be the most common interval in human experiences, because that's also how long it took me to explain the situation to Grandma, including the fight with the lindworm and our dinner with Hannah. From there, Shelby and I took turns relaying what happened at the apartment—slightly edited, of course, since I had no interest in discussing my sex life with my grandmother.

When we finished, Grandma nodded, and then looked to Sarah. "What do you think?"

"They're telling the truth, and four times four is sixteen," said Sarah, still looking thoughtfully up at the ceiling. "My head hurts. You were hurting a lot last night."

"I'm sorry about that," I said.

"You aren't a candle." She lowered her head, fixing me with an accusing stare. "You can burn and burn, but you'll never give any good light. And I don't think it would smell very good, either."

Shelby snorted laughter. "She's got your number down to rights, Alex. No playing candle."

"You got burned worse than I did," I said defensively. Then, to Sarah, I said, "I promise to do my best not to get set on fire, but I can't promise it's never going to happen again. We have dangerous jobs. You know that."

"Knowing that and knowing it aren't the same thing, even if they use the same words," said Sarah. She sounded frustrated. Pushing back her chair, she stood and walked out of the kitchen.

I sighed. "Grandma, I'm sorry. I—"

"Alex Price, I could kiss you right now."

"What?" I blinked at her. "What are you talking about?"

"Haven't you noticed that's Sarah's making a lot more sense these days? You just had a whole conversation with her, and yes, it was unsteady in places, but she knew who you *were*. The whole time, she was talking to her cousin Alex, and not to some college professor whose class she audited or a character from one of her PBS shows." Grandma beamed. "She's coming back to us. She's putting the pieces of herself back into the order they're supposed to be in, because she knows you need her. This is wonderful."

"Great, I should have arranged for someone to start trying to kill me sooner." I stood. "I need more coffee. Shelby?"

"I'm good, thanks." She looked at my grandmother, expression uncharacteristically earnest. "I know we didn't meet under the best of circumstances, what with that whole 'I came here intending to kill you' aspect of things, but I hope you do understand that I'm genuinely sorry about all that."

"It's a common reaction to my species," said Grandma. "Since you didn't start dating my grandson just to get access to the house, I'm not angry. Now, if you'd actually shot me, it might be a different story."

"If I'd actually shot you, I think Alex would've shot me immediately after, and my story would be finished now," said Shelby. "I'm not in a hurry to wind up in a shallow grave."

"Hey," I said, stung. "I'm a professional. Shallow graves get discovered. No one would ever find your body."

"Oh, yes, that's very reassuring," said Shelby. "Anyway, Ms. Price, what I'm trying to say is . . ."

"It's Baker, actually," said Grandma. "I'm Alex's mother's mother. His father's mother is Mrs. Price. We didn't get along at first, and I think calling me by her name might convince her that we're not getting along now. Alice can be a little . . ."

"My paternal grandmother is about as stable as the San Andreas fault right after it's been ripped open by a rock elemental," I said. "Love her. Love her lots. But, yeah, we try not to push her buttons when there's any possible way to avoid it, because she habitually carries a backpack full of grenades."

Shelby blinked. "That doesn't sound safe."

"And now you're starting to understand Grandma Alice." I stood and walked over to the counter, where I refilled my coffee cup.

"I . . . see." Shelby shook her head, almost as if she was trying to physically force the weirdness away. Sitting up a little straighter, she looked at my grandmother, and said, "To return to an earlier topic, I would greatly appreciate it if you would accept my apologies for the way we met, especially as you've been so hospitable during what could have been a genuinely trying time. Well. *Is* a genuinely trying time. I think my apartment burning down counts as a trying time."

"So does everyone else, dear," said my grandmother, cutting Shelby off before she could begin another round of awkward apologies. "You'll be staying with us until the police have finished their investigation of your building, of course. Maybe longer, depending on how bad the smoke damage is."

Shelby's eyes widened. "Oh, I couldn't impose, it would be — "

"The sensible thing to do, under the circumstances." Grandma shook her head. "Maybe whoever burned your building was after Alex, and you simply had the bad luck to be in the wrong place at the wrong time. He usually stays here, after all, and only a fool would approach this house with malice on their mind."

Shelby, who had done exactly that, reddened.

Grandma was polite enough not to say anything, for which I was profoundly grateful. She continued calmly, saying, "But it's also possible that whoever burned your building was trying to kill you."

"*Me*?" squawked Shelby. "What in the world would someone have against me? I'm just a visiting zoologist. And I'm quite charming; ask anyone who's met me. I'm not the sort of girl who inspires murder attempts, not unless I'm really working at it."

"You *did* go with me to the gorgon community," I commented, as I returned to the table. "Someone could have seen you, and decided you were a threat. Maybe they would have tried to burn the building even if I wasn't there, and getting us both was just two assassination attempts for the price of one."

"You're an optimistic lot, aren't you?" Shelby crossed her arms, slumping in her seat. "So maybe whoever torched my place was trying to kill me, not you, or me *and* you, or just you. Regardless of how you slice this, you're looking at someone trying to kill someone I'm fond of."

It took me a moment to untangle her sentence. Then I smiled. "I'm fond of you, too. And there's a way we can find out whether someone is trying to kill one or both of us."

"Oh? How's that?"

"First things first. Hey, Grandma, do we have anything Shelby can borrow?"

Slowly, my grandmother began to smile.

"I'm going to kill you."

"You look fine."

"I'm quite serious. I'm going to murder you. I'm going to murder you to *death*. And then, after I've finished doing that, I'm going to kill you again, just to be sure you got the point."

"Shelby, honestly, you look fine."

Shelby sank deeper into the passenger seat of my car, folding her arms, and glared at me. I had enough of a sense of self-preservation not to snicker, but it was a close thing. It wasn't the outfit, either. Sarah's clothing might not fit Shelby's sense of style—somehow, I couldn't picture Shelby ever voluntarily donning a knee-length green skirt and a white peasant blouse that looked like it had been stolen straight out of the 1960s—but it was clothing, it was clean, and I'd seen stranger, usually on one of my sisters. Being the only male in my generation has made me very flexible where female fashion is concerned. (Artie doesn't count. Artie divides girls into three categories—"terrifying," "related to me," and "Sarah." Near as I can tell, the only category he actually *looks* at is Sarah.)

No, it was the sulking. My sisters, again. Having two of them, both younger than me, meant I'd learned that the only way to survive a sulk is to mock it: a sulking sister, rewarded for her efforts, will proceed to push her sulking to ever-greater heights, until an entire platoon of pigeons could perch on her out-thrust lower lip.

"I look like a first grade teacher from the pioneer days," said Shelby.

"I don't think they had machine stitching in the pioneer days," I said, turning onto a narrow residential street lined with attractive brick houses, each on its own privately landscaped stretch of land. Even the air smelled like money. It was something of a relief to see a few fallen leaves clogging the gutters in a distinctly unartistic manner. If not for that, I would have been afraid we were driving into a completely fabricated community, and started looking for signs that we'd discovered a new form of ambush predator, one that looked like a pleasant suburban neighborhood right up until it slammed its jaws closed on your car.

"Fine, then, I look like a first grade teacher from the 1970s."

"Your sense of history is very brief." I consulted my GPS before pulling to a stop in front of one of the attractive brick houses. "We're here."

Shelby forgot her sulk long enough to peer past me at the house. "Are you sure?"

"What did you expect? A hole in the ground? Wadjet are civilized people. Chandi's mother is a doctor." And Chandi's father was an impressively large spectacled cobra, which was why Chandi's fiancé lived at the zoo. Male wadjet don't coexist well.

"Are you sure she's home?"

"I called first." Never surprise any member of a venomous species with a home visit. It's not only rude, it's potentially hazardous to your health.

We walked up the narrow path to the front door, Shelby shamelessly gawking at the landscaping, me watching for signs that we'd been followed. No one drove down the street, but that didn't mean anything; any tail smart enough to stay with us this far would probably be smart enough to park farther down the block and observe our activities from a distance.

There are times when I hate being as paranoid as I am. Life with my family makes paranoia a vital survival trait, but that doesn't mean I enjoy it. It can be a lonely way to live. I glanced at Shelby out of the corner of my eye.

Then again, maybe it wasn't so lonely after all.

I stepped up onto the porch and rang the doorbell, which made a pleasant chiming sound before tapering off. Running footsteps replaced the sound of the bell, and a familiar voice called, "I've got it!" just before the door was wrenched open to reveal Chandi. She blinked at us, eyes wide and bewildered. Then they narrowed, and she demanded, "What are *you* doing here?"

"I came because I wanted to speak with your parents," I said. "Ms. Tanner accompanied me because she needs to be formally introduced as a visiting cryptozoologist."

Chandi wrinkled her nose. "Ew. Are you running a breeding program for *those*, too?"

I gaped at her, not quite sure how I was supposed to respond. I was still gaping when she turned and ran back into the house, leaving the door ajar.

"Mooooooo-om! Dr. Price from the zoo is here and he brought a *girl!*"

Shelby stepped up next to me. "Look at it this way," she said. "That's one little girl who's never going to need the facts of life explained to her."

"That's one little girl whose explanation of the facts of life looks nothing like whatever you're picturing," I replied.

Fortunately, Shelby's reply was cut off by the appearance of Chandi's mother. Dr. Sarpa was a tall, slender woman with skin the same deep, rich brown as the scales on a spectacled cobra's back. She had her long black hair pulled into a ponytail, and was wearing a pencil skirt and a flowing white blouse. Her shoes were three-inch heels that my sister would have coveted, but which made me wince in sympathy. She'd only dressed this fancily for me once, and that was the first time that we met; this was all for Shelby's benefit.

"Alex," she said, with considerably more warmth than her daughter usually managed. She even smiled at me in the human style, showing her teeth without baring them. "This must be Dr. Tanner from the zoo. I've heard so much about you. Won't you both please come in?"

"Thank you for your hospitality," I said, stepping over the threshold and bending to remove my shoes. Shelby nodded quickly, indicating that she got the hint, and copied my actions. There was a low bench near the door. We placed our shoes on it.

"Daksha is waiting for us in the back garden," said Dr. Sarpa.

"Thank you," I said again. "Kumari, may I please properly introduce you to the scholar, Shelby Tanner, who has come here seeking only knowledge?"

"You may," said Dr. Sarpa, and turned her human-style smile on Shelby. "You are welcome in my home so long as you travel with Alex, who is known and beloved to us, and do not offer any harm or threat unto my family. Do you agree?"

"Yes, of course," said Shelby, looking puzzled but still agreeable. I understood her confusion; I shared it, the first time I had to deal with wadjet in a social setting. Humans are primates, and primates generally wait to see whether something is a threat before inviting it into their homes. Wadjet are something different. For Kumari, bringing us inside put us within striking distance. If we were going to pose a danger to her family, she wanted to control the environment. She wanted us in her den.

"Good." Kumari's smile died, taking the implied threat with it. "This way." She turned, heading deeper into the house. Her heels clacked sharply against the floor, while our bare feet made no sound.

Shelby paced herself to walk beside me, looking faintly ill-at-ease. That was a good reaction, all things considered. I followed her gaze and saw that she was looking, not at the artwork on the walls or the general design of the house, but at Kumari's shoes.

"We can't wear shoes indoors because we might step on something we shouldn't," I murmured. "People are heavy. You're more likely to realize what's happening and pull back before putting your full weight on someone's tail if you're barefoot. Kumari gets to keep her shoes on because this is her home. She's demonstrating dominance over you."

"Just me?"

"She demonstrated dominance over me a long time ago." I paused, realizing how that sounded, and winced. "That isn't what I meant."

"No, but it's what you said," said Shelby, clearly amused. I decided to stop trying to correct her. Amusement was better—much better—than any of the alternatives.

Kumari was waiting by the sliding glass door to the backyard, which was already standing open. When we reached her, she calmly removed her heels, leaving them on the mat, and stepped through the doorway, onto the cobblestone path that wound its way through their lush rainforest of a yard.

The back fence of the Sarpa residence was high enough to brush up against the restrictions laid down by the local homeowners association. I knew that well, since I'd helped Kumari deflect three attempts to have her fined for building her fence too tall. It had to be the height it was in order to conceal their private greenhouse from prying eyes. Anyone flying over would realize the Sarpas were essentially maintaining a backyard hothouse, but as it was perfectly legal and all their building permits were in order, none of us were particularly worried.

I'm a herpetologist, not a botanist; I couldn't have named any of the trees, climbing vines, or flowers that filled the enclosed glass box of their yard. A fountain chuckled quietly to itself in one corner, feeding into a pond filled with decorative fish. Birds flashed by in the canopy, as captive as any denizens of the zoo. And in the middle of it all, coiled on a large, flat stone intended for that very purpose, was the master of this household, a spectacled cobra fully seventeen feet in length. As we approached him, he lifted the first third of his body into the air, looking down his nose at me as he opened the great flare of his hood. Shelby's hand closed on my upper arm, fingers clenching convulsively tight.

I smiled. "Hello, Daksha. It's nice to see you again. Your scales look remarkable. Did you shed recently?"

The massive cobra continued to study me, his tongue flicking in and out three times before he closed his hood, lowered himself back to the basking stone, and slithered down to the garden path. Moving fast enough to be the stuff of nightmares, he zigzagged to Kumari and twisted his way up her body, moving like the stripe on a barber pole. She held perfectly still, helping him along, until his head was resting on her right shoulder and his body gathered in a thick belt around her waist and torso.

"He greets you, and thanks you for your continued hospitality toward our daughter," she said, walking over to take his recently abandoned place on the central stone. "As you ask, yes, he did shed recently, and is pleased with his pattern brightness in this current molt." Daksha arranged himself around Kumari as she sat, moving with her to avoid any unpleasant accidents, like her settling her full weight on his tail. Her lips turned downward in something that was closer to a frown than I liked, and she said, "He wishes to know why you have brought your colleague from the zoo here, as he did not believe she was aware of our nature."

"If you didn't think I knew what I know, why are you telling me what you think I didn't know but might have come here looking to find out?" Shelby paused. "I'm sorry. I'm not sure even I understand what I just said."

"Dr. Tanner is from an organization with goals much like those of my family," I said, taking a seat on one of the decorative benches. I tugged Shelby along with me, and she settled to my right. "She studies the cryptid world in Australia, and hopes to someday bring the human and cryptid populations of her home continent into a peaceful coexistence. This meant that when people at the zoo began dying of petrifaction, I couldn't keep her from becoming involved with the investigation of their deaths, and she found out about a great many things. At this point, I feel that it is safer for all of us if she knows as much as possible about the local community. That way, no one can slip and tell her something she's not meant to know."

"I agree with Alex, husband," said Kumari, speaking in a slightly more casual tone now that she was speaking for herself and not the great snake that she wore around her waist and torso. "He called before he came, and I agreed to this visit."

There was a pause while Daksha adjusted his grip. She nodded, and said, once more in the formal tone that meant she spoke for her husband, "He knows what I have told him, but wanted to hear your reasoning for himself. It seems sound; he does not question your motives as much as he did before you came here."

"That's good," I said sincerely. Wadjet are incredibly venomous. Having Daksha question my motives could end in my untimely demise. "I do trust Shelby with my life at this point: she's saved it several times."

"Bringing her here means you are trusting her with ours, and that you are trusting us with hers," said Kumari, a faint edge on her voice. "It is not a trust to be cheaply given."

"It hasn't been," I assured her. "There was, however, a motive for bringing her to meet you now, rather than waiting until things were calmer. I assume Chandi told you about what was happening at the zoo before I did?"

"She's very put out," said Kumari. "She was counting on spending more time with Shami before she had to resume her schooling at the end of the summer. If the deaths continue, her bond could be set back by a matter of years."

Shelby sat up a little straighter. I put a hand on her knee, squeezing, and hoped she would read the touch as a request that she not say anything. She shot me a quick look, confusion writ large across her face, but nodded, and kept silent. I smiled gratefully before returning my attention to Kumari.

(For Shelby, and for most human beings—myself honestly included, when I didn't make an effort—referring to the deaths at the zoo so casually was almost like erasing the suffering of the victims. For Kumari and her family, while the death of a few humans was sad, it was by no means a tragedy. The human population of Ohio was in no danger. For Chandi and Shami, however, failure to properly bond could mean they would never be able to have children. It could also mean she would fail to develop the appropriate adult physiological responses to his venom, which would make her vulnerable to him later in life. Wadjet biology is not forgiving of things like zoo closures, and they only had one shot at a happy ever after.)

"The zoo closures are likely to continue, but if necessary, I can help smuggle Shami out of the reptile house," I said. "The difficulty will be finding a place for him to stay until we're ready to reopen. I'm terribly sorry, but my grandparents' house isn't an option, due to the presence of a colony of Aeslin mice. I know Shami is well-mannered and would do his best to abide by the local rules, but . . ."

"But there is no sense in testing his resolve in such a direct and potentially damaging way," said Kumari. "I quite agree, and I appreciate that you have both considered this, and rejected it for good cause. I will ask around about arranging another safe house for him. If only my husband," she caressed the head of the great snake that encircled her body, "could already tolerate the presence of his son-in-law to be, this would be so much easier."

"Yes, it would," I said, and tactfully didn't ask any more questions about the situation. I might not like the answers I got. "Do you mind if I go back several steps in the conversation?"

"Not at all; I was the one who derailed us. You were asking whether I was aware of the deaths. I responded that I am."

"Shelby and I went to visit the local Pliny's gorgon community, to see whether they might be able to tell us where the cockatrice we believe is haunting the zoo came from. We have some good leads to follow. In the meanwhile, we needed to sleep, and we returned to her apartment for the night. I woke to the smell of gasoline ..."

It only took a few minutes to tell the full story, including our escape via the second-floor window. Kumari looked appropriately shocked and dismayed. Daksha remained wrapped around her the entire time, his tongue occasionally flicking out to taste the air. Normal snakes don't hear, exactly; they soak up vibrations with their bodies. I wasn't sure how male wadjet were able to listen to verbal communication, but knew from my dealings with Shami that they could, probably due to an inner ear structure that was dramatically different from their serpentine cousins. When I finished, the male wadjet turned his head away, letting out a long, low hiss.

"My husband is shocked and saddened by the trouble you have experienced, but wonders what it has to do with us," said Kumari. "Surely you don't think that we had anything to do with the burning of Miss Tanner's building."

"Actually, I came here because I thought the opposite, and because we need your help," I said. "The local bogeyman community has never been exactly friendly toward me."

"They mistrust your grandmother," said Kumari.

Shelby snorted. "A Johrlac not being trusted. What are the odds, really?"

I eyed her but didn't say anything. Instead, I returned my attention to Kumari, and said, "They have their reasons. That doesn't change the fact that I need to know who is trying to have me killed—or whether I was the target in the first place. The arsonist could have been attempting to murder Shelby, and been willing to take me out as collateral damage."

"I find it more likely that they were hoping to kill both of you," said Kumari. "I will ask around, however. Perhaps someone has opened a contract, and your life is now valued in a small but viable number of dollars."

"What a lovely way of putting it," Shelby said, wrinkling her nose.

"Everything has a price." I stood. "Thank you for your hospitality. Will you call me if you learn anything?"

"Everything has a price," agreed Kumari. "Will you help us find a place to house Shami if it proves needful?"

"I will."

"Then, yes. I will call you." She stood, her husband slithering into a new position around her shoulders. He looped himself there, head bobbing like a wax museum prop. The temptation of Eve, as recreated by cobra and pediatrician. "For both your sakes, I hope the killer was trying for the two of you together."

Shelby blinked. "Why's that?"

Kumari smiled. "Because it will make you twice as difficult to destroy."

Twenty

"Being smart isn't good enough. You need to be educated, and you need to be open-minded, and you need to remember that what you don't know can most definitely hurt you."

—Martin Baker

Driving through downtown, returning to an only moderately creepy suburban home

"ALL RIGHT," said Shelby, once we were back on the road and moving away from the Sarpa household. "Do you want to explain to me how a woman can be married to a cobra? Because I'm afraid that's where I got lost."

"Kumari may look like a human woman, but she and Daksha are the same species," I said. "Wadjet demonstrate extreme sexual dimorphism. Kumari is female, Daksha is male." That wasn't necessarily a given. Kumari had more in common biologically with an alligator than she did with either Sarah or Dee. Specifying gender seemed like the safest way to go.

Shelby blinked several times. Finally, she asked, "Is that why the bossy little girl who let us in is always lurking around the reptile house when she thinks you're not looking?"

"Yes. Her fiancé, Shami, is the zoo's spectacled cobra.

It's only temporary, until Chandi gets old enough to move into a place of her own. Male wadjet don't coexist well." That was an understatement. Male wadjet had a nasty tendency to try to kill each other. "He was placed here shortly after I arrived in Ohio. I figured I could handle his care along with my basilisk breeding program and the fricken survey."

"What's a fricken?"

"Uh—little frog with feathers."

"You have those here?" Shelby sounded delighted.

"We do, and I've been researching them in my spare time. I can take you out to see them next time we have a minute to ourselves."

"Is this part of your research?" Shelby twisted in her seat enough to face me as I drove. "Explain it."

"It's boring," I cautioned.

"I'm dating you," she countered.

I snorted. "All right," I began. "We've been seeing a dramatic decline in amphibian populations lately ..."

The explanation of what I was doing with the state's fricken population took most of the drive home, especially since I'd never tried to discuss the details with another biologist outside my own family. Shelby asked several questions that required actual thought to answer, forcing me to assess my replies more carefully. I finished as we were turning into the driveway.

"All right; let's go see if your clothes are back from the dry cleaner's," I said, reaching for my seat belt. "If not, we can always stop by the Old Navy and pick up something you'll be more comfortable in before we head for our next step."

"Hold on," said Shelby. She hadn't moved, and was still watching me thoughtfully. "Isn't the end thrust of your research basically that the discovery of the fricken by mainstream science is inevitable, due to the ongoing decline of the frogs and such?"

"Yes," I said. "The problem becomes managing that discovery. I can't be the one to make it. We'd really rather have warning. So that means navigating someone into a position where they can find out that frickens exist without realizing they've been managed. This is going to have huge repercussions for the cryptid world. Among other things, it may force the reexamination of a lot of 'rumors' that science currently dismisses out of hand."

"Like snakes with wings," guessed Shelby.

I nodded. "And fish with fur, and all the other 'that could never happen' hybrids. This isn't going to lead to someone discovering the vegetable lambs or barnacle geese—not yet—but it's going to open a lot of doors, and if we're not braced when that happens, things could turn ugly, fast."

"Sounds fun." Shelby finally undid her belt and got out of the car. I followed suit, and we walked together up the pathway toward the house. Outside the door, she paused and asked, "Are you sure your grandmother isn't going to mind me staying with you for a little bit?"

"If she minded, she'd tell you. Grandma is pretty good about mimicking human behaviors—she grew up with humans. But she never quite picked up the habit of social lying. It makes her uncomfortable." Probably because normal cuckoos are the most dishonest things in the world. Grandma never did like being compared to her relatives.

"Good," said Shelby, looking relieved.

"Nothing to worry about," I said, and opened the door. "Grandma? Are you home?"

"I'm in the kitchen," she called back. I glanced at Shelby, shrugged, and pushed open the kitchen door.

Grandma was sitting at the table, which was covered in a thick layer of financial reports from one of her clients. Most of the people whose accounts she handled were cryptids or otherwise involved with the cryptid world; when it came to accountants, you couldn't find one who was better with nonhuman spending patterns than my grandmother. She looked up as we approached. "How did it go?" she asked.

"Not too badly; Kumari is going to ask around and see if she can get us more information about who might be trying to hurt us." I walked past her to the fridge. "How have things been here?"

"Calm. The police came by."

I nearly dropped my can of V-8. "*What?*"

"*What?*" echoed Shelby.

"Don't worry about it. They know you had nothing to do with any of the current troubles, and they won't be questioning you again. You could probably commit murder in front of the officers and they wouldn't notice." Grandma turned over a piece of paper, studying the back. "You're welcome."

I gaped at her, but it was Shelby who spoke, saying, "I thought you weren't a receptive telepath."

"Brainwashing is projective, as it turns out. Who knew?" Grandma raised her head and smiled sunnily. "Again, you're welcome."

"Thank you," I said hastily, as I closed the fridge. "Has the dry cleaner called yet? We need to get Shelby into something a little less obtrusive before we break into the zoo."

"They have, and her clothes are upstairs," said Grandma. "It's amazing what a fifty-dollar tip will do for a rush job."

Shelby's eyes widened. "I—"

"Don't worry about it." Grandma dismissed the matter with a wave of her hand. "If our little arsonist hadn't burned down your apartment, they might have come after Alex here, and there's no way we would have been able to get the mice out in time. Consider it hazard pay, and go get your clothes on. I don't want you getting that skirt dirty."

"Yes, ma'am," said Shelby, before turning and fleeing the kitchen for the dubious safety of my bedroom.

"She thinks you don't like her," I said, opening the V-8. "Brainwashing the police probably doesn't help, although I think she'll understand your reasons once she's done being unnerved."

"I don't," said Grandma, with a shrug. "But you do, and that's good enough for me, at least for right now. If she hurts you, she's going to learn the real reason you shouldn't mess around with cuckoos." She stood, walking over to ruffle my hair. "It's nice to see you with a girl of your own species. I want great-grandchildren someday, and let's face it, you're my best bet."

"Grandma!" I said, scandalized.

"What?" She shook her head. "Verity won't have children as long as she's dancing professionally, Antimony is . . . well, she's Antimony and requires special considerations, and even if she completely recovers, Sarah is unlikely to ever get within ten yards of a male Johrlac without screaming her head off."

"There's always Artie," I said.

Grandma sighed. "Oh, believe me, I know there's always Artie. He called again this morning to find out whether I was ready to have him come for a visit."

"That might not be such a bad idea," I said carefully. "Sarah's more focused lately. Seeing him could be what she needs to pull herself the rest of the way together."

"Or it could make her fall further apart when she panicked and tried to put herself together without being ready," said Grandma. She shook her head. "No. Artie won't be visiting until she can ask for him herself. And even if those two eventually figure things out, they're not genetically compatible."

"True." Artie was a blood relative, half-human, half-incubus. Sarah was well, Sarah. "But that doesn't mean I'm going to jump straight into the baby-making business with Shelby."

"Maybe, maybe not," said Grandma, with a smile. "Either way, she's good for you. Now go do something illegal and dangerous with your girlfriend."

"My family did not prepare me to date like a normal human," I muttered.

Grandma just laughed.

Even closed, the zoo was easy to access; it had its own road, after all, and they couldn't seal that off from the public. Still, we didn't want to head down the main drive. We would have been too obvious. I turned off onto one of the maintenance roads as soon as the opportunity arose, driving through the trees as we paralleled the zoo's rear retaining wall.

"There's a skeleton crew on the grounds taking care of feeding and vital maintenance and security's been stepped up, although that's just going to take it from 'joke' to 'slightly better joke,'" said Shelby, reading from her phone. Management had sent us all an email with the updated schedules and information on the closure. "I'm supposed to be on duty tomorrow to clean out the lion enclosure. Seriously? The zoo's closed, I'm not even the one doing the feedings, and I still have to change the kitty litter?"

"Do you actually use kitty litter?" I asked, pulling off the road and parking behind a particularly thick copse of oak trees. They would almost completely hide my car from anyone who wasn't really looking for it. As long as we didn't somehow trigger a full police sweep, it should be fine here.

Shelby gave me a withering look. "Of course not. It's a figure of speech."

"Hey, I don't look at you like that when you ask dumb questions about snakes," I said. I got out of the car, easing the door carefully closed behind me. The forest was quiet; out here, a slammed door could echo like a gunshot.

"I don't ask dumb questions about snakes," she protested. "I'm Australian. We're born knowing more about snakes than you will ever learn."

"Uh-huh." I crouched down, studying the loam around the car. "I don't see any cockatrice tracks here. We should be safe, for the moment. Put on your glasses, okay? I really don't want to explain to your parents that I have no idea where you went." Explaining her disappearance to the police would be even less fun. Getting involved in a murder investigation after my girlfriend went missing would be a guaranteed way to blow this identity.

"Are you sure these are necessary?" asked Shelby, producing a pair of wire-framed glasses from her pocket and slipping them on. The non-prescription lenses were polarized, and would give her a measure of resistance to petrifaction.

Besides which, maybe I'm shallow, but I'm also a science geek. Shelby in glasses was *hot*.

"Yes, they're necessary," I said, straightening. "You should try not to lock eyes with a cockatrice if you can avoid it, since there's always the chance that your glasses could be knocked askew or something, but they'll buy you time. Even if it's only a few seconds, a few seconds can save your life."

"All right," said Shelby.

"Follow me."

We slunk through the woods parallel to the fence, watching our feet as we tried to minimize the amount of noise that we were making. I grew up in the woods outside of Portland, Oregon, and while I didn't have Verity's knack for moving through the landscape like it was just another dance floor, I did all right for myself. Shelby, on the other hand, had a nasty tendency to step on branches and slip on patches of dried leaves, making it very apparent that *something* was moving through the trees, even if it wasn't quite clear *what*. I tried to focus on forging the quietest trail possible, rather than getting angry with her for not knowing the terrain. This wasn't the kind of forest she'd trained in. Of course she wouldn't know how to use it to her advantage.

A gnarled old oak pressed up against the fence about two hundred yards from our parking spot. The bricks were warped and bowed around the trunk of the ancient tree, and I estimated that we were less than ten years away from the zoo management needing to make a decision about either removing the tree or rebuilding the fence around it. I hoped they'd decide to keep the tree. It had been there a long time before the zoo showed up.

"This overhangs the alligator enclosure," I murmured. "This time of day, they'll either be inside, or they'll be sunning themselves near the interior fences. We should have a clear shot to the access door." Better, zoo security was unlikely to come anywhere near the place, since only a suicidal idiot would use this method of breaking in.

Shelby looked at me like I'd just proposed we grow wings and fly into the zoo. "Alligators? That's your brilliant plan? We climb a tree into a pen filled with *alligators?*"

"It's perfectly safe, as long as we're careful, and don't drop directly onto a gator's head or anything." I reached up and grabbed a low-hanging branch. "You can wait here, if you'd prefer."

Shelby muttered something under her breath that sounded suspiciously like "madman" and climbed after me. I somehow managed not to laugh.

The old oak was broad enough and bent enough that climbing wasn't difficult; in no time at all, we were inching our way along a branch that extended over the alligator enclosure. It was suddenly very obvious how Chandi had been able to use this method to break into the zoo. I made a mental note to talk to the groundskeepers about cutting this particular branch off the tree, and then dropped down to the soft grass below—

—only to find myself crouching almost nose to nose with Big Ted, the largest of the zoo's three American alligators. I blinked. He blinked, looking as surprised as I was, in his slow reptilian way. I heard a soft thump as

Shelby landed behind me, followed by the sound of her whispering, "Aw, fuck me."

Evolution has been kind to the alligator. It discovered a form that suited the alligator's function millennia ago, and rather than forcing the alligator to change, it backed off, leaving a living fossil to prowl the swamps and wetlands of the world. The alligator is the cardboard box of nature: perfect just as it is, and needing no further refinement.

Fortunately for us, that means the alligator is not the sharpest tool in the shed, since it's never needed to be. I straightened and began backing away, hands raised, less because I thought Big Ted would understand what I was trying to tell him, and more because he'd learned to associate humans with raised hands with a coming mealtime. Sure, promising food I didn't have to the giant reptilian killing machine was a potentially bad idea, but if he was waiting for me to drop a chicken, he might hesitate before taking a chunk out of my thigh.

Footsteps behind me told me that Shelby was following my lead. Good.

Big Ted appeared to finally finish processing the shock of our presence. He opened his mouth and hissed. It was a horrible, primeval sound, and I was probably going to be dreaming about it for the next few nights.

"Shelby," I said quietly, as I continued to back up, "look behind you. Do you see any other alligators?"

"No," she said. "I don't see security, either."

"That's good. Do you see the door in the fence over there?"

"Yes."

"That's better. All right. American alligators can sprint at a speed of about eleven miles an hour when they really try." Big Ted was growling now. That was worse than the hissing. I kept backing away, trying to put more distance between me and the massive reptile. "Hu mans can run much faster when they're properly moti vated. I'm feeling motivated. How about you?"

"I have never been this motivated in my life."

"Good. On the count of three, run. One, two—"

Big Ted reached a decision: we were a threat to hi territory. Jaws open, he lunged forward, aiming for my legs. I jumped backward, feeling my shoulder impac Shelby's chest, and his mouth snapped shut on empty air

"*Run!*" I whirled, putting my back to the alligator— not the most comfortable thing I'd ever been forced to do—and ran like hell for the door. Shelby was two steps ahead of me, not wasting time. Good. Big Ted was an noyed, but he didn't seem angry yet, and for a well-fed reptile his size, chasing us all the way to the door would be a serious commitment of energy and resources. I wa hoping that he would give up before we had to deal with the lock. If not . . .

Humans evolved from monkeys. Maybe it was time for us to put our primate climbing skills to good use.

When we hit the fence, I looked back. Big Ted was stil in virtually the same spot, mouth open, staring after us If alligators could look smug, he did. He had scared away the threat, and he'd done it without needing to put in much of an effort. He was still King Lizard.

"Thanks for that," I said, half-panting, and turned to open the door. It was a safety model that required a key to open from the outside as a precaution against idiot trying to sneak into the alligator enclosure, but which was always unlocked on the inside, in case one of those idiots actually managed it. "After you."

"I'm really glad you didn't say that when we went up the tree," said Shelby, and stepped out of the enclosure onto the narrow strip of grass between the chain-link fence and the low stone retaining wall. I followed her and together we hopped the wall and stepped, unsteadily onto the walking path beyond.

"I try not to get my girlfriends eaten by alligators,"

said. "I mean, it's a tidy form of breakup, but it's so hard to explain to their families."

Shelby punched me in the shoulder.

"Ow," I said, rubbing the spot. "What was that for?"

"You dropped me into an alligator pit," she said. "I don't think I needed any reason beyond that."

"Fair enough." I adjusted my glasses, stealing a look back at Big Ted. He was still in the same place, mouth open, content with his world. I turned to Shelby. "We're clear on the plan."

"Check the underbrush for signs of cockatrice, which will look a lot like signs of chicken, only bigger. If I find anything, come find you. If I don't find anything, come find you. If anyone finds me, tell them that I stopped by to pick up some notes from my office, and I got distracted thinking about whatever it seems like they're most likely to believe."

"Right. And if you see the cockatrice?"

"Shoot it." Shelby's lips thinned into a hard, uncompromising line. "I'm as fond of conservation as the next girl, but three people are dead, and it's not an endangered species. It has to go."

"Right." I hated sanctioning the death of any cryptid, but a cockatrice in this ecosystem was a ticking time bomb. It wasn't just killing people: by now, it would be killing rats, mice, and any other small animals that it came across. The cockatrice was innocent: it was just following its instincts. That couldn't matter anymore. "I have my phone if you need me."

"Same here," she said, and stepped forward to give me a quick kiss before she trotted away down the path, her ponytail swinging behind her and flashing golden in the light.

I was pretty sure that I was in love with that woman. I was even more sure that she was going to be trouble, one way or another. Turning, I made my own slower way toward the portion of the zoo that we had reserved for me to search.

Walking through the zoo in broad daylight with no children staring raptly at the animals or demanding answers from their teachers was a surreal experience, like suddenly finding myself in one of those movies where most of the human race has died off overnight. The animals clearly found it as strange as I did, because they were restless, staring at me with their wide, alien eyes as I walked past their enclosures. The Columbus Zoo was built on an open plan, giving each of our residents plenty of space within a semi-natural environment, and it seemed like every one of those residents was out, waiting to watch as I walked by. I split my attention between them and the ground. It was entirely possible that the cockatrice was roosting in the trees of the zebra enclosure, or hiding amongst the flamingos. So I studied them, looking for signs of illness or petrifaction, and I studied the ground, looking for scat or tracks that could lead me to my prey.

The zoo's claims of enhanced security were either idle boasting or failed to account for people's tendency to gather around coffee pots and snack machines when not supervised. I didn't see anyone.

I was halfway through my part of the zoo when I heard frantic quacking up ahead. I broke into a jog. Coming around the curve, I saw one of the many flocks of ducks that inhabited our open-air enclosures clustered on the bank of the artificial pond we provided for the capybara. I came closer. The ducks were directing their fury at the water.

Capybara aren't great climbers, and they're not a species that's particularly interested in escaping from any location that contains food, water, and a lack of predators. I boosted myself over the stone retaining wall and was inside the enclosure without even breaking stride. The ducks, long since accustomed to the presence of humans, ignored me as they kept quacking at the water. I crouched down, peering closer.

If I hadn't known better, I would have taken the stone

drake that was mired in the mud at the bottom of the pond for a particularly well-sculpted bit of garden statuary. I reached in and carefully freed it from the muck, shaking it a little to clear the worst of the mess away before pulling it out of the water. It was frozen in mid-paddle, its legs fully extended, as if it had been swimming when it met the cockatrice's deadly gaze.

The ducks continued to squawk and complain around me, although my presence seemed to be calming them somewhat. Humans brought bread and other tasty things. Humans might throw rocks or kick, but they never really *hurt* ducks. Humans were safe.

"Sorry, guys," I said to the ducks, straightening up as I continued to study the petrified drake. I couldn't tell how long ago the petrifaction had been complete; the drake was smaller than either a human or a lindworm, so the process wouldn't have taken long. Death would have been virtually instantaneous. I'd need to crack the drake open to know whether the entire thing was stone, or whether it was still flesh inside, but that wouldn't tell me anything. It would just destroy something beautiful. That seemed unfair, somehow.

If the ducks were still this upset, however, the cockatrice must have been here recently. I peered at the mud. Duck tracks obscured any tracks the cockatrice might have left on this side of the pond, and so I inched carefully around the water, aware that I was breaking a good dozen zoo rules as I made my way deeper into the enclosure. No capybara showed themselves, but I could hear them grunting and huffing at me from inside their artificial jungle. That was reassuring. They were mammal noises, nothing like the hiss or croak of the cockatrice. If it was still lurking here, it hadn't petrified the capybara.

Not yet, anyway. I moved faster, scanning the ground . . . and there, at the edge of the pond, I found what I was looking for. They could have been mistaken for chicken tracks, if they'd been smaller, and if we'd had any free-range chickens at the zoo. As it was, they were clearly out of place.

The trail began in the bushes, made its way to the pond, and stayed there, driven deep into the mud. The cockatrice had stopped for a drink. That was probably when it petrified the duck. I followed the track to the other side of the enclosure, hoping that it wouldn't disappear into the underbrush.

It didn't. Instead, it just disappeared. "Shit," I murmured, and peered closer. There were no scrapes to indicate that the cockatrice had taken flight; it was walking, and then it was gone. I straightened, trying to take in the enclosure around me. I was almost to the back, and that meant I was probably near the wall. I reached into the foliage. My fingers penetrated only a few inches before I hit stone. Feeling around, I found the latch that would allow the zookeeper standing on the other side to open the feeding hatch and toss in treats for the capybara—or, if they had a more nefarious goal in mind, allow them to lean in and lift out a runaway cockatrice.

Whoever was using the cockatrice as a murder weapon was still here at the zoo.

I pulled my phone out of my pocket, dialing Shelby's number. It rang until the call rolled to voicemail and her cheerful voice offered me the chance to leave her a message. There was a killer loose in the zoo, and my girlfriend wasn't answering her phone.

Somehow, I managed to walk non-disruptively through the enclosure to the retaining wall. The ducks quacked angrily as I bent to press the stone drake into the mud at the edge of the pond. Then I hopped over the wall and broke into a run, heading as fast as I could for the far side of the zoo, and hoping that I was being paranoid. God, I hoped that I was being paranoid.

Even though I knew I probably wasn't.

Twenty-one

"Nothing good has ever come from splitting the party."

— Thomas Price

Ohio's West Columbus Zoo, running like a bat out of hell toward the big cat enclosures

THE GEESE HAD TAKEN over most of the zoo's walkways without humans to shoo them away. They scattered as I ran, spreading outward in feathery waves to either side of me. Between the motion and their angry honks and hisses, there was no chance I'd have the advantage of surprise on my side: anyone with eyes or ears would know that I was coming. So I put my head down and focused on speed. The faster I could get to Shelby, the faster I could convince myself that everything was all right; that I was the first person in the history of my family to be paranoid for no good reason.

I actually found myself wishing that security would spot and stop me. At least then I'd have some backup.

The roar of a big cat—lion or tiger, I didn't know, although Shelby would have—sounded from ahead, loud and angry and filled with a territorial possessiveness that I didn't need to speak feline to understand. The cats never roared at Shelby like that. They'd eat her if she gave them the chance, but they didn't see her as an intruder. I ran faster.

The geese tapered off as I got closer to the roaring. They knew a predator when they heard one, and they wanted nothing to do with what they heard. The smaller big cats were outside in their daylight enclosures, prowling and snarling, clearly agitated. The zoo's two snow leopards were crouched atop their rock, tails puffed out to three times their normal size, snarling in low, almost subsonic tones that put my teeth on edge. Eyes flashed from the darkness of the lynx enclosure as I ran past it, and I found myself grateful for the fences between us.

Humanity is on top of the food chain because we have weapons, and fences, and the ability to run from danger. I was running *into* danger, and since I didn't want to get tackled by any security guards I might happen to run into—possibly literally at my current speed—I was doing it without my gun drawn. This was stupid. It might actually cross the line into suicidal. And it was what I'd been training for since I was a kid who didn't understand that someday, the world would come with consequences.

The door to the big cat house was ajar. I managed to slow down before charging inside, putting a hand on the gun I had concealed beneath my jacket as I eased my body through the gap.

The hot stink of cat hit me as soon as I was inside: raw and primal and vitally alive in a way that was entirely different from the smell of my reptiles. There was blood beneath the surface stench, freshly-spilled and lingering in the air. That didn't necessarily mean anything. The big cats were obligate carnivores, and they required a lot of meat to get through their days.

The cats themselves were watching me as they prowled their cages, growling in agitation. A big male lion occupied the enclosure to my left, while an equally large tiger of indeterminate gender was to my right, lips drawn back to display massive canines. Looking at them, I guessed that the lion had been the source of the roaring. He still looked unhappy, although he wasn't roaring anymore. I couldn't tell whether or not that was a good sign.

Moving carefully, so as to minimize the amount of noise my footsteps would make, I made my way down the length of the big cat house. The lion and tiger followed in their enclosures, matching their steps to mine. Eerie as the giant predators were, I was strangely grateful. Their growls and the thudding of their paws would cover any noise I happened to make, muffling it and making it easier for me to reach my destination.

The layout of the big cat house was linear, with an entrance at either end. The door leading to the offices and zookeeper back-channels was at the other end of the room from the entrance I had used. Naturally. Circumstances never conspire to deposit me near the door I need. As I approached the door, I saw that it was also standing slightly open. Not enough to be obvious from a distance, but enough that it was obvious someone had been through very recently, and in a hurry.

Stealth was abandoned again as I jogged for the open door. The big cats matched my stride, although they were stopped by the edges of their enclosure, and snarled in obvious frustration as I went through the open door and stepped into the narrow white hallway of the backstage area of the big cat house.

There was blood on the floor.

Not much—just a few drops, small enough that they could almost have been dismissed as runoff from feeding the cats. Except that the big cats didn't get live prey, no matter how much they wanted it, and nothing dead bleeds like a living body. This blood was bright red, almost artificial-looking, with none of the watery clarity of blood that came from pre-butchered meat.

The halls were silent. I stopped long enough to draw my gun and continued forward, listening for any sign that I was not alone. The blood trail led deeper, curving away from the offices and into the channel that was used to carry food to the big cats. I followed it, trying to focus on the entire area, and not just on the question that those bright drops of blood forced me to keep asking. Who was bleeding? Shelby, or someone else? How badly were they hurt? There wasn't enough blood to be fatal, but that didn't have to mean anything. There are a lot of ways to keep blood from hitting the ground.

The trail led into one of the feeding pens. I hesitated only long enough to be sure that the channel connecting it to the cage on the other side was closed. Then I un-latched the door and stepped inside.

It was a small, concrete space reminiscent of the zoos of old, the ones where the animals slept on bare stone and were little more than prisoners of man's eternal war against the natural world. The walls, floor, and ceiling were all designed to be easily hosed down, and there was a drain in the middle of the room, making it clear that the hosing happened on a fairly regular basis. In addition to the entrance and the broad, portcullis-like barrier that separated the feeding room from the open enclosures, there was a narrow, solid metal door set deep into one wall. In case something went wrong during a feeding, the keeper was to retreat into the tiny built-in "panic room," giving time for the other keepers to run for help.

The blood trail led to the panic room door.

Cautiously, I approached the closed door. When I was close enough, I whispered, "Shelby? Are you in there?"

"Alex?" There was no mistaking the relief, or the pain, in her voice. "Is that really you?"

"If not, I was replaced so long ago that it doesn't make any functional difference," I said, which may not have been the most reassuring answer possible. I was too wor-ried about her to think straight. "Can you open the door?"

She laughed a little, unsteadily. "No. It's not meant to be opened from the inside. I wasn't thinking too clearly when I ran in here."

"Okay. Can *I* open the door, or will you shoot me if I try?"

"Are you sure you're Alex?"

"Believe me, no one else is going to claim my family."

This time, her laughter was a little more sincere. "All right. Yes, you can open the door."

"Thank you." After one last glance back to make sure that no one was sneaking up on me, I holstered my gun and opened the panic room door. Shelby, who had been crammed into the small space with little room to move, or even turn around, tumbled out. I managed to catch her before she could hit the floor. She cried out—a small sound, quickly swallowed, but that was enough to tell me that the blood was definitely hers. "Shelby?"

"It's nothing." She paused before laughing unsteadily. "All right, it's not nothing, but it's not that bad. Let me up."

I let go of her, and she straightened, pulling away from me. The motion revealed the blood soaking into her khaki top, turning it a plummy purple. "Shelby . . ."

"No, really, it's nothing. Look." She pulled up the bottom of her shirt, revealing a cut that slashed across her ribs, deep enough that it was going to need stitches. It was surrounded by a thick crust of dried blood. "Hurts like nobody's business, but it's not going to kill me."

"What happened?"

"I barely believe it, and I'm the one who got stabbed," she said, pulling her shirt back down. She shook her head slowly, confusion written plainly across her face. "It was Lloyd."

"Lloyd? The security guard?"

Shelby nodded. "The same. He saw me checking the bushes outside the cat house. Came over to ask what I was doing here when the zoo was closed, and I said I'd dropped my wallet in the bushes the day before, and that I was trying to find it. He offered to take me back to the office to check the lost and found, and I would have gone with him so that I didn't seem suspicious, but . . ." Her voice trailed off.

"But what?" I prompted.

"But when he saw that I was wearing glasses, his whole face changed. He didn't look like Lloyd. He looked like a stranger—an angry stranger, who wanted to hurt me. He asked whether I'd always worn glasses, and I said no, they were new. I should have pretended, I should have said I wore contacts for work, but I wasn't thinking. I was just reacting. As soon as I said that . . ." Shelby paused again before looking up, meeting my eyes, and saying, "He said he wasn't going to let me stop him. That he'd always liked me, but that he couldn't let that change anything. And then he drew a knife. On me!"

"What kind of knife?"

"A stupid big one, that's what kind of knife," snapped Shelby, looking annoyed. "Does it matter what kind of knife? He pulled it out of his coat and he *stabbed* at me in broad daylight, where anybody could have seen."

"That means he wasn't worried about getting caught," I said. "That's a bad sign."

"You think?" Shelby shook her head. "I turned and ran into the cat house. I figured he might not follow me inside. The cats get a little unhappy when people fight in front of them, and they were already all up in arms about something."

"If the cockatrice was nearby, that would have given them plenty to be upset about." Animals were more adept than humans at knowing when there was danger close by them. Better senses of smell, better instincts, and less arrogance. It wouldn't necessarily keep them safe, but it could turn them into early warning systems. "Did Lloyd say or do anything else?"

"You mean beyond stabbing me? Because believe me, that was more than enough to convince me that I didn't want to be anywhere near the fucker." Shelby pressed a hand against the cut in her side. "He said I wasn't fooling him. I wanted to ask him what I'd been trying to fool him *about*, but he didn't leave me much time. The stabbing was already in process, and running away was a much more important goal."

"Right. We need to get you out of here." I looked at the door that would lead us back into the big cat house. Shelby was injured; she needed medical treatment. But unless we wanted to explain the entire impossible situation to the Columbus police, I needed to get her out of the zoo without either of us being seen, and without running into Lloyd, who had somehow been transformed from a mild-mannered security guard to a knife-wielding maniac.

"No big deal, right?" I muttered. More loudly, I asked, "Shelby? Where do you keep the bleach?"

Shelby had almost stopped bleeding, and while her injuries were bad enough to make me want to scoop her into my arms and carry her back to the car damsel-in-distress style, they weren't bad enough to be life-threatening if we got her looked at soon. Much as I hated to take the time, leaving a trail of human blood through the big cat house would cause us a lot more problems than we had the energy to deal with right now.

Fortunately, zookeepers are experts when it comes to dealing with bloodstains. I found bleach, meat tenderizer, and a bloodstained mop in the janitor's closet, and set about mixing Shelby's blood with the blood of a whole lot of dead animals as I vigorously mopped up the trail I'd used to find her. She sat tiredly on an overturned bucket, watching me work, pointing out when I missed a spot, and trying not to get any more blood on the floor. She was still responsive and alert, and she swore she wasn't bleeding anymore. I wasn't certain I believed her. I wasn't certain it mattered.

When the mess on the floor had been reduced to just another stain of indeterminate origin, I returned the mop, bucket, and cleaning supplies to their places. Shelby was waiting when I came back. "All good?" she asked.

"All clean," I said, offering my arm. "We're going to have to find another way out of the zoo."

"What about the delivery gate?" asked Shelby. "That's how you had Dee get Chandi out before."

"That might work. Can you walk?"

"I could hike a mile without noticing it, but only if we left now," said Shelby. Her grip on my arm belied her careless tone. She was worried, and frankly, so was I. "I'm sorry we didn't find the cockatrice."

"No, but we know it's here." I began walking toward the exit, taking it slow out of consideration for Shelby's injuries. This time, I was hoping we *wouldn't* see any other security guards. As we walked, I explained what I'd found in the capybara enclosure, including the poor, petrified duck.

She laughed, sounding a little bit perplexed as she asked, "So what, you just walked off and left him there? Won't someone notice?"

"Maybe. But everyone will assume someone else did it. In five years, everybody will swear the duck came from one of the fountains, or that it was put there as a prank by one of the summer trainees. It'll become part of the landscape. Trust me. Denial is a powerful force in the human psyche, and anyone who works around animals gets extremely good at it."

"Swell. How do you think they'll explain away us if we get petrified? Will we be a tribute to the two zookeepers who mysteriously decided to abandon their posts after a few people got murdered?"

"Since statues wearing real clothes aren't exactly considered high art in Ohio, probably not." I kept scanning the bushes as we walked, watching for signs of the cockatrice. "They'd remove us quickly and without making a fuss, and write it off as a terrible prank committed by someone with no social skills whatsoever."

"Sounds like you've really thought this through."

"I think most things through, even when it might be

better not to." The zoo was built in a mostly circular design. Every path curved slightly, either conforming to the shapes of the enclosures, or leading the guests inexorably toward the money-making points on our local compass: the gift shop, the café, the exit. We were trying to avoid falling into that easy passage, working against the shape of the land as we pressed on toward the gate that was used for large deliveries.

We could have taken the back passages, hidden from the main facility by clever fencing and building placement, but those were narrow and confined, and much more likely to be observed by the skeleton crew of security on the premises. Counterintuitive as it seemed, cutting straight through the middle of the zoo was the best way to move unobserved.

Then there was the matter of Lloyd. I kept the hand that wasn't supporting Shelby on my gun as we walked. I didn't know why the old security guard had stabbed my girlfriend, and if he put in a repeat appearance, I wasn't going to give him the luxury of explaining.

Something rustled in the bushes. I looked over and saw another smug, well-fed goose waddling out, tail wagging as it approached us. "Just a goose," I said, shoulders relaxing slightly.

Shelby didn't answer.

"Shelby?" Even as I said her name, I realized she wasn't walking so much as stumbling along, more than half-dragged by my own momentum. I turned toward her. She was sagging on my arm, shoulders slumped, head dangling like it was simply too heavy to be held up. "*Shelby?*"

"'M okay," she slurred. "Just a little shocky, that's all. 'M fine . . ."

"Liar," I said. Speed was suddenly more important than safety. I took my hand off my gun and swung her up into my arms, only staggering slightly under the weight of her before I started jogging down the path toward the delivery gate. She gasped a little at the jostling. I winced, and kept going. "I'm sorry, sweetheart, I'm so sorry, but we need to get you looked at as soon as possible, and that means we're running."

She didn't say anything. I chose to take that as an admission that this was the only way, and jogged faster, trying to keep myself as calm as possible under the circumstances. Panic would just slow me down and reduce Shelby's chances.

How deep had the knife actually gone into her body? How much blood had she lost? Questions warred with my absence of answers, but only briefly: then guilt showed up, and was more than happy to take over for everything else that I might be feeling. I ran, and kept running, until I reached the wood gate that would lead to the loading area. I shifted Shelby enough to free my right hand, undid the latch, and slipped quickly through, trying to tell myself that her unresponsiveness wasn't a bad sign.

I wasn't really listening by that point.

Luck was with us, in a small way: there was no one in the loading area. I was able to carry Shelby to the outside gate without anyone questioning what I was doing or what we were doing at the zoo while it was supposed to be closed.

The delivery gate was closed and padlocked. Of course. There wouldn't be any deliveries today, not with no one here to accept them, and this would have been seen as a potential security risk. One that I'd very much been looking forward to exploiting. There were no cameras on the delivery gate. Why did they need a damn lock?

"I'm going to put you down for a moment, all right?" I didn't expect a response from her, but I wanted her to know what I was doing as I carefully lowered her feet to the ground and propped her against the side of the gate. There was a chance she'd leave bloodstains behind, but I couldn't worry about that, not now. I needed to worry about getting her out of here. That took priority over everything else.

The lock on the gate was a straightforward one, probably purchased from the local hardware store when someone realized that having unfettered access to the zoo could result in drunk teenagers breaking in and getting eaten by alligators. I produced a set of lock picks from the inside pocket of my jacket and set to work.

"I don't know what your childhood was like, but my parents began teaching me the basics of breaking and entering when I was five," I said, trying to keep my voice neutral, like I was having a conversation with my girl-friend and not babbling at her semiconscious body. "The day I can't take out a lock like this in thirty seconds is the day I find myself disowned—ha." The tumbler snapped open. "Today is not that day. Come along, darling, your ride to much-needed medical care awaits."

With Shelby in my arms, I was able to close the gate, but not relock it. Hopefully, everyone would assume someone else had left the padlock open. If not, that would become one more problem that we would have to deal with later. I had my hands full with the problem I was dealing with now.

The frontage road used for zoo deliveries ran around the back, following the curve of the fence. That was a good thing; the trees were thick between us and the highway, and unless one of the delivery drivers had missed the memo, we would be able to walk here undisturbed. And that was the bad thing: we would have to walk for quite some distance, because my car was safely hidden in the trees on the other side of the zoo.

Shelby wasn't moving at all. Only the slow rise and fall of her chest told me that she was even alive. If I tried to run to the car, I'd face the risk of dropping her, and even if I didn't drop her, the bumpiness of the trip wouldn't do her any favors. It would be a shorter trip through the woods, but that would be even harder on her—and on me. If I was being truly honest about the situation, I wasn't sure I could carry her that far. Shelby was a slim woman, but she was muscular, and almost as tall as I was.

"Shelby? Can you hear me?"

She mumbled something. Or maybe that was my imagination assigning meaning to a random gasp. It didn't matter. Either way, I knew what had to be done if I wanted there to be any chance for her.

"I need to leave you here while I go and get the car," I said, stepping off the road and into the trees. I walked a few yards in, positioning us so that we wouldn't be visible to anyone who happened to be passing by. "I'm sorry. It's the only way I'm going to get you to a doctor in time. I'll be back for you as soon as I can."

She didn't make a sound as I lowered her to the ground, propping her up against a nearby tree. The temptation to check her stomach wound was high. I quashed it, forcing myself to turn away from her and head back to the road. I broke into a run as soon as my feet hit the pavement.

I felt incredibly light without Shelby in my arms, and the guilt and fear that nipped at my heels drove me to break all my previous records for distance running as I covered the half mile between my starting point and the car. It was still where I had parked it, thank God; if it had been gone, I would probably have stood frozen in the woods outside the zoo until the police found Shelby's body and came to collect me.

Throwing myself into the front seat, I jammed my key into the ignition and broke several speed laws pulling out and turning around, heading back to where Shelby was waiting. *Just hold on,* I thought desperately, thankful for the short distance, and even more thankful for the fact that there was no one else on the road. *I'm almost there, so just hold on.*

Cars are wonderful things. I was back where I had left Shelby only minutes after I got into the driver's seat, and less than fifteen minutes total after leaving her behind. I stopped the car in the middle of the road, stumbling out onto the pavement, and ran into the trees. I pushed through the branches to the place where I'd left her—

—and stopped, blinking in confusion at the scene in front of me, or rather, at what *wasn't* in front of me.

Shelby was gone.

Twenty-two

"There is a moment, just before the bullet
hits, just before the serpent strikes, when
you will realize that your life is about to
change forever, and not in a good way. That
is the moment when you will try to make a
bargain with God. That is the moment when
you will become an atheist."

—Jonathan Healy

*Outside the wall of Ohio's West Columbus Zoo, somehow
missing a girlfriend*

"SHELBY?"

The question hung in the air unanswered, making me feel foolish for asking it. Shelby wasn't there, and
with her injuries, there was no way she'd recovered
enough to move on her own while I was getting the car.
I still took a few precious seconds to scan the nearby
brush, looking for the blood trail she would have left if
she'd tried to move on her own. It wasn't there. Someone
had taken her.

I took a deep breath, trying to force down the wave of
panic clawing at my chest. She was gone. That was a fact;
that was something I was going to have to deal with. All
it really meant was that I was going to need to get her
back.

I stepped deeper into the brush, watching the ground

for signs of disturbance. Lindworms don't normally have territories that span more than a few miles, but she'd killed the local male's mate. If it had somehow tracked her, it might have—

No. I rejected the thought as quickly as it came. Shelby had *not* been dragged away by a hungry lindworm. This wasn't *Jaws*: an animal that consisted of nothing but hunger and survival instinct wasn't going to come looking for revenge. Even if it was, it wouldn't come near the zoo—too many people, too many large scavengers. And besides, there would be traces if something that large had been through here. The brush was almost undisturbed. Nothing larger than a human had passed recently.

The trunk of the tree where Shelby had been leaning was damp and sticky with her blood. I touched the bark, unsure whether or not I should be reassured when my fingers came away red. Then I looked down, and began trying to sort through the broken branches as I looked for a direction. *This* trail was where I'd carried Shelby from the road, and *this* trail was where I had forged my way back in . . .

When I was done, there was only one trail unaccounted for, wider and slightly more uneven than the others, like whoever had walked there had been dealing with an unexpected weight. I followed it to a spot on the road a few yards from where Shelby and I had originally entered the trees. Crouching down, I studied the pavement, looking for tracks. There were some muddy scuffs, like someone had walked here recently. And there was a single drop of blood.

Someone had taken Shelby. Someone had followed us out of the zoo and taken her.

I wanted to be sick. Instead, I pulled out my phone and walked back to the car, scrolling through my contacts until I came to the number labeled "dry cleaning." I pressed it and raised the phone to my ear.

"Yes?"

"Grandma." I closed my eyes. "I need you. Please come."

I was still standing next to my car when my grandmother pulled up, parking her own car so that it blocked the entire road. She launched herself from the driver's seat at me, and Crow was close behind her, his wings spread wide as he arrowed for my chest. He hit me like a small feathery missile, and I wrapped my arms around him, automatically supporting his hindquarters in order to keep him from shredding my shoulders.

"You're projecting panic, Grandma," I said, fighting to keep my voice level. Maybe it was my anti-telepathy charm taking the edge off, and maybe it was the fact that I was panicking quite well without any outside help, but I didn't want to run for the woods. I just wanted the extra waves of fear to stop. "Please pull it back. I don't know how much I can take."

"I'm sorry," she said, stricken. Her eyes flashed white, and the foreboding in the air decreased. I only wished she could take my panic away as easily as she'd stopped projecting her own. "What can I do?"

"You've already done it. You brought Crow." I walked back to the place on the road where that last drop of blood glittered dark and foreboding against the pavement and knelt, putting Crow carefully down. He looked up at me and cawed, tail lashing. "Shelby, Crow. Where's Shelby?"

He sat down and croaked at me.

"Shelby. You liked Shelby. I know you can track by smell. You've tracked me through five miles of dense forest because you thought it was time for dinner. Now where is Shelby?"

Crow looked at me for a moment, head cocked to the side. Then he leaned forward and sniffed the ground, wings half-mantling, before he launched himself into the air. In seconds, he was gone, flying up over the zoo and disappearing.

I gaped. When I asked my grandmother to bring the Church Griffin, I hadn't been counting on the fact that he had wings and I didn't. "Oh, shit," I said, and ran back to my car. "Southeast, he's going southeast. What's southeast of here?"

"Lots of things, Alex, that's not exactly a small question!" said Grandma, following me. "Woods. Some cave systems. Dayton . . ."

"The gorgons." I raised my head and looked at her. "That's where the cockatrice came from. That's where this all started. And they're to the southeast, too. Someone from the gorgon community has Shelby."

Grandma stared at me. Then, in a dangerous tone, she said, "I don't have to move my car. I can keep you here."

"No, you can't." I got into the driver's seat, fastening my seat belt on autopilot. "I'm going after her, Grandma. I *have* to go after her. I'm the reason she got involved in all of this to begin with." She was the reason I was distracted. I'd spent *years* keeping myself from forming any attachments that could interfere with my work, and then Shelby goddamn Tanner had come along and fucked everything up. And all I wanted now was to see her safely home.

"Then I'm coming with you," said Grandma. "I can't let you run into a nest of snakes alone."

"That's racist," I said automatically. Then I shook my head. "No. Grandpa's at work, the cockatrice is still somewhere in the city, and you can't leave Sarah alone for as long as this is going to take. I'm trained for this. Now please. I'm not going to argue with you while Shelby's out there bleeding to death." Assuming Shelby still had blood; assuming she wasn't a statue by now.

That kind of thinking wouldn't get me any closer to saving my girlfriend. I shut the car door, rolling down the window so that I could say, "I'll call as soon as I know anything. Trust me and my ability not to get myself killed over something stupid, all right? Now please. Move your car."

She looked at me sadly for what felt like hours but was probably just a few seconds before nodding and walking back to her own vehicle. I rolled up my window and clutched the steering wheel, waiting for her to get out of my way so that I could follow Crow's flight path across the city.

The second her car had rolled far enough to leave me room to maneuver, I hit the gas, blasting past my grandmother and heading for the main road at an unsafe speed. I made matters worse by pulling out my phone again, driving one-handed as I pulled up the number for the Sarpas.

Chandi answered the phone, sounding surprisingly polite as she said, "You have reached the Sarpa residence. Who may I say is calling?"

"It's Alex Price," I said, and swore under my breath as I swerved to avoid a VW bug that seemed to think the appropriate place to slow down and smell the roses was in the middle of a major thoroughfare. "I need to speak to your mother. Can you put her on the phone?"

"What? Why are *you* on my phone?" Her tone turned irritated and slightly scornful, which was much more normal for her. "You were just in my house. Why are you on my phone?"

"I need to speak to your mother," I repeated. "If you want me to open the reptile house tomorrow, you'll put her on the phone."

"*What*? You can't threaten—"

"I'm not threatening anything. I won't be able to open the reptile house if I'm dead. Now put your mother on the *phone*."

There was a pause as Chandi considered my words, weighing their meaning. Then she said, "I'll get my mother."

"Thank you."

There was a clunk from her end of the phone, followed by the distant sound of her bellowing for her mom to come to the phone. I gritted my teeth as I merged onto the freeway, still driving one-handed. It was easier than I expected, maybe because I was too angry and too afraid to really pay attention to what I was doing. Things are always easy when you refuse to let yourself remember how dangerous they are.

"Alex?" Kumari sounded worried. That made sense: I didn't normally call the house several times in the same day. "What is going on?"

"Have you made any headway with who might be trying to kill us, Kumari? Because Shelby's missing, and it looks like whoever took her went back to the local gorgon community, or someplace near there. What haven't you told me? What do I need to know?"

Kumari gasped. If not for that, I would have thought that she'd hung up on me as the seconds ticked past without her saying anything.

"Kumari. I'd like to put both hands back on the wheel before I flip the car. Please."

"I didn't . . . it was just a rumor. I gave it no credence."

"*What* was just a rumor?"

"The mother of the community in the woods, she was a crossbreed. Father of one strain, mother of another."

"Yes, I know that," I said impatiently. "I had dinner with her."

"Most crossbreeds are sterile. She was not."

That was a surprise. "Meaning what?"

"Meaning she had a son, but he was born malformed and twisted. Genetics were not kind. He was an outcast among his own people, always seeking a way to earn his place. He disappeared some years ago."

"This is fascinating from a biological standpoint, but what does it have to do with Shelby?"

"When I contacted the local bogeymen and explained what I needed to ask, they told me to look for the gorgon's son. That while many of them would be quite pleased if you and your family were killed, no one had been asking about it lately, save for the gorgon's son."

"I thought you said he disappeared."

"Yes," said Kumari. "I did."

This time, her silence extended until I pulled the phone from my ear and checked the screen. The call had ended. I had five bars of service; we hadn't been disconnected. She hung up on me.

"Swell," I muttered, dropping the phone into the passenger seat. Finally gripping the wheel with both hands, I hit the gas and sped down the highway, heading as fast as I could for what might well be certain doom.

There are species in the cryptid world that are cross-fertile with each other, just like there are in the scientifically accepted world: as a wise man once said, life finds a way. Life is extremely bloody-minded, and often finds the worst way possible, preferably with a body count somewhere in the triple digits. Hannah's existence was biologically no stranger than the existence of, say, mules, hinnies, or ligers. It happens. But crossbreeds of that type are almost always sterile, because while nature likes to find a way, biology likes to set limits. Those limits say "no, at some point, we're pushing things too far, now stop before you get silly."

There have been a few recorded cases of mules and the like having offspring, but they're few and far between, and almost nothing is known about how those babies will mature, or what traits they'll inherit from their crossbred parents. If Hannah was fertile, that changed everything.

I hit the gas a little harder.

Kumari hadn't named Hannah's impossible offspring, calling him only "the gorgon's son," but based on Shelby's experience at the zoo, I had a decent idea of who it was.

Lloyd, who should have been the man at the gate when the second guard was killed, yet was somehow conveniently missing from his post when the cockatrice came to call.

Lloyd, who always wore his hat, and who knew the zoo inside and out.

Lloyd, who had looked so surprised to see me after I saw the cockatrice in my backyard.

He wasn't a zookeeper, but that would actually make it easier for him to move unobserved. Who watched the guards to see if they were in the right place? Management, presumably, and yet no one else on the property would have reported him for snooping around a restricted area. He could have hidden his cockatrice anywhere in the zoo without needing to worry about being caught.

Lloyd always wore his glasses, thick, Coke-bottle things that looked too heavy for his face. What if they weren't intended to improve his vision, but rather to protect the zoo's staff and patrons from the full effect of his gaze?

I'd always taken Lloyd for human. It was an assumption, but it was a statistically safe one: even in an area with a large cryptid population, nine out of ten people on the street, if not more, will be human beings. We are the dominant sapient species on this planet, numberswise. So assuming that the little old man who checked my badge at the front gate was human wasn't arrogant; it was reasonable. And it may have gotten Shelby killed.

I broke the speed limit for the entire drive, and saw no police on the roads; so much for Ohio's finest. Then again, with a killer in the area who was somehow turning his victims partially into stone, it was possible they just had better things to worry about than speeders—and depending on the strength of Grandma's whammy, they could have been choosing not to see me out of a vague sense of self-preservation. I barely slowed down in time to avoid missing my turnoff into the forest, where the trees promptly closed in.

Illusions can't actually keep you out if you're determined to keep going; they just mess with the visual aspects of the world, and do nothing to change the physical. I tightened my hands on the wheel, hoping my memory of the road was correct, and kept going into what should have been unbroken forest—

—only to emerge onto the curving road surrounding the gorgon community. On a hunch, I leaned forward and peered upward. In the sky, high overhead, a black shape that didn't quite look like a bird was circling. "Good boy, Crow," I said, and continued on my way down, through the spiral, to the cluster of mobile homes below.

A crowd was gathering by the time I reached ground level, gorgons appearing in every doorway and around the sides of every building. I slowed enough to give them time to get out of my way but kept driving until I reached the spot where Dee had instructed me to park on my first visit.

She emerged from a nearby trailer as I turned off the engine, making it clear that she'd been watching my approach. Her snakes were up and hissing, mirroring the distressed look on her face. I adjusted my glasses to make sure they would shield me from accidental petrifaction, unfastened my seat belt, and got out of the car.

"Alex!" Dee skidded to a stop a few feet away from me. Frank was approaching from the back of the crowd; he must have been in his office, leaving him farther to walk before he could find out what I was doing here. "What in the world—?"

"Look up." I pointed, to make my meaning perfectly clear.

It's interesting: even when they're not primates, most things that *look* like humans will *react* like humans under normal circumstances. That includes following simple directions that don't make sense. More than half the crowd, Dee and Frank included, looked up to where Crow was doing his slow circle.

Of the gorgons who did look up, only Dee gasped, her

hand flying to her cheek before she said, sounding un-nerved, "Is that Crow? What's he doing?"

"Hunting." I waited until she looked back down be-fore I continued, "Shelby's missing, Dee. She was hurt while we were searching for the cockatrice at the zoo, and in the time it took me to go and get the car, someone took her. When I asked Crow to find her, he came here. When I called Kumari and asked if anyone might be in-terested in hurting us, she told me a really interesting story. About Hannah, and the son no one bothered to tell me she had."

Dee's eyes widened further, and her snakes stopped hissing as they coiled close against her head, becoming a tightly-knotted pile of serpentine curls. "I don't under-stand what you're talking about."

"She spoke to the local bogeymen. I asked her, since they won't talk to me. And according to what they told her, I should be looking for 'the gorgon's son' when I'm trying to find the person who took Shelby. So is there anything you'd been wanting to tell me, Dee? As a friend? Because now would be the time."

One of the gorgon men to my left took a step forward, the snakes atop his head hissing menacingly. I had the gun out of my belt and pointed in his direction before he could take a second step. I didn't turn, but he stopped moving, which told me my aim was true. Not taking my eyes off Dee, I continued, "Also, we're all friends here, right? I mean, I know I'm outnumbered, so you could technically go ahead and jump me, but I have eight bul-lets in this gun, and I'm a real fast shot. Right now, we're having a chat. No hostilities. I'd like to keep it that way. But if you decide we're going to have problems, I'm not going to be the guy who tells you no."

"Paul, stop it," snapped Dee, dropping her hand to her side. The gorgon to my left took a big step backward. I lowered my gun. Dee focused back on me. "Alex, I swear, I don't have any idea what you're talking about. I've been here all day. We all have."

"I believe you," I said wearily. "That's the hard part. But someone tried to burn down Shelby's apartment building last night, and now she's missing. I want her back, preferably alive and intact. Crow led me here. You didn't tell me Hannah had a son. Now do you want to help all these things make sense, or are you just going to keep standing there?"

Frank pushed his way through the crowd to Dee's side. He put a hand on her shoulder, looking dispassionately at the gun I was holding, before he asked, "What do you want us to do?"

"I want you to tell me where to find Hannah's son."

"I wish we could." Frank shook his head. "No one here knows."

I looked up to where Crow was still endlessly circling, like a carrion bird above its prey. I wished there were a way I could call him back to land and make him show me where to go next. Sadly, even a smart animal is still an animal. He'd done as much as he was going to do. I looked back down.

"Fine, then," I said to Dee and Frank. "If you can't take me to Hannah's son, I'll settle for the next best thing. Take me to your leader. I want to talk to Hannah."

Twenty-three

"Underestimate the power of gravity, if you like; underestimate how many bullets you'll need to take out a chimera. But never, if you value your life, underestimate what a parent will do for the sake of preserving a child."

—Alexander Healy

At a hidden gorgon community in the middle of the Ohio woods, which is probably a terrible place to be right now

IT WASN'T A SURPRISE when Dee and Frank led me away from the buildings that made up the bulk of the community, heading toward the woods. We were heading away from the fringe farms, I noted; that was a little more unexpected. The fringe must have come later.

"I wish you'd called," said Dee, for the third time.

"I wish you'd told me Lloyd was a gorgon," I said, my temper beginning to fray around the edges. "Maybe it wouldn't have made any difference. Maybe it would have made *all* the difference. Now people are dead, and Shelby's missing, and we're never going to know."

"You cannot blame Deanna for protecting her people," said Frank.

"Like hell I can't." I kept walking, locking my eyes on the tree line. Nothing was moving there. Any deer that lived in this stretch of the Ohio woods would have learned to be cautious, to avoid the smell of both humans and snakes. They would have had to be stupid not to have learned.

Snakes have a distinctive smell, dry and ancient, like the wrappings of a mummy or the rot that sleeps at the heart of a rainforest. Pliny's gorgons like Dee and Frank have a bit of that same smell, but it's only noticeable if you get right up on top of them, moving into their personal space, which is never a safe place to be. The closer we got to the woods, the stronger the smell became, until it was like we were walking into an old, primal version of the reptile house at the zoo. The hair on my arms stood on end as my mammalian sense of self-preservation kicked in, trying to tell me that I was doing something incredibly stupid. Dee and Frank didn't seem to share my nerves, probably because they didn't have any mammalian instincts to tell them that walking into the lair of a giant snake was a suboptimal plan.

I kept walking. No matter how uncomfortable the situation made me, if I wanted to find Shelby, I needed to find Lloyd, and if I wanted to find Lloyd, I was going to need to talk to Hannah. We reached the tree line. Dee and Frank stopped where they were.

"You don't have to do this," said Dee. "We can go ahead and ask her if she'll see you. We can—"

"There's only one way you're getting me to stay behind, and I don't think you're ready to take that step yet," I said.

"Don't be so sure," said Frank darkly. "You endanger us."

"No, I don't. I am *saving* you." I glared at him, fighting the urge to start shouting. We were wasting time. Shelby could be bleeding out, and I was standing here arguing about whether or not I had the right to rescue her. "Do you think this can keep happening and no one's going to notice? You're one dead body—one more disappearance—away from the feds sweeping in here like the wrath of God, and one rumor on the Internet away from the Covenant coming to see what that raid *really* uncovered. Lloyd isn't a professional. Do you get that? He doesn't know how to make problems go away. He's making a mess that's going to land on *your* heads. Now you can take me to Hannah and I can continue to pretend that I have any interest in being on your side, or you can force me to find her on my own. And after that happens, we are *not* playing for the same team, got it?"

"I take it you think your team will be the winning one?" asked Frank, a dangerous glint in his eye. His snakes rose into a strike position, hissing. Some of them opened their mouths, displaying dangerously sharp fangs.

"We always have been so far," I said. "You're five feet, eight inches away from my current position, Frank. Do you think you can close that distance before I put three bullets in your chest? It's a math problem. I am very good at math. Unless you're *sure* of the answer, I don't recommend you try to run the numbers."

"Frank." Dee put a hand on his arm, her own snakes hissing and slithering over each other like in an eternally moving knot. "We can trust Alex. We *have* to trust Alex. He's right. If this doesn't stop soon, we're going to be discovered."

"Mammals," spat Frank. Then he turned and stepped into the woods. Dee glanced back at me, expression somewhere between apologetic and resigned, and went after him.

I was about to follow two angry gorgons into the woods. I had no cell service, and no one knew where I was. My only potential backup was injured, missing, and presumably being held captive.

"No turning back now," I said, and stepped into the trees.

The smell of snake was stronger once we were past the tree line, like they had somehow been holding it back, preventing it from coming out into the open. Dee and Frank picked a confident trail through the underbrush, following a series of landmarks that I couldn't distinguish from everything else around us. I tried to stay close behind them, even as my monkey brain shrieked louder and louder, telling me that I needed to turn back at the first possible opportunity.

As we walked, I started to see glimpses of rock face through the trees. Finally, we moved around a particularly dense clump of elms, and there it was: a cave, cut like a gaping black hole into the side of the Ohio hills. Moss grew thick on the rocks around it, and roots overhung the edge, some of them dangling almost down to the ground. Dee and Frank stopped, allowing me to catch up with them.

"Hannah lives here," said Dee needlessly. The smell of snake emanating from the cave was so strong that there was no way Hannah could have lived anywhere else.

"I got that," I said. Neither of them looked inclined to go any further. I eyed them. "Are you staying out here?"

"You've been a great boss, Alex, and that's rare," said Dee. "You're even a pretty good guy, which may be rarer. Most of the time these days, I almost forget that you're a mammal. And none of that is good enough reason for me to go into that cave with you."

Frank didn't say anything. He simply stood there, stone-faced and silent, save for the soft hissing of the snakes atop his head.

"Fine," I said. "Cowards."

"Better a live coward than a dead hero," said Dee.

"Dead heroes are sort of the family business," I replied, and started walking toward the cave. The smell of snake got stronger with every step I took, underscored with a thick layer of old blood and older decay. I took my last breath of semi-clean air, put my hand on the pistol at my waist, and stepped through the curtain of roots into the darkness.

The temperature dropped several degrees as soon as I was inside the cave. The air grew cool and damp at the same time, creating a strange sort of cognitive dissonance. Snakes normally prefer to den in warm places, and the smells of both serpent and decay are hot smells, like chili peppers or sunbaked rock. I slowed my pace, giving my eyes time to adjust to the dimness.

"Hannah?" I called, hand still on my pistol. "It's Alexander Price. I need to talk to you."

Something slithered in the dark ahead of me. I swallowed hard, fighting back the wave of panic unleashed by my monkey brain. There were a hundred good reasons not to do this. There were a thousand good reasons to turn around and run.

There was one good reason to be exactly where I was. Her name was Shelby Tanner, and there was a better than good chance that I was in love with her. I kept walking.

"I'm not here to hurt you, and I don't want to cause any trouble, but I *need* to talk to you, and I'm not leaving until that happens," I said.

The sound of slithering came again. It was louder this time, which meant that it was probably closer. I had a real hard time thinking of that as a positive thing.

"I know about Lloyd, Hannah. I know what he's been doing, and I know you're protecting him, because he's your family. I understand how important family is. But do you remember Shelby? The woman who was here with me before? Lloyd hurt her. He stabbed her, and I think he took her, because there's nowhere else she could have gone. She's going to die if I don't find her. Shelby is *my* family, Hannah. She's my family, and she didn't do anything to deserve this."

Slithering, followed by silence.

"You said my great-grandfather helped you. You said he helped your parents find each other. That means you wouldn't be here to refuse me without him. Honor his memory. Help me."

"You would make me choose between you and my son?" Her voice was closer than I'd expected from the slithering; I somehow managed not to jump, but it was a close thing, based more on the fact that I was too terrified to move than on any aspect of my training. "How *dare* you. I may owe my life to your great-grandfather, but that is *all* I owe him. I owe the life of my son to no one at all."

"Your son's life is his own," I said. "He's killing people. You know what that means."

"You came here to kill us. I knew that as soon as I set eyes on you."

"I came here for reasons of my own. It was Lloyd who made this a hunt."

"Yet you have always been a hunter."

"I'm not here to hunt anyone but Lloyd," I said. "I just want to stop the deaths and get my girlfriend back."

"You lie. Humans always lie."

"Did Jonathan lie to you?"

Silence fell in the cave, broken only by the low, constant sound of hissing. I hadn't noticed it when she was speaking; either it had just started, or the silence was really that absolute. Finally, she said, "Yes, he did. He told my parents they would be happy here in Ohio. He told them they would be safe here, that they would have good lives here, and that they would never have children. They were happy with their choice and with each other, but were they happy with me?" Her face loomed out of the dark, close enough that this time I *did* jump, taking an involuntary step back. "He lied when he said I would never be, and when they learned to love the thing I was, he lied *again* when he said that I would never have children of my own."

"Biologically speaking—"

"Do not speak to me of science, little mammal," hissed Hannah, and slithered into the light. Yes, *slithered*: her legs were gone, replaced by a tail that gripped the rocks like a rock python. Shapeshifting is a trait of the greater gorgon, one they share with the gorgons of legend. She circled me, creating a barrier with her tail when she stopped, her human half raised off the ground in parody of a standing woman. She was naked, having eschewed the trappings of humanity here in her cave, where no one with half a brain would dare to bother her. "Science did not stop my birth, and it did not stop the birth of my son. His father left me when the egg hatched; when he saw what we had done together. Children should be a blessing. Your family took that from me."

I thought of Sarah, who came from a species the entire world—including Shelby—was ready to write off as beyond redemption, monsters from birth. "Children *are* a blessing," I said. "Nature doesn't define everything that we're going to be. Love can change us."

"You think I didn't love him? I loved him more than any mother has ever loved a hatchling. I cradled him to me and protected him from the world. But the world kept forcing its way in. The world couldn't let us be." Hannah scowled, a flash of fang showing through the dimness. "The world deserves whatever it gets."

"Does Shelby? Do the people you built this community for?" I gestured behind me, trying to indicate the mouth of the cave. "Dee and Frank are outside. They respect your privacy too much to come inside with me."

"They fear me," she said.

"They *respect* you," I said. "They introduced you to me as their protector, their founder, the reason they've stayed safe here while so many gorgon communities have failed. They love you. Whatever may have happened in the past, they love you. But if Lloyd isn't stopped, if he doesn't see reason, all of this is going to be lost. Do you get that? You're not giving the world what it deserves. You're hurting the people who love you."

Hannah stared at me, the snakes atop her head hissing. Then, slowly, they began to settle, dropping back into a neutral position. She dipped a little lower, still holding herself off the ground. "You're here to kill him," she accused.

"Yes," I said. "I am. I'm sorry, Hannah. He's been responsible for the deaths of three people so far—that I know of—and that makes him a danger to all of us."

"So you will kill him and then what?" Hannah tilted her head, watching me. "Will you walk away? What if your woman is dead?"

"I'll be honest: I don't know," I said. "My first response is that if she's dead, I'll burn this place to the ground, but I know that's not fair to people like Frank and Dee, who didn't do anything. I'll do my best to restrain myself. It's not going to be easy. So really, the best thing would be for me to find her alive, and that means I need to find her soon. Will you please tell me where Lloyd is, Hannah? For Shelby's sake, and for his?"

She sighed. It was an old, tired sound, like wind blowing over bones. "And what if I kill you right now? Won't that solve the problem for everyone?"

"I'm getting really tired of playing chicken," I muttered. "If you kill me, I guess I'll be dead, and Shelby will probably be dead too, since no one's going to show up in time to save her. But my grandparents will come looking for me, and when they find out what happened, they'll call my parents, and my sisters, and a lot more people will die. None of that has to happen. If you tell me where to find Lloyd, we can end this all today."

"You'll kill him. You'll kill my son."

"Yes." I looked at her, a strange calm spreading over me. "So I guess this is where you decide. You need to kill me right now, or you need to tell me where to find Lloyd. Otherwise, I'm going to go looking for him, and I'm going to find him, and you're going to have no say at all in what happens next."

Hannah froze, holding herself still as only a snake can, like she no longer possessed even the potential for motion. Then she dipped lower, until her eyes were level with mine, and her entire body seemed to slump, giving the impression that she was barely holding herself away from the floor. "He was a good boy once," she said dully. "It wasn't his fault."

"Where is he, Hannah?"

She looked at me. "It is fitting that you're of Jonathan's line," she said. "This is all *his* fault."

And she told me where to go.

Dee and Frank looked surprised when I emerged from the cave, probably because they'd both expected to be sending me off to my death. I straightened my coat, pulled the pistol out of my belt, and said, "You need to take me to the old barn."

"The old barn?" said Dee. "But that was abandoned years ago."

For a moment, I just stared at her. "You abandoned the old barn years ago, and you didn't take me there *first?*" I asked. "You people need to watch more horror movies. Yes, take me to the old barn—just you, though. Frank, you need to go back to your office."

"What?" He frowned at me, the snakes atop his head hissing quizzically. "Why?"

"Because Shelby's hurt. Go get your first aid kit, and meet us at the barn." Hopefully, she would still need whatever help he could give. Hopefully, we weren't already past the point of her needing any help at all.

To my surprise, Frank nodded and turned without argument, walking briskly into the woods. He was still in sight when he broke into a run, leaving me alone with Dee. She looked up at me and sighed, the hissing of her snakes providing a strange counterpoint to the sound.

"This way," she said, and beckoned for me to follow her through the trees in yet another direction. Lacking any better options, I matched her stride, letting her lead me.

"It was nice working with you, Alex," she said, after we'd been walking through the woods for about a minute and a half. "I appreciated having a boss who didn't mind that I wasn't a mammal."

"Why would I have minded? You did your job." The frickens were creep-creep-creeping in the trees, their tinny, piping voices providing a degree of background reassurance. We were alone here, or at least, there was nothing nearby that the frickens recognized as a threat. "You still have a job, you know, unless this is how you turn in your resignation—and if it is, you have shitty timing, since I can't really focus on anything but Shelby at the moment."

"I sort of figured I was fired."

I bit back the urge to swear. "Look, I know human-gorgon relations aren't always peaceful, what with us hunting you for your heads and you turning us into stone, but I thought we had worked past that, and I really, *really* don't want to have the speciesism conversation when I'm preoccupied with wondering whether or not my girlfriend is *dead*."

Dee nodded quickly. "I know, I just . . . this might be the last time I see you. And I didn't want to let that slip past without my telling you how much I respected you as a boss, and as a friend. You did a good job."

"Ah." I gave her a sidelong look as I stepped over a fallen branch. "You're pretty sure I'm about to get myself killed, aren't you?"

"Lloyd is older than anyone here, except for Hannah. If you're walking into his lair, you're walking into more than you can handle."

"Age isn't everything," I said. "You should meet my little sisters."

Conversation died as we reached the edge of the woods. I thumbed off the safety on my pistol, standing for a moment at the tree line as I scanned the decrepit old barn in front of us for signs of life. The structure was the sort of classic Americana that looked like it had been assembled over a weekend by the cast of *Little House on the Prairie* before being left to the elements for twenty years. Patches of iconic barn-red paint remained, but most of it had been ripped away by wind and weather, exposing wood slats the color of old bone. I couldn't get a real feel for the roof from where I was standing, but it looked like it was on the verge of caving in.

"Alex . . ."

"See you later, Dee," I said, and walked toward the barn, gun raised and ready. Whatever was ahead of me, I was going to face it, and I was going to bring Shelby home. There wasn't another option. There never is when things get bad.

Dee remained behind, lurking in the trees as I made my way into the shadow of the barn. I couldn't blame her, although I felt obscurely betrayed, like she should have been able to put her personal feelings above her loyalty to her species. It was unfair of me and I knew that, but fairness sort of falls by the wayside when the people I love are in danger.

The weeds had been beaten back around the foundation, reducing the fire hazard and probably prolonging the life of the structure itself. That was enough to make it clear that someone had been living here for quite some time. I glanced up. Crow was still circling, and now that I was here, I could see that his loops were centered directly above the barn. It was a risk, but it was a risk worth taking: I put two fingers in my mouth and whistled, short and shrill.

There was a moment when I thought Crow hadn't heard me. Then his flight path altered, turning from a tight circle into a descending spiral as he arrowed toward the ground. He landed on the nearest tree, tail puffed out to twice its normal diameter, and cawed angrily. I didn't speak griffin, but I didn't need to understand him to know what he was saying: Where was Shelby? I'd sent him to find her, and he'd found her, so why wasn't I getting on with saving her?

I made a hush motion, which he ignored as he cawed again. There was a banging sound from the back of the barn. I froze, recognizing it as the sound a door made when it was slammed open. Lloyd was coming out of the barn, and here I was, standing out in the open, arguing with my Church Griffin.

"Crow, *hide*," I hissed, hoping he'd hear me, and took off at a run, heading for the opposite side of the barn. Crow had wings. He could take care of himself, if it came down to that.

I made it around the corner of the building and out of sight just before I heard Lloyd say, angrily, "What in the hell—?"

There was a screech, like a bobcat trying to scare off an intruder, followed by the infinitely welcome sound of wings beating hard. Crow was making his retreat. "Clever boy," I murmured, and turned my attention to the barn itself.

There was a door not six feet from me, held half-open by a choking mat of weeds. Gun still in my hand, I crept forward and slipped through the opening, into yet another snake's lair.

The inside of the barn was brighter than I'd expected, largely due to the aforementioned issues with the roof: there were large holes where the wood had rotted away, allowing the sunlight to slant through them into the room. A makeshift sort of home had been built around those holes, with everything pushed into the spaces where the rain wouldn't reach. There was a table with two old, rusty lawn chairs; a wardrobe that looked like it had been mended with pieces of cardboard; and a kitchen area that consisted primarily of a fire pit and two racks of chipped old dishes. A faint smell of snake hung over the whole place, overlaid with the twinned scents of mold and ancient, rotten wood.

I took all that in as I scanned the space, waiting for my eyes to adjust and searching frantically for some sign of

Shelby. Then, in the darkest corner of the barn, I made out what looked like a bed. It was a big, amorphous shape, lumpy with what could either have been too many pillows piled into a heap ... or Shelby.

It took all my waning supply of self-control not to run across the room, potentially knocking things over and almost certainly bringing Lloyd back into the barn. Instead, I made my way carefully around the edge of the barn, until I was close enough to that dark corner to whisper, "Shelby? Are you there?"

There was no reply. My heart sank, and I took the last steps into shadow feeling considerably less hopeful.

Despite the broken patches in the roof, there was enough shadow that I couldn't see any real detail I reached out with my free hand, leaning down until my fingers hit the cool skin of a humanoid shoulder. I closed my eyes and ran my hand along the curve of the shoulder, identifying it as belonging to a female. Reaching a little higher, I touched her hair. Human. I brought my fingers to my nose. Unless Lloyd was fond of kidnapping women who all used the same shampoo, it was Shelby. She wasn't moving, but when I placed my fingers against the side of her neck and focused, I could find a pulse. It was faint, weak enough that I could just as easily have missed it. It was *there*, and that was all I had it in me to give a damn about at the moment.

"Shelby." I knelt, blinking as I tried to force my eyes to adjust faster. I slid my hand along the side of her torso, trying to figure out how best to pick her up without making too much noise or attracting too much unwanted attention. To my surprise, my questing fingers encountered expertly applied bandages circling her stomach, wound tight enough to stop the blood, but not so tight that they would cut off circulation. Lloyd had provided her with basic medical care. Thank God.

The bandages made it more likely that I would be able to move her, although I wasn't sure how far I'd need to carry her through the woods in order to get her back to the car. It didn't matter. "It's going to be okay, baby," I murmured. "I'm getting you out of here."

"That's a pretty sweet thought, Mr. Preston—or should I call you Mr. Price now, since we're not on the zoo grounds anymore?" Lloyd's voice was as familiar as always, holding its customary mix of deference and apologetic nosiness. For the first time, however, I could hear the hard edge underneath it. He sounded like someone who'd been given plenty of reasons to be angry with the world, and was planning to make use of every single one.

"Hello, Lloyd," I said, turning slowly to face him.

Even through the shadows, I could see that he wasn't wearing his hat. Short, stunted-looking snakes cast malformed shadows on the wall.

"Hello," he said. "Mighty kind of you to save me the trouble of hunting you down." That was all the warning he gave before he lunged.

Twenty-four

"Once upon a time there was a little boy who lived with monsters, and the monsters swore that they would never hurt him, because even monsters dream of living happily ever after."

— Kevin Price

Facing a gorgon hybrid in a supposedly abandoned barn attached to a hidden gorgon community in the middle of the Ohio woods, which is absolutely a terrible place to be right now

SHELBY WAS IMMOBILE AND unconscious; I had to save myself before I'd have any hope of saving her. I dodged aside and allowed Lloyd to slam into the mattress. He whirled, hissing, but I was already halfway across the barn, my pistol in my hand and aimed at him.

"You didn't have to follow me," he said.

"I thought you just said I'd saved you a lot of trouble," I replied.

"You did and you didn't. I was going to hunt you down, and I don't have to do that now, but it might have hurt you less if you'd just let my cockatrice take care of business." He shook his head, his snakes setting up another chorus of hisses. "I liked you well enough, while we both worked at the zoo. You were always nicer to me than you had to be, given our positions. Had to lie to you, of course; couldn't just go announcing I was a freak of nature, given your family history. I could still have offered you a mostly painless death."

Spoken like a man who had never been partially petrified. Phantom pains flared in my eyes as I offered the only reply that I could think of: "We left the Covenant generations ago."

"But you still hold yourselves as judge, jury, and executioner when you feel like it's appropriate, don't you? You wouldn't be here otherwise." Lloyd remained next to the bed, straightening slowly, until he stood taller than I had ever seen him. It wasn't just a matter of hunching or not hunching; his torso seemed to have elongated, adding a serpentine cast to his silhouette. "That's why you had to go before I could have my revenge. Andrew was an accident, you know. I was planning to put my cockatrice in your office, take care of the biggest threat around before things got started. So I put it in your yard, and even that couldn't get rid of you. Slippery bastard."

"Sorry I didn't want to die."

"I shouldn't have expected anything different from a Price. Self-appointed saviors of the cryptid world, who know what we need better than we do."

"You know, I'm used to people being mad at me because of who my ancestors were, but most of the time, they're pissed off because someone I'm related to killed someone they were related to, not because my great-grandfather helped their parents get married."

Lloyd laughed bitterly. "You'd best change your thinking, then. You do more damage when you let us live than you ever did when you let us die."

"So you put the cockatrice in my yard—then what? Why keep letting it kill random people? Why set Shelby's building on fire? Why did you need revenge in the first place?"

"You would have caught me eventually. I needed to get rid of you, even if it meant hurting *her*." Something about the stress he put on the word "her" made me profoundly uncomfortable. "As for why I needed revenge . . . those bastards told me I'd be retiring at the end of the year. They said I was too old to do my job and that it was an oversight I'd been allowed to stay as long as I had. Said their insurance didn't like it when they kept on old men past a certain point. No telling what kind of health problems we could have. Wouldn't want to see us dropping dead in front of the paying customers. So they were cutting me loose after sixty years of service, and all because I had the nerve to survive past the point where I was *convenient*."

"There are other jobs," I said, aware of how inane that sounded almost as soon as I spoke.

It was too late to take the words back. Lloyd sneered. "Maybe for you. When I took that job, no one asked for high school diplomas or proof of residency. It was enough that I showed up for work every day. But you humans, you never stopped hunting us, did you? Not really. You just built different traps. Red tape and fences everywhere. I'm trapped."

"I could help you . . ." I tried.

Lloyd wasn't listening. "You humans, you make your rules, and you never consider what they'll do to the people who get in their way. Retirement ages and well-meaning meddling, and for what? So you can feel powerful when you're the only damn things in the world who don't have an advantage past 'thumbs'? Lots of critters have thumbs. You don't see us prancing around shouting about being the lords of creation."

"Hold on a second, okay? Just . . . hold on." I shook my head. "What are you mad about? Are you mad that you were born, or that you got old, or that the zoo fired you, or that paperwork exists, or something else altogether? Because people have died over this, and I'd really like to understand why."

"I'm mad about all those things," said Lloyd. "And I'm mad about you and Doctor Tanner, too."

I froze. "What do you mean?"

"You're not much of a catch, are you, Price boy? She's a pretty girl, and she could have done a lot better than a weedy science boy with glasses and scuffed shoes. But she didn't look twice at anybody else, especially not the old man at the gate. Not even when I brought her flowers and didn't check her ID on mornings when she was running late. She didn't *see* me. I was willing to let her burn for that, but I came up with a better idea." He shook his head. "She's going to see me now. And then she's going to stay with me forever."

"But . . . you're not even a *mammal*," I said, before I could think better of it. The horror of him turning Shelby to stone and keeping her as his captive bride was too much to focus on, and so I went to the safe haven of biology.

"You think that matters?" Lloyd's voice took on a sneering tone. "My mama is a crossbreed, and my daddy was a Pliny's gorgon who wanted nothing to do with me. He couldn't even look me in the face. My species cast me out a long time ago."

"They still take care of you. They let you live here —"

"Only because they're so scared of Ma that they don't know what else to do," Lloyd spat. "Pa founded a whole new place because he didn't want to look her in the eye."

"The fringe," I guessed grimly.

"Why do you think I went there for my cockatrice?" He laughed. "Can't keep your hands clean forever, no matter how hard you try. Can't hide forever, neither. Eventually, the world's going to figure out we're still out here, that *all* the monsters are still out here, and then there's going to be hell to pay. You can't blame me for trying to hurry that along."

Actually, yes, I *could* blame him. At least three people were dead, assuming no one had died in the apartment fire, and a lot more people had been hurt, either physically or emotionally. Not all damage is visible to the eye. "You didn't have to take Shelby. She needs medical care."

"We have a doctor," said Lloyd. "Once I get rid of you, Frank will have to patch her up. Then, when she's awake, I'll offer her a deal: be my girl like she was yours, and I won't feel the need to look her in the eyes."

"No thank you," said Shelby's voice, weak and welcome. Relief flooded through me. Until she'd spoken, I hadn't realized just how afraid I was that she was never going to speak again.

"What?" Lloyd whipped around to face her. She hadn't moved so much as a muscle, and was still a dark, huddled form on the bed. That forced him to lean in closer, and I saw my chance, beginning to cautiously pick my way through the darkened barn as I tried to line up a clear shot on him.

Hannah, I'm sorry, I thought. It was him or me, him or Shelby, him or a lot of other people . . . maybe Lloyd was right, and my family was too quick to judge the cryptid world. Most of us were human. So what made us qualified to decide who lived and who died?

He had a point. I didn't care. If I had to choose one of them, I chose Shelby.

"I said, no thank you," repeated Shelby. Her voice was a broken echo of itself, washed out by pain and blood loss. "I have no particular interest in becoming your next meal, or your tethered love slave, or anything else that you may have been considering for me. Alex is quite sufficient to suit my needs. Now do me a favor and go fuck yourself."

"You . . . you . . . you *mammal,*" hissed Lloyd, and did exactly what I had been hoping he wouldn't do: he grabbed her, pulling her halfway into a sitting position and shaking her. Shelby made a small sound that was halfway between a whimper and a gasp. "Forget healing you. Open your eyes! You stupid human bitch, open your eyes!"

"No thank you," said Shelby, for the third time.

I couldn't get a clean shot, not in the dark with him half-blocking her from sight. With as much blood as she'd already lost, I wasn't sure Shelby would survive even being grazed by a flying bullet.

"Put her down, Lloyd," I said. "She's not the one you're mad at."

"I'm mad at all you bastards," he said, and shook Shelby again. "Open your eyes and *look at me*."

"Shoot him, Alex," said Shelby, still hanging limply in Lloyd's hands. "Don't worry about me. Just shoot him."

"You bi—"

Lloyd's insult was cut short by Crow, who came screeching through the door with talons extended and feathers fluffed until he looked twice his actual size. He slammed into Lloyd's arm, slashing with his beak and feline hind claws for an instant before releasing and rocketing toward the rafters overhead, where he proceeded to start shrieking at the gorgon below. The whole thing happened in seconds. Lloyd dropped Shelby back to the bed, screaming and clutching at his bloody arm.

And then, as if that weren't chaotic enough, a lindworm crashed through the barn wall.

Where there is one lindworm, there is probably another: this is a fact of the natural world, much like "don't put your hand in the manticore," and "try not to lick the neurotoxic amphibians." We'd killed the female lindworm in the forest, and tagged the male back in the swamp. I hadn't thought to check and see whether he'd come looking for his mate. Apparently, my Church Griffin was smarter than I was.

The lindworm let out an enraged bellow and charged for the most distinctive smell in the room: the smell of blood, which was flowing freely from Lloyd, thanks to Crow. Lloyd shouted. The lindworm roared, which would have been an impressive sound even if we *weren't* all stuck in a confined space.

"We're going to die," I said, dazed, just as the lind-worm crashed into Lloyd.

The gorgon security guard shouted something incomprehensible as he grabbed for the lindworm's head, trying to force it to meet his eyes. It responded by snarling and snapping at him, driving him farther back against the wall. I stared for another few precious seconds, knowing I was wasting time, and yet unable to tear myself away. This was something no one had ever seen before, so far as I knew; it might be something no one was ever going to see again.

And that didn't change the fact that Shelby needed me. I made my way quickly around the edge of the barn, trying to avoid doing anything that might catch the lindworm's attention. I wasn't nearly as worried about catching Lloyd's attention, which was a nice change. I made it all the way to the bed where Shelby lay crumpled without being seen.

Shelby made a protesting sound when I touched her arm. I shushed her quickly. She recognized my voice and dared to crack one eye open, sagging into my arms with relief. I smiled as encouragingly as I could, grimacing a little as I realized how much blood had soaked into her clothing. Lloyd's shaking must have reopened her wound, and given where the damage was located, I couldn't even throw her into a fireman's carry, which would have left my gun hand free. Instead, I had to carry her with both arms, and hope that we'd make it out of the barn unchallenged.

The lindworm was still roaring as I made a beeline for the door, and the sound masked my footsteps enough that I actually started to believe that I might get away with it. Then I heard Lloyd shout behind me, sounding offended and enraged all at the same time. I glanced back to see him shoving the lindworm away from himself, that strange, serpentine bend in his torso expanding as fabric shredded and he emulated his mother's "turn your lower body into a giant snake" trick.

The lindworm might not have been very smart, but it was a predator, and it knew when the odds had shifted. It fell back, snapping and snarling at the transformed Lloyd. As for Lloyd himself, he ignored the lindworm in favor of pursuing a much more appealing target: me.

I ran.

It wasn't easy with Shelby in my arms and an uncertain terrain beneath me—the lindworm had ripped gouges in the floor, which complicated my escape. I could hear Lloyd slithering after me as I reached the hole in the wall and ducked outside, Shelby dangling heavy and unmoving in my arms.

I had barely stepped onto the flat ground outside the barn when strong hands grabbed me and yanked me roughly to the side, nearly causing me to lose my grip on Shelby. I took a breath to protest, and stopped when I realized that the man who had grabbed me was familiar: it was Walter, Dee's brother. The current leader of the fringe.

"Give the girl to me," he said, speaking quickly. "I'll see her to the doctor."

"But—"

"Give her!"

I could still hear Lloyd's scales against the barn floor. He had stopped, for whatever reason, without crossing the threshold. Swallowing hard, I transferred Shelby into Walter's arms. He nodded curtly, like this was the only sensible thing that I could possibly have done, before he turned his back and walked away into the woods.

Shelby's blood was hot and sticky on my shirt and hands. I pulled my gun back out of my waistband as I turned to face the barn, ready to challenge Lloyd more openly now that Shelby was out of the line of fire—and stopped as yet another surprise layered itself on top of what was already a surprising afternoon.

Lloyd hadn't emerged from the barn because his way wasn't clear. Dee was standing in front of him, the snakes atop her head coiled in full strike position, her mouth open and her fangs extended. I'd never seen my normally mild assistant look so terrifying.

"Dee?"

"This isn't your fight, Alex," she said, voice only slightly distorted by her mouthful of fangs. "Run, and don't look back."

I wanted to. It had been a long time since I wanted anything as much as I wanted to do exactly as I was told. If I ran, I could catch up with Walter and Shelby, and leave Lloyd to be handled by his own people. And if something happened to Dee?

If something happened to Dee, I would never be able to forgive myself.

"I can't," I said, and walked over to stand beside her, bracing my gun against my left wrist as I aimed with my right hand. Lloyd's outline was clearly visible against the doorway, standing a good nine feet off the ground now that he had a serpent's tail to lift him up. "Come out, Lloyd. Maybe we can still end this peacefully."

"Any chance of that ended a long damn time ago." Lloyd's head turned. I couldn't see his eyes, but I knew from the way that he was angling himself that his attention was on Dee. "Isn't that right, little sister?" The lindworm lurked in the shadows behind him, clearly steeling itself for another attack.

"It was always going to end badly, but it didn't have to end like this," replied Dee. "You chose this when you killed those people—when you endangered us. Why did you do that, Lloyd?" There was a pleading note in her voice that hadn't been there before, and as she spoke, the impact of Lloyd's words hit me. He was her brother. His father had left Hannah and gone on to find a mate of his own species, one who could give him children who wouldn't be outcast like he was. Walter and Dee were Lloyd's half-siblings. They were his *family*.

It was unfair on so many levels that I didn't even know where to begin. There wasn't time for me to decide. Lloyd slithered forward, emerging from the shadows of the barn. I had just enough time to see the ragged, diseased-looking line where his tail joined with his torso, half-formed scales melting into blotchy skin. There were gaps in the flesh of his tail, places where his legs hadn't quite merged properly. He hissed, displaying outsized fangs. I adjusted my aim, preparing to take the shot, and Lloyd lunged—

—not at me, but at Dee. She shrieked, backpedaling, and I turned, calculating the shot in the instant before I pulled the trigger. My aim was true. My aim has always been true.

Gunshots are always loud. This one seemed louder than most. It sounded like it should have carried for miles.

Somehow, we still heard Lloyd hit the ground.

Dee ran to Lloyd as soon as he fell, gathering him into her arms and sobbing into the motionless snakes that were his hair. The fact that he'd been preparing to hurt her was forgotten in her sorrow. Crow was already in flight, arrowing toward me. I managed to shove my gun back into my waistband before Crow hit my chest and buried his head under my arm, tail lashing. I wrapped my arms around him and held him, letting him shiver himself back to calm.

"Good boy," I murmured, watching as Dee cried over the body of her brother. "You're always such a good, good boy."

A soft scuffling sound from inside the barn drew my attention. I glanced over to see the lindworm's tail pass by the opening, heading back out into the forest. I smiled a little despite the seriousness of the moment. The lindworm hadn't done anything but allow itself to be annoyed by Crow, who was admittedly very good at being annoying. There had been enough blood shed already, and I didn't need to add another lindworm to the total.

Blood . . . "Dee, where did Walter take Shelby? Which way is Frank's office?"

"West," she said, voice muffled by her position. "Walk west, and you'll find it."

My day had included a homicidal gorgon crossbreed and an angry lindworm, and there was still a cockatrice somewhere around here that needed to be accounted for. This wasn't the time to worry about any of that. Shelby was hurt. Shelby might be dying. And she needed me.

"I'm sorry about your brother," I said softly. Then I turned, still holding Crow against my chest, and ran into the woods.

My parents insisted that my siblings and I learn how to navigate by the cardinal directions before we were allowed to start first grade. It didn't come easily for all of us; Verity used to get confused, and nearly had to repeat kindergarten. I'd always been good at that sort of spatial orientation, and I ran without hesitation, somehow managing to navigate the uneven terrain without tripping over anything and slamming face-first into the dirt.

It was something of a shock when the woods finally ended and I emerged into the open field surrounding the gorgon community. I didn't slow down, but kept running, tossing Crow into the air as I went. He took wing, cawing angrily. Hopefully, his irritation would be enough to keep him in the trees and prevent him from accidentally locking eyes with any gorgons. It was a miracle that he hadn't been petrified yet, and I wanted to keep it that way.

I work hard to stay in shape, but that doesn't involve very many sprints through the forest. I was panting and weak-kneed by the time I reached the door to Frank's trailer. The door was closed. I stopped myself just short of pounding on it, managing to make myself back off enough to knock politely.

The door opened a moment later. Frank's form filled the doorway, and his expression as he looked down at me was utterly impassive.

"Where is my wife?" he asked.

"In the woods, with her brother," I replied. "He's dead. She's not. Where's Shelby?"

"Here." Frank stepped aside, allowing me into the trailer.

I've entered homes that had been taken over by ghouls. I've walked into Apraxis wasp hives. And I don't think I had ever taken a single harder step in my life. I stepped inside and turned toward where I'd seen the surgical beds when we were in the trailer before.

Shelby was lying there with a blanket pulled up to her shoulders. Her eyes were closed, but her face wasn't covered. I took a slow step toward her. "Is . . . is she . . . ?"

"She lost a great deal of blood," said Frank. "I've sent a car to get some supplies from the hospital. She's stable for now. He missed her major organs. She was, if you can believe it in a situation like this, lucky."

"Lucky," I echoed, as I walked to her bedside. Her cheek was warm beneath my fingers. She didn't open her eyes. I sat down in the chair next to where she lay, leaning forward to rest my forehead against the edge of the bed. I would wait there for the next emergency.

I fell asleep in that position. The emergency never came.

Epilogue

"Good for you. Now survive the next one."
—Thomas Price

The reptile house of Ohio's West Columbus Zoo, a private back room where no one reasonable goes

Six weeks later

THE BASILISKS WERE AWAKE, circling each other in their carefully darkened enclosure with their wings outstretched and their tails lashing in what was either a mating dance or a precursor to bloody combat. I kept my eyes glued to the glass, waiting for the moment where one of them would make a move.

The male stopped circling, picked up a piece of the hard rocky shell that had protected him while he hibernated, and placed it gently at the female's feet. She hissed. He offered her another bit of rocky shell. She lashed at him with her tail. He offered her a third fragment. She accepted it, striking him with her tail again—but this time it was less of an attack, and more of a caress. Beginning to croon, she turned and walked away into the high grass. He followed, head bobbing in what could only be interpreted as a victory dance.

"You go on with your bad self," I murmured, smiling.

"Who's going where, then?"

I turned, my smile widening at the sight of Shelby Tanner standing behind me in the dimly-lit room. She was the second person to have the code—not for any scientific reason. Just because I wanted her to. Crow was cradled in her arms, his tail swishing lazily back and forth. He'd been spending as much time with her as he could since we came home from the gorgon community. He loved having a second human to cuddle with, especially one who was endlessly willing to give him the petting and adoration he deserved. I didn't begrudge him the attention. He'd earned it when he saved us both.

"I think my basilisks are finally mating." I gestured toward the enclosure. "It's not much to look at right now, but in a few months, we'll have chicks."

"Oh, yay, more horrible things to turn me into stone," said Shelby. But she was smiling, and she kept smiling as she walked over to kiss me on the cheek. "Ready for lunch?"

"In a minute," I said. "And basilisk chicks are surprisingly adorable. They have blue feathers."

Shelby had been stable but very weak for the first few days after Lloyd attacked her. She hadn't been strong enough to come home, and her injuries would have been hard to explain to the human hospital, unless I wanted to be arrested for assault. Luckily, Frank had done a more than competent job. He was a very talented surgeon. She couldn't have been in better hands. Thank God.

She walked over to peer into the enclosure, where only the rustling of bushes betrayed the location of my basilisks. "Blue, you say. All right. What happens after the chicks come?"

"We raise them to maturity and then send them off to the people who need them. Walter has agreed to take these two on a long-term basis, and trade their offspring for whatever the fringe requires." It was a tidy way for them to make a little money without betraying their ideals. Much. "Are you still coming to dinner tonight?"

"What, like I'd miss the opportunity for your cousin

to school me at Scrabble again?" Shelby laughed. "I'll be there at six, as planned."

"Oh, good."

Sarah wasn't exactly "schooling" anyone at Scrabble, since half the words she used were made up, but she had fun, and she was getting better at keeping up with the conversation. Really, she was getting better at everything. She could reliably tell me from Shelby, which was a real accomplishment, considering how far gone she'd been when I'd first come to live with my grandparents. I was actually starting to think she might get back to her own personal definition of normal.

Shelby wrinkled her nose at the rustling bushes. "This is getting dull," she said. "Anything else going on around here?"

"Just the usual," I said, plucking Crow from her arms and dropping him on the floor. "It's been blissfully dull all day."

"Oh, really?" Shelby took her cue, sliding her arms around my shoulders as Crow croaked in aggravation. "Sounds like you need a little excitement."

"Honestly, you're about all the excitement I can handle right now."

I'm a scientist. Excitement is supposed to be something that happens mostly to other people, and I'd been right at the center of way more than I wanted over the past few months.

Hannah had been devastated by Lloyd's death, even if she wasn't surprised. She'd been expecting this for a long time, and it had just been a question of when and how it would happen. I was pretty sure Shelby and I were no longer welcome at the gorgon community. I didn't mind. We didn't belong there, and any debts between us were paid.

Dee had kept her job at the zoo, thankfully. Shelby had been bedridden for several weeks after I brought her home, and I wouldn't have been able to take the time off to care for her if Dee hadn't been at the reptile house, keeping things running smoothly. I was glad she'd decided to stay. I would have missed her.

Lloyd's cockatrice was still out there somewhere. It hadn't shown up in any urban areas, and we were all assuming Lloyd had taken it back to the woods with him when he abducted Shelby. A cockatrice loose in the woods near the gorgon community was nowhere near the threat that a cockatrice loose near humans had been. As long as we didn't see any further signs of it, we were willing to live and let live.

Shelby leaned forward and kissed me slowly. I slid my arms around her waist, shutting out Crow's angry squawks as I focused on the business at hand. When she finally pulled away, I was a lot less interested in basilisks, and a lot more interested in her.

"Lunch?" she asked again.

"As long as it's not in the tiger garden, that sounds good to me," I said, before kissing her again.

I had my work; I had my family; I had my friends; and I had Shelby, who was a distraction from everything else, but only in the best of ways. Things were changing. I was changing with them. That was all right, in the balance of things; after all, people have paid a lot more to come away with a lot less. As I tightened my arms around Shelby's waist and sank into another kiss, I couldn't help thinking I was a very lucky man. I was a very lucky man indeed.

Price Family Field Guide to the Cryptids of North America
Updated and Expanded Edition

Aeslin mice (Apodemus sapiens). Sapient, rodentlike cryptids which present as near-identical to noncryptid field mice. Aeslin mice crave religion, and will attach themselves to "divine figures" selected virtually at random when a new colony is created. They possess perfect recall; each colony maintains a detailed oral history going back to its inception. Origins unknown.

Basilisk (Procompsognathus basilisk). Venomous, feathered saurians approximately the size of a large chicken. This would be bad enough, but thanks to a quirk of evolution, the gaze of a basilisk causes petrification, turning living flesh to stone. Basilisks are not native to North America, but were imported as game animals. By idiots.

Bogeyman (Vestiarium sapiens). The thing in your closet is probably a very pleasant individual who simply has issues with direct sunlight. Probably. Bogeymen are close relatives of the human race; they just happen to be almost purely nocturnal, with excellent night vision, and a fondness for enclosed spaces. They rarely grab the ankles of small children, unless it's funny.

Coatl (Coatl arbore). The coatl is a classic example of the plumed or feathered serpent. They are morphologically similar to boa constrictors (with feathers), but are likely evolutionarily derived from large monitor lizards. There are more than twenty-seven separate subspecies of coatl known, and many more have probably gone extinct, victims of urban expansion and people having an atavistic aversion to the idea of flying snakes.

Church Griffin (Gryps vegrandis corax). A subspecies of lesser griffin, these small, predatory creatures resemble a cross between a raven and a Maine Coon cat. They are highly intelligent, which makes them good, if troublesome, companions. They enjoy the company of humans, if only because humans are so much fun to mess with.

Cockatrice (Procompsognathus cockatrice). Venomous, largely featherless saurians approximately the size of a large chicken. This would be bad enough, but thanks to a quirk of evolution, the gaze of a cockatrice causes petrification, turning living flesh to stone. Cockatrice are not native to North America, but were imported as game animals. Again, by idiots.

Dragon (Draconem sapiens). Dragons are essentially winged, fire-breathing dinosaurs the size of Greyhound buses. At least, the males are. The females—colloquially known as "dragon princesses"—are attractive humanoids who can blend seamlessly in a crowd of supermodels. Capable of parthenogenic reproduction, the females outnumber the males twenty to one, and can sustain their population for centuries without outside help. All dragons, male and female, require gold to live, and collect it constantly.

Ghoul (Herophilus sapiens). The ghoul is an obligate carnivore, incapable of digesting any but the simplest vegetable solids, and prefers humans because of their wide selection of dietary nutrients. Most ghouls are carrion eaters. Ghouls can be easily identified by their teeth, which will be shed and replaced repeatedly over the course of a lifetime.

Gorgon, greater (Gorgos medusa). One of three known subspecies of gorgon, the greater gorgon is believed to be the source of many classic gorgon myths. They are capable of controlled gaze-based petrifaction, and mature individuals can actually look a human in the eyes without turning them to stone. They are capable of transforming their lower bodies from humanoid to serpentine. This is very unnerving. Avoid when possible.

Gorgon, lesser (Gorgos euryale). The lesser gorgon's gaze causes short-term paralysis followed by death in anything under five pounds. The bite of the snakes atop their heads will cause paralysis followed by death in anything smaller than an elephant if not treated with the appropriate antivenin. Lesser gorgons tend to be very polite, especially to people who like snakes.

Gorgon, Pliny's (Gorgos stheno). The Pliny's gorgon is capable of gaze-based petrifaction only when both their human and serpent eyes are directed toward the same target. They are the most sexually dimorphic of the known gorgons, with the males being as much as four feet taller than the females. They are venomous, as are the snakes atop their heads, and their bites contain a strong petrifying agent. Do not vex.

Johrlac (Johrlac psychidolos). Colloquially known as "cuckoos," the Johrlac are telepathic hunters. They appear human, but are internally very different, being cold-blooded and possessing a decentralized circulatory system. This quirk of biology means they can be shot repeatedly in the chest without being killed. Extremely dangerous. All Johrlac are interested in mathematics, sometimes to the point of obsession. Origins unknown; possibly insect in nature.

Lamia (Python lamia). Semi-hominid cryptids with the upper bodies of humans and the lower bodies of snakes. Lamia are members of order synapsedia, the mammal-like reptiles, and are considered responsible for many of the "great snake" sightings of legend. The sightings not attributed to actual great snakes, that is.

Lindworm (Lindorm lindorm). These massive relatives of the skink have been found in Europe, Africa, and North America, which makes them extremely well-distributed armored killing machines. They tend to pair off at maturity, and while adult lindworms will have very little territorial overlap, they are constantly aware of the location of their mate and any juvenile offspring still being tolerated in the area. Lindworms are very difficult to kill, more's the pity.

Oread (Nymphae silica). Humanoid cryptids with the approximate skin density of granite. Their actual biological composition is unknown, as no one has ever been able to successfully dissect one. Oreads are extremely strong, and can be dangerous when angered. They seem to have evolved independently across the globe; their common name is from the Greek.

Tooth fairy (Pyske dentin). Tooth fairies are small—no taller than the length of a tall man's hand—and possess dual-lobed wings. Its dietary habits are unpleasant, and best left undiscussed. Do not leave unsupervised near children.

Wadjet (Naja wadjet). Once worshiped as gods, the male wadjet resembles an enormous cobra, capable of reaching seventeen feet in length when fully mature, while the female wadjet resembles an attractive human female.

Wadjet pair-bond young, and must spend extended amounts of time together before puberty in order to become immune to one another's venom and be able to successfully mate as adults.

Waheela (Waheela sapiens). Therianthrope shapeshifters from the upper portion of North America, the waheela are a solitary race, usually claiming large swaths of territory and defending it to the death from others of their species. Waheela mating season is best described with the term "bloodbath." Waheela transform into something that looks like a dire bear on steroids. They're usually not hostile, but it's best not to push it.

PLAYLIST:

Everything's better with music! Here are some songs to rock you through Alex's trials.

"Boats and Birds" . . . . .Gregory and the Hawk
"Splatter Splatter" . . . . .OK Go
"Lovers in a Dangerous Time" . . . Barenaked Ladies
"The Frog Prince" . . . . Keane
"Viva la Vida". . . . . .Coldplay
"I Am a Scientist" . . . . The Dandy Warhols
"Walk Away From the Sun" . . . . Seether
"One Normal Night". Company (The Addams Family)
"Narrow Your Eyes". . . . . . . They Might Be Giants
"To the Ghosts Who . . . . Low Anthem
    Write History Books"
"Strange Conversation" . . . . Kris Delmhorst
"Headlights On Dark Roads". . . . . Snow Patrol
"The End". . . . . .John Wesley Harding
"Don't Set Foot Over . . . . .Thea Gilmore
    the Railway Track"
"You Are a Tourist" . . . . Death Cab for Cutie
"Dragging the River" . . . . .Idgy Vaughn
"The Space Between" . . . . .Ally Rhodes
"Don't Say Okay" . . . . Mary Black
"Fire" . . . . Delta Rae
"Crocodile Man". . . . . Dave and Tracy
"Blood Red Sky". . . . . Seth Lakeman

ACKNOWLEDGMENTS:

So here we are again, as *Midnight Blue-Light Special* takes the floor, and Verity takes a well-earned break: the next two books will focus on her brother, Alex, as he deals with some problems of his own. Thank you all so much for reading, and for supporting this series so enthusiastically. Cheese and cake for everyone!

Betsy Tinney, to whom this book is dedicated, remains my ballroom pixie godmother, explaining all the nuances of dance culture. Phil Ames is still to blame for a surprising amount of this whole mess, while my webmaster, Chris Mangum, continues to tolerate my introducing cryptids into every single conversation we have.

As always, the machete squad provided proofreading and editorial services, doing everything in their power to make this book as good as it could possibly be. Kory Bing illustrated my fantastic Field Guide to the Cryptids of North America, which you can visit at my website—I want a fricken of my very own. Tara O'Shea continued to design amazing wallpapers, icons, and internal dingbats for these books, helping to create a large, unified world. I couldn't be more thrilled.

My agent, Diana Fox, remains my personal superhero and one of my favorite human beings. My editor at DAW, Sheila Gilbert, looked at my first draft, saw what needed fixing, and made everything better. Huge thanks to everyone at DAW, and to my cover artist, Aly Fell, who continues to bring these people to life in an amazing new way.

Thanks to my Disney World girls—Amy, Brooke, Patty, Vixy, Rachel, and of course, Mom—and to Barfleet, for service above and beyond the call of duty. Thanks to Borderlands Books, for tolerating my large, often chaotic book events. And of course, thank you. I couldn't write these books without you.

Any errors in this book are my own. The errors that aren't here are the ones that all these people helped me fix. Thank you.

Seanan McGuire
The October Daye Novels

"...will surely appeal to readers who enjoy my books, or those of Patricia Briggs." —*Charlaine Harris*

"I am so invested in the world building and the characters now.... Of all the 'Faerie' urban fantasy series out there, I enjoy this one the most."—*Felicia Day*

ROSEMARY AND RUE
978-0-7564-0571-7
A LOCAL HABITATION
978-0-7564-0596-0
AN ARTIFICIAL NIGHT
978-0-7564-0626-4
LATE ECLIPSES
978-0-7564-0666-0
ONE SALT SEA
978-0-7564-0683-7
ASHES OF HONOR
978-0-7564-0749-0
CHIMES AT MIDNIGHT
978-0-7564-0814-5
THE WINTER LONG
978-0-7564-0808-4
(Available September 2014)

To Order Call: 1-800-788-6262
www.dawbooks.com

DAW 142

Tanya Huff

"The Gales are an amazing family, the aunts will strike fear into your heart, and the characters Allie meets are both charming and terrifying."
—#1 *New York Times* bestselling author
Charlaine Harris

"Thoughtful and leisurely, this fresh urban fantasy from Canadian author Huff features an ensemble cast of nuanced characters in Calgary, Alberta.... Fantasy buffs will find plenty of humor, thrills and original mythology to chew on, along with refreshingly three-dimensional women in an original, fully realized world."   —*Publishers Weekly*

The Enchantment Emporium
978-0-7564-0605-9

The Wild Ways
978-0-7564-0763-6

and coming soon...
The Future Falls
978-0-7564-0753-7

To Order Call: 1-800-788-6262
www.dawbooks.com

DAW 200